I never saw the attack coming.

The streetlight flickered and went out with a pop. In the next instant, the bare lightbulbs flanking Morgan's back door went dark, and the air filled with shadows and rustling.

Darklings.

I sprang up. The street behind Morgan's was narrow—barely wide enough for a delivery truck to squeeze through—and the creatures coming for me swarmed across the pavement gracelessly, a feral cluster. A screech rang out as one of them dragged a talon across a Buick, sparks bright against their black robes.

Two options: I could try to outrun them—Darklings rarely hunted in populated areas, especially if there was no raw magic to draw them. If I could make it to Western Avenue, with its lights and traffic and witnesses, they might call off their pursuit.

The second option was to duck back into Morgan's—but that would mean running directly toward them.

And there was a third choice. Luc.

Also by Erica O'Rourke

Torn

Tangled

BOUND

ERICA O'ROURKE

KENSINGTON PUBLISHING CORP.
www.kensingtonbooks.com

K TEEN BOOKS are published by

Kensington Publishing Corp.
119 West 40th Street
New York, NY 10018

ISBN-13: 978-0-7582-6707-8
ISBN-10: 0-7582-6707-X

First Kensington Trade Paperback Printing: July 2012
10 9 8 7 6 5 4 3 2 1

Printed in the United States of America

To Danny, my very own ever-fixed mark.

And to my girls, whose futures are
as wide and bright as the sea. Dive in, my loves.

ACKNOWLEDGMENTS

It is a strange and humbling feeling to look back at this trilogy and remember all the people who have nudged, guided, and encouraged me along the way. Writing Mo's story has brought an astonishing number of wonderful people into my life, and I am so very thankful for them—and for my readers. Without them, this story would never have been written.

I owe a tremendous amount of thanks to Alicia Condon and her team at KTeen/Kensington, for their faith in me and in this story, for bringing it to life, and for always encouraging me to dig a little deeper. They gave me the chance to make my dreams real and cheered me on every step of the way, and I will always be grateful to them.

I could write a million words and still not adequately express how fortunate I am to have the brilliant Joanna Volpe as my agent. She knows exactly how to handle every situation, from stubborn plot holes to a zombie apocalypse. Working with her has made me a far better writer, and I would cheerfully walk through fire for her. I am equally indebted to the rest of the NCLMR team, especially Nancy Coffey and Kathleen Ortiz for their savvy and support at every turn. Sara Kendall's kindness and humor are unmatched, and her keen eyes have improved this story a thousandfold. Thank you all, for the infinite number of awesome things you've done.

Chicago-North RWA has been with me since the very first pages of Mo's story—they taught me how to be a writer, and it's a debt I can never repay. The 2010 Unsinkables and MargaRITAs have cheered me on without fail, as have the Broken Writers. The YA community has brought so many wonderful people to my life, I can't possibly name them all, but Loretta Nyhan, Jenn Rush, Lee Nichols, and Monica Vavra deserve special mention for their support and general awesomeness.

My friends, both writerly and otherwise, have kept me sane since this roller coaster started: Paula Forman, Lisa McKernan, Lynne Hartzer, Ryann Murphy, Keiru Bakke, Clara Kensie, Lexie Craig, Joelle Charbonneau, Heather Snow, Erin Knightly . . . I could not have done this without them. KC Solano, Vanessa Barnevald, and Kimberly MacCarron have come to the rescue so many times, in so many ways, and I can't wait to return the favor. Lisa Tonkery cheerfully answers my rambling two a.m. e-mails, makes me laugh until I cry, and always understands without explanations. Hanna Martine is one of the smartest, strongest, most talented authors I know, and an inspiration in both writing and life.

Eliza Evans has been an unending source of support and friendship throughout my journey in publishing, and I could not have written this trilogy without her cheering me on. From writing sprints to pep talks to brainstorming to patiently explaining pop culture, she has done it all. Having her in my life is proof positive that I am one of the luckiest girls on the planet.

I can't overstate how thankful I am for my family, especially my mother, father, and sister, who have always been my loudest, most devoted cheering section. Time and again, they have provided child care, a sympathetic ear, research, marketing expertise, food . . . the list is endless, as is my love and gratitude.

I am so proud of my three beautiful, independent, intelligent, generous, funny daughters. If there is such a thing as karma, I must have rescued a boatload of nuns and puppies from a burning orphanage in my last life to get kids this amazing. They have been understanding and patient beyond comprehension, and I hope watching me work to achieve this dream has shown them their dreams are just as reachable—

and that I would move heaven and earth to help them get there.

Last, there is Danny—my true north, my true love, and my favorite person in the whole world. He makes everything possible, and he makes everything better, including me. Thanking him properly would take an entire book, so I will leave it at this: Thank you for being exactly who you are, always.

CHAPTER 1

The problem with terrible ideas is that the people who have them don't recognize how truly awful they are until it's too late. After all, nobody deliberately chooses the worst possible course of action. They have great plans and good intentions. They're caught up in the thrill of the moment, seeing the world as they wish it to be, blind to any hint of trouble. You can warn someone that they're running headlong into disaster, beg them to stop, plant yourself in their path. But in the end, people have to make their own choice.

Even if it's a terrible one.

My father's coming home party was a perfect example of good intentions gone awry.

"This is ridiculous," I said to Colin. "Who throws a huge party for someone fresh out of prison?"

My mom, that's who. I'd tried to talk her out of it—I felt less than celebratory at the prospect of my dad's return—but she'd insisted. Then I'd argued that a small family gathering at the house might be more appropriate. But for once, my mother wasn't concerned with propriety.

So I was stuck at my uncle's bar with everyone we'd ever known, waiting for my dad to walk in the door for the first time in twelve years.

Around me, the crowd was growing impatient, their small talk taking on an irritable note. I should have been setting out bowls of peanuts and pretzels, but instead I slumped against the back wall and watched a game of darts. "You know she's hoping for one of those big reunion scenes. Like we're all going to hug and cry and be a happy family again."

Colin's hand found mine and squeezed, but his eyes swept across the sea of people, searching even in the dim light of the bar. "Just hang in there a little bit longer."

"I don't know why I even agreed to come," I said.

"Because it's important to your mother," my uncle said, appearing beside us. Irritation flickered across his face at the sight of my fingers linked with Colin's. "Be grateful I told her you had to work, or you'd have been off to Indiana along with her. They'll be arriving any moment, so start practicing your smile."

I bared my teeth. "How's this?"

"I'll not have you spoil her day, Mo. She's waited a long time for this."

"Longer than she needed to, right?"

Billy's eyes narrowed, and beside me, Colin made a low noise of warning. "Don't bait the bear," he was telling me, and any other day I would have listened. But tonight, my nerves were stretched to breaking.

Ignoring the ripple of tension along Colin's arm, I lifted my chin and stared at my uncle. A moment passed, and finally Billy made a show of looking around the room. "Make sure everyone has something to toast with, and then you're free for the night. I'll need you back on Monday."

With that, he was off to mingle. I leaned my head against Colin's shoulder and he murmured, "The sooner we get The Slice up and running, the better. I don't like you working for Billy."

I wasn't a fan of the arrangement, either, but I had no choice. As long as I worked for my uncle, Colin was safe. He didn't know about the deal we'd struck, and he definitely wasn't aware my job was more than wiping down tables and carting empties to the recycling bins out back. He assumed, like almost everyone else in my life, that I was working at the bar until my mom's restaurant was rebuilt, at which point life would go back to normal.

I had learned the hard way that normal was not an option anymore.

I went up on tiptoe, brushed a kiss over his lips. His hand tightened on my waist for an instant before he edged away.

"What? Everyone knows we're together." I sank back down, trying not to feel hurt.

"I'm not crazy about having an audience."

I glanced around. There were a few people eyeing us—not many, but enough to make Colin uncomfortable. "Fine. But we're not staying here all night."

He grinned and ducked his head, his breath warm against my ear. "Wasn't planning on it."

I made the rounds of the bar, my back aching from carrying a full tray back and forth. The whole time, I could feel Colin watching me, an anchor in a stormy sea, and I clung to the sensation. But gradually, I became aware of another one, a prickling awareness that made me rub my arms to ward off a chill, despite the overheated room.

Around me, voices faded to a murmur. I spun, looking for Colin, but the crowd hid him from view. The magic stirred—anticipation and stress and dread waking up the force inside me. Something was happening.

Luc? He had a knack for showing up at the worst possible moment, and I couldn't imagine a worse one than tonight. The connection between us had lain dormant for nearly three months, a welcome break while I got acclimated to my new life and the constant presence of the magic inside me. I'd always known he would come back. I'd just hoped to have things under control before he turned my world inside out again.

My hands clutched the empty tray to my chest like a shield. I squeezed my eyes shut, feeling along the lines for the vibrating tension that would indicate an Arc was here. But the lines were quiet, their power held in abeyance. There was no sign of Luc or anyone else in the room working a spell—

even a concealment. I opened my eyes and searched for a familiar green gaze and sharp cheekbones, but they weren't there. Better that way, I told myself.

People stood three deep in front of the oak counter running along the side of the room. Behind them I could see the backs of the regulars hunched over their drinks, and Charlie, my favorite bartender. He was pulling beers and gauging who'd hit their limit, working his way down the line in a steady rhythm. He seemed to pop in and out of view as the people milled in front of him.

It was a familiar sight, but something seemed off-kilter. Like a puzzle in a kid's magazine, where you compared two pictures of the same scene and circled the differences. What was the difference? The bar. Charlie. The customers. The party. What was out of place?

A gap opened in the crowd, giving me a clear view of the bar for only an instant. But it was enough.

The regulars all faced Charlie or the front door. From my spot at the rear of the bar, only the backs of their heads were visible. Except for one guy, facing the opposite direction.

Facing me.

For a split second, I could see him as clearly as if I'd taken his picture—eyebrows raised mockingly, mouth twisted in a caustic smile—and then the shutter closed as the crowd filled the gap again.

Not Luc.

Suddenly, I wished it was.

Anton Renard. Leader of the Seraphim. A renegade Arc who wanted me dead.

The feeling was mutual.

I forced myself to walk toward him, but when I reached the barstool, he was gone, and the lines were silent as the grave.

"Problem?" Colin asked from behind me. He rested his hands on my shoulders, the weight reassuring.

I drew in a shaking breath, turning to him. "I thought I saw Anton. Here."

His expression hardened. "You're sure?"

"No." If it was Anton, I would have felt the spell he'd used to hide himself as it resonated along the lines. Either I was mistaken, or he'd managed to blend convincingly into a Flat bar on the South Side of Chicago. But the Anton I knew was too arrogant for blending.

Something had triggered the magic's fretfulness, but maybe it was my own unhappiness. Three months ago, I'd willingly given myself over to the magic—taken it inside of me, bound myself to the source of the Arcs' power—and discovered that it wasn't just a supernatural energy source, but a sentient being. Alive. Since then, our connection had strengthened. We couldn't carry on a conversation, but I was getting better at interpreting its moods, and it responded to mine: a pleasant hum beneath my skin when I was content, a tremor every time I crossed the threshold of Morgan's. I didn't know which one of us was responsible for the disturbance I felt now.

From the front of Morgan's, someone called, "They're here! Where's Mo?"

Colin took my hand, tugging me toward the narrow front doors as they opened. The crowd drew a collective breath as my mom stepped inside, cheeks flushed with cold and excitement. And I forgot all about half-seen faces, because immediately behind her, blinking at the noise of the crowd's shouts of "surprise" and "welcome home," was my father.

I hadn't seen him in five years.

From behind a wall of people, I studied him carefully. He was still my dad, sharp greenish-brown eyes framed with heavy black glasses. His dark red hair, curling at the collar, needed a trim, and his narrow face managed to look surprised, even though the expression was a beat too slow to be genuine. But there were lines at the corners of his eyes that hadn't been there before, and his hair was streaked with gray. His posture was a little more stooped, as if he were trying to withdraw into himself. He looped one arm around my mother, drawing her close as people lined up to greet him.

Billy spotted me trying to fade into the crowd and grasped my elbow. "Don't you dare ruin this," he muttered, and towed me into the circle surrounding my parents. His voice suddenly brimmed with good cheer. "Jack! Welcome home! Look what I've brought you—a sight for sore eyes, don't you think?"

He stepped back, releasing me. The expectation of the crowd, waiting for our tearful reunion, weighed on me like the air before a storm.

After a moment, my father let go of my mom and took a tentative step toward me, spreading his arms wide. "There's my girl," he said, his voice cracking in the suddenly quiet room. "There's my Mo."

I wanted to turn away, punish him for all the pain he'd caused us. I wasn't going to let him back in, and there was no reason to pretend otherwise.

Until I saw my mom blinking back tears, a wobbly smile on her lips. All her hopes for our family crystallized in a single moment, and my reaction would either let them grow or shatter them on the worn oak floorboards. I licked my lips and swallowed the dust clogging my throat.

"Hi, Dad." I wound the apron string around my fingers until it cut off the circulation, untwisted it again. "It's . . . good to have you home."

He was across the room in three strides, wrapping me in the same bear hug he used to give me when I was five, and for a second I let myself believe Mom was right. Tonight could be a fresh start, a chance for us to be a family again. His return might not be such a terrible thing after all.

And then, still squeezing me tightly, my father whispered one word to me. "Liar."

CHAPTER 2

An hour later, there was still a knot of well-wishers surrounding my father, but my own goodwill was used up. I sat down at the bar, accepted a Diet Coke from Charlie, and poked at the maraschino cherries he'd garnished it with. Colin leaned against the railing, scrutinizing every face despite his casual stance.

"See anyone?" I asked.

"Nobody that shouldn't be here," he said, and laced his fingers with mine. "You look beat."

"I thought he'd be nicer," I said without thinking.

Colin's mouth twitched. "He probably thought the same thing about you. The guy's been in prison for twelve years, Mo. Nice doesn't last long there."

"He went to prison for Billy. Added an extra seven years to his sentence to keep us safe. That's nice, right?"

"Not nice. Desperate. He'd do whatever was necessary to protect his family." He finished the beer he'd nursed all night, set it back on the bar with a crack. "Don't confuse nice with good."

"You think he's a good guy?" Colin saw my family a lot more clearly than I did. If he thought my dad deserved another chance, maybe I could bend a little.

"I think he's on his way over."

The crowd had thinned out, but my dad took his time

crossing the room, his attention riveted on us. Colin started to draw away, but I held fast.

"Aren't you going to introduce me, Mo?" my father asked. Without waiting for my response, he said, "You're Colin Donnelly."

"It's good to meet you, sir."

"Annie's told me a lot about you. Says you've done a good job keeping my daughter out of trouble."

I bristled at the words, but Colin's voice was cool. "I try my best. You know Mo."

My father's jaw clenched as he caught the implication—he didn't know me at all. "The good news is, now that I'm home, things will settle down. I don't think we'll need your help for much longer. Annie says you're a carpenter?"

He was getting rid of Colin? "But . . ." I started to protest, but Colin's hand brushed mine, reassuring.

"With all due respect, sir, I work for Billy." Now the words held an edge.

My dad looked disappointed. "I figured you'd say that."

My mom joined us, worry creasing her brow, and my dad settled an arm around her waist. She brightened instantly. "It's a nice party, don't you think? Everyone's so happy to see you."

He dropped a kiss on her forehead. "You did great. Never saw it coming."

Looked like I wasn't the only liar in the family. I coughed, and he frowned at me. "Don't spoil her fun," his look telegraphed. "Can I bail, please?" I asked. "I'm wiped out."

"Honey, it's your dad's party!"

"Yeah, with your friends. Not mine." Like I would have invited any of my friends to this. "Look, I helped set up, and I did the big welcome. Why do I have to stay?"

"Oh, Annie, let her go." Billy approached us, a tumbler of whiskey in hand, doing his best impression of the doting uncle. "What fun is she going to have with a bunch of old people? Besides, we've things to discuss."

Her mouth thinned, and she glanced at my father, who shrugged. "It's fine. We'll have plenty of time to catch up."

"I suppose." She gave me a quick hug. "We'll be home in a bit."

While Colin went to warm up the truck, I popped into the back room and clocked out. The sudden quiet was a relief, and I took a minute to steady myself. I'd survived. While I was still reeling from my dad's greeting, the other guests had swarmed in to welcome him, and I'd slipped off to the side. Other than the brief exchange between my dad and Colin, I'd managed to steer clear of my family for the night. It could have been worse.

It could have been much worse. It could have been Anton on that barstool instead of a random stranger.

I'd worked so hard to keep my real life separate from my magical one. If Anton had shown up, it would have meant only one thing: He and the Seraphim, his genocidal cult, were back. Anton and his followers wanted to release the magic from the ley lines that carried it safely through the world. But doing so would be lethal to weaker Arcs and any Flats—ordinary people—who came in contact with untempered magic. They called it The Ascendency, when members of the Seraphim would destroy the Arcs' society and rise to their rightful place. They'd been the ones to order Verity's death last summer, and they'd been after me ever since. We'd defeated them a few months ago, but I knew they would regroup. I just didn't know when.

But Anton never passed up an opportunity to attack me. I'd had no word from the Arcs that I was in danger. The ley lines around Morgan's had been quiet all night. For now, at least, I was safe.

I bent over, trying to untie my apron.

The string was so badly knotted, I was going to have to cut it off or try to wriggle out. Behind me, the door opened and the noise from the party swelled, grating on my nerves.

"The stupid string won't come undone," I told Colin. "Can

you help me get this off?" I turned, tugging at the white canvas hem.

It wasn't Colin.

"Nothing I'd like better," said Luc, stepping inside and shutting the door with a wave.

I gaped at him. He looked ordinary—or at least, as ordinary as it was possible for Luc to appear. Dark jeans, dark green shirt, black leather coat, cut close to display his lean swimmer's build. It wasn't his clothing that set him apart. It was the eyes, the smirk, the way he walked into a room and instantly, effortlessly took command, like it was his due.

Which he probably figured it was.

"What are you—" I sighed as the pieces fell into place. "Some people actually say hello, you know. They don't lurk in corners."

He looked offended. "Neither do I."

"You've been watching me all night. It's a little creepy."

"Just walked in the front door." He crossed the room, took my hands in his ice-cold ones. Up close, I could see water beading on the surface of his coat. "City's a hell of a lot less charming in the winter, by the way."

I pulled away, crossed my arms over my chest. "I felt you. Earlier tonight. The magic knew you were here."

"Magic doesn't know anything." He blew on his hands, enveloping them in a red-tinged glow. Show-off. As my words sank in, his brow furrowed. "Wasn't me. What happened?"

I hadn't seen Luc for months—since our last run-in with the Seraphim; since I had once again fixed the Arcs' magic; since he'd left me for dead, then risked his own life to save me. All winter, he'd left me in peace, our only contact the small gifts he left in my locker or my coat pocket. Messages without words. A clutch of sweet olive blossoms, a single praline in a white cardboard box, a tiny silver fleur de lis, a glass vial of brick red dust. Each time, my heart stuttered, simultaneously pleased and nervous. I'd try to put him out of my mind, tuck the reminders of him away in a dresser drawer, but every so often he would slip back into my thoughts, and I'd study the odd little collection. And then I'd put them back, annoyed with myself all over again.

Luc had made no secret of the fact he was going to pursue me, but so far he'd given me space and freedom. The two things I could never get in Chicago. Telling him about what I'd seen—or thought I'd seen—would change everything between us. Again.

I wasn't sure I was ready for that.

I wasn't sure I was strong enough.

Waving a hand like it was nothing, I said, "I thought I felt something, and I assumed it was you."

"Someone worked a spell? Here?"

"I don't think so." I chose my words carefully, not wanting to give too much away. There was power in a secret. I might not want it, but I wasn't going to hand it over unthinkingly, either. "I can feel it in the lines when someone does magic. I can see it, if I try hard enough. Like now, when you warmed up your hands. There's a ley line on the west side of the building. I sensed it responding when you drew on it to cast the spell. But this was different. It was inside me, like it came from the source of the magic, not the lines." I tugged at my apron again, regretting I'd ever brought it up. "It was nothing, Luc. Probably just stress."

"You're positive?" He searched my expression, and at the same time I felt the connection between us strengthen, as if he were trying to get a magical read on me.

The familiar contact jolted me, a reminder of how we'd once been, and I responded without thinking. "I'm not sure. I'm not sure about anything."

"That so?" His eyes glinted.

I couldn't change the subject fast enough. "Why are you here, anyway? Did the Quartoren send you?"

God, that was the last thing I needed tonight. A summons from the Quartoren, leaders of the Arcs. Unlike the Seraphim, they didn't want me dead—but they weren't my biggest fans, either.

"This is all me," he said with a shrug. "Big night, with your daddy coming home. Figured I'd check in, see if you needed a hand. Or a fast getaway."

"You're sweet." I'd forgotten how kind he could be, small acts that revealed more about him than he liked to admit.

"That's the last thing I am." There were circles under his eyes, worry lines etched into his forehead, and he turned away, tracing a rectangle in the air. A door of flame, open to nothingness, took shape. "If the magic acts up again, call for me. You remember how?"

"Like I could forget?" Reflexively, I touched my wrist, felt the connection that bound me to Luc, a magical reminder that my life and his would always be intertwined. "There's more, isn't there? This wasn't just a social visit."

"There's always more. But tonight was about me missing you. Even if the feeling ain't mutual."

As he stepped closer, our connection began to hum. I held perfectly still as he brushed a finger over the snarled mass of apron strings at my waist. The air quivered as the spell curled around the knot, and he caught the apron midfall.

"Thanks," I said, taking the fabric from him and crumpling it in my hands.

"Pleasure's all mine," he murmured, and vanished through the door.

CHAPTER 3

Outside, the air was clear and biting, the sky tinted with the orange glow of the city lights. I buried my nose in my scarf and ran for the truck.

"Everything okay?" Colin asked as I climbed in. "You look rattled."

I took a deep breath, bracing myself. For an instant, I considered not telling him, but dismissed the idea. Bad enough there was already one huge secret between us. Two seemed like a habit.

"Luc stopped by," I said, and watched for his reaction.

There. A quick curling of his fingers, a muscle tightening in his jaw. When he spoke, though, his voice was unchanged. "Problem?"

"He knew about the party. I think he was offering moral support."

Colin made a skeptical noise. "What did he say about Anton?"

"I didn't mention it. Once I tell him, he's got an excuse to come back whenever he wants." I curled up against him, relaxing for the first time that night. His canvas coat was rough against my cheek. "We survived the party. That's something."

"You're going to have to talk to your dad eventually," Colin said. "You've got six months before you leave for New

York. That's a long time to avoid someone who lives in the same house."

"He's up to something," I said, trying to shift his attention from my college plans. "Did you hear Billy? They have to talk business? The man's been out of prison for less than a day, and he's already back working for the Mob."

"Maybe it's about reopening The Slice," he said. I wanted to believe him, but he didn't sound like he believed it himself.

The yellow beams of the headlights illuminated the half-finished shell of my mom's restaurant. The framing was in place, plywood covering where the windows would be installed soon. A tattered sheet of weatherproofing twisted like a wraith in the night air.

"How much longer till it's open again?"

"Depends on the weather. Couple months, we hope."

"It means a lot to my mom that you're helping with the rebuilding. She's kind of crazy about you."

"Yeah?" His eyes crinkled with amusement.

"It might be the only thing we agree on."

He dipped his head, his mouth finding mine. I curled my fingers around his shoulders, pulling him closer, crowding out thoughts of my family and unexpected faces.

Eventually he eased back, voice husky. "Time to get you home."

As we drove, he said, "Do you think it was Anton?"

"I barely saw him. But if he was there, he wasn't using magic, and that's not really his style."

Inside me, the magic had settled into a soothing, pleasant hum. Whatever had riled it earlier was gone. The magic wasn't centered in me, but I was perfectly attuned to it—every cell in my body picked up on its movements and inclinations, the way it flowed to and from the lines. Sometimes it focused its attention elsewhere, and sometimes it zeroed in on me, reacting to my experiences like they were its own, like a willful shadow. Gradually, I was refining my understanding of its feelings, like a child learning the nuances of emotions. Not just happiness, but delight or quiet pleasure. Not just sadness, but grief or annoyance.

The one thing I didn't need to be told was that the true nature of the magic was a secret.

If the Quartoren were to find out—or worse, the Seraphim—it would be a disaster. They'd try to take control, to grab as much power for themselves as they could. They'd be completely indifferent to the fact that the magic was a living being, only see it as a tool to be bent to their will. Even Luc was dangerous. As the Heir, his obligation was to his House. The magic and I weren't even a close second. The only person I'd trusted enough to tell was Colin, whose only concern was whether the bond was dangerous to me.

I couldn't keep the truth about the magic hidden forever. Someone—Luc, or one of the Quartoren's scholar-scientists—would figure it out. But for now, it wasn't my secret to tell, and it was safer to stay quiet. I'd learned too well the dangers of acting on impulse.

"Do you want to come in?" I asked when we'd pulled up in front of my family's orange brick bungalow. "They won't be home for a while longer."

He pointed to the car across the street. One of my uncle's men, there for protection. Ironic, since Billy was the greatest threat facing me right now. "I don't like an audience."

"I don't care what they think. Or what my family says."

"We have six months before you leave, Mo. Do you really want to have a knock-down, drag-out with your family over this?"

"Absolutely." We had a lot longer than he realized, because I wasn't going to New York. I just hadn't found a way to tell him yet. "We never talk about it. My leaving."

"What's to talk about? You're going to New York. I'm staying here." He touched my cheek. "Six months. Don't wish them away, Mo."

I didn't believe in wishes, but I didn't need to. I'd fix this myself.

CHAPTER 4

Y ou knew things were bad when school looked like a welcome alternative to home. But by Monday morning, I'd fended off as many of my mom's attempts at family togetherness as I possibly could. I'd walked in on my parents kissing so many times, my retinas would be scarred for life. When they weren't making out, they were talking about my dad's job—or rather, his lack of one. Nobody was interested in hiring an accountant who'd done time for embezzlement. Nobody except my uncle.

It was a relief to walk into St. Brigid's, despite knowing I was the center of attention. My dad's return had put the spotlight on my family once again, but I had plenty of practice ignoring the whispers and smirks. The trickiest part of the day to navigate, as always, was lunch. The social scene in the cafeteria was an ever-shifting landscape. It was smarter to map out the terrain before committing to one location. There were land mines and bogs and deserts of pariahs. I wasn't looking to be an island, but I didn't have much interest in the heavily trafficked areas, either. Safer to sit somewhere with a view of the action and an easy escape route.

I'd lost my taste for running away, but it never hurt to have options. And it was always better to know what was coming. Forewarned is forearmed, as my uncle always said.

So when I saw Jill McAllister making her way toward my table, her cronies snickering and gawking, I pushed away my limp Caesar salad and prepared for a showdown. The back of my neck buzzed slightly. Jill always put me on guard, and by now the magic was clued in, too. I ignored the now-familiar sensation and concentrated on the problem at hand. Jill, beautiful and pouty and spoiled rotten. She was wearing the same St. Brigid's uniform as the rest of us—navy plaid skirt, white blouse, blue V-neck with the school crest embroidered on it—but the studs in her ears were real diamonds, not cubic zirconium, and her shoes probably cost more than I made in a month's worth of tips.

At first, she didn't sit down. She loomed over me—the expensive heels were also impossibly high—until I looked up, casually rubbing my nape.

"Did you want something, Jill?"

"You're sitting by yourself." She dropped into the chair next to mine with an uncharacteristic thump. I fought the urge to scoot away.

"I *was*." And enjoying it.

"We never talk, Mo." She leaned an elbow on the table, propped her chin in her hands. "Why is that?"

Because you're a bitch. "What would we talk about?"

"You *know*," she said, glassy eyed. She shoved playfully at my arm. "Stuff. School. Boys. Like that cute guy."

"Colin?" I asked absently. The buzzing sensation spread across my scalp. Jill didn't usually provoke this kind of reaction. I scanned the room, looking for the source as she droned on.

There. Traces of magic, like glittering sunlight, swirled around Constance Grey, my best friend's little sister, at a table with a bunch of freshmen. Verity's death had transformed her, almost as much as me. Sweet, bright, the tiniest bit spoiled, Constance had tagged along after us since she could walk. Verity had pretended annoyance, but mostly she'd treated Constance with equal measures of exasperation and affection.

Then Vee died, and Constance was lost. I should have done more—stepped in right away, tried to help her. But I'd been so focused on finding out who killed Verity, I'd left Constance to flounder, and her grief had turned to blame. I'd accepted it, because I'd blamed myself, too.

When her powers as an Arc had come through, I'd made a deal with the Quartoren so she'd have someone to guide her. Penance, I guess. But Constance hadn't seen it that way, especially once she'd discovered that her great-aunt, Evangeline, had been the one behind Verity's death—and that I'd killed Evangeline in turn.

Over the past few months, as Constance had gained control over her own abilities, she'd slowly reemerged from her hard, angry shell and we'd formed a very cautious truce. I'd kept tabs on her from afar, and she'd kept most of her snark to herself. Because she was a freshman and I was a senior, the only time our paths crossed was when Niobe—Constance's tutor, who posed as our guidance counselor—needed to speak to us.

It was good to see Constance interacting with her friends again. But now she watched us openly, barely paying attention to the other girls at her table. When she realized I'd spotted her, she looked away guiltily. Eavesdropping, probably, amplifying the sound with a spell. I started to frown at her, but my attention was drawn away by Jill, who was tapping her fingers impatiently.

"Not Colin. The other one," Jill said, eyes boring into me.

"Other one what?"

"The other guy. Luc."

My palms turned damp. "You know about Luc?"

Her voice dropped to a whisper. "Was he supposed to be a secret? We know all about Luc. You're the real secret, Mo. Don't you want to tell?"

I tried to shove away from her, but she swung both hands up, clapping them against my temples. The noise of the cafeteria faded, but the buzzing I'd felt before grew to a full-on shriek, reverberating in my head as the magic reacted to the attack.

This wasn't Jill. She was a bitch, but she wasn't an Arc. Someone was using her like a puppet. Her face was contorted and her pupils were blown, a thin line of blue ringing the black. Images flashed before me: Luc's palm pressed against mine; the silhouette of a Darkling against the moon; Verity dying by the feeble glow of a street lamp, the tumbling nexus of energy that was raw magic. I tried to wrench free, but Jill—or whatever was controlling her—was too strong.

She dug through my thoughts, ferreting out information, leering at the memories she saw. The Seraphim, I thought dimly. I'd imagined a shadowy attack, not an assault in broad daylight. I tried to picture something empty—a blank screen, a placid lake, a dense fog—and begged the magic to quiet itself. The Seraphim knew I was bound to the source, that hurting me would deplete the magical energy that sustained the Arcs, but this wasn't just a physical blow. It was a violation, the way they rifled through my most private thoughts while I stood trapped and helpless.

Not helpless. I reached for the plastic fork on my tray, but it was too far. My arms flailed, and her fingernails dug into my scalp. I kicked, connecting with her shins, and the pressure eased slightly. Not enough to break away, but enough to catch my breath. I hooked my feet around the legs of the chair and wrenched, causing us to both topple over.

The crash was earsplitting, and everyone stopped to watch as Jill scrambled up, lunging toward me. Would they kill me in full view of the school? The Arcs did everything in their power to conceal their existence from Flats. Why would the Seraphim risk something so public now? I circled the table, careful to stay out of reach.

"Do you really think you can run from us? From what is coming?" hissed the thing that wasn't Jill. "You live yet because you've something valuable within. Once we split you open to get it, the Darklings can have the rest."

I sought for the bond between me and Luc, trying to summon him. A quick glance showed Constance had disappeared, and I hoped she'd had the sense to go for help. The Seraphim had never invaded my mundane life before. This was a new tactic. And it was unacceptable.

Anger focused me, and the magic pounding through my veins gave me strength. I looked at the person before me, kept my voice low. "I beat you. *Twice.* No magic, and I still beat you. And that was when I didn't know what I was doing." I smiled, cold as the winter sky outside. "Imagine what I'm capable of now."

She straightened, stuffed her hands in the pockets of her skirt. "All the better, Maura Fitzgerald. I'd hate to be bored."

Anton. I had a sudden memory of him watching me at the Allée, where I'd bonded with the magic. Hands tucked in pockets, careless posture, sly tilt of the head. He was the one controlling Jill, I was sure of it.

From behind me, Niobe said, "Leave now. That body won't sustain you."

She placed one hand at my shoulder and gestured elegantly with the other one. The concealment rose up around us, the air wavering slightly. Meanwhile, I looked more closely at Jill. Beneath her fake tan, her skin was pale, her lips tinged with purple. Her breath came in uneven pants. Whatever spell they'd worked was killing her.

"I'll use her up and take another one."

"You can't work a Rivening and defend yourself at the same time. And I would imagine the Quartoren will be sending forces to take care of you right about"—Niobe paused, tilting her head to the side, listening to something I couldn't hear—"now."

Jill jerked, her chin dropping to her chest, and looked at me again. Her eyes were back to their usual sapphire, and she dropped into the chair. "God, Mo," she said. Her voice was weak, but the malice ringing through it was definitely her. "You're so boring I can't even stay awake when you talk."

Niobe touched her shoulder and whispered a few quick words. Jill's complexion transformed from sallow to sun-kissed. "The chair was unstable and you fell. Perhaps you should go see the nurse?"

Jill blinked at her. "My head hurts."

Niobe beckoned to one of Jill's friends, standing across the cafeteria, watching us uncertainly. "Go with her. She's not herself."

If Niobe had been a real guidance counselor, she would have walked Jill down to the nurse herself. But she'd made it perfectly clear that her position at St. Brigid's was only a cover to keep an eye on Constance's training. She'd also made it clear she was less than pleased with the assignment.

When Jill left, the buzz of the crowd subsided faster than I'd expected. "Did you do something to them?" I whispered.

"Let's discuss this in my office," she said pointedly, pitching her voice to be heard by the remaining gawkers.

Appetite gone, I dumped my lunch in the trash and gathered up my books. Niobe studied the room through narrowed eyes, watching for a second attack. I stayed close as we walked back to her office.

Constance was pacing back and forth outside Niobe's office. "You're okay! I went to get Niobe, but she was gone already."

"Inside, please." Niobe ushered us in, locking the door with a wave of her hand and a soft, foreign word. I could feel the lines shifting in response to the spell. If I let my eyes unfocus, I could see the casting as it traced through the air in twisting golden ribbons. But I still couldn't use the magic, make it trail from my fingers the way Niobe and Constance could.

"Are you sure you're all right?" Niobe asked.

"I want a shower." I wanted to scrub myself clean, erase the feeling of a stranger invading the memories I had locked deep within me. But the hatred I'd felt was too personal to be a stranger. "It was Anton, wasn't it? I could tell."

Constance made a startled noise, but Niobe merely nodded. "The Seraphim are going on the offensive, it would seem."

"What did he do?" I rubbed at my temples. "And how does Jill fit into this? She's Flat."

"Anton worked a Rivening," Niobe said, setting out cups of green tea. "Two, actually. The first was to direct Jill's actions. Her dislike of you made it easier—it lowered her resistance to his instructions. The second was on you, but only to see, not control."

Constance shuddered. "Rivening's not allowed. You told me it was, like, one of the Ten Commandments."

Niobe gave her a pitying look. "Does Anton Renard strike you as someone who cares about Arc laws? The Seraphim want to tear down our society and rebuild it according to their whims. Rivening's the least of what he'll stoop to. Which means you are in grave danger, Mo."

What else was new? I'd been in danger since the day Verity died. But Niobe was right. Until now, the Seraphim had gone after me only when I got involved in Arc affairs—fulfilling the Torrent Prophecy, working with the Quartoren. Coming into my world was a dangerous shift in tactics.

"You told Anton that the Quartoren were coming for him."

"Rivening is no small magic, especially when worked from a distance. I felt it a moment after he'd taken over Jill, and the Quartoren traced the spell back to his location." She paused. "He can't defend himself while working a spell of such magnitude."

"They caught him?"

"I doubt it. We'd have heard."

"What would they do to him?" Constance asked.

I was curious about that myself. The Seraphim had ordered Verity's death, and Anton was their leader. Ultimately, he was responsible, and I wanted him to pay.

"You know what they say about killing serpents—cut off the head and the rest will die quickly enough. Anton is the head of this particular serpent."

"They'd kill him?" Constance whispered.

"He killed the Vessel. He tried to start the Torrent. He's

been Rivening Flats with the regularity of a metronome. He's violated neutral ground and advocated treason on more than one occasion. Did you think they would give him a slap on the wrist? This isn't a student council election, it's war."

Constance flushed at Niobe's condescending tone.

I thought back to the scene at Morgan's. It must have been Anton after all. He'd sully himself with the Flat world if he had to, it seemed . . . but how had he found me there? How had he tracked me when I couldn't cast spells? "The Seraphim's been quiet for months. Why come after me now?"

"You'd have to ask Dominic."

I didn't trust Dominic DeFoudre to tell me the truth about the weather, much less the Seraphim's plans. "You know just as much as the Quartoren do. You hear things they don't. What's changed?"

She paused, her eyes sliding to Constance. Then she sighed. "It's time to choose Evangeline's successor."

Constance gripped the teacup so tightly I was afraid it might shatter, but that was her only reaction. Niobe had been trying to teach her to control her emotions. Obviously, the lessons were working.

For a long time, Constance had blamed me—wrongly— for Verity's death. But in Evangeline's case, the blame lay squarely on my shoulders. It was something we didn't really talk about, but the fact that I'd killed her great-aunt hung over us like nuclear fallout.

"What's that got to do with me?"

"Right now, the Quartoren are at a disadvantage. Many Arcs view them as weak and outmoded, and the Seraphim have used that to their benefit. They've gained traction. But now that the Water House has concluded its mourning, and is prepared to name a successor, the Quartoren stand to gain strength."

"The Seraphim see it as now or never?"

"Yes. They need to assert their dominance. Strike a blow to the old ways. Starting the Ascendency will do just that, and harming you is the easiest way to accomplish it."

The room blurred as her meaning became clear.

The Ascendency was Anton's endgame. He and his vile little cult believed only the strongest of the Arcs deserved their powers. Currently, raw magic was dispersed through the world via ley lines, which tempered the source's lethal power and made it safe for all Arcs to use. The Seraphim wanted to destroy the lines, triggering the Ascendency—raw magic sweeping across the world, killing the weaker Arcs or stripping them of their abilities, leaving the magic to Anton and the other survivors. They didn't care if Flats were caught in the crossfire, either. A new age, he called it. Purification. I called it genocide.

"Luc said if I'm hurt, the magic is, too. If Anton kills me, there won't be any left—they need *some* magic, right? The Ascendency won't work otherwise."

The magic needed a protector. Someone to keep its secret. If people knew about its power, and the depth of our connection, they would exploit it. Without any powers of my own, I wasn't much of a protector . . . but I was an expert on secrets. Maybe that's why it had chosen me.

"He doesn't want to kill you. Not yet, anyway. He'll look for a way to break the connection. Should it prove unbreakable, he'll find a way to use it to his advantage. With the Succession looming, he's growing desperate."

"The Quartoren knew this was his angle?"

"Of course. You would have, too, if you'd been willing to meet with them. You chose not to deal with them, and they've respected that decision. Until now."

"The last time I worked with the Quartoren, they tried to trap me inside the heart of the magic. *Forever.*" I wouldn't have died, but it wouldn't have been much of a life, either. "Sorry if I didn't feel like going out for coffee."

I'd cut ties with the Quartoren after I'd realized that their interest lay not with protecting the magic—or me—but in their own position. They weren't evil, like the Seraphim. But they were willing to sacrifice me to preserve the status quo, and I wanted nothing to do with them.

Niobe's words clicked, and surprise slackened my jaw. Not quite betrayal—she had never pretended to be on my side—but surprise, and annoyance that I hadn't figured it out earlier.

"You've been reporting to them. That's why you're here, isn't it? To spy on me?"

"I'm here because of the Covenant *you* forged. I'm tasked with looking after Constance until she is fully prepared for life with the Arcs and in control of her talents. But considering your importance in our world, it seemed sensible to keep an eye on you as well."

"I don't need a babysitter," Constance said, slouching back in the chair. I'd almost forgotten she was there.

Niobe ignored her. "You are the Vessel. You're bound to the Heir. Whatever difficulties you're having with Luc, you should have known he wouldn't leave you unprotected."

"I don't want his protection." I was tired of Luc coming to my rescue, of needing him to navigate the labyrinth of Arc society. Was this why he'd come to see me yesterday? Was his concern about my dad's return all a show? I wanted to believe otherwise—that for once he'd been genuine. That I was still free for a little while longer.

But I knew Luc. Once he heard about today's attack, my freedom would disappear. "We don't have to tell him about Anton," I said, hating the pleading note that crept into my voice. "Not right away."

"He already knows."

I bit my lip, suddenly nervous. I didn't have enough defenses against Luc—against his charm and his challenges. He'd never hurt me, but deep down I knew he posed a different type of danger.

The bell rang, and Constance stood. "I have an algebra test. Can I go?"

"For now, yes." Niobe waved a hand at the door, the lock turning over with a muffled thunk.

After Constance left, I slumped in my chair. The rapidly cooling tea was bitter on my tongue, and I made a face. "I never thought they'd come after me at school. It's supposed to be safe here. Separate."

She shook her head. "It's always been this way with you. You've bound yourself to the Arcs, but you insist on maintaining your Flat life as well. So long as you do, *neither* world is safe. You're going to have to choose."

I rubbed at my temples, unable to dispel the headache brewing. "Luc told me that once. Ask him how it ended."

"What makes you think this is the end?" she asked.

CHAPTER 5

"You cannot let Jill mess with your head like that," said Lena Santos.

I dropped my Chem binder, startled, and tried to compose myself when I bent to pick it up again. "I'll do my best. Where have you been?"

Lena had missed the entire day, and she hadn't responded to a single one of my texts. She was pretty much my only real friend at St. Brigid's, and I'd been terrified that Anton might try to use her against me, too.

"I had stuff," she said vaguely, waving a hand. "It took longer than I thought, so I'm just grabbing my books. I heard lunch was interesting."

"You've been gone all day," I said. "When did you have time to hear anything?"

She shook her head in mock disappointment. "I'm hurt you would even ask a question like that."

It wasn't quite right to say Lena was a gossip. She was a sponge. She soaked up all the news and scandal around the school but rarely spread it around. She was the most relentlessly inquisitive person I'd ever met, and people were happy to talk to her. Sometimes I thought Lena used her curiosity the way I used my camera—as a way to deflect attention. If you ask enough questions, keep the lens on the other person, they usually forget about you. I'd used it to my advantage for years, and I was beginning to think Lena had learned the same trick.

"Well? Lunch? Come on, spill."

"Pretty much the usual," I said, hoping my bland tone would discourage further questions.

"Jill McAllister went after you in front of the entire cafeteria. Even for you two, that's not really the usual."

"She said that?"

"No. She's telling people she wanted to ask about your NYU application and she got a migraine so bad she passed out."

"There you go, then." I slammed the locker shut and hefted my bag, settling the strap across my chest.

"You don't think I actually believe that, do you? Someone said she grabbed you."

"She was showing me where the headache was."

We'd been heading toward the front doors of the school, but she stopped. "The secretive act again? I thought we were past that."

Lena knew the truth about my family's Mob connections, and that was dangerous enough. She was completely, blissfully unaware that magic existed. If the Seraphim wanted to hurt me, she was an easy target. I needed to keep her out of this, for her own good.

I ignored the whisper of conscience that reminded me how much I hated people doing things for my own good.

"If you'd been there, you could have seen it firsthand," I pointed out. "Seriously, where were you?"

She looked down, her voice soft. "Family thing. I needed to help my mom."

"With what?"

"Work stuff."

"What exactly does your mom do, Lena? I don't think you've ever told me. I don't think anyone here knows." I was genuinely curious, but I also had a point to make. Wrapping my scarf around my neck, I continued, "You know more about my life than anyone in this school, but you never tell me anything. And I've never pushed. Not once. Maybe I'm not the one with trust issues here."

"I trust you." Her hand crept to the St. Anne medallion she always wore. "But I can't talk about it. It's not mine to tell. I'm sorry, Mo."

I was sorry, too, both for shutting her out and for prying when she wanted to leave something hidden. I'd done enough digging in people's lives to know that what you uncovered was usually the last thing you wanted to find.

"If Jill says she got a migraine, why argue?" I said, peering out the window. No rusting red truck yet, and I tugged my gloves on. "I feel the same way whenever I'm around her."

"A migraine," she said slowly, staring out at the courtyard. "Got it."

Colin's truck pulled up to the snow-covered curb. "I'll see you tomorrow. And Lena?"

She turned back to me. "Yeah?"

"It works both ways, you know. If you need help, or want to talk."

"Sure," she said, but I knew she didn't mean it. "Thanks."

I hurried out into the frigid afternoon. Chicago in late February is winter at its least appealing. The mountains of snow from the plows have turned gray from exhaust, the sidewalks are lumpy with ice, the cold air slaps you across the face. No matter what the calendar says, everyone knows spring is months away, not weeks, and summer seems like a myth.

Before I could run for the warmth of the truck, a familiar voice called my name.

"You couldn't have come inside?" I asked Jenny Kowalski. Her fleece hat was pulled low over her ears, her face buried in the collar of her jacket.

Jenny's dad had been the homicide detective assigned to Verity's case. Convinced her death was related to my uncle's Mob connections, he'd followed me into a Darkling attack and was killed by a blast of raw magic. The Arcs had covered it up, putting out the story that he was caught in a gas leak explosion that had leveled the Chicago Water Tower. Jenny didn't look like her father, but she was following in his footsteps—she blamed my uncle, and she wanted me to help take him down.

"Would you rather I come to Morgan's? Or your house? There's an idea," she said. "I could meet your dad. My invitation to the party got lost, I guess."

"This isn't exactly discreet," I pointed out. "Colin's right there."

"I'll be fast. Nick wants to know if you still have access to your uncle's books." Nick Petros, a political reporter for the *Chicago Tribune* who was working with Jenny.

"The hard drive was a fluke," I said. "I told my mom I threw it out when we put the new one in, and she never asked about it again. Usually, I don't have that kind of access."

"It helped a lot," she said. "They're really close to making their case against your uncle and the Forellis, but they need more evidence. Something ironclad."

I hugged myself to keep warm. "Isn't that what the cops are for?"

"You can get things they can't. The Forellis don't suspect you. Mo, we need this. I need this. You promised to help."

I sighed. Teaming up with Jenny had seemed like a good idea at the time. She'd appeared at The Slice one afternoon, brandishing a file on Colin's history and information about my dad's trial, offering a trade: answers for evidence. Now it was a complication, but I couldn't go back on my word, and she knew it. "I'm working tonight. I'll see what I can do. Now go away, before Colin starts asking questions."

When I hauled open the door of the truck, a blast of warm air enveloped me and I sighed with relief. Colin laughed. "You were out there for all of ninety seconds. I think you'll live."

"Try wearing a skirt in this weather. We'll see how long you last." I pulled my gloves off and blew on my fingers to warm them. By now I should have gotten used to the jolt of pleasure that ran through me every time I saw him. But it was always the same—his eyes would meet mine, gray and knowing, his mouth would tug up on one side, and the happiness flashed through me, like stepping into an unexpected patch of sunlight on a miserable day. "Hi."

"Hi." He leaned over and kissed me, slow and thorough. I slid my hands beneath his coat, feeling worn flannel, hard muscle, and sanctuary. Eventually, he pulled back and studied me, rubbing a thumb along my jaw. "Bad day?"

Of course he knew. Colin knew me better than anyone. It was pointless to try and hide things from him, so I almost never did.

There's a lot of wiggle room in almost.

I'd seen so much evil in the last six months. I'd seen killers and madmen and betrayal and greed. At times, I'd thought it would break me.

But compared to Colin's past, everything I'd witnessed was a fairy tale.

His story was horribly, horribly true. He and his siblings had been abused for years by their stepfather, but a run-in with Child Services caused the man to snap. He'd killed Colin's mom and brother, beaten his little sister so badly she'd suffered brain damage. He'd only stopped when an eleven-year-old Colin shot him to death.

That's where my uncle came in. He'd known the stepfather—the guy was a low-level enforcer for the Mob. When Billy heard what had happened, he swooped in, pulled strings to bury what should have been a front-page story, and arranged for Colin and his sister Tess to come back to Chicago. Doctors said Tess's catatonic state was part physical, part psychological, and most likely permanent—so Billy had placed her in a nursing home and taken care of the bills, made sure she was safe and cared for. Colin had been loyal to my uncle ever since.

Until we met.

Not surprisingly, Billy did not approve of our relationship. Bodyguard was one thing; boyfriend was another. The only thing keeping Colin alive was the deal I'd cut with my uncle after he found out—Colin's life and Tess's continued care in exchange for my promise to stay in Chicago after graduation and work for the Mob.

It was the one thing Colin could never, ever know. The day he discovered what I'd learned and what I'd done would be the day he walked away. I had survived a lot, but I wasn't sure I could survive Colin hating me.

"Mo?" He jostled me lightly. "Something happen?"

I couldn't mention Jenny's visit, but there was still plenty to tell. "Promise you won't freak out."

"Very reassuring. Something with the magic?"

I twisted my fingers together. "The Seraphim. They came after me at lunch."

"In public?" He sounded incredulous.

"I think they've passed the point of being subtle."

He scowled and put the truck into drive, the movements jerky as he worked through all the implications.

"Morgan's or home?" he asked.

"Morgan's." My uncle's bar was the last place I wanted to be. Curled up on the couch with Colin was infinitely more appealing, but I'd made a promise, and Colin's life depended on me keeping it.

"You're not hurt," he said as we drove.

"Just a headache." His hands flexed, and I was quick to reassure him. "A regular headache, I swear."

"Was Luc around?"

"Niobe came in at the end, but I had it under control."

He glanced over, eyebrows raised. "You did?"

"There wasn't time to wait around for a rescue."

He drew a deep breath. "We need to get you out of this. Hide you somewhere."

"Where would I go? The magic's everywhere. I can't hide from this. And I won't abandon it, either." I knew that with absolute clarity. It wasn't about escaping one world for the other. It was finding a way to balance my Arc life and my Flat one. "And let's say I did hide. You stash me somewhere the Arcs would never find me. Would you come with me?"

Amazing how he could withdraw in a space as small as the cab of his truck. "We've been over this. I'm not leaving Chicago."

Of course he wouldn't. He could never leave Tess. If I wanted them to be safe, I couldn't leave, either.

"Then I'll stay, too."

"Don't do that," he said. "Go to New York, the way you and Verity planned. Or we find a place to hide you away from the Arcs. But don't stay here because of me."

I tried to look out the window, but it was frosted over, obscuring the familiar sights of my neighborhood: the auto parts shop, the dry cleaners, the insurance agency. I scraped at it with my thumbnail, concentrating on the lines instead of the pain of his words. "You want me to leave?"

"I want you to be safe. If you stay here, you're going to get caught up in Billy's world. You deserve better than that."

"I deserve to make my own choices," I said. "Why do you get to decide what's right for me?"

"Because I love you."

I twisted to face him, shocked. And then thrilled, giddy with delight, my seat belt the only thing keeping me from throwing myself across the cab at him.

He checked his mirror and changed lanes, then glanced over. "What? You knew that."

"You've never said it. Not really." He'd never said the actual words. Holding back, the same way he held back the truth about his past, and I'd assumed it would stay that way. So I'd been careful not to say it, either, afraid talking about our future would only end badly. We'd slipped into that conversation, anyway, like a river where the most dangerous eddies and rocks were hidden under the surface. The kind of discussion where we had to navigate carefully or risk being smashed to bits. His words felt like someone had thrown me a life preserver.

He jerked a shoulder, but I could see the nervousness in the way his eyes flickered between me and the road. "Now I said it. Does it change things?"

I looped my arm through his. "Yes, you jerk."

He loved me. Maybe I could tell him the truth about what I'd done, and he'd forgive me. You forgave the people you loved, right? Wasn't that what my mom was always saying? Maybe we'd be okay.

He parked a few doors down from Morgan's. "Does it mean you'll listen?"

"Depends on what you're saying, I guess." I unbuckled my seat belt and slid across the bench seat until I was close enough to see the stubble along his jaw, glints of gold and caramel and auburn. His skin smelled like Ivory soap and pine shavings.

He slid a hand around the back of my neck, meeting my eyes. "I love you. I want you safe. I want you happy."

"I'm very happy." More so every minute. His words turned my blood effervescent.

"But you're not safe."

"I haven't been safe since Verity died. You can't stash me away somewhere. I'm not—" *I'm not Tess*, I'd almost said, but caught myself in time. I wasn't ready to reveal I knew about Tess just yet. "I'm not going anywhere."

He pulled me closer, onto his lap, his mouth crushing against mine. The steering wheel dug into my back and I didn't notice, too intent on sliding my hands underneath his Carhartt, feeling the tension in the way his muscles bunched under my fingers, feeling it smooth away as we kissed. The awfulness of Anton rifling through my mind melted away, and when Colin's hand slid underneath my sweater, his thumb rasping along the base of my spine, I forgot all about Anton and Arcs and anything except Colin. Here. Mine. Now.

And then someone tapped on the window, three sharp raps. I pulled back as Colin swore.

The figure behind the fogged glass was familiar, and I slid off Colin's lap onto the seat, wincing at the cold vinyl through my polyester skirt.

I dragged a hand across my mouth as Colin rolled down the window, letting in cold air and frigid disapproval.

"Hey, Dad."

CHAPTER 6

"You're late for work," my father said, voice tight. "Get inside."

I stared at the dash and refastened my coat, cheeks burning.

Colin touched my shoulder. "Let me go with you."

My father was waiting on the curb, arms folded, and I deliberately turned my back on him. "No. I'll deal with him."

With a quick kiss for Colin, I slipped out of the truck and stalked past my dad into the bar. I liked Morgan's better this time of day—dark and peaceful, ESPN turned low on the plasma TV while a few regulars offered their own commentary on last night's basketball game. Charlie was puttering behind the bar, a smile splitting his face as I pulled off my coat and scarf.

"Hey, Mo! How about this girl of yours, Jack? She turned out to be something, huh?"

"Yeah." He frowned at me. "She's a piece of work."

Charlie's smile faltered, and he turned back to the bar while my dad guided me to a table—not Billy's booth in back, but one near the front windows. The wooden blinds were opened, but the pale winter sunshine barely made it inside.

"What the hell was that?"

"Private," I said, laying my coat on the table and dropping my bag on top. "None of your business."

"You act like that in broad daylight, ten feet away from your mother's restaurant? It damn well is my business. I don't want to see it again."

"Don't look." I wasn't going to let him make me feel guilty.

"You're worrying your mother, you know. And she has enough to worry about right now."

"Mom adores Colin."

"Your mom isn't always the best judge of character."

I eyed him. "No kidding."

His face turned a deeper red than his hair. "I'm still your father. I made mistakes, but I'm trying to put them right. And I'm trying to keep you from making a mistake, too. You can do better than Colin Donnelly. He's too old for you."

"I'm almost eighteen."

"It's not about years, it's about the life he's lived. Steer clear of him."

"Okay, first of all? He's my bodyguard. It is physically impossible to steer clear of someone whose job is to watch me all the time. Second of all, I don't want to steer clear of him. And third? You can't stop me."

"I absolutely can. I'm your father, and if I say—"

"You've been gone for *twelve years*. We're way past the stage where you tell me what to do." I glanced around the bar. "Why are you here?"

He sighed. "Working. Same as you, which is another thing I'm not happy about. I know about Ekomov. I don't like this arrangement, Mo."

"Welcome to the club." I gathered my things. "I'm late."

I headed for the back room as he shoved out the front door. Whatever job my dad was doing for Billy, he must have finished it. He'd head home soon enough, filling the house with the sound of cable news, taking back his old seat at the table, leaving his work boots on the back porch, where I kept tripping over them. But of all the changes since his return, my dad's newfound interest in my life was the worst. It was like he wanted to cram twelve years of parenting into the few months I had left at home. My mom was overprotective, sure, but I'd learned how to defuse her worries, how to work around them. We had rules in place, about what things were left unsaid, areas where she gave me slack. Areas like Colin.

My dad didn't know the rules. He was perfectly willing to ask why my hair was a mess when Colin dropped me off. And he wasn't interested in cutting me any slack. Of course, I felt the same way about him.

I ducked into the tiny office to change clothes. When I came out, Billy was waiting for me. "Words with your father?"

I yanked my hair into a ponytail. "Like you care."

"Don't be unpleasant," he said sharply. "I warned you there'd be consequences if you stuck with Donnelly. Just like you to choose the rockiest path you could find."

"Charlie needs me," I said.

"I've got a job for you first," he replied. He pulled a folded piece of paper from his pocket and held it out to me.

I didn't take it. "Another one?"

"If he asks, you saw it sitting under some other papers on my desk and made a copy with that fancy printer. It wouldn't hurt for him to think you're worried about getting caught."

Him, of course, was Yuri Ekomov, a Russian crime boss. And I *was* afraid of getting caught. I'd been passing along information for months to lull him into a false sense of security, so he wouldn't be prepared for my uncle to move against him.

"I am. What's in there, anyway?" I asked, thinking of Jenny. Over the past few months, I'd slipped her the same information Billy had given me. Delivery routes. Addresses. I didn't know how useful the stuff was, but every little bit helped, she assured me.

"Nothing you need to worry about. We've given him enough good information. He thinks he's made inroads. He's overconfident, and now it's time to start slipping him the false bits. For a man in Yuri Ekomov's position, mistakes at this stage are costly."

Not good. The false information wouldn't help Jenny and her people. I'd have nothing for them. "What if he blames me?"

"We'll pull you out before he realizes what's happened," Billy said confidently. I wished I shared his optimism. He pointed to a neat stack of boxes already loaded in a grocery cart. "There's the delivery."

I didn't move, and his nostrils flared. "Don't tell me you're having second thoughts, Mo. Donnelly walks the earth as a free man, but only if you keep your end of the bargain."

"He's not really free." I took the folded-up paper. "Not while you hold Tess over his head."

Billy shrugged. "I've told you, family comes before anything else. Donnelly's a finer example of that than anyone I've met. Frankly, I'm amazed he ever risked Tess for you."

"Thanks," I said dryly, and grabbed the cart, wheeling it back through the restaurant.

But when I peeked through the front window, Colin and the truck—and my dad—were gone. Cold gathered in the pit of my stomach.

"That's bound to be an interesting conversation," said Billy, holding out my coat for me. I trusted his courtesy less than his coldness. "Can you handle going there yourself?"

"I think I can manage." I stared at the spot where the truck should have been. What was my dad doing? Reading Colin the riot act? Threatening him? It took a lot of work to get a reaction out of Colin. He could stay silent and immovable as a boulder for a maddeningly long time, but when he finally broke, it was with the sweeping violence of an avalanche. And if my dad brought up Colin's past, all bets were off.

My hands fisted at my sides. I didn't know my dad's style—was he like Billy, sly and manipulative and always three steps ahead? Or was he more blunt, laying his cards on the table? I had no idea what he was capable of or how far he'd go. It was possible I'd misjudged. It was possible that he was an even bigger threat than Billy, I realized, and my anger was suddenly laced with fear.

It was a short walk to Shady Acres, the senior apartments where Ekomov was hiding out. Edie, the manager, buzzed me into the building with a wave and a smile. I took a deep breath, squared my shoulders, and headed toward the kitchen. The magic nudged me reassuringly, but it didn't change the fact I was on my own. And defenseless.

The kitchen was empty and echoing, my shoes squeaking on the linoleum. I slid the pies onto the long stainless steel counter, taking my time, listening for the sound of footsteps and a cane. A minute later, I heard them.

"What did you bring us today, Mo?" Yuri Ekomov thumped his way across the room and peered at the labels on the boxes. "Lemon squares! They might be the only sunshine we get this week. Your mother is too good to us. Any other treats?"

He was older than my uncle—shoulders drooping; face heavily creased; and dressed, as always, in a suit that seemed just a little too small for him.

I dug in my pocket for the folded paper. "I found a paper on my uncle's desk. It's not the original—I scanned it so he wouldn't know I'd taken anything."

Ekomov nodded and plucked it from my hand. "He doesn't suspect?"

"He's kind of busy right now."

He looked over the paper, then folded it twice and tucked it inside his suit. "Yes, how is your father settling in? Back to his old ways?"

I twisted my hands together, uncomfortable with the suggestion. "I don't know. We haven't spent a lot of time together."

"Understandable. It would be nice if his time away had instilled a sense of caution. I am fond of you, Mo. And your mother, though I only know her through her baking. But I've told you before that a war is coming, and if your father has gone back to his old lifestyle, there's nothing I can do for him."

I picked up the envelope on the counter—Shady Acres' payment to my mom. The payment I got from Yuri Ekomov wasn't cash. It was the promise of protection, a line of credit I'd built up. Of course, since the information I was passing along to him was false, it was a pretty empty promise. And if he found out what I was doing, I'd be the one paying up. "I know."

"Good. All on your own today? I'd have thought your uncle wanted you better protected."

"I think he figures this place is pretty safe." He was wrong. Ekomov inspected me like a piece of fruit at the grocery store, trying to find any soft spots.

"Good. It's better for everyone this way. You and Mr. Donnelly are still an item." His smile held a touch of delight. "It must make your uncle deeply unhappy."

"He's not thrilled."

"How did you manage it?"

I gave him the same story I'd given Colin, but I felt a lot less guilty about it. "I said I'd tell my mom the truth about the fire."

He patted my hand. The magic pulled away briefly, the equivalent of a flinch, and the envelope in my free hand felt damp. "I knew you were an unusual girl. Perhaps we should consider a shift in your responsibilities," he said. "The sooner you're free of your uncle, the better. If we could hasten that process, we'd both benefit."

"What kind of shift?"

"One of your uncle's greatest strengths is the loyalty of people around him. It's what cost you your father. If we knew more about his most trusted employees, we could offer them better terms. Inducements."

A bribe, he meant. Or blackmail. It was exactly the sort of thing Billy would do, and I marveled at the similarity between the two men. If they weren't so busy trying to destroy each other, they'd probably get along really well. "You want me to recruit people for you?"

"No, no. You leave that to us. But if you could get to know them better. Help us get to know them better."

"I . . . don't know." It was one thing to pass along information about shipments and deliveries, but names? It might stop Billy, but Ekomov would simply take his place. Swapping one evil for another wasn't my intention. And what if he wasn't interested in recruitment at all? What if he was just going to start eliminating Billy's people?

"Think about it," he said. "And before you choose, think about where your future truly lies."

CHAPTER 7

Colin's truck was back in front of Morgan's. So was a black Ford sedan, crookedly parked, sporting municipal plates. An inspector from the building department, maybe. The health department.

Or the police.

Inside, the room felt watchful, like everyone was holding their breath. Charlie was somberly polishing glassware at the far end of the room. In the booths lining the wall, the customers kept their heads down and conversations low. Colin stood at the window, pivoting to follow my movements as I entered.

"Everything go okay?" he asked. I nodded, focused on the bar where my father stood with two men I didn't recognize. Judging from their smug demeanor and lack of clipboards, I was pretty sure they weren't the health department.

"You can look all you want," my father said, leaning against his push broom. "Nothing to hide."

"Really, Jack? You were in a hurry to come back here. Twelve years in Terre Haute and your first stop is your old job? Your old boss? Seems like maybe you haven't changed."

"I've changed," he said evenly. "But I have a family to support. If a man wants to take care of his wife and child, you can't hold that against him."

The two men exchanged glances, and one of them scoffed. "You're saying you've learned your lesson? That's great to hear. A valuable contributor to society. We need more of those. You won't mind if we come visit now and again, will you? Make sure you aren't forgetting?"

The other cop called to Charlie. "I like my Scotch on the rocks. Two cubes. Might as well start remembering."

Charlie sent him a look that would blister paint, and turned back to his polishing.

The second cop chuckled and turned around, catching sight of me. "This your girl, Jack? We've seen her around before. You knew Joseph Kowalski."

Slowly, my father straightened, shifting his weight like he was about to pounce. He lifted the broom slightly, adjusting his grip on the wooden handle. But it was the look in his eyes—splintering rage and absolute determination—that had the two cops stepping back. I did, too, bumping up against Colin.

"Come on," he said, mouth at my ear. With the slightest pressure, he nudged me toward the door, but I stood my ground, transfixed by the sight of my father's transformation into something ruthless and deadly.

"No," my father said simply.

"No?" The cops exchanged glances, part puzzlement, part nervous humor.

"No. Do not talk to my daughter. Do not go near my daughter. She does not exist for you."

Just then, Billy stormed up. "What the sweet hell is this?" He raked a glance over the cops. "You have a warrant?"

"Came in for a talk. Nobody invited us to Friday's party."

"No one here wants to talk to you. Either show me a warrant or get out of my bar."

"Sure. We'll stop by another time, Jack, just to catch up. Make sure you're adjusting to life outside."

"Maybe a bunch of other times," the other cop chimed in.

They walked, the shorter of the two men pausing to meet my eyes. Colin's hand tightened on my arm, but we were all silent as they ambled out.

When the door had swung shut behind them, Colin spun me around to face him. "You okay?"

"I'm fine." Confused, more than anything. I wondered if they worked with Jenny. If they knew about our arrangement.

Billy and my father were deep in conversation at the bar, glancing at me every few minutes. "What did they want?" I asked.

"They're warning your dad. He's the weak link in the chain, and everybody knows it."

My father and Billy approached. The murderous look in my dad's eyes was gone, replaced by a wearier, more familiar one. The sound of idle chatter and clinking glasses resumed.

"I didn't mean for you to see that," my dad said.

"Guess I should get used to it." Yet another benefit of my dad's homecoming.

"They're trying to intimidate us," Billy fumed. "Disrupting my business. I won't have it."

"Go ahead and tell them so," I said, pulling the delivery cart toward the back room. "I'm sure they'll listen."

He followed me into the back room. "You gave him the papers?"

"Yeah. It was fine. But . . ." I paused, trying to decide if I should tell him that Ekomov was targeting his employees. I couldn't get those names on my own—the only information I had access to was what Billy gave me. I had to let him know. "He thinks he can recruit some of your guys."

"Does he, now? And what was your answer?"

"I didn't give him one. He said I should think about it."

Billy smiled thinly. "He trusts you. We can use this, you know."

"Use it how?" He was always looking for an angle, but I couldn't imagine what this one would be.

"He's not the only one who wants to know who they can trust." He pushed open the door and barked, "Donnelly. Take her home."

"I just got here." I hated working at Morgan's, but I still needed the tips. Whether I got into NYU or not, I needed to save as much cash as I could. I was determined not to rely on my family for money.

"You've done what was needed. We've business to discuss, and you'll only be underfoot." He shooed me out of the back room. "Off with you."

My father glanced up. "Tell your mother I'll be late for dinner."

"Whatever," I said, rebuttoning my coat. When we got into the truck, I twisted to face Colin. "Business. You know what he means."

"Ease up a little," he said.

It took a minute to get over my shock. "You're taking his side?"

"No. But it wouldn't be the worst thing in the world to cut your dad a little slack."

"If he gets thrown back in prison, it *will* be the worst thing in the world. I can't believe he'd do this to my mom again."

"To her? Or to you?" He touched my hand, and I drew away.

"This is so not about me. I don't want my mom to get her hopes up and think we're going to be some happy family, and then he leaves again. That's it. I don't expect anything from him."

Colin checked the mirrors instead of looking at me. "Good to know."

"What did he say to you? Did he try to pull the over-protective dad act?"

"I don't think it's an act," he said, and this time when he reached for me, I didn't pull back. "He wants to know how you're doing. For some reason, he thinks you're not likely to open up. So he asked me about you."

"And warned you off."

He shrugged and laced his fingers with mine.

"He has no right to interfere. No right at all," I said. "Let's go back to your place."

"Your mom's expecting you."

"Not till after work. She doesn't know I left early. Besides, it's not like I'm violating curfew or anything. I even have my bodyguard with me."

We stopped for a light, and Colin tapped the wheel, considering. "My place?"

"Come on," I wheedled. "My mom's just going to nag me about school and my dad. And we haven't had any time alone in ages."

"We're alone right now."

"In a moving vehicle. That doesn't count." I paused, noting the way the corner of his mouth twitched, like he was biting back a smile. When I spoke again, my voice was innocent and mild as cream. "Unless you're afraid to be alone with me."

He kissed me, fast and hard. When I caught my breath again, I asked, "That's a yes, I take it?"

"Yes and no. Yes, we can go to my place. No, I'm not afraid to be alone with you."

I leaned into him, smiling as his arm wrapped around my shoulders. "Good."

We didn't talk much until we were back inside his apartment. The outer door was new, heavy steel with a reinforced frame. My uncle's men had battered down the old one in the fall. Colin had installed this one as soon as his cracked ribs had healed. He could turn the building into a fortress, but the truth was, the only thing keeping us safe was the deal I'd cut with Billy.

At the time, I'd been convinced I could find a way out, hatch a plan that would set all three of us—Colin, his sister, and me—free. I was working every angle I could, but so far we were still stuck. The possibility we'd stay stuck was looking more likely.

"Coffee?" he asked, helping me out of my coat. "You make it, and I'll get a fire going."

"Sure." In the past few months, I'd gotten familiar with Colin's place—enough that I knew my way around the kitchen, and it felt right. Easy. I waited while he stowed his gun in the locked cabinet, then pulled him over for another kiss.

I loved these moments. Small and quiet, the two of us alone, hidden from the rest of the world. We didn't get them nearly enough these days, with my mom working less and my job at Morgan's. When Colin wrapped his arms around me, resting his chin on top of my head with a satisfied sigh, I could almost believe we were a normal couple. Almost.

He gave me a gentle push toward the coffeemaker and crossed the living room to the wood stove in the corner.

I watched him crouch in front of the open door and begin building the fire, and then busied myself with filters and beans.

"What else did you and my dad talk about?"

"He wanted to know about your college plans." He made some minute adjustments to the layers of newspaper and kindling and cordwood. "Have you heard from NYU?"

"Not yet. Besides, I might not get in. Jill McAllister's already got a spot, and they don't usually take more than one girl from St. Brigid's."

He glanced over his shoulder at me. "Do you have safety schools?"

"Of course." Acceptance letters and e-mails from my safeties had been trickling in—as well as some of my "reach" schools, but I'd stayed quiet, waiting for the right time to tell him. Hoping I could find a way out for both of us. But now was as good a time as any to lay the groundwork. I concentrated on pouring water into the coffeemaker, not meeting his eyes. "Maybe I'll go to school in the city."

I heard the rasp of a match and the whoosh of the newspaper catching fire. "You're supposed to leave. That's always been the plan."

"Are you trying to get rid of me?" Worry began to gnaw at my rib cage, but I kept my voice light and punched the start button.

"The longer you stay, the more danger you're in. When someone knows as much about the Forellis as you do, they figure you're either an asset or a liability. You're nothing more than a weapon to them, Mo. And if they can't use you, they'll get rid of you. The only safe thing to do is get out of town."

A weapon. That's what I'd be if Anton or the Quartoren found out about the magic, too. I was right to keep quiet. About everything.

"But you won't come with me."

"I can't."

"Then neither can I." Sadness twisted sharply inside me, guilt welling up. I'd promised Verity that I'd go to New York. It had been our dream for so long, a goal I'd worked toward for years. But I had already lost one person I loved. I wasn't interested in losing another. I tamped down on the unhappiness and perched on the arm of the couch. "We both stay."

He slammed the stove door shut with a clang. "No."

"You love me," I said. "That should count for something."

"Don't make it leverage, Mo. Don't use it to force my hand." Something cold crossed his expression.

I'd heard girls at school say that to their boyfriends all the time. *If you loved me, you'd give me your class ring . . . let me borrow your car . . . blow off your friends.* It had always seemed whiny. Petulant, even, like a little kid throwing a tantrum. But the look on Colin's face made it seem more insidious—like using someone's love against them.

"I know you won't leave. I'm not even asking you to. But . . . you should let me stay. You should love me enough to let me choose."

He sat down, taking my hand in his. "What if you choose wrong?"

"You have to trust that I won't." It shouldn't be such a leap, trusting me. How could you love someone if you couldn't trust them? I'd made my choice. Now I had to make it the right one. "If I stayed here, would it be so terrible?"

Before he could answer, I pressed my mouth to his, hungry for reassurance. Whatever he said was lost in the kiss, and then I was lost, too, and he was all I had to hold on to. His hands slid underneath my sweater, under my T-shirt, his fingers dipping to the waistband of my jeans, and I whimpered, not sure how to ask for more but wanting it all the same.

The coffeemaker beeped from across the room, and he broke off. "Wait."

"No." I slid my arms around his neck, pulling him back to me.

"Mo. Wait. What about your uncle? Your parents?"

I looked around, deliberately. "They aren't here. I can handle them, and I swear to God if you use them as an excuse to put the brakes on, I will beat you with that fireplace poker."

He glanced at the poker in question, then turned back to me, eyes crinkling.

"Don't laugh," I warned. "I am out of my mind with wanting you, and I am done waiting. Done. Got it?"

And just to wipe the smirk off his face, I dragged off my sweater and T-shirt, the warmth of the stove a solid presence at my back. He swallowed visibly and his hands tightened on my waist. "Got it," he said, and pulled me down to him, our bodies tangling together, his teeth scraping along my collarbone.

I tugged off his shirt, wanting to kiss away the scars along his back.

"Jeans," I mumbled while he kissed my throat. "Off."

"Mo . . . slow down." He paused, his breathing fast and shallow.

"Seriously? Did you not hear the part where I said I was done with waiting?" I shook my head. "You should listen better."

"So should you. I said slow down, not stop."

"Why? No one's expecting me home for hours. We have all the time in the world."

"Exactly," he said, eyes serious, so dark they seemed bottomless, and I wanted to forget myself in them. "Why rush?"

"Oh." I laughed then, and shoved him back onto the couch. His hands roamed over me, even better and hotter than I remembered. In a moment, he'd reversed our positions, leaning over me while I sank into the worn velvet of the couch. I shimmied out of my jeans, and he groaned.

"I'm not sleeping with you," he said, trapping my hands above my head easily.

"Noted," I said, trying to wriggle away. "No sleeping."

"I mean I'm not having sex with you."

"Really? Because . . ." I arched against him and smiled when his eyes drifted shut. "I'm not saying I'm an expert, but that kind of seems like the direction we're heading."

He kept my wrists pinned with one hand and held my hip with the other, putting too much distance between us. "How many guys have you slept with?"

"That's kind of a personal question."

"Considering how much clothing you're wearing and where my hands have been, I think we've reached the stage where we can ask personal questions."

I felt a flush spread over my body. "How many girls have you slept with?"

His fingers stilled on my hip. "Enough to know what I'm doing."

"And you think I don't?" I yanked a hand free and flipped open the button of his jeans.

He kissed me, mouth open and searching, and I whimpered, trying to press myself closer.

"How many?" he asked again.

I scowled at him. "Why does it matter?"

"None, right?"

I twisted away, wrenching out of his grasp. I might not have had much experience with guys, but this was definitely not how it was supposed to go.

"I told you before, Mo. I don't want to be the guy you sleep with and then keep a secret."

"So I should shout it from the rooftops?"

"I would prefer you didn't," he said. "And I'd rather not have your first time be on my couch."

"You have a bedroom," I said. "If that's the problem. . . ."

"That's not the problem, and you know it. It's a big deal. It should be special. Not an impulse thing. It doesn't work so good that way."

"You know what's not going to work? If you're a condescending jerk," I snapped.

"I'm not saying we can't do anything, Mo. Just not . . . that. Not yet. It's illegal," he pointed out reasonably.

"I'm eighteen in three months."

"Great. In three months, we can do this again, and I won't stop you. But for now . . . no."

I huffed out a breath, partly out of frustration and partly to see how his eyes tracked the movement. "Three months is a really long time."

He grinned. "We'll manage." His hand slid down my body, and his mouth followed, and as I felt myself go completely weightless underneath him, I decided he might be right.

CHAPTER 8

I missed dinner entirely.

By the time Colin dropped me at home, the house was silent. I could see the silhouette of my mom in the upstairs window, getting ready for bed. I eased open the door and punched in the alarm code. The kitchen was dark, and I crept across, grateful I would be spared an interrogation until the morning.

"Where have you been?" my father asked.

I jumped, but managed not to shriek. "Jesus, Dad!"

"I asked you a question." He stood in the basement door-way—not a big man, but managing to fill it all the same.

"I called Mom," I said defensively. "I had dinner with Colin."

"It's ten o'clock at night. No one eats that late."

I gestured to my messenger bag. "Homework. I'm not grounded, you know. I'm in before curfew. I didn't do anything wrong."

He snorted. "Please, Mo. If you're going to lie to my face, put a little more effort into it."

I froze. He might suspect, but he didn't know. Skin didn't show fingerprints. And he hadn't been around enough to figure out when I was lying.

"Good night," I said, brushing past him on my way up the stairs.

"About today," he called after me. "The police, at the bar. It's not what you think."

I paused, glancing at him over the banister. "Tell you what, Dad. How about you stay out of my business, and I'll stay out of yours. That seems like a fair trade, doesn't it? And neither of us has to lie."

He dragged a hand over his face, looking exhausted. "I'm trying, Mo. It's not easy, but I'm trying to be a better man."

"Good luck with that."

Three hours later, I jolted awake to the sound of the world splitting open and a hand clamping roughly over my mouth, cutting off my scream before it began.

An instant later, the lamp next to my bed switched itself on, revealing Luc. His eyes were bright and hard, like emeralds. I sank back, pulling the quilt up to my chest. There was no hiding from Luc, though. Even the magic seemed cowed by his temper. After a moment, he pulled his hand away from my mouth, clamping it around my wrist instead. I felt the lines swell, cloaking us so that my parents wouldn't wake up.

"Niobe told you."

"Better." Our binding crackled with his fury, but his voice was brutally calm. "Dominic. Loved every second of it, too. Came waltzin' into the Dauphine with a full complement of guards, tellin' me you'd been attacked, askin' how I hadn't known that *the girl I'm bound to* was in mortal danger."

"I was fine. And Niobe said you knew." But it must have hurt him, to hear it secondhand—and I could only imagine how much his father had enjoyed delivering the news in the most humiliating way possible—punishing Luc for daring to put me ahead of the Quartoren's needs.

"Because *Dominic* told me. You promised to summon me if there was trouble, and three days later, you're breakin' your word. Makes a man lose faith. And then I can't get a moment alone with you, between school and your family and whatever the hell you were doin' at Cujo's tonight."

"I told you not to spy on me."

"It ain't spying if you jump the man in broad daylight," he said, and my cheeks burned.

"I'm sorry. I should have told you about Anton."

He dragged his free hand through his hair. "Damn straight. Remember when I first met you? You were all about findin' out the truth. Couldn't stand bein' lied to. It was the one thing you couldn't forgive. Now look at you—there's not a single person you're straight with."

"I didn't lie to you! Niobe said . . ."

"Niobe said you saw Anton at the party. That's what you felt, wasn't it? Not just the lines. *Anton.* And you kept it from me."

"I thought I imagined it. What was the point worrying you over nothing?"

He laughed bitterly, and I flinched. "Nothing? You're my heart, Mouse. You're my fate. I don't care if you don't like it, if you love someone else, if you're going to run from me till you've circled the earth. You're not nothing. Not to me. And if Anton is coming after you now, I am your best shot at staying alive."

"I'm sorry." But this apology was bigger. It was about more than Anton, or keeping things from Luc. It was an apology for not being the girl he wanted me to be. The one he needed me to be. Fate guided him like a touchstone, but I turned away from it, determined to find my own path. We were bound—magically, irrevocably tied to each other—and yet I'd chosen Colin and a life with the Flats over the one we were supposed to have together, leaving Luc to deal with the fallout. It had hurt him so terribly. Sometimes, I thought it had hurt me, too, in ways I couldn't quite understand. But I couldn't let him see me waver. Couldn't open the door to regret. Because the moment I did, it would ruin everything I'd fought for.

"The Quartoren want to see you."

"I don't want to see them."

He sat down next to me, and I shifted to give him more room. "They don't much care. If it was only your life at stake, they'd stay out of it. But it's the magic, too, and they've got a responsibility to their people." He waited a beat. "To my people, Mouse. Something happens to you, to the magic. . . . They all suffer. I can't let that happen." His grip on my wrist loosened, and he rubbed a thumb over the scar on my palm. "Don't think you can, either."

You had to hand it to Luc—he knew exactly which buttons to push. It was one thing to spite the Quartoren, who had proven they cared nothing about me. It was another to walk away from the well-being of an entire society.

"I need to get dressed," I said, climbing out of the bed.

He sighed and flopped back, pulling one of the pillows over his face.

I changed quickly, pulling on jeans and a long cardigan over my T-shirt. I caught a slight movement out of the corner of my eye.

"You're peeking."

"Can't blame a man for tryin'." He tossed the pillow aside, unrepentant, and rolled out of bed with a languid, cat-like grace that made me feel clumsy standing still. "All set?"

"No."

He laughed as we went Between.

CHAPTER 9

We came through in a familiar white, high-ceilinged room, the thunderclap sound of going Between echoing off the walls. I breathed in the scent of beeswax from the candles overhead, steadying myself. It was no longer dangerous for me to go Between. Now that I'd bonded with the magic, the only side effect was dizziness, instead of feeling as though my internal organs had been rearranged. Even so, it took a minute to orient myself.

Luc kept a hand on my waist, the other curving over my shoulder. "You okay?"

"Yeah." When his eyebrows lifted, skeptical, I shrugged. "I'm fine. It's different now."

He let go of me grudgingly as the doors to the main chamber opened.

"Mo!" exclaimed Marguerite. "Welcome back, my dear."

She nodded at the guard standing next to her—an Arc I didn't recognize, who melted back into the shadowy room. Luc's mother was blind, though she moved with such innate grace, it was easy to forget. Small and lovely, she barely came to Luc's shoulder as he guided her forward. I caught the faintest wisp of freesia as she embraced me.

"Your father's inside," she said to Luc, her hand on my arm. "And in a temper. Did you have words before you left?"

He shifted uncomfortably. "Nothing new."

She sighed. "I suppose it's good that someone stands up to that man. I certainly can't."

Luc allowed himself the slightest smile. "You don't need to stand up to him, *Maman*. He's always fallin' at your feet."

"Go on, now," she said with a shooing motion, a pleased blush tinting her cheeks. I suspected Luc was absolutely right. Dominic might be the Patriarch of the House, but Marguerite was head of the family. "Tell him we'll be along in a minute. And to mind his manners when we get there."

"As if he'll listen," Luc grumbled.

I liked watching the easy, obvious affection between them, the way Luc seemed to forget about his responsibilities and the weight of his position. It was a side of him I rarely saw, and unexpectedly sweet.

"Son," she called, and he paused to glance at us over his shoulder. "You mind your manners, too."

"Yes'm," he said with a distinct lack of enthusiasm.

When he'd left, she turned to me again. "It is so good to have you here, Mo. I've wondered how you've been getting on."

It should have been easier to lie to Marguerite, since she couldn't see my expression. But I didn't even try. "I'm scared."

"Of course you are. Anyone with an ounce of sense would be scared. Rivening's a terrible thing, and for that alone Anton Renard should be drawn and quartered." She sniffed, adjusted the cashmere wrap around her shoulders. "I was referring to the magic, though. Are the two of you . . . adjusting?"

The two of us. Marguerite knew. I'd wondered, after our last encounter, if she realized what had happened, if she'd guessed at the true nature of the magic. Clearly, she had. And just as clearly, she hadn't said anything to Luc. I wondered why—and if it meant I was right to keep quiet.

"I'm getting there. It's kind of a gradual process."

"I would imagine. You haven't told Luc."

"No." How to tell Marguerite that, even after he'd risked his life for me, I didn't know where Luc's loyalties lay. If he sided with the Quartoren, I couldn't trust him. If he sided with me . . . it would mean something I wasn't capable of handling. Safer to keep the truth hidden, at least for now.

"Your fear is understandable," Marguerite said. "And you're right to guard such a powerful secret. But you'll tell him eventually."

I swallowed. She wasn't asking me—she was telling. "When?"

"That's for you to decide." She paused. "I can't see everything, you know. Only slivers of the future, taken out of context."

"That must . . ." Suck, I wanted to say. "Be difficult."

"It's better that way, actually. I knew I'd have Luc. Can you imagine my surprise? All that time, his brother practically grown. And suddenly, I saw another son, years before he appeared. If I'd known the fullness of what would happen, I wouldn't have enjoyed it. Might have resented him, even, and that would have been a terrible thing."

"I don't understand." Luc had a brother, I remembered, but he'd died. Luc never talked about it. The loss must have devastated Marguerite, but I couldn't imagine why she would have resented her only remaining child.

"Luc's lost so much already. He carries burdens I can't begin to fathom. But I know what I've seen, Mo. All of the prophecies are clear—your fate and his are tied so tightly, more than anyone realizes. Like you and the magic, in some ways. If you hold back the truth from him, you'll both be hurt." She touched her hair, tucking a stray wisp back into its elaborate twist. "I know you don't want to leave your Flat life behind, but you are meant for so much more."

"That was Verity, not me." The old hurt surfaced again. The pain of losing Verity, and of knowing I couldn't measure up. The fatigue of fighting against a force I didn't even believe in.

"This is more than a single prophecy. It's a chance to shape the future of our world. Verity was never called for such a task. Only you."

"I don't know what I'm supposed to do," I said softly.

"Become what you're meant to. There's no heavier charge, but it can't be helped." She smiled regretfully. "And I'd ask you to do a kindness for me, as well."

"Anything." Marguerite had been nothing but kind to me. I was eager to return the favor.

"Help Luc. He needs to see that becoming his own man is just as important as any destiny he's taken on."

I'd given so much thought to what the Arcs considered my destiny, I rarely thought about Luc's. But his future had been laid out in prophecies as well—his place as the Heir, bound to me, charged with saving the magic and stopping the Ascendency. I wondered what sort of life he would have chosen, left to his own devices. He'd probably never considered the possibility.

"He won't believe that, coming from me." Not when I'd railed against the idea of destiny all along.

"Oh, Mo. You're the only one he will believe." She stood. "Come. I imagine Dominic is near to bursting, we've kept him so long."

I guided her toward the doors Luc had gone through, massive metal slabs, and she reached out, rapping five times in quick succession. The metal glowed where she'd struck it, and the doors swung open.

Inside was the Assembly, the seat of the Quartoren. I'd been here before, to sign the Covenant that protected Constance. Like before, it was empty, the rows of seats reaching upward. But my attention was riveted on the group clustered onstage, seated at a massive black table that nearly vibrated with power.

Luc met us halfway down the aisle. "Good chat?"

Marguerite smacked him lightly on the arm. "Don't pry, son."

He guided her to a chair along the side of the stage as I approached the Quartoren, my smile falling away.

"Maura," said Dominic coolly. He didn't rise from the table. Luc's father was a broad-shouldered man with mahogany skin, narrowed eyes, and an air of unmistakable

command. Patriarch of the Fire Arcs, he was the strongest of
the Quartoren, and the one I trusted the least.

"Dominic." I inclined my head. It came across as a gesture
of respect, but really I wanted to see the symbols shifting
along the table in front of me. If I squinted, I could almost
bring them into focus enough to read. But like letters in a
dream, they wiggled away just as I started to understand.
They were the language of the magic, I'd been told once. My
nerves tingled as the source strained to connect with them,
like calling to like.

"What do they say?" I asked as Luc rejoined me, fingertips
brushing the back of my hand.

"I don't see why you'd need to know." Orla, Matriarch of
the Air Arcs and the lone woman of the Quartoren, sniffed.
She was old and plump, fussy about protocol, and absolutely
despised me. She frowned as we neared the dais. Of the three
Arcs in front of me, she was the least dangerous—her hostil-
ity was out in the open, and easiest to defend against.

"It's the language of the magic in its purest state. The symbols form the charter of our people. They delineate the
Houses, and by extension, the Quartoren," Pascal said, giving her a quelling glance. "No Arc can speak it perfectly, but
these are the original words of power. Everything else is a dis-
tortion, no matter how slight."

As always, Pascal stood off to the side. His face brightened, studying me with undisguised curiosity. He was the scientist of the group. According to Luc, no one knew more
about how the magic worked than Pascal. I'd always gotten
the sense he viewed me as a particularly fascinating experiment, which was unnerving, but kind of a relief. He left the
subterfuge and manipulation to Dominic. It was one less battle to fight, and I'd come to view every interaction with the
Quartoren as a skirmish.

"We're not here to discuss spellcasting," Dominic said.

I folded my arms. "Why *are* we here? It's the middle of the
night."

"Anton managed to elude us this afternoon," Dominic

said. You could almost hear him grinding his teeth at the admission, and he straightened the lapels of his suit. "Seems likely he'll try for you again. You need protection."

I scoffed. "Like I'd trust you guys to protect me."

Orla puffed up like a outraged pigeon. "Do you think we're asking your permission?"

The Quartoren didn't ask permission of anyone—especially not a lowly Flat.

"I don't need protection. I need a way to fight them."

"Happy to show you some hand-to-hand," Luc said.

I rolled my eyes at him.

Dominic nodded approval. "Not a bad idea. There are other steps we can take as well. But the fact is, you need us."

"And you expect something in return, of course. Are you offering another Covenant? Because I'd rather take my chances with the Seraphim."

"We'll protect you no matter what, because it's what our people require," said Orla. "Whatever else you think of us, you know our Houses are our first concern."

Pascal spoke, pushing his glasses up the bridge of his nose. "Be logical, Maura. The Seraphim are aware that you and the magic are interdependent. Anton's willingness to hurt you signals he's willing to hurt the magic, too. It's only reasonable to conclude that his goal is to use the connection between you to trigger the Ascendency. He'll continue to attack you until the magic is weak enough to do so."

Understanding flashed through me, and as it did, the magic reared up in alarm, streaming through the lines like a broken levee. The symbols carved into the table before me glowed and trembled, light beaming out from them. Orla gasped, stumbling backward, and Luc thrust me behind him.

"It's okay." I dropped to my knees, dizzy. Luc sank down next to me, his body a shield, his arms caging me in. "It's okay," I repeated, and concentrated on calming myself, calming the magic, slowing my breathing and the rush of blood through my veins.

Gradually, the terrible brilliance dimmed. My heartbeat

eased. The room came back into focus, and the first thing I saw was Luc, eyes roving over me, his hands gently cradling my face.

"Mouse? You hurt?"

Our connection trembled, and I laid a hand over his. "Everything's fine." I didn't know if the words were for him or for the magic, one last bit of reassurance. "What about you?"

"Never seen that before," he said, brushing away my concern. "What was it?"

"Maura felt threatened," Pascal said from behind the table. He rested a hand on the blackened wood. "And the fear triggered a reaction from the magic, likely as a result of the bond you've formed."

I glanced at Marguerite, who remained in her chair, hands calmly folded in her lap. She tipped her head toward the sound of Luc's voice, the gesture a message. Luc needed to know, but not the Quartoren. Now wasn't the time.

It was strategy, not cowardice. That's what I told myself.

Luc's grip on my shoulders was firm, as if he could divine the truth just by holding on long enough, and I shrugged away, directing my words to Pascal. "You're the expert."

"We need your help," Dominic said, clearly loathe to ask. "You know what's at stake here."

I did, even more than Dominic realized. But knowing the stakes didn't change the facts—I was still powerless.

"How could I possibly help you?" The bravado I'd shown Anton at school was a bluff. If the Seraphim attacked, I'd be helpless—whether it came in the form of Rivening or Darklings or something entirely different.

"Come to the Succession," Dominic said. "You're a member of the House, by virtue of being the Vessel, so you've got a right to attend."

"I'm the reason they *need* a Succession," I pointed out. "Everyone knows I killed the last Matriarch, thanks to Anton's display at the Allée. Somehow, I don't think the Water Arcs are going to throw me a welcome party."

"Actually," said Orla, "the events of that night are not common knowledge. While you've been off taking tests and carting drinks around a pub, we've spent the last few months ensuring that our people know it was you who stopped the Torrent and repaired the breach in the magic. Anton's followers blame you, of course, but many people are appreciative of what you've done. And many are still loyal to the Quartoren."

Loyal to the Quartoren and loyal to me were different things entirely, and I was about to say so when Dominic spoke. "Fact is, we're at a disadvantage. Anton's promising the Ascendency before the Succession is complete, and with only three members, The Quartoren looks weak. You've saved our people twice. Standing with us at the Succession confirms what they know deep down. That the old ways— the Quartoren, the Houses, the very foundations of our society—are the ones that should hold."

"Even if I don't know that myself?"

Orla reared back. "Would you prefer the Seraphim take over? They will decimate our people. They'll come after yours as well, mark my words. Don't forget what they did to Verity."

As if that was a possibility? I remembered every day, and I hated Orla more than I ever had before, simply for suggesting I would ever let it go.

She carried on, oblivious to my anger. "You would really let the people who killed your best friend achieve their ultimate goal? What happened to the vengeance you've always spoken of? Your willingness to sacrifice in order to give her justice?"

"Don't," said Luc in a low voice. "Don't you dare guilt her into this."

Dominic spread his hands wide, affable, warm. It was a deliberate contrast to Orla, and I didn't fall for it. "We have to protect you, Maura. All we're asking is that you stand up with us publicly. Show our people we're still strong. Once the

Quartoren is restored to its full authority, we can crush the Seraphim underfoot."

"I do this, and the Seraphim will be finished? How?"

"No need for you to worry about that," said Dominic. "For now, the key is to keep you alive."

Luc touched my hand. "That's where I come in. We can put wards around the places you go, give you a guard. Conceal you from the Darklings, like Evangeline did before. And then we take the fight to Anton." He raised an eyebrow. "You up for it?"

I knotted my fingers together, listening to the magic's response. Fear, and a desperate longing for peace. And I heard something else, the faintest whisper in the back of my mind, that this could be the opening I'd sought. Not the magic, but the sly and hungry part of me that still wanted vengeance.

Killing Evangeline hadn't been enough. There had been others who'd ordered Verity's death. It wasn't right that they should live and not her. It wasn't fair that I had to face this new world without her by my side. It wasn't fair that all the plans we'd made had been ruined and I had to carry them out on my own. They deserved to be punished, every last one of them. For once, I agreed with Orla. Defeating the Seraphim was exactly what they deserved. It was what Verity deserved. In a way, I deserved it, too.

Still, the Quartoren had deceived me before—traded on my loyalty to benefit themselves. I needed to tread carefully.

"I'll go to the Succession. But that's it. I'm not going to stand there and argue your case to the rest of the Arcs."

Orla sniffed. "We want your appearance, not your opinion."

I gave her a patently false smile. "So glad we understand each other."

Pascal cut in. "The first night of the Succession is less than two weeks from now. If Anton and his people hope to trigger the Ascendency, they'll strike before then."

Luc elbowed me, trying to lighten the mood. "Sounds like we'll be spending quality time together, Mouse."

"Time . . ." I breathed, and looked at my watch. It was almost three.

He caught my meaning and asked, "We about done here?"

Dominic was tracing the symbols of the table, seemingly distracted. "For now."

"Good." We said good-bye to Marguerite, and Luc led me out of the Assembly; through the candlelit entryway; down the wide, shallow cathedral steps; and into the street. Unlike last time, when our night wanderings had revealed a hauntingly beautiful, quiet city, the streets were jammed with people milling about, large plastic cups in hand. It was like the Taste of Chicago, only . . . more. Noiser, pushier, friendlier, gaudier, messier.

"What happened?" I asked as Luc took my hand, leading me away from the revelry.

"Carnival," he said. "Mardis Gras starts today. Nonstop party since January, and this will be the worst of it."

A group of shirtless, drunken frat boys leaned over one of the ornate balconies, shouting lewd comments and suggestions for how I could earn beads. I ignored them, but Luc's expression darkened, and he flicked a finger, muttering something that started with "Damn tourists," and ended in magic. The lines flexed as he drew on them.

"Hey, baby! Show us your—"

The metalwork glowed white hot in the night air—the frat boys yelped and howled, backing away, waving their hands wildly. Burn marks marred their bare stomachs where they'd leaned on the railing, and they fled into the apartment, shouting for ice. I stumbled after Luc, who had picked up the pace.

"Not a fan?" I asked.

People scattered out of our way, and since I couldn't feel Luc using the lines to clear a path through the crowd, I had to assume it was the ferocity of his expression. "I'm all for misbehavin' now and again. But you shouldn't do it if you ain't prepared for the consequences."

"I don't think anyone's prepared for those kinds of consequences," I said. "It was a little extreme, Luc."

"Maybe they'll think twice before they do it again. Maybe they'll stay in tonight, rather than going to a bar and harassin' every girl who has the misfortune of runnin' into them. Speaking of which, you okay?"

"I hear worse on the El. I can handle myself."

He snorted. "Know you like to think so. Different world, Mouse."

We turned down a side alley, and the press of bodies eased. There was a gentle breeze, scented with flowers instead of sweat and trash and cigarettes. I sighed in relief and studied the narrow brick street.

"This is one of yours, right?"

"Yeah. Two blocks or so. We've got little pockets all over the city." Streets that wouldn't show up on maps, enclaves of Arcs living unnoticed by Flats. Luc stopped in front of a familiar courtyard, opening the gate and drawing me through.

"I need to go home," I said. "I have school. My parents will be waking up soon."

"We can talk here, or in your bedroom. Your choice."

"Here's good."

"Thought you might agree." We climbed the narrow staircase, the line of his shoulders stiff with pent-up frustration.

Once inside, I crossed to the French doors, peering through the wavy glass at the teeming mass in the Quarter. Music filtered in, jazz and zydeco warring with each other. "Will it be like this all day?"

"Gets busier. Parades start in the mornin', Uptown. By afternoon, every street in the Quarter is one big masquerade."

"Do the Arcs participate?"

"Sure. We don't mingle much the rest of the year, but Carnival's different." He joined me at the window. "Are you sure you're okay?"

"I told you, it takes more than a drunk guy with a big mouth to freak me out."

"I meant Anton. The Rivening. You handling it?"

Just the mention of it made me feel dirty, long for a scalding hot shower, but I didn't want to appear weak. "It was a shock. But he didn't have enough time to really hurt me." To keep from looking at Luc, I wandered over to the mantel and studied the objects there—a primitive-looking wood carving, a small oil portrait of two boys, a cluster of white roses in a tarnished silver cup.

"Anton was after something," Luc said. "What was it?"

"I don't know. He said I had secrets." And he'd seen so many of mine. Even the ones I tried to keep from myself.

"Right on that count, anyway."

"What's that supposed to mean?"

"It means you're not telling me everything. Anton's run you to ground twice now. In your world, not ours. There's a reason for it. You think I believe the table lighting up at the Assembly was because you're scared? Told you," he said, standing a shade too close, near enough that I caught the scent of him, cinnamon and smoke. "You can't lie to me. I see through it. I see you."

"Since when have we operated under full disclosure, Luc? You keep things from me all the time."

"Used to," he corrected. "Nothing to hide these days. Unlike you."

I toyed with the buttons of my cardigan. "I need to understand it better before I tell you."

"It's the magic," Luc said. "When it flared up, you were surprised, but not scared. Can you work a spell? Use the lines?"

"No. Nothing that simple."

"We can help you figure it out," he said. "Pascal would know what's going on."

"Pascal would make me his latest experiment. And he'd dissect me if it helped him figure everything out. I'm not going to the Quartoren about this."

I had a sudden vision of Luc telling the Quartoren everything, handing me over because he believed that beneath their robes, they were dedicated to saving the magic. I knew better.

He tapped the mantel, his concern turning to irritation.

"Seraphim will come after you again. They will Riven your mind and turn you inside out. You don't trust the Quartoren, fine. But I'm not them, not yet, and I will do my damnedest to protect you."

"From the Seraphim? Or the Quartoren?"

He didn't have an answer, and it stung more than I expected. "That's the problem. You keep saying I have to decide which life I want—Flats or Arcs—but I'm not the only one with a choice to make." I checked my watch again. "It's late, Luc. Can I please go home?"

"Sure thing. But Mouse . . ." He pulled me closer with one hand, cut a doorway into the air with the other. His voice was low and amused, though there was an unmistakable strain to it. "What makes you think I haven't already decided?"

CHAPTER 10

It didn't seem fair that I could be connected to so much power and yet couldn't tap into it—not even to keep myself awake the next morning. I slogged through breakfast, dozed on Colin's shoulder during the ride to school, and prepared for a day of sleepwalking through my classes. But as we approached the school, I started to feel jittery, like I'd had a pot of coffee instead of a cup. And when I got out of the truck, my adrenaline spiked higher.

St. Brigid's had plenty of ley lines crossing the grounds, but they were fairly quiet. Occasionally, I'd feel Niobe or Constance using them, particularly when they went Between, but for the most part they were practically unnoticeable.

But this morning, every single line that bordered or crossed the building was quivering with energy. Arcs from every House were drawing on them. I held on to the door, feeling the power charging the air around me like an electrical storm.

"Problem?" Colin asked.

"I don't know." I leaned back into the cab, and he kissed me, a momentary sweetness that grounded me. "Arcs. Lots of them."

He couldn't see them but looked anyway. "Should we leave?"

"It's better to face them down. I'll go talk to Niobe."

No one else seemed to notice the hum in the air as I crossed the courtyard, but I was acutely aware of a hundred unseen eyes watching me. Niobe met me inside the doors.

"Tell me this is not permanent," I said, gesturing to a nearby current.

"The Quartoren were adamant, Mo. You need protection."

"It's making me crazy." The constant thrum of the lines raised goose bumps along my arms. "There's got to be at least twenty people here. Doesn't it bother you?"

Her brow furrowed. "I can only feel my own lines, and they're not bothersome. Perhaps you're more sensitive due to your abilities. It's actually better this way—the guards will alert us if Anton approaches, and I can remove you to a safe place while they deal with him."

Like a magical version of the Secret Service. I wondered if they had little earpieces. Then I wondered if all the energy pumping through my system was making me a little loopy.

"They have to go," I said, trying to focus. "Call Orla and tell her to pull them out. I can't spend all day like this."

"You should count yourself fortunate. The Quartoren were all for locking you away until after the Succession. For your own good."

A coldness crept into me. "They can't . . ."

"They're the Quartoren, and they're entitled to do what they deem necessary to protect the magic. Luc argued against it and won. This time. But if you can't find a way to ensure the magic's safety—and defeat the Seraphim—you'll spend your life in protective custody, no matter how hard Luc fights for you."

"Protective custody?" I started to argue, enraged, and the rest of her words filtered through. "Luc stood up for me? Against the Quartoren?"

She eyed me speculatively. "I've known Luc for a long time. The mantle of the Heir would have stripped the humanity from anyone else, burned away the softness and decency and left behind only the duty and the power. He's managed to avoid that, but if you continue putting yourself at risk, you'll force him to leave himself behind completely."

Before I could ask more, Lena strolled up. "You coming? All-school assembly in five."

"Then you'd best get under way." Niobe turned on her heel and strode off.

"I thought guidance counselors were supposed to be warm and fuzzy," Lena said. "That woman makes Sister Donna look like a Care Bear."

"She takes some getting used to," I said. "Any rumors about the Lenten Service Project this year?"

"Not that I've heard. But we'll know in a few minutes."

Every Lent, the school administration chose an all-school service project: forty days of donating our time to those in need. Last year it had been tutoring disadvantaged kids. The year before, reading to veterans at a nearby VA facility. It was a graduation requirement, a yearly tradition, and two months' worth of shortened classes.

As we filed into the gymnasium, the magic—and my nerves—settled, acclimating to the vibrating lines. As Sister Donna strode to the podium, habit flapping behind her, the fidgety feeling faded. She droned on about the purpose of Lent, the same speech she gave every year, and the magic washed over me like white noise. I struggled to stay awake despite the uncomfortable wooden steps.

"Wake up," Lena hissed, elbowing me in the side. "You drool on my sweater and I will shove you off these bleachers."

"Sorry," I whispered. "Late night."

She waggled her eyebrows. "Colin?"

"Nothing so fun." Sister Donna concluded her speech, the girls around us applauding dutifully, and I clapped, too. "Okay, I missed it. Where are we going?"

"Soup kitchens and homeless shelters."

From across the bleachers, Jill McAllister caught my eye and I tensed up again, searching for any sign of Anton.

"Twenty bucks says she's in our group," Lena grumbled. "We start the day after tomorrow, by the way. In case you slept through that part, too."

"Lovely." We headed out of the gym and joined the slow-moving crowd, heading toward second period.

"So, if you weren't out with Colin last night . . ."

My stomach fluttered, remembering my visit to Colin's.

"I was, for a while. But when I got in, I had work to do." My time with the Arcs could definitely be considered work.

"You know we're seniors, right? Our applications are in, our fates are sealed. We can let things slide a little bit."

"I wish." I still hadn't heard from NYU. At this point, I wasn't even sure what I was hoping for—that I'd get in, and have to decline, or that I'd be rejected, and have the decision taken out of my hands.

"Mo!" Constance called my name across the hallway. "Wait up!"

"This is a first," Lena muttered.

"Did you see all the—" Constance broke off at the sight of Lena. "Do you mind?"

"Yes." Lena put a hand on her hip. "We were having a conversation."

"Well, I need to talk to Mo. It's important."

"I'll catch up," I said to Lena. "Save me a seat."

She eyed Constance, not bothering to hide her suspicion. "If you say so."

"Did you see the guards?" Constance asked when she was gone. "What's going on?"

"It's to prevent Anton from coming back in."

She blinked. "It's a trap?"

"I don't think it's a trap if he knows they're looking for him," I said, but inside I knew differently. The Quartoren assumed he might try it, anyway. And that made me the bait. "Have you heard any talk?"

"Me? Nobody tells me anything," she said with a pout. "Not even Niobe. She's supposed to be teaching me, but she never tells me any of the good stuff. It's all 'control your emotions' and 'focus your will.' She knows everyone. Like, *everyone*. And they're all a little afraid of her, too. I think she's kind of a big deal."

"Probably." Luc relied on her for information, and I'd seen how well they worked together. They seemed to move in different circles, though, and their interactions had just enough friction that I had to wonder about their history. I brushed aside my annoyance. "Listen to her, okay? She can keep you safe."

"Whatever. It's not like I'm in danger. You're the one they want."

"Go to class, Constance." I didn't bother to see whether she listened.

"I'm trying to remember to feel sorry for her," Lena said as I slid into the seat she'd saved for me. "It's kind of an effort."

"I know the feeling," I said. More and more, my guilt over everything that had happened to Constance was turning to annoyance. I'd lost Verity, too, but instead of sniping at everyone, I was going after the people responsible. Having a purpose had helped my grief. Maybe Constance needed to find one of her own.

I operated on autopilot for the rest of the day. The lines stayed quiet. Jill McAllister stayed out of my way. Even Constance and Niobe seemed willing to give me space.

"You need a nap," said Colin as I climbed into the truck.

"I need a vacation," I said. "Someplace with blue water and white sand."

He traced the curve of my cheek, the gesture careful and tender. "Wish we could. Do you want to crash at my place for a little while?"

That sounded like an even better plan than a tropical beach. And equally impossible. "I have to work."

"We should find you another job," Colin said. "At least until The Slice opens again."

I yawned hugely. "Billy wouldn't let me. Besides, my mom likes having me close. She feels safer."

"Your dad doesn't. He's worried."

I sat up straight. "When did you two discuss this? During your joyride yesterday?"

"This morning. Your dad's joined the crew working on The Slice. Should make for some nice quality time for the two of us," he said dryly.

"You have got to be kidding me."

"He needs a paycheck. Not a lot of people are willing to hire him. And he seems to think that getting you out of Morgan's is in everyone's best interests."

"Funny how everyone wants me out, but they're not willing to leave themselves."

"It's not always a question of wanting," he said. "Sometimes it's not possible. But for you, it is. We're trying to keep your options open."

I laughed, the sound strangled. "You and my dad are on the same side?"

"We both want you safe," he said. "And happy. That puts us on the same side, and Billy on the other."

My dad didn't have any idea what made me happy, and it wasn't his place to decide it. We stopped behind Morgan's, and my stomach clenched. I had a sudden vision of the thugs who'd once broken into my house, the fear returning fresh. I blinked and the image was replaced with the memory of Billy's face as he watched The Slice burn, as he spun out more lies for me. Fear and lies and greed, the magic seemed to warn me, and I braced my hands against the dash.

"You okay?" Colin asked, sliding his arm around me.

I let myself relax into him. This was how we were supposed to be—solid and together. I'd managed Billy; I'd convinced my mom. It was supposed to be okay. My dad's interference was a threat I hadn't anticipated.

"Under control," I said through gritted teeth. Through sheer force of will, I calmed my stomach and my temper. "Pick me up at eight?"

He nodded and touched his lips to mine. "Just because you're angry doesn't mean your dad's wrong, Mo."

"And it doesn't mean he's right, either."

Inside, Morgan's was busier than usual for a Tuesday night. Even Billy was helping out behind the bar. I felt a faint tension in the lines, and traced it back to a guy sitting near the front door, who was casually, continuously surveying the room. He caught my eye and nodded slightly, and I realized it was the guard Luc had mentioned. The Quartoren weren't taking any chances.

I made my way to the back, unwinding my scarf, my hair crackling with static. I checked the wire delivery cart. Empty. My breathing came easier.

Then my phone beeped, and my heart slammed into my ribs all over again.

I checked the number. Jenny.

Anything? read her text.

I started to respond, but paused. Everyone was busy out front. If there was ever a time to snoop, this was it.

Billy's office, like my mom's, was in a closet off the back room. I locked the door behind me and looked around. Haphazard stacks of papers—order forms, old electric bills—were scattered across the desk, and the computer whirred softly. I nudged the mouse, but the screen saver asked for a password. I eased a drawer open and found only invoices from liquor distributors and glassware companies. Nothing Jenny could use.

"Mo?" called Billy, rattling the doorknob. "What are you doing?"

I was so startled I knocked over the stack of papers I'd been riffling through. "Getting dressed," I shouted, switching out of my uniform and making as much racket as possible. Finally, I flung open the door.

"Sorry," I said. "I didn't have a chance to change at school."

He looked past me at the paper-covered floor. "What happened?"

"I tripped. Banged my funny bone." I rubbed at my elbow. "I'll clean it up."

"Never mind," he said brusquely, and shooed me out. "Charlie needs you out front."

I fled, hoping I'd masked the guilt on my face.

Back out on the floor, I waved to Charlie and started working my way around the room, taking orders and delivering drinks. It was easier than working at The Slice, in a lot of ways—a shorter menu, and people rarely ordered trendy, complicated drinks. Despite the crowd, the simpler routine meant I had more time to think about Colin's words.

Working for Billy was risky—even more than Colin realized, since he didn't know about Ekomov. If the Russians found out the truth, I'd end up at the bottom of the Chicago River, or in a landfill somewhere outside of Gary. I'd banked on the idea that Jenny Kowalski and Nick Petros could help me take down both organizations. And I'd bought time to figure out how to save Colin and his sister.

But with my dad's return, my plans were in jeopardy. I'd built a house of cards and he kept jostling the table. I didn't know his motives, his loyalties, or what he was up to. All I knew was, if he kept interfering, Colin would find out the truth. Everything would come crashing down, and I'd be left with nothing.

I'd learned to live with risk over the last six months—my interactions with the Arcs and the Mob had given me little choice—but the idea that Colin would discover what I'd done still made my skin slick with sweat. Even now, setting down glasses of Guinness and plates of curry fries, my hands shook.

"Go take your break," Charlie said as I bobbled my tray. "I can drop these off."

I pushed damp wisps of hair away from my face and smiled, but the expression felt as unsteady as the tray I'd nearly dropped.

"Go on," he said firmly, and shooed me away.

"I'm fine," I said, loudly enough for the Quartoren's guard to hear me. "Back in ten, okay?"

He dipped his head in understanding, and I made my way into the back. There was no reason to be worried. Billy wouldn't tell Colin, or he'd lose my cooperation. My dad wouldn't tell, because he'd lose me. But the panic wouldn't subside. Images flitted through my mind—Colin's file from social services, Verity in the alley, the fire at The Slice—and the room felt stiflingly small.

My uncle called my name as I grabbed my coat from its hook. "Charlie said you're ill."

"Just getting some air. I'm on break." I yanked on the gray metal door, gulping down icy air.

I let the door swing shut behind me with a solid thunk. The alley was dark, a single streetlight casting a weak glow onto the snow piled at its base. One of the parking spaces had been reserved with a couple of folding chairs, a time-honored Chicago tradition, and I made my way toward them. A few more minutes, I told myself, already feeling the cold penetrate my heavy coat. The magic trembled in response to my own anxiety, and I tried to think of something soothing—the ocean, with gulls wheeling overhead, a cup of hot cocoa during a gentle snowfall—but the images were interrupted by the same ones that had crowded in earlier, all terror and loss. I took slow, deliberate breaths, anchoring myself with the sting in my nose and lungs. A few minutes to wrestle down the fear, and then I could go back in and pretend everything was fine. I'd had practice at pretending, after all.

I never saw the attack coming.

The streetlight flickered and went out with a pop. In the next instant, the bare lightbulbs flanking Morgan's back door went dark, and the air filled with shadows and rustling.

Darklings.

I sprang up. The street behind Morgan's was narrow—barely wide enough for a delivery truck to squeeze through—and the creatures coming for me swarmed across the pavement gracelessly, a feral cluster. A screech rang out as one of them dragged a talon across a Buick, sparks bright against their black robes.

Two options: I could try to outrun them—Darklings rarely hunted in populated areas, especially if there was no raw magic to draw them. If I could make it to Western Avenue, with its lights and traffic and witnesses, they might call off their pursuit.

The second option was to duck back into Morgan's—but that would mean running directly toward them.

And there was a third choice. Luc. Concentrating on the faint tension of our binding, I eased away, toward the far end of the block. Better to try and lose them, I thought. They were moving slowly now, keeping pace with me as I edged backward. Any moment, they would attack, and I needed as many escape routes as I could find. The end of this block— with its cross-streets and Dumpsters and cars—was as good as it was going to get.

I stretched one arm out to the side, feeling my way down the row of cars, never taking my eyes from the horde. I envisioned my free hand curling around the chain that connected me to Luc, trying to focus enough to summon him. Before I could, someone spoke.

"Predictable." The word was singsong, pitched high enough to scrape along my nerves. "Do it, and they'll attack. By the time Luc arrives, he'll find what's left of you on the ground, well past saving. Déjà vu for the Heir."

"Anton?" I tore my gaze away from the Darklings, who had halted at the interruption. Where was the guard from inside? The ones monitoring the wards? Why hadn't they noticed something was wrong? And then I realized—Anton hadn't triggered any magic. He'd snuck in, disguised as a Flat, just like before. No one was worried. No one was coming.

He stood at the end of the alley, his suit so dark he seemed to be made of shadows, his skin so pale it nearly glowed. He glanced up at the streetlight, and it flickered back on, turning his complexion jaundiced. "They say imitation is the sincerest form of flattery, but wouldn't you prefer to be an original?"

"Take me Between," I said. Crazy to be asking him, of all people. But there was no reasoning with Darklings. They'd kill both of us. "Please. Get me out of here."

He chuckled, ambling down the alley, skirting heaps of snow, lightly skipping over slush-filled puddles. "Why should I help you? Flat girl. Interloper." He paused as he drew even with me. "Murderer."

The Darklings were pressing forward. Still not attacking, just prowling, too loose-limbed to be human. Their joints moved in the wrong direction—too many directions—I couldn't tell which. Tattered hoods covered what was left of their faces. Their words sounded as if they were missing parts—guttural, sibilant noises that must have meant something. But all I understood was that both my nerves and the magic were screaming at me to run.

"You need me alive," I said, voice cracking. "You need some magic to make the Ascendency happen, right? If they kill me, you'll lose, too."

He appeared to consider this. I could sense water lines nearby, the power swelling within them. If I could get him to use that power, to let some of it leach out, it might transfer the Darklings' attention to him. I could escape, at least long enough for help to arrive.

There was no need to pretend terror as I took another step, trying to position him between me and the Darklings.

"We do need you alive," Anton mused, stroking his chin. And then he smiled, expression clearing like he'd just solved a particularly tricky riddle. "But not *very* alive. Only partly."

"I don't think they do partly," I said as the Darklings picked up speed, coming toward us with fresh intent. If Anton didn't act soon, we'd both be dead in the next couple of minutes.

"It's all in how you ask," he said, and threw back his head, calling out in the same horrible language the Darklings used. Two of the four leapt overhead and landed with a scraping, clattering noise, blocking my way out of the alley. He turned to me. "If I ask nicely, they should stop just before your heart does. Which will give me exactly what we need."

"You can talk to them." The words sounded heavy and stupid as I said them, as pointless as all my plans to flee.

"Even better, I can control them. Do you see what a favor I'm doing you? Without my command holding them back, they'd be feasting on your marrow by now."

My heart lurched, my vision turning grainy with fear. No wonder he wasn't afraid. He'd been sending them after me for months—at the park, when I'd put on Verity's ring; at the Water Tower; at the Allée; even at the golf course where Pascal had tested my connection to the magic. The Darklings weren't just drawn to magic—they were his own personal death squad.

"You should thank me, Flat." There was no cruel humor in his voice this time. He meant it. He *expected* it. He took another step toward me, grabbing my wrist. The connection to Luc went cold and inert, pain shooting up my arm. "I'm waiting."

"Thank you." My lips formed the words, but no sound came out.

"Better," he said with a nod. "I want to know about you and the magic. There's something there you haven't told anyone. Some truth that no one knows but you."

I shook my head in frantic denial. Inside me, the magic writhed, and I closed my eyes, trying to calm us both. But all I could see was the Darklings, attacking Verity in the alley, remembering how easily they'd thrown me aside. Anton grabbed my chin roughly, forcing my face up to his, and my eyes snapped open again.

His breath was sour and hot against my face. "You like free will, and now you get to exercise it. I want to know about the magic—what you can do with it, why you've survived. And you are going to tell me. But I will let you choose. I can work a Rivening—you sit quietly and let me drag those secrets out of your clever little brain—or I can let the Darklings at you. Slowly, because you'll need enough breath to tell me the truth." His hand slid down to my throat and he squeezed. Black spots bloomed before my eyes. "It would start the Ascendency, but that's fine. What's that saying? Killing two birds with one stone?"

He released me and I fell to the ground, gasping for air, the slush soaking through my coat and jeans. The Darklings shuffled closer, the scent of blood, like scorched metal, thick in the air. I scrambled away, but one reached out and snagged my coat. The fabric ripped wide open, and I fell again.

I swallowed down the bile flooding my mouth. Inside me, the magic thrashed, and I willed it to burst free, to incinerate Anton and the Darklings. I'd seen how much damage raw magic could do. Surely now, when we were both in danger, it could protect us.

But even as it battered against my veins, I couldn't find a way to release it.

Anton reached for me with both his hands and his magic, and I wanted to scream. I started to scream—sucked in the night air, felt my throat ready itself—but the sound died before it reached my lips, because there was another, inhuman shriek, and the head of a Darkling flew above us, landing heavily on the lid of a nearby Dumpster.

"Touch her again, it won't be birds I'm killin'."

Luc stood at the entrance to the alley, the body of a Darkling at his feet, ruby flames dancing along the edge of his sword. The symbols inscribed along the flat of the blade seemed to burn golden white, and I could sense the power within, a hunger fueled by rage. He stepped forward, ducking under the reach of the second Darkling, and buried his sword to the hilt in its chest, yanking upward until the rotting flesh cleaved in two. "Mouse?"

I bit back a sob. "I'm okay."

Anton whirled to face him, face twisting, shouting orders at the remaining Darklings. They bounded past, intent on Luc and his blazing sword, forgetting I was even there.

I'd never seen such berserker fury on Luc's face, but the numbers still weren't good—especially when I felt Anton draw on the nearest line, power surging up, centering a deep blue light in the palm of his hand.

It was instinct that propelled me forward, coming out of

my crouch like a sprinter off the blocks, shoving Anton the instant before the energy left his hands. The bolt went wide, blowing the door off a car and knocking down a telephone pole.

"Stupid little bitch," he snarled, and reached for me, but I scrambled away, scooping up the chair I'd sat on earlier, swinging it wildly. I managed to get in one blow, knocking him back again, and then he spoke a word and the chair disintegrated in my hands.

"Luc!" I shouted. He looked up from the fight. Blood was running down his arm, and he shouted something that knocked both Darklings back several yards.

"Behind you!" he called. I glanced back, expecting to see some new, horrible threat. Instead, there was a gash in the air—a pocket of emptiness I'd seen him use before, and I thrust my hand in, hoping I wasn't going to fall through and find myself lost in Between.

Instead, my fingers found something wrapped in cloth, slightly larger than a football and heavy for its size. I pushed past layers of linen until I felt metal, burning with cold, against my palm. Anton grabbed my hair and yanked me toward him, tears springing to my eyes.

The magic rose up, vengeful, as I grasped the handle and whirled, blade extended, and felt it slice Anton's arm. He cried out and let go, and I ran toward Luc.

"Down!" Luc cried, and I dropped to the ground. He sent a bolt of energy along the sword, aiming for Anton. There was only one Darkling left, but I could feel Anton gathering magic—huge swaths of it, readying a strike. Luc was chanting; the Darkling was making wet, sucking sounds as it stalked around him; Anton was muttering incantations of his own; and my breath was so loud and ragged in my ears, I shouldn't have been able to hear anything.

But when the back door of Morgan's flew open, the sound of the metal door smashing into the wall was louder than a rifle. And for an instant, as my uncle strode into the midnight-dark alley, we all fell silent.

"We've a bar full of—" He broke off as he took in the scene before him. "What in the name of—Mo?"

"Go back inside," I shouted. Anton flashed me a grin, shifting his stance toward Billy as Luc and the Darkling continued to battle.

I don't know what made me protect Billy, but without thinking, I threw the knife at Anton, aiming for the center of his back.

I missed, of course. You can learn a lot of trick throws with darts—fancy moves that impress the regulars, especially if you're eight and looking for a few bucks to spend on the ice-cream truck. But darts and daggers are very different things, and my throw dipped, catching the back of Anton's calf instead. He went down, but the blue glow spreading across the injury told me he'd be up again in a minute, completely healed.

Behind me, Luc hacked apart the remaining Darkling. The air was thick with the scent of decay. I staggered, nauseated as Luc sent another bolt of energy sizzling across the alley, forcing Anton back several paces.

Billy sagged against the door frame, ashen faced.

"Go inside," I repeated, and tried to push him back into Morgan's. But he shook free, staring as Luc and Anton faced off.

"I can call more Darklings," said Anton.

"I can call more guards," Luc countered. There was a flash of light, a cracking sound, and he grinned. "Already did, in fact. And they've got orders to kill you on sight."

Anton scoffed. "I'd like to see them try."

"That can be arranged. But actually"—Luc's voice dropped to a conspirator's whisper—"I'm plannin' on doing it myself."

Anton shifted, his eyes flickering to the group of Arcs rushing down the alley. "Next time," he said with a mocking little bow before he went Between.

Luc grabbed my arms. "You okay?"

"No. But . . ." I gestured to my uncle, whose mouth was opening and closing soundlessly. "What about him?"

"Hold on," Luc said, and strode to the guards that had halted a few yards away, barking orders. The group snapped to attention, hung unquestioningly on his every word. It was yet another side of him I hadn't seen before—a leader. It suited him. Everything about this life suited him, and I wondered at his insistence that someone like me should be a part of it.

Billy braced an arm against the Dumpster, his eyes wide and fearful. "Mo—"

"I can explain," I said to Billy, as my teeth started to chatter. I bent down and picked up the dagger I'd thrown, the blood on the blade so dark it looked like oil.

"You should clean that before it rusts," Billy said, his voice hollow.

I nodded, wiping it on my slush-soaked apron, afraid to ask how he knew that.

"That thing," he said finally, gesturing to the spot where the Darkling's body lay crumpled. "What . . ."

"It's called a Darkling. They're assassins. Hunters."

He stared at it and crossed himself. "Not human."

"No."

"You've seen them before."

"Yes."

He nodded at that, and I watched him take it all in, assemble the clues like a crossword, seeing how the different parts connected. And finally he looked at me. "Those things . . . they killed Verity?"

I swallowed. "Yes."

Luc approached us. The sword was gone, but he still wore a fierce, deadly expression. It softened as he took in the sight of me. "You're soaking wet, Mouse."

"I fell."

"I noticed." He brushed a hand along my sleeve, along my back, the warmth spreading through me and drying my clothes. With a few words, the rip in my coat began reweaving itself. "Hypothermia ain't a good look for anyone."

Billy was regaining control—no longer leaning against the Dumpster, smoothing his hair down, retreating to the role he played best. He folded his arms and stared Luc down. "And who would you be?"

"Luc." He said it carelessly, as if Billy's discovery didn't put us in jeopardy. I knew differently.

"I've not heard of you."

"I've heard of you," he said. "The uncle, right? You'll want to forget what you just saw."

"What I'll be wanting is an explanation," Billy said ominously.

Just then, Colin's truck rounded the corner, the headlights capturing us in an unlikely tableau.

"Hell, Mouse. You're the only person I know turns a back alley into Grand Central Station." Luc scowled at the truck.

"This isn't my fault," I shot back. "It's not as if I asked Anton to attack me."

"You've someone else after you, Mo?" Billy asked.

Colin strode toward us. "What the hell happened? What's he doing here?"

I didn't know if he was referring to Billy or Luc, so I covered both. "Anton showed up with a bunch of Darklings, followed by Luc. Billy came looking for me in the middle of the fight."

"Are you okay?" He inspected me carefully, eyes going steely at the sight of the dagger in my hand. I nodded, and he pulled me into his arms. "How'd he get so close?"

Behind me, Luc sounded as weary as I felt. "He didn't use magic, so he didn't trigger the wards. Darklings don't use lines, so they didn't, either. Nobody realized what was going on until he started the Rivening."

"You knew about all of this?" Billy demanded, drilling a finger into Colin's chest. "You've known all along these creatures were after her? That such things existed? And you said nothing to me?"

"You wouldn't have believed him," I said.

"Magic," he said, and his tone wasn't fearful. It was . . . wondrous, like he'd had a celestial vision. The shift alarmed me. "This changes everything."

"It absolutely does not." I turned to Luc. "Isn't there something you could do to make him forget? Erase all of this?"

"Nothing but a Rivening," he said. "And that's a line I won't cross. Not even for you."

I shook my head, remembering the sensation of Anton digging through my mind. I wouldn't wish that on anyone. And I didn't want Luc to be capable of it. "You can't talk about this," I said to Billy "Not a word."

"But, Mo, darling girl . . ."

I gathered up every last bit of strength I had, tightened my grip on the knife, and said, "I am not your darling girl. I am tired and I am cold and I am really, really sick of people trying to kill me. You don't talk to anyone about this. You forget tonight ever happened. You leave it alone, Billy, because if you don't, someone's going to get hurt. Maybe even you."

Luc smiled, even as he pried the dagger out of my hands and tested the blade with his thumb, his eyes on Billy the whole time. "No maybe about it."

Billy glanced from me to Luc and back again. His mouth opened and shut with a snap.

"Home," Colin said firmly. "Now."

"My bag . . ." I trailed off at the look on Colin's face.

"Donnelly's right," Billy said. "Best we get you home. I'll come around with your things later. We'll have a chat, you and I."

The warmth in his smile turned my blood to ice. Without another word, Colin steered me toward the truck.

Luc followed. Voice low, he asked, "You sure you ain't hurt?"

I pressed my lips together. I wasn't hurt—not really, though my hands and knees stung from falling, and my neck ached where Anton had grabbed it. But this was everything I'd tried to avoid—the magic and the mundane parts of my life crashing together, endangering everything I'd worked for. Billy knew the truth now, and that made him dangerous.

From the moment I'd taken Verity's place as the Vessel, Luc had insisted I would have to choose between a life with the Flats and one with the Arcs—and he'd made no secret about which one he believed I was meant for. Until tonight, I'd thought I could handle both. I'd argued and pushed and run and refused. Now I had to wonder if he was right. If he was right about where I belonged, what did that mean for my relationship with him? And for my future with Colin?

Colin, who bristled beside me as if Luc were the danger. "Can it wait until morning?"

Luc dragged a hand through his hair. "We can talk tomorrow. But you'll need protection from here on out."

"How did you know?" I asked, finding my voice. "He told me if I called for you, the Darklings would attack."

He touched my chin, the gentle movement replacing the memory of Anton's grip. "The binding works both ways. When you got scared—big, bone-deep scared—I could feel it."

And he'd come for me.

Before I could reply, Billy sidled across the alley and extended a hand to Luc, some sort of man-to-man gesture designed to put them on equal footing. When Luc didn't move to take it, Billy dropped his hand, cleared his throat. "Think what you might of me, but she's my family, and you have my thanks."

Luc strode away, not deigning to respond, every inch the Heir. Outrage flashed across Billy's face, quickly hidden, and I pretended not to notice, even as his gaze trained on me like he'd scented fresh prey.

Colin, of course, didn't care about either of them. He bundled me into the truck, helping me with the seat belt when my fingers shook too much to manage. Billy waited until Colin walked to his side of the truck, and leaned in.

"Later, then," he said. "We'll have our talk."

I didn't answer. Colin drove away, but in the side mirror I saw Billy waving us off, more good-natured than you would expect for a man who'd just seen his world turn inside out. That couldn't possibly be a good thing.

Colin blasted the heat on the way home, but I burrowed into him, unable to warm up, trying to press inside his skin through will alone. His hand moved shakily over my hair, a gesture of reassurance for both of us.

"I don't like Luc," he said eventually.

"He's not—"

"Listen to me." His voice sounded strangled and halting. "I hate his guts. I think he's dangerous. I think he drags you into things you aren't ready for, and asks you to do things no one has a right to ask. I think he wants you for himself, and he'll use anything he can get his hands on to make it happen. I think he's sneaky and manipulative and untrustworthy in a thousand different ways. He makes my trigger finger itch every time I see him."

"Can we not do this right now?"

"*Listen to me.* None of it changes the fact he's the only one who can protect you. I've seen the way you push back at him and the Arcs. Partly, you're trying to keep them from hijacking your life. That's good. But another part of it is because you're afraid Luc will come between us, and that's bullshit. We're better than that. So when he comes to you and says he's got a plan to keep you safe, don't turn him down because you're worried about my feelings. I don't give a rat's ass about the Arcs and their prophecies. All I want is you. Safe. Everything else—everything—comes second to that."

"The Seraphim want to destroy their whole world. I might be able to stop them."

"But you don't need to. You don't owe them."

"It's not about owing them. It's about standing up when no one else can. Even if the cost is terrible."

"There has to be another way. With all that magic, Luc can hide you. He would, if you asked him to."

I wasn't so sure. Not if he thought the Arcs needed me.

"I don't want to hide. You do it. Every day, you hide. Even from me. Does it make you happy?"

"This isn't about my past," he said.

"No. It's about my future. Our future."

"Our future isn't worth your life."

"That's where we disagree," I said, and tried to keep my voice light.

We pulled up in front of my house, and he kissed me—desperately, like he was exorcising demons, trying to crowd out fear with wanting, and I kissed him back just as hard, telling him everything I couldn't say with words. I'd taken another step into the Arcs' world, to a place he couldn't follow, and we both knew it. But tonight had taught me I could fight back . . . and win.

CHAPTER 11

I woke from a dream about the magic—the Quartoren's table alive with symbols, light dripping from them like tears, and the dagger Luc had given me slipping out of my grasp, reopening my scar, the blade gleaming with my blood—and my mouth was cottony with fear. I reached out to the magic and felt the Quartoren's wards in place just like at school. Like my very own supernatural alarm system. I was safe here.

Safe and terrified.

I lay in bed for a long time and listened to the familiar noises of our house—the radiator knocking, the foundation settling. The occasional snore from my parents' room. Comforting noises. But they didn't soothe me the way they used to.

I threw the covers back, wincing at the icy floorboards underneath my feet. Warm milk. As a kid, whenever I couldn't sleep, my mom made me a mug of warm milk with vanilla. I eased open the door, left the hall light off so as not to wake my parents, and felt my way downstairs to the kitchen.

Nerves jangling, I flipped on the stove light, casting a comforting glow around the room. I pulled a mug from the cabinet and filled it with milk, then crossed over to the spice cabinet, where Mom kept the vanilla extract.

"I thought you might want your books," said my uncle, strolling in from the pitch black living room.

I stifled a scream, my heart pounding crazily. "What are you doing here?"

He'd been sitting in the living room, some part of my mind registered. He'd watched me stumble past him through the darkness and stayed silent. He'd waited until I was distracted and then cornered me.

"You spilled some milk there," he said, pointing to the counter. "I told you I wanted to chat."

Hands trembling, I grabbed a towel and mopped up the milk. "It's the middle of the night. And there's nothing to talk about."

"Isn't there? After everything I've seen tonight?"

"I told you—you need to forget what you saw. It's only going to bring you trouble."

He waved my words away. "Trouble I'm better suited to handle than you. You're not thinking this through, Mo. The possibilities. What this could mean for us."

I stared at him. "You can't deal with these people. They don't care about you. You're inconsequential to them."

"But you aren't." He smiled again, thin and unpleasant. "You matter quite a bit, I'll wager, judging from the look on your friend's face tonight. We can use that."

My stomach turned. I wouldn't. I wouldn't use Luc, wouldn't let Billy have access to that kind of power. He had too much already. "Get out," I said, trying to keep my voice strong.

"You don't give the orders, Maura Kathleen. Have you forgotten that?" Billy drew himself up, storm clouds gathering, fist clenched as if he was about to strike.

The door to the screened porch swung open, and Luc stepped inside. "Problem here?" he asked.

I let out a long, slow breath, and Billy's expression transformed to one of welcome. "Luc! Just dropping off my niece's books, as I promised. Good to see you again."

Luc nodded, a curt gesture that didn't bother with sincerity. "Little late for family to be droppin' by."

"It is," I agreed.

For once, Billy took the hint. "We'll continue this another time, Mo. If I were you, I'd tread lightly."

"Excuse me?" With Luc standing next to me, it was easier to inject disdain into my voice.

"Your mother's a light sleeper. I'd be careful on those stairs."

And with that, Billy left.

Luc's hand cupped my elbow, keeping me steady. I took a long, slow breath and said, "Your timing is impeccable. Again."

He smiled grimly. "Saw him come in. Didn't want to interrupt, but he looked like he was about to go after you."

"You've been watching the house." After the night's events, the idea didn't bother me like it once would have.

He'd changed out of the blood-stained clothes from the fight. Now he wore a pair of ancient jeans and a white T-shirt so pristine it seemed luminescent against the black leather of his coat. "You've got guards, but . . . I wanted to be sure."

I almost told him to leave. Billy wouldn't return, and it wouldn't make sense for Anton to come after me tonight. No doubt he was off licking his wounds, plotting his next attack, whipping his followers into a frenzy. But Anton was insane. Nothing he did made sense. And the idea that Luc would be watching over me suddenly felt secure, not stalkerish.

"Come upstairs," I whispered. He took my hand, concealing us as we crept back to my room. "Did the Quartoren tell you to come?"

"They know I'm here." I turned on my lamp and settled on the bed, watching him prowl the room. He moved to my dresser, poked idly at the tumble of jewelry and detritus—ticket stubs, last year's school ID, pens, hair clips. He picked up a bottle of perfume and sniffed, nose wrinkling. "Doesn't smell like you."

"I never wear it. What did they say?"

"Told me to bring you back." He shrugged, a quick angry jerk of his shoulder.

Of course they had. They were probably rubbing their hands together in glee and practicing their "I told you so." I pulled my knees to my chest and tried to keep the weariness from my voice. "Tonight?"

He moved on to my desk, picking up the geode I used as a paperweight and tossing it from hand to hand. "Figured you could use some rest, so I volunteered to stay with you instead."

"And they went for it?"

He grinned, teeth gleaming as white as his shirt. "Rumor has it I am hard to say no to."

I couldn't help smiling back. "Never been a problem for me."

"Exception proves the rule." He crossed the room and sat down next to me. "And you are one hell of an exception."

Chin on knees, I studied him. Dark smudges under his eyes, a crease between his brows that was on its way to becoming permanent—the night had taken a toll on him, too. "You're exhausted. You can't stay up all night just to watch me."

"Not sure I can sleep. I keep seein' Anton grab you, like a movie in my head. Can't make it stop. Does it hurt?"

"A little," I said, remembering Anton's fingers pressing into my throat, cutting off my air. I inhaled deeply, just because I could.

Carefully, Luc pushed my hair to the side, baring my neck. His voice was hard, but his touch was light and tentative. "Bastard left marks."

"I know." I'd already tried to figure out how I would hide them. Makeup wouldn't cover the purple welts. A scarf would be better, but a violation of the dress code. I hadn't owned a turtleneck since the fifth grade. And no matter how I hid the marks, they'd still exist. I'd still feel them and remember.

I straightened, pressing the heels of my hands against my eyes, unable to stop the hitching of my breath.

"Let me fix it," he said.

"No. It'll hurt you." Arcs could heal wounds—and Luc was particularly good at it—but our bond meant that any time he healed me, he injured himself. "What if Anton comes back while you're recovering?"

"He won't. Please, Mouse. Bad enough it happened at all. Neither one of us needs a reminder." He reached out, saw me flinch, and took my hand instead.

"You promise it won't hurt you too badly?" I couldn't stand the thought of causing him more pain than I had already.

"Can't hurt more than looking at 'em," he said. "Tilt your head back."

I did, pulling my hair into a ponytail, and closed my eyes. His hand moved over my throat, and I started to choke, panic stealing my air. Immediately, he pulled away.

"Breathe for me. Nice and steady. In and out."

I opened my eyes. "Sorry. I freaked a little."

"My fault," he said easily. "Let's try somethin' different. Look at me this time."

So I did. He sat across from me on the bed, cross-legged, and I mirrored him, feeling self-conscious in my thin T-shirt and ratty flannel pants. I forced my fingers to still, gripping my knees, and let myself fall into his eyes.

Even if I hadn't known Luc was magical, his eyes would have given it away. No one had eyes that green, unless they wore colored contacts. Green flecked with gold, and depending on the mood, they could flash like emeralds or turn soft as summer grass. Lashes the color of soot, indecently long, like they might tangle together when he blinked. The corners of his eyes crinkled slightly, as if he was smiling, but I didn't dare look away to check. I felt his touch on my collarbone and my windpipe started to close.

"It's only me," he said. The world narrowed down to the low, musical drawl of his voice and the pools of his eyes. "Keep looking at me."

His finger hovered above my neck, separated by a few molecules of air. No pressure, only a sensation of warmth, shimmering and sinking inside of me, and the magic responded, unfurling like a flower in sunshine. Luc's eyes turned a deeper, glinting green, and he covered each of the bruises in turn as the magic built between us, our bond strong and silvery, impossible to ignore.

Slowly, he ran his thumb along the side of my neck, across my collarbone, stopping at my shoulder. And then he blinked and fell back, the air whooshing out of his lungs.

"Are you okay? Can you breathe?" I scrambled across the bed and knelt next to him. "Luc?"

"No worries," he gasped. For a long minute, he sounded like he'd run a marathon, and then he propped himself on one elbow, studying me.

"You're sure?" The circles under his eyes were darker, but his breathing had evened out.

He threaded his fingers through my hair. "Pretty damn sure."

I went still at his touch—startled, but not afraid—and my own breath came more quickly.

"We should get some sleep. It's really late."

He sighed. "Whatever you say."

I pulled back and made a show of reaching for my alarm clock, fighting for normalcy. "I say you should take a pillow. And you're sitting on the spare blanket."

When he'd settled into his makeshift bed on the rug, I turned out the light, oddly nervous. Not afraid, exactly, but the air felt charged, full of things we hadn't said, words that might be easier in the darkness. I wondered if Luc felt it, too.

"You ready to come clean?" Apparently, he did.

"About what?"

"I've healed you plenty of times. Before the binding and after. This was different. If I didn't know better, I'd say the magic was gearin' up to protect you. When it realized I wasn't a threat, it boosted my spell instead of blockin' it. Like it was trying to help you."

"So?" I rolled onto my back, stared up at the ceiling. "That would be a good thing."

"*That* would imply the magic made a conscious choice.

Like it has a mind of its own. Which is about as crazy as saying gravity decided to keep the planet in orbit another day."

I wanted to tell him the truth. Even the magic seemed to
yearn for it, in tandem with my heart. But some part of me
resisted, wary and skittish. I didn't know if I was guarding
the magic or myself. "You're the one saying it."

"You ain't denying it, either."

I didn't answer. It was the best I could do, for now.

"I don't know how to make you trust me," he said.

"You can start by not trying to *make* me do anything."

"Fair enough. But let's say I'm right—and the magic is
aware. Alive." He sounded awestruck at the idea, and more
somber than I'd ever heard him. "It's a game changer, Mouse.
You've got a connection to the magic, and if you can tell it
what to do . . . if it'll listen . . . everyone will want at you.
Not just Anton. The Houses, too. The Quartoren."

"I'm aware." But hearing Luc state it made it more real.
More dangerous. And it made me feel more alone than ever.

"I bet. You can't tell them. I can't make you do anything,
but I'm asking you to promise. Promise you won't tell anyone."

"Not even the Quartoren?" Was he really warning me
against his own people? Putting me before his duties as Heir?
If he was truly on my side, I could almost believe we'd get
through this. "I thought you trusted them."

He sighed again, heavily. "I trust them to do right by the
Arcs."

"I'm not an Arc."

"Exactly."

Chapter 12

My mom woke me the next morning. For a brief paralyzing moment, I was afraid she'd spotted Luc. But she looked impatient, not incensed. Luc was gone.

"Your father and I are going to the early service," she said. "You'll have Mass at school, right?"

"Ugh. Yes." Ash Wednesday. Start of Lent. It would be nice to give up mornings. I dragged the covers back over my head, but she yanked them away.

"You need to get up. Colin will be here soon."

I stumbled out of bed, took the hottest shower I could stand, and finally made my way to the kitchen. I should have been stiff from the fight, but Luc had evidently healed that, too.

My mom was wrong. Colin was already leaning against the counter, eyeing the plate of egg and cheese biscuits on the table, a mug of coffee in hand.

"She left them for you," I said. "Go ahead."

He handed me the mug and kissed me at the same time, tasting of toothpaste and coffee and concern.

"Did you sleep at all?"

"A little. Luc stood guard." I waited for a reaction, but all he did was pause midbite and nod in grudging approval.

"Smart. Where is he now?"

"Probably dealing with the Quartoren." I tested our connection, reassured by its presence. The wards from last night were still in place, and more had been added. The Quartoren had been busy.

"We need to figure out what to do with Billy."

"You think he'll try to use this against Ekomov?" I already knew the answer. I was hoping, for once, to be wrong.

"It would be his style. He's already tried to use you once."

I looked down, hoping my face didn't give me away. Colin grudgingly accepted the fact I needed Luc's protection when I dealt with the Arcs. I didn't want him to know it was Luc who'd rescued me from my Mob problems as well.

"You know I'm right," he said.

"And I know your next sentence is going to be about how I should leave town. Save your breath." I slammed the mug down. "I have school."

He caught my hand. "Hey. I'm not the bad guy, Mo."

"I know. The problem is, you're too damn good." I leaned against his chest, listened to his heart beating true and steady, and tried to tell myself we could find a way out.

Ash Wednesday marked the beginning of Lent—and the next day kicked off the Lenten Service Project. We sat through another all-school Mass, and spent the second half of the day on a field trip to our volunteer sites. We were broken up into teams, loaded onto buses, and sent off with the standard reminder that we were ambassadors for our school and our faith, so we'd better behave or face the wrath of Sister Donna.

Lena's prediction came true, unfortunately. Jill McAllister was in our group, and so was Constance. And our chaperone was none other than Niobe, bearing a clipboard and a scowl. Our site was a Catholic church a few neighborhoods east of the school. Dutifully, we tromped from the bus to the basement where the kitchen and dining room were located. Niobe began handing out assignments, and I caught my first break in a long time. Lena and I would be dishing out food in the dining room, while Constance was assigned to the kitchen, mixing up gravy and instant mashed potatoes. Jill pulled dishwashing duty.

"I don't see why I have to be stuck in the back," she sniped. "I am a people person. There are other people here with experience in menial labor. Why not let them make the most of their skills? I could do a lot more good fund-raising, especially with my father's connections."

"It's good to broaden your horizons," said Niobe, and walked away without further comment.

Jill reapplied her lip gloss, ignoring the stack of dishes in the sink. "Speaking of horizons, Mo, have you heard from NYU yet?"

"Soon."

She nodded in mock sympathy. "The waiting must be really hard. God, I'm glad I went with early decision. I can't imagine how stressed you must be, especially since you blew the interview."

"I'm managing," I said, resisting the urge to dump a pan of gravy on her head.

"Come on," Lena said, tugging at my arm. "They're waiting for us."

I lugged the gravy into the dining room, where the day's meal was set up on a long table, cafeteria style.

"Would have been a waste of food," Lena said, tapping the gravy pan with a ladle.

"But satisfying."

"This is true. I think half the reason I want you to get into NYU is to piss off Jill." We began dishing out mashed potatoes and slices of turkey.

"Yeah, well, don't get your hopes up."

She looked at me sharply. "You really think you'll have to stay here?"

"A lot of things have to go right for me to get in. I'm not sure I'm that lucky."

"But if they did. If you managed it. You'd go, right?"

I shrugged, watching Niobe circulate around the room, greeting everyone—homeless person, student, shelter manager—with the same unsmiling look.

"Ugh." Lena plopped another spoonful of potatoes onto a plate and gestured toward Niobe. "Why couldn't we have had Ms. Corelli?"

"Because the universe isn't that kind." I leaned over, setting a slice of turkey on a little girl's plate. Enormous eyes in a too-thin face tracked my movements. "Here you go, sweetie. Do you like potatoes?"

The girl's mother tried to smile, but her eyes darted around the room, her shoulders hunched defensively. Lena took the girl's plate. "Here . . . I made a mountain with a hole in the middle. You can put the gravy in and pretend like it's a volcano. A potato volcano," she said, her voice unexpectedly gentle.

The girl gripped the plate of food and followed her mother down the line. Lena was silent, watching their progress.

"So sad," I murmured.

She nodded, and turned her attention back to the line, greeting the people who shuffled past. "Is Colin chaperoning, too?"

"He's outside, I'm sure. But he won't come in unless something looks off or I text him."

"Your dad has to be freaking out about you two."

"Not freaking out, exactly. But he's not happy about it, and he tells me so all the time."

"Has it been weird since he got home?"

"My mom's a lot happier, so that's nice. It's just . . . he's always around, trying to be a part of things. My mom's overprotective, but she gives me my space, too. He's not so interested in that." I sighed, dished out more food. "I think he's back to working for Billy."

She whistled. "Bad news, chica. Does he know about your deal?"

"Yeah. I'm worried he's going to tell Colin." He hadn't yet, though. I wasn't quite sure why, but it was definitely a point in his favor.

"How do you keep it all straight? Is there anybody who knows the whole truth?"

I considered. "No."

"Lonely," she said softly.

She was right. I hadn't thought of it that way, but it would be nice to have one person who knew everything. Someone I didn't have to watch my words with or monitor my reactions for. I'd lost that when Verity died. And it made me sad that she'd never been able to tell me the whole truth, either. I wondered how Lena had pegged the feeling so quickly. If she felt that way, too.

The line had petered out, and we started to clean up. "Back in a minute," Lena said.

She picked up one of the few remaining cookies and casually crossed the room toward the little girl from earlier. She crouched down to talk with the kid, handing her the cookie, which disappeared instantly. The mother hadn't lost her hunted, stricken look, and Lena spoke with her, still in a crouch, her expression intent. She pulled out a pen from her pocket and scribbled something on a paper napkin, folded it twice, and pressed it into the woman's hand.

"Are you nearly finished?" Niobe asked, and I jumped.

"Sorry. I was distracted." Lena was still talking to the woman and the little girl. Worry seemed to coalesce around them, almost visible. "Did you hear about last night?"

She nodded briefly, glancing around with obvious distaste. "You were lucky. Again."

"Not that lucky. My uncle saw everything. He knows about the Arcs. I think he'll try to use it." I bit my lip, imagining Billy with magic at his disposal. So much power—and I'd already seen how much he'd risk to go after what he wanted.

"Your uncle is not an issue," she said. "Who among us has a reason to help him? Luc might, if he thought it would win your favor. But knowing what I do about your family, that seems an unlikely scenario. You have more pressing concerns, Mo. Your uncle and his world are a trifle."

"Maybe for you," I muttered.

She shifted impatiently. "How many more of these visits?"

I bristled. "What's the matter? Too many Flats for your taste? You don't like homeless people?"

She rolled her eyes. "I spend all day surrounded by Flats. A few more wouldn't make a difference. Not everyone here is a Flat, Mo. Pay attention to what's in front of you."

I tuned in, trying to read the lines, and I nearly dropped the platter I was holding. At least ten of the people in the room were Arcs, but you couldn't tell from their appearance. Faint, almost untraceable magic drifted around them, but they didn't seem to notice.

"What's wrong with them?"

"A variety of things." She seemed oddly shaken, watching them. Her hands moved restlessly, plucking at her bouclé suit. "Some of them don't have enough power to draw on the lines. Others could not withstand the force of their powers manifesting, and the magic burned through them, like an overloaded lightbulb."

"But what are they doing *here?*"

"Surviving. You're supposed to be cleaning up, yes?"

I started stacking platters and serving utensils, but I couldn't take my eyes off the Arcs dotting the room. The magic around them tapered off to a tattered silver thread, or a burnt ember glow. Some were so weak I couldn't discern their element. To anyone else, they would simply look like some homeless people. Everything about them—matted hair, unwashed clothes, empty eyes—seemed drained, the color of dust.

"This is the underside of the Ascendency. The Seraphim promise great power to those who survive. But they will cull our society of those deemed weak or unworthy. Render them powerless and adrift. They'll end up like this. Only the very strongest of our kind would still have magic."

"Would you?"

She shrugged. "I'd like to think so, but there are no guarantees. No one knows for certain who would benefit."

"But the Seraphim have lots of followers. Why would they support the Ascendency if most of them would end up like this?"

"It's the rare individual who enters a battle assuming they'll lose," she said. "It calls for an uncomfortable level of self-scrutiny."

I ferried dishes between the dining room and kitchen, but I couldn't stop looking at the Arcs. They hunched over their plates, shoveling in food as if this was their only meal of the day. It probably was.

"Why doesn't someone help them?" I asked Niobe when she passed by. "Their families, their Houses? The Quartoren?"

"They try. But sometimes our help isn't welcomed. The people here aren't the only ones, you know. Some manage to live quite convincingly among Flats. Some rely on their connections in our world. But sometimes . . ." She looked out over the room. "Sometimes people would prefer to walk away, rather than live surrounded by what they cannot have.

"There's nothing more to do here," she added. "Round up your friends from the kitchen. It's time to leave."

"What's up with her?" Lena asked as we pulled on our coats. "Not that she ever gives off the warm and fuzzy vibe, of course."

"I'm not sure," I said, staring at Niobe's ramrod-straight posture. We made our way outside, "Speaking of warm and fuzzy, that was nice of you—slipping that little girl another cookie."

She toyed with the zipper of her coat. "She was such a skinny little thing. I figured one more wouldn't hurt."

"You were over there for a while. Did you know her?" We circled the church, heading for the parking lot where Colin was supposed to meet me.

"I've never seen her before," Lena said. There was more to the story, I was sure, but before she could tell me it was complicated or something I wouldn't understand—the same excuses I'd been giving her all year—she caught sight of something over my shoulder, her face lighting up.

"This ought to be entertaining," she said, and I turned to see Colin and Luc, staring each other down. "We should charge admission."

We crossed the parking lot quickly. "Hey, Colin," said Lena. "Nice to see you. And not bleeding, even. It's a good look."

"Lena." The corner of his mouth twitched.

"And . . . Secret Guy. Luc, right?"

Luc bowed slightly. "Always a pleasure. Never met a girl with timing like yours."

She grinned. "It's a gift. So, what are we not-talking about today?"

"Wondered if Mouse would agree to a bit of a field trip," said Luc easily. I was certain what destination he had in mind.

I looked at Colin, slouched against the truck. His collar was turned up against the cold, and I straightened it, an excuse to touch him. "Cover for me?"

"Do I have a choice? I want you home in one piece."

"Me too." I glanced at Lena, who was watching the three of us like she was trying to crack a code. "I promised Lena a ride. Can you still take her home?"

"School," Lena cut in quickly. "My car's at school. It's not a great car or anything. But it's reliable. Starts every time and the radio works. It's not quite as old as your truck, though. What year is that thing, anyway?"

Colin's eyes narrowed. He'd heard the same thing I had—the note of panic in Lena's voice. The clumsy attempt at deflecting attention. He was like a human polygraph, and Lena had just failed. Big time.

"Get in," he said, and glared at Luc. "Take care of her."

"Always," Luc replied.

CHAPTER 13

I watched them pull away, wishing I could go along. "Let me guess. The Quartoren would like a word."

"Just Dominic today. The others are doing some damage control after last night. You still need to be on your guard, though."

I figured as much. In some ways, Dominic was even more dangerous without Orla and Pascal to keep tabs on him.

We came through behind a white building, its bright-green awnings flapping cheerily in the breeze. Nearby, the Mississippi made a rushing, roiling sound, the smell of damp and mud mingling with a sweet, yeasty scent. I could see the triple spires of the cathedral across Jackson Square, but Luc headed for a tiny window counter set into the back corner of the café.

A moment later, he passed me a to-go cup and a paper bag. "Let 'em cool a bit or you'll burn your tongue."

I peeked inside the bag, saw a square of dough topped with a mountain of powdered sugar. "Did you and Verity do this a lot?"

"Get beignets? Fair amount, yeah. It was a nice treat if she'd had a rough day."

I didn't like reenacting one of their traditions. And when I took a sip of the scalding café au lait, it tasted too rich and milky for proper coffee, even with the bite of chicory underneath. "Are you thinking this will be a rough day?"

"You've had a string of 'em."

Not a reassuring answer.

"I don't know what her life was like here. I can't picture it at all."

"She was training, most of the time. Spells with a bunch of tutors from her Houses. Protocol with Orla. Spent time with Pascal getting a feel for how the magic worked. Evangeline schooled her in history."

"What about after all her training? Once you two stopped the Torrent, what was she going to do?"

"With as much power as she had, I'm guessing she would have served as a mage in the Houses. Worked closer with Evangeline, since she'd have been the Heir of that House, but she could've helped in all of them. She had a responsibility, Mouse, but she had choices, too."

I was careful not to ask what the future would have held for them as a couple. Some things it was better not to know. I took another sip of my café au lait and tried to envision what my own life here might be like. It was impossible. Despite its charm and its lush, overblown beauty, New Orleans didn't fit me correctly.

Once inside Luc's apartment, I stood on the balcony overlooking the Quarter. A light rain had started to fall, one of New Orleans' frequent afternoon showers. Sanitation crews were sweeping up beads and broken glass, empty cups, the odd shoe, and indefinable substances I didn't want to think about. I turned back to Luc, who held out the bag of beignets.

"Try one," he said.

I pulled out a square of sugar-covered dough and bit in. Sweet and hot and chewy, like a refined doughnut. I closed my eyes to better savor the taste. "Okay," I said. "You are starting to win me over."

"Hell, Mouse. Beignets? That's all it took?"

"No. But it helps your case." I laughed a little, then looked down at my navy sweater, dusted with enough sugar to make me look like I'd been caught in a snowstorm. "Lovely."

Luc fought a smile, brushed a hand along my side. Instantly, my sweater was clean again, and the air rich with the scent of burnt sugar. For a moment, everything between us felt like a reprieve, like we'd stopped battering each other with expectations.

Then his face turned grave. "They're here."

Moment, ruined. Leave it to Dominic.

I straightened my skirt, brushing away the last bits of powdered sugar, while Luc went for the door. Dominic stepped in, followed by Marguerite, and I relaxed a little. It couldn't be too bad if he'd brought Marguerite. She kept him in line. Luc kissed her cheek and she squeezed his hands tightly, relief evident.

"Maura," said Dominic. "Glad to see you looking so well."

"Thank you." He was after something, of course. Dominic's kindness was a mask, as much as any I'd seen the night of Carnival.

"Let's sit," Marguerite said, and Luc guided her to a chair. I perched on the edge of the couch, back straight, skirt tucked under me, hands clenched into fists. With an effort, I relaxed them. Only Dominic remained standing, pacing back and forth in front of the balcony.

"I'm so sorry about last night," Marguerite said, unexpectedly tentative. "It must have been horrifying."

"I survived." Barely. Luc rubbed at his throat unconsciously.

"You aren't the only one the Seraphim are hunting. Anton is escalating his attacks," Dominic said. "A number of mages—the scholars of our people—have been attacked. Rivened. Some of our brightest minds, and they will never fully recover. What did he want from you?"

My voice was soft, as if speaking still hurt. "He gave me the choice between letting the Darklings torture me until I told about my bond with the magic or letting him Riven me."

Marguerite paled, hand flying to her mouth. Even Dominic looked repulsed, but all he said was, "It was an empty threat—he can't risk killing you, and Darklings don't have the self-control to stop at torture."

"Still could have Rivened her," Luc said, his voice like a dagger. "That sure as hell wasn't an empty threat."

Dominic gave me an apologetic shrug. "But why risk the Darklings? Once they're on a hunt, they can't be called off."

"Anton did. He told them to stop and they listened."

"Darklings don't listen," he said sharply. "When someone enlists a Darkling to hunt, it's a simple command—you give them a target and a taste of magic, and off they go. It's not a conversation."

The fact that Dominic knew how to send Darklings after someone was not a comfort.

"Well, Anton speaks their language. Don't you have people who can do that?"

"It's not done," said Marguerite. "It's simply not done."

Luc shook his head. "I heard him. Thought it was a fluke at first, but she's right—he spoke, they listened. Worse, they obeyed."

Dominic frowned. "They're loyal to him. That settles it, then. Time for you to come home."

I shot up, my first instinct to head for the door. No one moved to stop me, and I realized how futile it would be to run. It made me want to smash every single object in the room to bits. "This is *not* my home."

"You've always planned to leave Chicago. We're offering you a way to do that."

"For New York," I said. "For *college*. Not to run away from the Seraphim or join the Arcs."

"You're already part of our world," he said. "You'd have entry at all four Houses—you can choose whichever one suits you. Even ours."

I thought about the Georgian mansion that served as the Fire Arcs' House. Living under the same roof as Dominic held zero appeal. *None* of the Houses appealed. "You think I'll be safer living with a bunch of strangers?"

Luc leaned forward and touched my elbow. "You could stay with me."

I whirled. "You're joking."

His expression darkened. "Nothin' funny about it. Next to the Houses, this is the safest place for you to be."

"There has to be another way." Colin had told me to go along with Luc's suggestions, but I doubted this was what he had in mind. Shock made me desperate. "Another option."

Dominic studied me for a moment. "We can cloak you. Set more wards. But the only way to truly protect you is to eliminate Anton."

"Then let's do that," I said. I hadn't forgotten Niobe's warning, that the Quartoren would lock me away in protective custody if I was in too much danger. "Let's go after Anton."

"That's got dangers of its own," Dominic said, but he seemed more pleased than worried. "I'd need to consult with the rest of the Quartoren."

"Fine. But in the meantime, I go home."

"You need training to prepare for the Succession," he warned. "There are spells you'll need to learn, even if you can't cast them. It'd be easier to do if you're here."

"Nonsense," Marguerite cut in. "Niobe can train her. She's a familiar face, she's at the school already, she can protect Mo if need be. Luc will work a cloaking, so the Darklings can't find her. Combined with the wards, that should be enough to keep her safe until the Succession. And she'll have Luc."

She smiled at him, but he stayed silent, gaze fixed on the fireplace mantel.

"I'll notify Niobe and the Water mages," Dominic said eventually. "Son? A word?"

They moved to the French doors leading to the balcony, and Marguerite leaned toward me. "Thank you."

"For what?" I said, trying to listen to the men's conversation over the sound of the rain outside, growing increasingly heavy. The press of Marguerite's hand on mine brought me back.

"For agreeing to help. For accepting some protection, instead of rejecting it outright. You didn't ask for this life, and it must be so tempting to run from it. To see it all as one giant trap."

"Not a trap, exactly. But I had a life before this one. It wasn't great, but it was mine. And it didn't stop when Verity died."

That might have been the hardest realization for me to make—harder than accepting the existence of magic, or the truth about my family. It was the knowledge that Verity's life had ended, and mine went on. I still felt guilty about it sometimes.

"And now you try to find a balance between your path and the Vessel's."

"You get it," I said gratefully. "Nobody else does."

"Luc does. He's starting to, anyway. He'll always be the Heir, but he's also my son, with a life of his own. Caring for you has reminded him of that. If he manages to reconcile the two, it will be thanks to you."

She smoothed her skirt. "We've imposed on you enough today, and if those two knock heads much longer, someone'll end up with a broken skull. My men," she sighed, with equal parts exasperation and affection.

I guided her to the balcony doors, where Luc and Dominic broke off their conversation.

"Leavin' so soon?" Luc asked.

"I suppose we could stay for dinner, if you'd like more time with your father," she said slyly.

"And here I am with nothing in the icebox," he drawled, matching her tone. "*À bientôt, Maman.*"

He brushed a kiss over her cheek, and she whispered something to him in low, rapid French. His brow furrowed as she drew back.

"Mo," she said as Dominic ushered her out. "Thank you." And then we were alone again.

"We should set the cloaking spell," he said, his voice cool. "Get you home."

"You're mad." I touched his shoulder, and he walked away, toward the mantel.

"Not mad. Just wish you didn't think so little of me."

"That's not true."

He scoffed. "I saw your face when I said you could stay here. Like someone had offered to set your hair on fire. I was tryin' to keep you safe, not seduce you."

"I know that." I could feel my cheeks turning scarlet. His intentions had been noble, but I'd panicked anyway—which said more about me than him.

"And yet you'd rather risk Anton finding you again. Anything to keep from being alone with me."

"I'm alone with you now."

"And itchin' to leave." There was a hardness in his voice rarely directed at me. "You like me well enough. I already said I'm not going to try and sweet-talk you into my bed. And I am fairly confident you're not going to be makin' any attempts of that nature. Which means something else has set you to running."

"You're insufferable," I snapped.

"And you still don't trust me."

I bit my lip. "It hasn't exactly been our strong suit in the past."

"I'm not interested in our past, Mouse. I'm interested in our future. Which is going to get grim pretty damn quick if we don't start trusting each other."

"You first," I said. He was right, but old habits died hard. "What did your mom say earlier?"

He ran a fingertip idly along the mantel. I expected him to

hedge, but instead he replied, "Told me the destination was fixed, not the path. Said it wasn't just yours, but mine."

I forced myself not to bolt. He'd trusted me with the truth. The least I could do was not run from it. "Prophecy, or motherly advice?"

"Hard to tell. Advice, more'n likely. She's never been shy with her opinions."

"It upset you," I said. I'd seen the look on his face—confusion, then frustration, bitten back so as not to hurt Marguerite's feelings.

"Strange thing to say, that's all." He touched the small painting. "She's a seer. She knows the power of a prophecy. She understands fate better than anyone." He sounded almost resentful. Sullen. I'd never heard him speak about Marguerite like that before.

"What do you think she meant by it?"

"How should I know? My path's always been clear, Mouse. While you were learning addition and subtraction, I was being schooled in my fate. Most important lesson I ever learned."

I tried to picture Luc in kindergarten. He would have been skinny, all knobby knees and sharp elbows, years before he built up the lean cords of muscle I saw now. And his hair would have been a mess. Always in his face, hiding those breathtaking eyes. I'd bet anything he had the same manner about him. Confident to the point of arrogance, quicksilver charm he wouldn't hesitate to use if it meant getting his way—whether it was ice cream or a girl.

I did not like thinking about Luc getting other girls. I didn't like thinking about why, either. I shut out those thoughts and tried to understand what was making him so edgy. "Kind of a big burden for a little kid."

He lifted a shoulder, staring at the picture. "You grew up hearing that the world unfolded according to God's plan. I grew up hearing that everything that ever happened to me, good or bad, was the hand of fate."

"And it was mostly bad, I'm guessing?"

He reached out, eyes glittering green, and touched a lock of my hair, wrapping it around his finger. "Not all of it."

"Luc . . ."

He let go and began to pace. "And then you come in, and you don't believe in fate at all. You change the world, Mouse, and you tell me it's because of your *choices?* Hard thing for a man to swallow after a lifetime of hearing otherwise, but I figure we can agree to disagree."

Which seemed like a reasonable approach. But Luc looked far from reasonable right now. He looked explosive. Carefully, I said, "I don't think she's denying fate exists. She's saying you can have a life of your own, too. That as long as you end up in the right place, you can choose your own path."

"I have freedom?" His mouth twisted, the word sounding like a curse. "What in the hell am I supposed to do with that?"

"Whatever you want." I intercepted him as he rounded the sofa. "That's the point. You don't have to be the Heir every single minute. You don't have to give your entire life to it."

"You don't know what you're talking about."

"I do, actually. Remember me? The Vessel?"

He looked at me as if he'd never seen me before. "Everything I've done, Mouse. Everything. It was fate. It has to be. Or I'm to blame."

Whatever it was that Marguerite had tried to tell him, he'd misunderstood. Her words had torn open an old wound, long buried and badly healed. And it had fallen to me to fix it.

I touched his hand, kept my voice gentle. "For what?"

He jerked back, and the lines nearby blazed up, sending a tremor through the room. Pottery and marble sculptures tumbled from the shelves, exploding into dust as they fell.

"Luc!" I reached for him, but he knocked my hand away. Paintings tilted drunkenly on the walls, the canvases in their frames glowing like the end of a lit cigarette, the scent of scorched cloth and burnt oil filling the air.

"I did it. My fault," he said. "All of it, and she knew, and never said."

With a whoosh, the drapes caught fire, flames licking their way up the heavy silk.

"Knock it off! You're going to burn this place down!"

"She wasn't giving me a gift," he said, his face drawn and older, suddenly. "It was payback."

Smoke was billowing, the crackling sound of the fire filling my ears. The magic twisted and shuddered, even as it was drawn into the lines like unwilling fuel for the flames. I took his face in my hands, forced him to meet my eyes. "You're going to kill us. Stop this. Turn it off."

He blinked at me.

"She loves you. She didn't say it to hurt you," I said, coughing from the smoke. "Please, Luc. Listen to me. *Please.*"

He closed his eyes, drew in a ragged breath, and the flames went out. The portraits lost their ominous glow, and the remaining sculptures ceased their trembling. With a wave, the French doors opened and fresh air flowed in, bringing the scent of sweet olive and rain.

"Listen to me," I said softly. The lines quieted, but the link between me and Luc felt dangerously tight, the bones of his face sharp against my palms. "Your mom loves you. I see it whenever you're around her. She loves you, and more than anything else, she wants you to be happy. She didn't say it as a punishment."

"She should." His voice was hoarse, eyes still shut. Whatever he was seeing wasn't in this room, and I needed to find a way to bring him back. "Not a soul who would blame her."

"For what? You've done what was expected of you your entire life. Why would she punish you for that?"

"Because if it wasn't fated, then it was my fault. That's the nice thing about fate." He smiled bleakly. "Something bad happens, you aren't to blame. Nothing you could have done. Isn't that what people say?"

It's what he'd said to me, eons ago, when Verity had died. *Nothing you could have done to stop it, Mouse.* Words both kind and honest. But they weren't absolution. And this wasn't about Verity. This went far deeper than a girl he'd met only last summer.

"Tell me."

He slid his hands to cover mine, and brought my fingers to his lips. "I scared you. Didn't want that."

"I'm not scared of you." Of our future—and the toll it would take on both of us—yes. But not him. Not anymore. "Tell me."

He ran a hand through his hair, the strands falling back into his face, hiding him from view, and slumped on the couch. I sat close enough that when he stretched his arm along the back of the couch, it brushed my shoulders, far enough that I could read his body language. Tucking my feet underneath me, I propped my chin in my hands and waited.

"I had a brother," he said quietly. "Theo. I was six. He was seventeen."

"Big age gap."

"They had the Heir," he said, and there was no rancor in his voice. "No need for another kid."

He trailed off into silence, and I prompted, "What was he like?"

"Thought he was God's gift. He got his powers real early, before he could even speak full sentences. Dominic said it was 'cause he was the Heir. He liked to show off, you know? Always doin' tricks to put me in my place, just because he could. Big deal to be the Heir to any House. Throw in the Torrent Prophecy, and it's even bigger. People telling you how amazin' you are, wanting to get close, like it might rub off."

I nodded. I'd seen it with Verity, how people always

wanted a bit of her shine, her vibrancy for themselves. It was not something I'd ever had to deal with.

"He was going off to see his friends, and I wanted to tag along. He said no, and I was mad. Told him he wasn't so special. Told him he wasn't any better than the rest of us." Luc's gaze went far away again, some place I couldn't follow. "I said the Vessel was the only thing that made him special. Once she was found, he'd be second string.

"He called me names, told me to go home. And I dared him. I said if he wasn't just the errand boy for the Vessel, he could do big magic without her."

"So he tried it?" I asked. "There was a line nearby—it'd always been unsteady, we knew not to mess with it, and he opened it up. It got away from him."

I felt sick, knowing what came next. What he'd witnessed. "Was it like Kowalski?"

"Raw magic kills a Flat almost instantly," he said. "Arcs . . . especially ones with big talents . . . it eats them from the inside out. Takes a while, sometimes. But you can't stop it."

"Oh, God. Luc . . ." I squeezed his hand.

"Dominic said it was fate. That if Theo had been the Heir, he wouldn't have died. But I'm the Heir, so I lived, and Theo had to die. That's what I've always thought. That's what they've always told me."

No wonder he put so much stock in fate. It was the only way for him to make sense of his brother's death.

I laced my fingers with his, my heart breaking for him. "You didn't make him open up that line. He was old enough to know how risky it was. He could have said no."

"I knew he wouldn't. He wasn't the type to back down from a dare, especially not from his little brother. He did it because of me."

"She said the destination is fixed, right? That means you were always supposed to be the Heir. You. Not him. He would have died anyway. The circumstances might have been different, but it would have happened anyway." It felt cruel to speak so bluntly, but I didn't know how else to make him hear me. "You didn't cause this."

"Easy for you to say. Seein' as how you don't believe in fate to begin with."

"The hell it's easy! I know a little something about living at the expense of other people, Luc. I don't have to believe in fate for that."

"Guess not," he mumbled.

I tried again. "She isn't saying you were to blame. She's saying you shouldn't make your entire life about one prophecy. Maybe it should be about your heart, too."

He glanced up at me then, and the anguish in his eyes was almost more than I could stand. "And if it comes down to the same thing?"

I didn't answer. The rain beat down steadily, filling the silence between us.

"Been enough truth for one day," he said. "Let's set the cloaking spell and take you home."

"Thank you for telling me. For trusting me with it."

"Trust you with my life, Mouse. With more than that, even. Give me your hand."

I did, managing to keep it steady. "This part hurts, doesn't it?"

"Sorry." From Between, he produced a small silver pocket-knife. "You don't have to look."

I turned my head, managed not to flinch at the jab of pain. He started to speak in the language of the Arcs, and the magic rose up and joined in, pulling the protection of his words deep into me, spreading under my skin like a flush. The damp air grew heavier, almost oppressive. Then it lightened again, and Luc's fingers were still pressed against my stuttering pulse.

"You can look now."

The cut itself was tiny—a quarter of an inch at most, and

shallow. A single drop of blood welled up, and Luc dabbed it away with a napkin.

"Darklings won't be able to find you now," he said.

"But Anton will."

"Yeah. Sure as hell would like to know how he's doin' that." He shook his head. "You'll still need protection."

"Not for long," I said.

CHAPTER 14

"Something's up with your friend," Colin said as we drove home. Luc had dropped me off at school, where Colin had been waiting. "Should I be worried?"

"You'll worry no matter what I say," I pointed out. "She doesn't want to talk about it."

He humphed, and I was struck by a sudden suspicion. "Did you follow her home?"

"She knows the truck," he said. "She would have noticed me."

"So you thought about it."

He smiled, just a little. "Are you sure whatever she's mixed up in isn't dangerous?"

"No idea. But it doesn't matter. She's my friend."

He scowled but didn't argue further, and we pulled up in front of the house. "Do you want to come in?" I asked.

"Your dad's home," he said. "And Billy has eyes on the house. It's a little crowded."

He kissed me good-bye and waited until I'd unlocked the front door. I flashed the porch light at him, and he pulled away, leaving me to a dark house and darker thoughts.

I climbed the stairs, waiting for my dad to come and greet me, but there was only silence. I poked my head into my parents' bedroom. It was strange to see evidence of my dad in what had been my mom's territory for so long. The night-stand no longer carried a neat stack of food magazines, but

The Economist and mystery novels. The top of the dresser held his wallet and keys, and the closet door was cracked open, revealing his new, post-prison, post-accountant wardrobe of jeans and T-shirts and flannels, so new the fabric was still crisp.

No wonder Colin hadn't come in. He'd spent the day working side by side with my dad. That was more than enough quality time.

My phone rang, and I checked the caller ID. Jenny Kowalksi.

"What?"

"You didn't answer yesterday. Did you find anything?"

It took me a minute to remember what she was talking about. Yesterday afternoon seemed like a lifetime ago. But I thought about the password-protected computer, the fruitless search of my uncle's office. Nearly getting caught. "He keeps all that stuff on a computer, and I don't know the password."

"Can't you figure it out? Try the street he grew up on, or his first pet, or something. We need that information to make the charges stick," she said. "Nick says without something solid, your uncle and the Forellis will just walk again. Nothing will change."

"I'll find it," I said. The furnace switched off, and in the sudden silence, I heard my dad's voice, oddly muffled. "I have to go. I'll let you know if something turns up."

I padded into the kitchen, noting the casserole dish on the counter. My mom had a church thing tonight, so she'd left us dinner. She'd be horrified to know, but I'd be eating mine over the kitchen sink. No need for a cozy family meal, after all.

The door to the basement stairs was just off the kitchen. The latch was tricky—you had to really tug on it to keep it closed, and my father must have forgotten that trick, because it stood wide open, letting in a faintly musty smell and blanketing the linoleum with cold air. My father's voice drifted up, echoing off the stairwell, and I stopped to listen.

It was a jumble at first—his voice was low, and I had to let the sounds roll around in my head until the words sifted through, like wheat from chaff.

"I told you I'll deliver the numbers," he said. "I keep my word. You should know that by now."

My hand stilled on the lid of the casserole dish, and the hollow feeling in my stomach wasn't from hunger.

"They'll be clean." A pause. "That's why you need me."

The blood pumped through me in a fury, and the magic stirred as well. There was a roaring in my ears like when you listen to a seashell. I thought of the ocean, envisioned endless blue water and forced myself to calm down.

". . . our deal," my father said.

The casserole lid slipped from my grasp and hit the floor with a ringing sound.

The conversation broke off. A moment later, my father stood in the doorway, sporting a too-hearty smile and a new cell phone, which he quickly tucked in a pocket.

"Didn't hear you come in. When did you get home?"

"Just now."

He bent to retrieve the lid, weighed it in his hands as he studied me. "You smell like smoke."

I rolled my eyes. "I don't smoke."

He sniffed again. "Not cigarettes. Like a fire. Where were you?"

"Studying with Lena."

"Arson techniques?"

I brushed past him toward the fridge and rummaged for something to drink. "Lena and I were studying. Colin brought me home. Who were you talking to?"

"Nobody you know. Trying to find work."

"Aren't you working for Billy?" My mom would have scolded me for leaving off the "uncle." My dad hardly blinked.

"It's never a bad idea to diversify," he said.

"It is if you end up back in prison." I popped open a Diet Coke. "Or dead."

"I don't plan on either of those things happening," he said.

"If you get caught again, it will kill Mom. If Billy and the Forellis find you're working side jobs, they will kill you."

He crossed his arms over his chest. "Did you know your mother sent me your report cards? Every quarter. Every year."

"I know." Part of her attempt to keep us a happy family, to ensure my dad knew me even in absentia. It had failed pretty spectacularly.

"You're plenty smart, but you don't know as much as you think you do. No more deliveries, Mo."

"I don't have to listen to you. I am almost eighteen, and I've been managing just fine without your input. Besides, in a few months, I'll be gone."

"I'm glad. But you're out of the business starting now. I will handle Billy."

"Why? So you can go to jail again? Break Mom's heart again? Do you know how long she's waited to have you home?"

There was something in his eyes, a hint of the anger he'd almost unleashed on the cops at Morgan's. "To the damn day."

"If you go back, it'll kill her. It really will." He'd leave us. Again. "Don't ruin this, Dad."

"I won't. You're doing a bang-up job of that yourself."

I sputtered, trying to form a response. None came—the accusation struck so deeply, I was afraid he might be right. And the consequences, if either one of us was caught, would be disastrous.

Headlights played across the windows as my mom pulled into the driveway. He jerked a thumb toward the stairs. "Go take a shower so she doesn't ask questions."

For once, I listened to him.

CHAPTER 15

By the end of my second training session with Niobe, it was painfully obvious the Quartoren had made a mistake. She shouldn't have been working at St. Brigid's as a guidance counselor. She should have been a PE teacher. She had the masochistic streak down pat. Whether we were studying protocol for the ceremony or fighting techniques, she took way too much pleasure in pointing out all the things I was doing wrong, then making me try again.

The fact that Constance sat in on our sessions only made it more humiliating.

"What's the point in learning all these spells? I'll never be able to cast them. I'll never be an Arc." Niobe had taken us to a training room in her House—a large, high-ceilinged room with mats on the floor and weapons hanging from the walls. I sank down on a low bench and tried to will away the headache brewing behind my eyes.

"It's a sign of respect. A Succession is a sacred event, and showing you've taken the time to learn our language will go a long way toward assuring the Arcs you take it seriously. That you're committed to our world." She hauled me up by the arm and pointed to the symbols she'd written on the opposite wall. "Try again. From the beginning."

She spoke in the liquid, silvery language of the Arcs, and I attempted to copy her. Every few words, she'd stop, breathe so deeply her nostrils flared, and correct me. Constance followed along; even though she'd only been studying with Niobe for a few months, she'd picked up the language quickly. My tongue felt stiff, almost frozen, as if I'd eaten an entire pint of ice cream.

"Tell me again how it'll work," I asked, angling for a break. Constance yawned and wandered away.

"The first session of the ceremony is for members of the House to declare their candidacy—they swear to take the test, and to serve the House if they are chosen. The second session takes place five days later. It's a public testing of the candidates, where they attempt to prove their worthiness. At the conclusion of the test, the House elevates its next leader."

"It's an election?"

"In a way. The test each candidate undergoes is to cast a spell in front of the membership. The results indicate who should be selected."

"That sounds like the magic tells them who to vote for."

"Of course not. The magic is merely an indicator. Like in one of your science experiments, when one chemical changes color in the presence of another. The magic reacts differently to those who are capable of handling the burdens of the station, allowing members to gauge each person's suitability. A Succession via ceremony is quite rare. It's most often hereditary, as in Luc's case. Luc said Pascal was chosen in a ceremony. He didn't really want to be on the Quartoren."

"That's my understanding as well. I was too young to remember it."

"Why would he try out if he didn't want the job? Why risk it?"

"A sense of duty, I suppose. Likely curiosity was a factor—Pascal never passes up a chance to better understand the magic. And then once he was chosen . . . it's not an honor one walks away from. Now," she said, "try the spell again."

Midway through the next halting, garbled incantation, she held up a hand. "Enough. It's like asking a toddler to recite Shakespeare. Let's switch to fighting techniques. You and Constance can spar."

Yet another area Constance outperformed me. Niobe let her use magic in our fights, dampened to keep me from getting seriously hurt. I'd pointed out it wasn't a fair fight, to which she'd replied that any fight with Anton would be twelve times more unfair. The most I could hope for was to keep myself alive until help got there.

"Anton likes to hurt," she added. "If he casts a spell from across the room, your odds are grim, to say the least."

"Comforting."

"It is, actually. Anton rarely attacks from a distance. He wants to feel it happening, and that requires proximity. If you let him get close enough, you can fight back."

"If he doesn't kill me first." My throat closed, remembering the pressure of his fingers.

"We've been over this. He needs you alive. And he continually underestimates you."

"Everybody does," I muttered.

"Then use it," she said, impatient. "You're accustomed to being overlooked. Your age, your family, your gender. Your lack of magic. It's a mistake for people to dismiss you for those reasons, but since they do, use it to your advantage."

I drained half my water bottle while considering her words. Wasn't I already doing that, playing the part Billy expected while I worked to take him down? Maybe it would work here, too. If I lulled Anton into believing I was an annoyance instead of a threat, I might be able to beat him.

Across the room, Constance was playing with her phone, barely noticing when I stood. "One more round, and then I have to leave."

Constance clambered up, pulling her caramel-colored hair back into a ponytail, and moved to the center of the room. "Ready."

Niobe nodded. "Go."

Constance struck first, a blast of gold light that caught my shoulder. I stumbled backward.

"Stay close," called Niobe. "This is hand to hand."

"We should have weapons," Constance said, following me. As I straightened, she swung, a wide right hook that I blocked with a grunt. "Lots of the other kids have them."

I shoved her with both hands while Niobe replied, "They've practiced much longer. And they focus—something you seem to lack. This is a sparring match, not a social event. Fight."

Constance tossed her ponytail. "Fine."

And then she went after me in earnest—a flurry of punches and kicks, and she didn't pull a single one. I skidded across the floor, managing to block a particularly vicious kick to my rib cage.

"Get up, Mo," Niobe called. "You need to take the offensive."

But it seemed impossible—Constance was fast, she could heal herself, and she was obviously in a mood. "I'm not even breathing hard, Mo."

There was just enough nastiness in her voice to blot out my tendency to go easy on her. Across the room, I caught Niobe's eye, and she dipped her chin, a small smile of approval.

I staggered to my feet and went after Constance again, but she slammed a fresh burst of energy into me. I went down, just like before.

Just like I planned.

I'd hunched over, panting. She approached me, smirking, hands spread wide. I launched myself sideways at her legs, knocking her down with a grunt. She landed hard on hands and knees. Before she could gather enough magic for a strike—I could feel her fumbling for the lines, startled into clumsiness—I pinned her, forcing her against the ground, wrapping her ponytail around my hand for extra leverage.

"Enough?" I said.

Her cheek was pressed against the floor, and I eased up enough for her to raise her head. She scowled.

Niobe answered for her. "Enough. Well done, Mo."

I scrambled up, extending a hand to help Constance to her feet. She ignored me and stalked over to her water bottle.

"Don't sulk," said Niobe mildly. "She beat you fairly."

"It wasn't fair—I had to hold back so I didn't hurt her."

"That was you holding back?" I tugged at the neckline of my T-shirt, displaying a reddish welt on my shoulder. "Maybe you need to work on control."

"Maybe you shouldn't be trying to fight Arcs," she said. "If I can beat you, what do you think Anton will do?"

"You didn't beat me today." I pulled on a hoodie over my T-shirt. "Can we go back to school now?"

"Certainly. Constance?"

"I can get back on my own."

"Very well." Niobe gripped my elbow, and an instant later we were back in her office. She scribbled a pass to the locker rooms so I could change back to my uniform.

"Thanks," I said. "Do you really think this is the best way to handle Anton?"

She lifted a shoulder. "It's a delaying tactic."

Not really an answer. Hefting my bag over my shoulder, I started to leave.

"Mo. You should also keep in mind that it only works once. Constance, for example, won't be fooled again."

"And she'll be twice as vicious next time." So would Anton. I'd get one shot at him. I intended to make the most of it.

CHAPTER 16

Our second trip to the soup kitchen was pretty much a rerun of the first. Only the menu varied: shepherd's pie, green salad, roll, fruit. Cookies for dessert. Once again, Jill and Constance were stuck in the kitchen while Lena and I worked the front. I looked for the weakened Arcs as they came through the line, felt sorrow deep in my chest when they wouldn't meet my eyes. I added a little extra to their plate, as if that would make up for everything they'd suffered.

Meanwhile, Lena kept a close watch on the door.

"Expecting someone?" I asked.

She shrugged. "Wondered if we'd see the little girl from last week. She was a cutie."

"Maybe they found a place to live," I said.

"Maybe." She poked at the giant bowl of salad, obviously not convinced.

In the kitchen, Jill was preening about getting into NYU—all the paperwork she was filling out, how her parents were taking her to visit the campus over spring break, how many of her AP credits would transfer. She pitched the words just loud enough for me to hear. I tried to tune her out, but the words managed to work their way under my skin, like some sort of poison ivy.

"Ignore her," Lena said. "You'll get in."

I passed out more shepherd's pie. "It was a waste of money to apply. I can't go."

"What if you get everything with your uncle . . . sorted out?"

"Even if." I tried to smile, but it didn't work. Lena didn't know about Tess. Colin could never leave.

"You know, I like Colin. I do. But you're a moron if you pass up your dream school because of a guy. Even one like him."

"It's not just Colin. It's lots of stuff."

She frowned. "If you say so."

"I do."

We didn't talk much for the rest of the meal. Jill left early, claiming she had a doctor's appointment, but we all knew she was actually going to the salon. The little girl and her mom were no-shows. We swept the floor and scrubbed the tables, and when everything was done, Niobe rounded up the remaining kids. I interrupted to ask if Lena and I could wait for Colin upstairs.

I was not enjoying the constant babysitting. Protective wards now crisscrossed St. Brigid's, Morgan's, my house— even the church we were in today. It was a constant barrage of vibrating lines, wearing on my nerves. The sooner we dealt with Anton, the better.

"Go ahead," she said, examining her roster in annoyance and making a shooing motion. "The wards will alert me to any problems."

We waited on the steps—the day had lost its painfully cold tinge, and the fresh air was nice after being cooped up. "Have you told Colin yet?" she asked.

"That I'm passing Billy's information to Ekomov? I will. I'm waiting for the right time."

"He's going to figure it out, you know. It would be better if you told him first."

Before I could respond, a man lurched across the sidewalk, his shadow stretched long and distorted in the late-afternoon sunlight. My heart thudded, imagining the odd joints of a Darkling in his silhouette, but he was just a man, backlit and bulky in a dark green parka.

"The afternoon meal is over," I said politely. "You can come back tomorrow, though."

"You know where my wife is?" he slurred. A whiff of beer floated toward us.

I shaded my eyes with my hand and reached out with the magic. Not an Arc. Not a Flat under a Rivening. Not one of Billy's men, either. Just a guy who'd had one too many drinks after work.

"Sorry," I said. "I don't think so."

"My wife," he said again, climbing up to the landing, stopping a few feet away. "And my little girl. My Emily."

"We don't know any Emilys," I said, and pointed down the street. "There's a police station just a few blocks that way. Maybe they can help you."

Help him right into a cell until he sobered up, I meant, but the guy barely glanced at me. "Wasn't asking you," he said, pointing one doughy, unsteady finger. "I'm asking her."

Lena went still, her face frightened for an instant. Then her eyes went huge and innocent as she twisted her ponytail into a knot. I'd seen that move before. Every time she covered for me. "I don't know either, sir. I'm sorry."

"My wife. My daughter. Where are they?"

"Is there a service tonight? Maybe they're already inside. You should go in and ask the priest." I searched for Colin, trying to sound nonchalant.

"Shut up," he snarled, and Lena flinched. "They're not *here*. Tell me where they are."

"I don't know," she said, a fear trickling into her voice.

"Lying little bitch!" He lunged at her, and she fell backward on the hard stone steps with a cry. He loomed over her, reaching down and grabbing the front of her jacket.

"Hey!" I tried to push him away, but he swung wildly, clouting me on the side of the head.

He loomed over Lena, who shrank back in terror. "You

know where they are. You took them, but they're mine. Mine, and I want—"

He broke off as he was jerked away, and Colin shoved him against the brick wall of the church. He wrenched the guy's arm up and back, impossibly high and incredibly painful looking.

"You want to leave," Colin ground out. "That's the only thing you want. Because if you don't, I will snap your arm like a toothpick, and then I'll snap your neck."

Colin's mouth was white with anger, his eyes nearly black. I crouched next to Lena and helped her to her feet, but watched him the whole time, saw him unraveling bit by bit, the threads of his control fraying as the guy struggled against him, calling us horrible names. Colin twisted harder; the guy stopped talking, alternating between hisses and whimpers.

"You okay?" Colin asked Lena over his shoulder.

Lena nodded, cupping her elbow, tears caught in her lashes. But when I tried to coax her away, she shook me off and stalked over to the man. "Emily is gone, you bastard."

"Walk," Colin said, shoving him toward the sidewalk. The guy stumbled away, clutching his arm and swearing. Colin trailed after him, calling over his shoulder to us. "Wait here. Both of you."

"Friend of yours?" I asked.

"It's complicated," she said. She was back to twisting her ponytail. "You know how it is."

I swallowed back a retort, reminding myself how many times she'd covered for me unquestioningly, cheerfully. Instead, I dug a tissue out of my bag and offered it to her. "Are you sure you're okay?"

She wiped at her nose. "It'll bruise like crazy, but I'll live."

I buttoned my coat. The fresh air no longer felt good. Just cold. Around us, no one seemed to have noticed the disruption. "Who's Emily?"

She swallowed and stuffed her hands in her pockets. "I don't know anyone named Emily," she said after a long pause. "Other than that junior in our history class."

"He thought you did."

I was missing something. Something huge. It was like someone had dumped out a jigsaw puzzle in front of me but taken the box away, leaving me with pieces I knew should fit together, but with absolutely no idea how. I tried again. "Do you know him?"

"I've never seen him before in my life."

Colin was walking back along the sidewalk, and I knew we only had a minute before he rejoined us. "Lena, a perfect stranger attacked you—in public—because he thinks you know something about his family."

"Men with guns broke into your house in the middle of the night," she retorted. "You disappear constantly. You run off with Luc at the drop of a hat, and Colin—who gets pissed when you're five minutes late to leave school—is okay with it. Do I interrogate you?"

"If I remember correctly, half an hour after those guys came to my house, you were going through my dad's court transcript. Without my permission. I'm not asking because I'm nosy. I'm asking because I care."

Colin marched up the steps. "Time to go," he said in his bodyguard voice: Remote. Focused. Stubborn as hell. Lena hadn't had much experience with it, but I knew better than to argue. "We'll drop you at your car, follow you home."

"You don't need to do that."

"I sure as hell do," Colin said. Before she could protest, he continued. "You want me to drop you somewhere else? Fine. We'll go someplace else, make sure he didn't follow us, and then we can go our separate ways."

"He won't follow me," said Lena.

"How do you think he found you here? It wasn't a coincidence. My guess is, he was watching you the minute you left school. He followed you here, had a few beers while he worked up his nerve, then decided to introduce himself."

"He doesn't know where I live?" she asked with obvious relief.

"If he knew where you lived, he wouldn't have approached you in a public place. Start walking."

Lena was not in the honors program for nothing. She stopped arguing and started walking. Just before I climbed into the truck, I glanced back at the church. Standing in front of the arched main door was Luc, expression troubled. Behind him stood Niobe, looking equally concerned. I gave a tiny wave and slid into the cab, taking the middle seat.

On the ride back to school, Lena kept her head down, Colin kept his guard up, and I tried to piece together everything I had witnessed—not just today, but in the last six months. Her ability to deflect questions. Her unblinking acceptance of my family's history. Her reaction to the break-in last November—scared but not panicked, the same way she'd reacted today. Her assurance that the secrets she kept weren't her own.

"Where are we going?" he asked her before she got out.

"El station," she said, clearly unhappy. "Leavitt and Archer."

"Fine. Do not try to shake me," he said. Lena nodded.

"You have excellent timing," I said after we'd been driving for a few minutes.

"How many times have we gone over this? You don't leave the building until I'm there. What if he'd been after you?"

"He wasn't." I paused. "Why was he after Lena?"

A muscle in his jaw jumped. "It doesn't matter. She put you in danger, Mo."

A warning sounded at the back of my mind as he continued, "You could have been hurt today. Maybe it's better to . . ."

I cut him off. "Drop her? She's my friend! She's stuck by me through all sorts of crap this year, Colin. School stuff and family stuff and Arc stuff, even though she doesn't realize it. Remember the break-in? She didn't bail on me, and that was a lot more dangerous than one drunk guy."

"Do you have any idea what she's mixed up in?" he asked.

I stared. "No. But you do, apparently."

He jerked a shoulder. "I've been asking around."

"You ran a background check on my friend?" My voice came out high, too close to a shriek for my liking, and I lowered it with an effort. "You have got to be kidding me."

"I needed to make sure you were safe. Find out if her family was connected. They're not, by the way."

"You are unbelievable. So, as long as you're doing it for a good reason, it's okay to snoop around in someone's life? Is that what you're telling me?" I wanted him to say yes. More than want—I *needed* him to, because it would ease my conscience and absolve me of what I'd done. The same way, I realized, that Luc needed to believe in fate.

"I'm telling you that I will do whatever I have to in order to protect you. I'm sorry if it offends you, but it's my job."

"Your job." My voice was brittle.

His hand found mine. "Not just a job. I take care of what I love."

I wished I could maintain the full force of my anger, but his words made it impossible. The question was, would the same rules apply when he found out what I'd done?

We pulled into the parking lot of the El station behind Lena. Everything looked muddy and tired. "I need to talk to her," I said.

She rolled down the window as I approached her little white Cavalier. "I'm sorry," she said.

"No apology necessary," I said. "Are you okay to drive?"

"Yeah. I'll ice the elbow when I get home."

"Good idea. Lena . . . Colin knows. He won't tell me, but he knows."

She pressed her knuckles to her mouth.

"I'm not telling you as a threat, okay? If you don't want to tell me, I respect that. I won't nag Colin or you. I promise."

She shook her head no, the gesture panicked. I'd never seen her this way before.

I leaned down, gripping the window frame with both

hands. "You don't have to tell me, but you should know . . . whatever this is about? It's not as secret as you thought."

"Nothing ever is," she said softly. "Tell Colin thanks, okay? I'm glad he was there."

"Me too."

CHAPTER 17

My uncle cornered me the next afternoon at Morgan's. "Have you thought more about our conversation the other night?" he asked, glancing around to see if anyone was in earshot. "About helping our cause?"

I checked off inventory on a clipboard, saying nothing. I'd managed to avoid discussing this with Billy for more than a week, but I knew I couldn't put it off forever.

"This Luc fellow. He seems quite attached to you. Who was the other one?"

I set down the clipboard. Might as well get this over with. "His name is Anton. He's the leader of the group that killed Verity."

"And now he's trying to kill you?" His face creased in concern. "Why? Can you do magic as well?"

"No. He thinks I have information, and he wants it."

"Ah." Finally, something Billy was familiar with. "Do you?"

"No," I said shortly, and went into the front to hand off the inventory to Charlie. Niobe and Luc seemed confident that Billy wouldn't be a problem, but that's because they didn't know him the way I did. He'd find a way to cause trouble, sooner or later.

Sooner, as it turned out.

A few hours later, Luc strolled into Morgan's, tossed his fedora on a table, and settled in. His eyes tracked me across the room, and I fought off annoyance that once again, the two halves of my life were mingling.

"What can I get you?" I asked, slapping down a coaster and a tattered menu.

"Minute of your time would be nice," he said. "Looked like you had some excitement yesterday."

"Lena did. I was an innocent bystander."

"You? Innocent?" One eyebrow lifted. "If you say so, Mouse."

I flushed. "Are you going to order?"

He glanced over at the bar. "Bourbon'll do."

"ID?"

He blinked at me. "Beg pardon?"

"The drinking age here is twenty-one." I smiled sweetly. "Is it different in Louisiana?"

He scowled at me. "Different for—" He broke off as a hand clapped my shoulder.

"Luc!" said my uncle cheerily. "Good to see you again!"

"Likewise," Luc replied, not even bothering to sound sincere.

"Mo, bring the lad whatever he's asking for. After all he's done, I'm not about to deny him a drink."

I sighed. "Bourbon. Neat or on the rocks?"

"Neat."

I didn't want to leave them alone, but Billy gave me a push toward the bar. "Top shelf," he called after me. When I returned, they'd moved to the back booth. "Mo, darling girl. Fetch me a cup of coffee and ask Charlie to mind your tables for a bit so you can join us."

By the time I'd brought Charlie up to speed and grabbed Billy's coffee, he and Luc had been talking for far too long. I set Billy's mug down with a thump and slid in next to Luc, my fingers knotted in my lap.

Luc patted my hands under the table, his bland smile unwavering, his eyes shrewd.

"I was just telling Luc how worried we've been about you, ever since Verity died. I'd say knowing the truth has been a burden lifted, but . . ." He lifted his hands, helpless. "It seems you're in as much danger as before."

"More," said Luc pleasantly. "You're trying to protect a neighborhood. Mouse and I are lookin' to keep a whole world safe."

"All the more reason she should be protected," said Billy.

"I *am* protected."

"Can Donnelly fight those things that came after you the other night?"

"No need," said Luc. "They won't come after her again."

"Your doing, I'd wager." When Luc didn't respond, Billy continued, "Don't you see, Mo? It's a gift, this world appearing when we need it most."

"It's not a gift," I said. "None of this is for your benefit."

"It's benefited you, hasn't it?"

My best friend murdered, my once-clear future now a twisted, murky path. Kowalski dead and the Seraphim attacking me every time I turned around. "Less than you'd think."

"But it could fix everything. Think of what it would mean—we could rout Ekomov. Take back our neighborhood. Even get out from under the thumb of the Forellis. All our dreams . . ."

"Your dreams," I said quickly. "Not mine. You can quit making plans. I can't use magic, and even if I could, I wouldn't use it to help you."

The mask dropped away; for an instant, his bafflement and rage were crystal clear. Luc saw it, too, and his eyes narrowed in warning.

Billy got the message and changed tack immediately, transferring his attention to Luc. "You've brought my niece into something dangerous."

"She made that call all on her own," Luc said. "And she's handlin' herself well enough."

"Still, I'd like some assurance she'll be safe."

"You have my word," Luc said.

Billy looked unimpressed. "I'd like something a bit more tangible. Proof. A demonstration would suffice."

"You've had a shock," Luc replied, draping his arm around me. "So I will not take offense at the fact you just questioned my word and impugned my character. And I will refrain from demonstratin' my ability to turn this place into a bundle of toothpicks. Let's leave it at this: Someone tries to hurt Mouse, or wrong her, or give her cause to grieve? I will drop them. Permanently. And that includes you."

Billy's hand went still on his mug, and then he smiled, so widely it couldn't be natural. "And that was the proof I needed, right there," he said. "I only want to see my niece with someone who'll treat her as she deserves."

"I'm not with him," I said through gritted teeth.

"Of course not. You're throwing your future away on Donnelly, for all the good it will do you." He shook his head in disapproval, holding Luc's gaze.

Luc drained his whiskey and set the glass down with a sharp crack. "I'll be going now."

I slid out of the booth, and Luc followed.

Billy stood, unhappy at the abrupt end of the conversation. "You're welcome here any time," he said. "Walk our guest out, Mo."

We made our way to the front, Luc looking sleek and dangerous compared to everyone else in the room.

"I thought you wanted to talk," I said.

"Some other time. Illuminatin' conversation," he added.

"I'm sorry. He's awful." Of all the emotions roiling inside me, it was embarrassment that was strongest. Mortification that Luc would have to deal with Billy's machinations, childlike compared to the circles Luc moved in.

"That he is. Fun to put him and Dominic in a room, see what develops."

I shuddered theatrically, and he laughed a little.

"So, now that I come with your uncle's seal of approval, you dead set against me?"

"No." I heard what it sounded like, and backpedaled. "Wait. I didn't mean . . . it's not Billy. He's not the problem." He touched my chin lightly. "Never thought he was."

Billy tried to pry more information out of me, but my shift was nearly over, and I wasn't in the mood to share. He was furious—all that power, and he couldn't get to it. He'd gotten so used to using me—as a courier, as a shield, as a bargaining chip—the fact he couldn't use me as a weapon practically had him frothing at the mouth. And while Billy's anger didn't faze me anymore, his desperation did. I'd seen the way he watched Luc—avarice and calculation oozed from his pores. He was looking for Luc's weak spots, and he'd zeroed in on me as the most likely possibility.

Colin came in as I was putting my tip money away. "Billy's in a strange mood. None of the usual dirty looks tonight," he said.

"Luc stopped by. Billy's too busy dreaming of how he'll use magic against the Russians to give you dirty looks."

"Great. That has disaster written all over it."

"I thought so, too. Luc doesn't seem interested in helping him out."

"For once, I agree with him." He bent to kiss me, then broke off. "Your mom invited me for dinner."

"Family dinner." I sighed. "Are you sure you want to brave it?"

"I think I can manage your dad over pot roast," he said.

"That makes one of us."

But I kept it together while we sat around the table, Colin's hand warm and familiar in mine as we said grace, his foot touching mine in a small, silent gesture of support. It was silly to rely on the nudge of his toes against mine as an anchor, but I did.

Right up until we started talking about the future.

"So," said my mother. "I've been talking with the architect about the renovations at the restaurant."

"Is there a problem?" my dad asked.

"No, no. The work's gone slowly, of course, because of the weather. But everything happens for a reason. I've always said so."

She smiled at my dad, and he returned it cautiously.

I had my doubts about divine providence and its relation to the construction industry, but I stayed quiet.

"He thinks it would be easy to extend the dining area into the parking lot next door. We could double the number of tables, at least. Maybe even wall it off so it could be used as a private room."

"You want to expand The Slice?" There was no real reason for the sense of foreboding congealing my stomach. But it did, nevertheless.

Colin seemed to consider the idea. "It wouldn't be too hard. You'd keep the kitchen where it is, right? We wouldn't have to run any more plumbing or gas lines. Just the electrical."

"Exactly," she said. "I could open for dinner, too. He's going to draw up the plans."

"Annie, I don't know about this," my dad said.

"They're just plans," she said, a defensive note creeping into her voice. "What does it hurt to make plans? To dream a little? Especially now that you're home."

"It's a gamble. Things could change. Our situation could change." When she looked at him blankly, he tried another approach. "Mo's going off to school soon. We could travel, if we wanted. Start fresh somewhere."

"Chicago is our home. Our family's here. Why would we want to leave?"

I didn't miss the look that passed between my father and Colin.

"We don't have to decide this minute," she said. "There's plenty of time. They're just plans. And speaking of plans, Mo, I was talking to Mrs. Sullivan after Mass last weekend. Chloe got into Notre Dame *and* Purdue."

"Great," I said, feigning enthusiasm. Anything to ease the strange tension running through the room. "Pass the potatoes, please."

My father handed me the earthenware dish. "When do you hear from NYU?"

"Soon. Seconds, anybody?"

Ordinarily, the suggestion someone was not being adequately fed would have sent my mother into a flurry of activity, but not tonight. No one was willing to be distracted. "What about the other schools you applied to? It seems late in the year to be waiting on a response."

I ducked my head. "I've heard back from a few."

My mom's fork skidded across the plate. "You have? Who?"

"University of Chicago. University of Washington. A couple of my safeties."

"And?" she pressed.

Colin frowned at me, which wasn't surprising, since I hadn't told him, either.

"And I got in." I shrugged, focused on making little crosshatch marks in my potatoes. "It's not a big deal."

"Of course it is, sweetheart! I can't believe you didn't tell us!"

"Me neither," said Colin, so quietly no one else heard.

I shifted in my chair, kept my eyes down. "I wanted to wait till I'd heard from all of them."

"University of Chicago! I'm so proud of you!" She paused. "Did they mention financial aid?"

"It's a pretty decent package."

Finally, my dad spoke. "But you'll take the NYU spot."

"I haven't heard if they've accepted me."

"But you'll take the spot," he repeated.

"Jack! Why would she go all the way to New York when she can go to school here?" She turned to me. "You could live at home and save money on room and board."

"I don't think I'd be living at home," I said quickly. I'd agreed to stay in the city, but nothing in my deal with Billy specified living here. I'd had a fantasy about staying with Colin—but that seemed more unrealistic every day.

Colin was silent, and I nudged his foot, trying to make him look at me. When he did, his eyes were flinty and unreadable.

"She'll go to New York because that's where her future is," my father said. "Not here. You think she should keep working for Billy? That's what you want for her?"

"She won't know a soul in New York. And anything can happen there. I don't think it's very safe."

"Neither is Chicago." There was sharpness to my dad's voice that I hadn't heard before, and my mother started in her chair.

"She has her family," Mom said, her voice trembling. "You just came home, and now you want to send her off halfway across the country all by herself? Who'd watch over her?"

Colin's silence was deafening.

"Mom, you're freaking out over nothing."

"It's not nothing!" Her eyes filled. "I've never liked this idea of New York. Never. Why would you encourage her, Jack? You know I don't approve."

"If she can go, she should. It's a fresh start." He helped himself to more pot roast, trying for nonchalance despite his death grip on the serving fork. I felt an unexpected rush of gratitude—he wasn't going to back down, no matter how upset my mom got. But he knew about the deal I'd made with Billy. He knew I was stuck. Why would he push for me to leave?

"Why are you so consumed with the notion of fresh starts these days?" Mom asked. "We've already gotten ours. How many do we need?"

From where I sat, it wasn't much of a fresh start—more like history repeating itself: my dad working for Billy, and me following his path. No matter what my reasons were, I was doing the same thing he had, all those years ago. What had Luc told me once? *What we hate most about other people? That's usually what we hate about ourselves.*

He'd been right. And the knowledge made me want to put my head down on the worn Formica table and weep.

But I didn't. Instead, I met Colin's eyes. "Right now, I'm planning on U of C."

He fumed silently, but he'd have plenty to say later. I tried to figure out how to stall the discussion as long as possible. And another one of those unreadable looks passed between him and my father, who also said nothing.

My mother reached across the table and patted my hand. "I'm so proud, sweetheart. And don't you worry about the money. We'll find a way."

I tried to smile but just couldn't make myself. We finished dinner quickly and quietly, as if talking about anything except the week's forecast would result in another confrontation. The minute my mom stood to clear the table, my father pushed his chair back with a scrape. "I need to run out for a bit."

Mom turned, startled, still clutching the dish of pot roast and vegetables. "Now? We haven't had dessert yet. There's apple crisp."

"I won't be long. Save me a piece." Before she could protest further, he caught her face in his hands and kissed her deeply. I stared at my shoes and Colin busied himself inspecting the caulking on the windows. "I love you, Annie."

"I love you, too, you impossible man."

My dad was gone before she could even set down the platter.

"Well," she said, cheeks pink. "I guess it's just the three of us, then. Mo, put on some decaf."

"We'll clean up," Colin said, scooting her out of the kitchen.

She mock-protested, like she always did when Colin came for dinner. It was a routine they'd established, and yet another thing that endeared him to her. She patted him on the cheek, and the fact that he let her made me fall for him all over again. "You are a keeper," she said.

He waited until she'd gone upstairs. I was in the middle of running a sinkful of soapy water when he leaned past me to slap the faucet off.

"When were you going to tell me?"

"When I'd decided, I guess."

"Seems like you already have."

I shoved him aside and started scrubbing pots and pans. "You're the only guy I know who would actively push his girlfriend to leave town, you know that? It's one thing to be supportive, Colin. It's another to torpedo a relationship."

"How many times do I have to say it? I want you to be free of Billy."

"Even if that means the end of us?" For the second time that night, I stuffed down tears.

He didn't hesitate. "Absolutely."

Temper took over. It wasn't fair. He kept secrets from me all the time. Not just Tess—I understood his need to keep her hidden—but other things. Information I had a right to, like the truth about Lena. The strange looks he'd been giving my father. But I was expected to tell him everything.

"So protecting me justifies anything else you might do. That keeping me safe matters more than anything else."

"I'm pretty sure that's what I've been saying since the day we met. Good to see you've been paying attention."

"And it works both ways?" I rinsed out the roasting dish and set it on a towel, wiped my soapy hands on my jeans.

He stopped loading the dishwasher and studied me. "What do you mean?"

I didn't answer.

"What did you do?"

I swallowed, trying to dislodge the fear choking me. "You said keeping me safe was the most important thing."

"*What did you do?*" He dragged a hand over his face. "Mo. Tell me you didn't . . ."

"They were going to kill you," I said. "He sent them there to kill you, and you wanted me to hide in another room and let them."

"They wouldn't have killed me."

"I'm not *stupid*," I said. "I know how Billy works. I had something he wanted, so I offered him a deal. A trade."

"Ekomov for me." His voice was rough, unrecognizable. A stranger's.

I pushed on, hoping I could make him understand. "He's got an apartment at Shady Acres. I make deliveries once a week or so. Billy gives me information to pass along—not every time, but enough to keep Ekomov happy. Sometimes he asks for specific stuff, so I tell Billy and he comes up with answers."

"What sort of information?"

"Different stuff. Delivery schedules. Routes. Right now, Ekomov's interested in figuring out which of Billy's guys he can turn. I think Billy's going to use it as a test. I pass along the names, wait for Ekomov to contact them. The ones who tell Billy about it are loyal. The ones who don't . . . he'll know not to trust them."

"Do you know what will happen to them? To the guys who double-cross Billy and the Forellis?"

"I don't care. It keeps you safe. Isn't that the rule? It doesn't matter what happens, as long as you're safe."

He leaned on the back of the chair, hands gripping the wood like he was going to throw it across the room. Then he released it, very deliberately, and paced the room. "You threw away your whole future. Everything you worked for. You never should have done that. Not for me. *Especially* not for me. And then you lied about it. What about New York?"

I stared into the sink. "New York was for Verity and me. She is *dead*. You are *alive*. Excuse me for wanting to keep it that way."

"What is it with you? Every goddamn time I turn around, you're risking your life for somebody else. You're like the queen of martyrs. Do you know why they're martyrs, Mo? Because they end up dead." He clenched and unclenched his fists as he walked.

"I won't. This is temporary. The police are almost ready to move on Billy and the Forellis. They just need a little more evidence, and then we won't have to worry about him anymore."

He massaged his temples, like I'd given him a migraine. "Wait. The cops? You're trying to double-cross the Outfit? Have you lost your goddamn mind?"

"It's only for a little longer. And then Billy will be gone, and we can be happy." I touched his sleeve, but he jerked away.

"You're kidding yourself," he said, the contempt in his voice like a kick to the stomach. "How the hell am I supposed to be happy about this? How are you? You're going to end up hating me. Ten years from now, you'll be stuck in the same place you are now, and you'll blame me for it."

"I *won't*. Do you blame Tess?"

He looked at me blankly. And then understanding crossed his face, followed by disbelief, and finally, anger that went so far beyond anything I'd seen from him that I stepped back, afraid of Colin for the first time in my life.

"Say something." The words came out in a whisper, but he flinched as if they'd struck him. "Colin. Please. Say something."

The sound of the door slamming echoed in my head, simultaneously final and infinite.

I couldn't move. I stood frozen in the cheery yellow kitchen as the truck started up and roared off. Even breathing seemed impossible, as if his rage had sucked all the oxygen from the room. I needed to sit down, but my legs wouldn't carry me to the table. Eventually they just folded underneath me and I thumped to the floor.

I wanted to be angry right back. I wanted to find someone to blame. A target for my anger. Someone to lash out at, to make hurt the way I was hurting. But the only target I could find was me. I'd been the one to hurt Colin. I'd gone behind his back and lied to his face. I'd taken his need to protect me and twisted it into something unrecognizable to justify my own actions.

With an effort, I stood and finished cleaning up the kitchen. I scrubbed dishes, wiped down counters, put everything away.

When I was finished, it was like the evening had never happened.

Except I was alone.

My mom appeared in the doorway. "Where did Colin go?"

"He left."

"Before dessert?" She shook her head. "And your father's not back?"

"No." I wrung the dishcloth in my hands, trying not to cry.

"I guess it's just us Fitzgerald girls again, isn't it? Like old times."

I choked out a laugh. "Guess so."

She nudged me toward my chair and began dishing out apple crisp. "Colin is a good man."

"I know." I was more certain of that than anything, a fact as irrefutable as gravity.

"Proud, I think. Stubborn. A bit like your father, maybe."

"Not helping," I muttered, poking at my dessert.

"He'll come around." I glanced up, startled, and she nodded. "It will take a while. But the two of you will sort it out. Whatever the problem is."

"How can you be sure?"

"People fail each other all the time, Mo, and they forgive each other, and start again. It's a question of knowing the other person's limitations. Knowing what's fair to expect of them. Knowing what's fair for them to expect of you." She spoke with absolute authority, knowledge gained from hard experience.

I took a bite of apple crisp, and pushed the rest away. I didn't have the stomach for it. "That's how you and Dad managed?"

"Every day," she said. "Go to bed. Things will look brighter in the morning."

I went upstairs, but I didn't go to bed. I sat at the window, watching the street for any sign that Colin might return. The cold seeped through the glass, through my sweater, sank into my bones. Lonely, Lena had said, when I admitted there was no one in my life who knew the whole truth about me. Now Colin did, and I was even lonelier than before.

I reached for my phone and texted Lena. She'd know what to do. She always did.

Can u talk?

While I waited for her reply, the magic stirred, trying to re-assure me. But this problem wasn't magical. It was all of my own doing, and I would have to be the one to repair it.

The phone chirped. *Tomorrow?*

OK.

No Lena, then. I fished Colin's file out of my desk and read it again, all the horrible details of his past, the tragedy that had befallen him and Tess. It had shaped the man he was now, guarded and hard and honorable, gentle and brave and fierce. I'd hurt him so terribly.

And I would do it all over again, to keep him safe.

CHAPTER 18

I'd never doubted Colin before. It left me feeling like I'd swallowed a cereal bowl full of worms as I waited for him at the front window the next morning. When he showed, I nearly threw up out of sheer relief.

Instead, I crossed the yard on shaking legs and climbed into the truck.

"Hey," I said, my voice almost inaudible.

He jerked his head in acknowledgement and pulled away, not waiting to see if I'd fastened my seat belt.

"Are we going to talk about this?"

"No." There was no heat in his words. No emotion. His expression was equally indifferent. In chemistry, we called it absolute zero—the temperature at which all movement ceases, even at the molecular level. Doctor Sanderson was always careful to remind us that it was a hypothetical concept only, a theory.

Now I had proof it existed. She'd be thrilled.

"So that's it? We're done?"

He didn't answer until we pulled up in front of the school. "I'll pick you up at the usual time."

"Okay." I waited for him to say something else, but he kept his eyes on the wheel and his mouth tightly closed. "Bye."

He pulled away the second I'd crossed the threshold. Doing his job, but no more.

Lena was standing by my locker, hugging herself and rocking, looking as miserable as I felt. When she saw me, she dropped her arms and took a deep breath.

"You look like hell," she said.

"Thanks. You too. You want to go somewhere and talk?"

"Yeah. Chapel?" she suggested. "No one will interrupt."

"Sure." We ducked out a side door and crossed the courtyard to the tiny stone building. Purple linens decorated the altar, and the usual flowers were replaced by stark arrangements of willow and forsythia, the buds tightly furled. A few candles were lit against the gloom. I sank into one of the last pews. Lena chose the one opposite me, braced her hands on the pew in front of her.

"When my mom was fifteen and living in Texas, she dated a guy from the next town over. She knew he was bad news, but she didn't care. When she got pregnant, he accused her of cheating. Then he beat her until she lost the baby. She stayed with him. They got married when she was seventeen. He continued to beat her. She got pregnant again. He beat her some more. She ran. When he found her, she tried to divorce him, but the court said she had to share custody. Let him have equal time with my big brother."

She paused for breath, deliberately loosened her grip on the pew, and continued. "She ran again, but this time people from a battered women's shelter helped her out. She was in Florida when she heard he'd been killed in a bar fight. She changed her name and my brother's. Went to school nights and weekends. Got a degree in social work. Met my dad. Had me. Went to law school."

She laid out the history of her life like a game of solitaire, neat and orderly and unemotional, one layer on top of another.

"I'm sorry," I said. "That's . . . awful." More than awful.

Lena brushed the words aside and took a deep breath. "Now she's a professor at Northwestern. She specializes in family law—specifically, custody cases involving battered women and children."

"So they don't have to go through what she did."

"Yes." Lena sat for a long time, hands folded in her lap, shoulders hunched. "You have to promise not to tell anyone."

"I promise."

"The man at the shelter," she said. "I don't know him. But I know what he's done."

I had a momentary vision of Raymond Gaskill's mug shot, and everything came together in my head. "He said you knew where his family was."

"I might have, at one point. But if they went missing recently, then they're probably moving around every couple of days. Emily might have been his daughter's name when he was hurting her, but I guarantee you it's something else by now. And he won't touch her again."

"He lost custody?"

She spoke precisely, no quaver in her voice despite the horror of all she'd relayed. "He was granted custody, despite overwhelming evidence he is an abuser. Because those are the families we help. The ones the system failed. We hide them. We give them new identities. We help them start over, far away, so they can have a shot at a real life."

I stared at her. Lena Santos, editor of the school paper. Honor student. Middle hitter on the volleyball team, left striker on the soccer team. "It's like witness protection for battered women."

"Right. Except it's illegal. Identity fraud. If there's a kid, we relocate them, too. But then it's kidnapping."

The secrecy. The practiced way she'd deflected attention. Colin's willingness to keep Lena's secret. Of course he would, considering his past. "The woman and the little girl at the soup kitchen?"

"She looked scared, like someone was coming after her. I gave her the number of a shelter where we have contacts." She shrugged, the gesture defeated. "They haven't shown up."

It made sense. Now that I knew what I was looking at, the

picture developed rapidly. "Jill said something once. About your family. It spooked you."

"She's always talking about how her dad is friends with the State's Attorney."

"You didn't want her to pay attention to your family." I knew the feeling well.

She made a face. "I know it sounds paranoid . . ."

I shook my head. "It sounds careful. What's your dad's take?"

"He's on board. He's a criminal attorney, actually."

"That's why you understood the transcript from my dad's court case." She'd had a better grasp of the situation than I'd realized. "Does your mom know you're telling me?"

"Yeah. I promised her you would keep quiet." She grinned, though it wasn't the full wattage of her normal smile. "Nobody keeps secrets like you."

"What about the guy at the soup kitchen? Is there going to be fallout?"

"My mom was pretty freaked out at first. She was ready to make me change schools, but she's calmed down. She was pretty happy about Colin being there."

The wormy feeling in my stomach returned.

"Your turn," she said.

"Colin knows. Everything. And now he hates me."

"He doesn't hate you."

"You didn't see him last night. Or this morning. It's like trying to talk to a glacier."

"He'll thaw out eventually."

"It's not just the deal with Billy," I said. "I did some digging, found out about his past. He'd told me to leave it alone, but . . ."

"Look, the man is overprotective, but that's his nature. And you threw him for a loop, because you switched it around—you protected him. He'll adjust, and he'll forgive you for snooping, and you'll go back to the way things were."

I picked up a hymnal and flipped through it, suddenly restless.

"Which is what you want," she added, peering closely at me.

I slid the hymnal back into its slot.

"Not a ringing affirmation, Mo."

"I want to take Billy down. Colin doesn't approve. He thinks it's dangerous."

"He's right. But you still need to do it."

"If we go back to the way things were, I won't be able to." Billy aside, there were still the Arcs to contend with. I'd be tied to them for the rest of my life, and I didn't know if Colin could stand it.

Luc had warned me I couldn't live in both worlds, and I'd ignored him. Now I had to wonder if he was right.

CHAPTER 19

I hadn't cut class since the fall, when Sister Donna had put me on probation and threatened to revoke my membership in the Honor Society. But when Lena headed back to class, I stayed behind in the chapel, soaking up the scent of beeswax and chilled stone. I lit a votive for Verity, and one for Kowalski, my hand so shaky the match nearly guttered out.

And then I sat on the pew and thought about Colin, scrambling for a way to fix things. But nothing came to mind—nothing that would break through the icy wall of anger he'd surrounded himself with. It seemed so impenetrable, I didn't even know how to begin chipping away at it.

A more sensible person would have given him time to thaw, but it was February. Thaws were a long way off. I needed to make sure that Colin and I were solid before everything else disintegrated.

He'd be at The Slice, most likely. If not there, at Morgan's. I shivered at the thought of Colin confronting Billy. Or maybe he'd be back at his place, lifting weights or finishing up a woodworking project. I knew him. I could track him down and make him listen. Eventually he'd talk to me. We'd work this out.

So I slipped out of the chapel, hurrying north to the CTA bus stop, hoping no one at the school happened to look out their window at that exact moment.

I'd gone all of fifteen yards before Luc fell into step next to me.

"Field trip?"

"Let me guess. Niobe?"

"She was a touch concerned. Anton's still runnin' around, you know. Just 'cause Darklings can't spot you doesn't mean you're safe."

"I don't really care about Anton right now."

"You should. Man's angling for you."

I stopped at the corner. Ten minutes, tops, before the bus came.

Luc frowned. "Really, Mouse? You so stubborn you won't even ask for a ride?" He held out his hand. "Where we goin'?"

I considered. "The Slice. But I need you to cloak us, okay?"

"And here I was plannin' on settin' you down in the middle of the street, maybe shoot off some fireworks while I was at it." He looked at me again. "It's that bad?"

Something in my chest ached so fiercely, I couldn't breathe. Finally, I said, "Pretty bad."

He didn't say anything else, just caught my hand and brought me Between.

I ducked my head inside the partially rebuilt restaurant. Workmen, including my dad, were swarming around, and the sound of power tools—saws, nail guns, belt sanders— was deafening.

Colin was nowhere in sight, but my dad spotted me across the room. "Aren't you supposed to be in school?" he shouted over the din.

"I'm looking for Colin."

He shook his head, gesturing for me to follow him outside. The noise dropped off somewhat, and he said, "You don't want to talk to him right now."

"Where did he go? Morgan's?"

"No. He was here this morning. We talked for a few minutes. Then he left. He didn't say where he was going, but it wasn't Morgan's." He shook his head. "Go back to school. If

Donnelly wants to talk to you, he will. You force it, and he'll only get angrier."

"You're giving me relationship advice? Really?" But he wasn't the one who'd told Colin, I reminded myself. He'd had the chance, every day, to warn him or enlist his help. To break us up. Instead, he'd let me handle it my own way, even though my own way had clearly sucked.

"Isn't that what fathers are supposed to do?" he asked. I turned to leave, and he caught my arm. "I don't like you and Donnelly together. But he cares about you. He'll keep you safe, if I can't. So don't screw this up by pushing too hard. That's what got you in this mess to begin with."

I pulled away and circled around to the back of the building, where Luc was waiting. *He'll keep you safe, if I can't.* My steps slowed, the packed snow crunching underfoot. Is that what he thought he was doing? Keeping us safe by going back to the Outfit?

"No luck?" Luc asked.

"Let's try his place."

Colin wasn't there, either. I pounded on the door until my knuckles were red, but there was no answer. The truck was gone, too. He wouldn't have left town, I told myself. The one thing he would never do was leave, no matter how angry he was. He wouldn't abandon Tess.

"The nursing home," I said. "He's with his sister."

"Mouse, I'm happy to take you anywhere you want to go. But maybe you should listen to your daddy this time. Wait a bit before you go barging in there."

"You were eavesdropping?"

"I have excellent hearing."

"You have *magic* hearing."

"Six of one," he said offhandedly. "Point is, your daddy was right. And I am not actually here on a social visit."

"You never are. What now?"

"The Succession starts tonight. You ready?"

"I've been working with Niobe," I said stiffly.

His mouth crooked upward. "I heard. Would've liked to see you knock Constance on her ass."

"You really don't like her, do you? Why? I figured you'd have more sympathy than anyone, considering . . ."

"Considering Theo? Sure. But sympathy's one thing. Spoiling her's another. You risked your life to help that girl, and all she does is slap at you. You might feel guilty enough to put up with it, but I don't need to."

"She's grieving."

"She's spoiled," he said firmly. "And she's trouble."

My teeth were chattering with cold. "Can you please take me to the nursing home?"

"Anywhere in the world," he grumbled. "My place, a tropical island, Paris. And you want to go to an old folks' home."

But he took me anyway.

With Luc concealing us, it was easy to slip down the hallways and find Tess's room. The facility was bright and spacious, with fresh flowers on hall tables and watercolors on the walls.

"You don't need to come in," I said. "I don't think Colin would appreciate more company."

"Don't imagine he would." He tapped my wrist and set off toward a waiting area. "Call if you need me."

I squared my shoulders and knocked, then pushed the door open, the magic shifting nervously within me.

"We're not . . . oh." At the sight of me, Colin's face shifted from politely neutral to coldly dismissive. "What do you want?"

Forgiveness. A chance to explain. A way forward. But it all seemed insignificant compared to the sight before me—Colin in a floral armchair, sitting opposite a wisp of a girl in a wheelchair. The same honey-colored hair and smoky eyes as Colin, but instead of his strong, solid features, she seemed insubstantial, her pointed chin and snub nose delicately shaped. She wore a long-sleeve pink T-shirt and white yoga pants, her feet tucked into fluffy slippers that looked brand-new. She watched me from the corner of her eye.

"I wanted to make sure you're okay." He didn't seem inclined to throw me bodily from the room, so I chanced another step forward.

"I'm fine. So you can leave now."

I ignored him, my attention riveted on the girl in front of me. "Hi, Tess."

She didn't respond, and I took another step. "I'm Mo. It's nice to meet you."

"She knows who you are."

"You told her about me?" I wondered if that was good or bad.

For a moment, his look was exasperated instead of angry. "Yes. Just go, okay?"

"I will. I just wanted to—"

"To what? Gawk? Pry a little more?" His voice was like a lash, and Tess's fingers scrabbled in her lap. "You're upsetting her."

"I'm not the one yelling," I said.

He turned his back on me, murmured to Tess as her eyes darted around the room. I studied the place. Pink walls, a neatly made hospital bed, a pale pink blanket folded at the foot. Pink roses in a silver vase on the table, and white curtains pulled back to display the courtyard beneath. A bird feeder hung within view, half-full of seeds.

"Well?" he asked, not looking at me.

"It's nice. Very . . . pink."

"She loved pink. Pink and Barbies and birds."

Loved. Because the girl in the wheelchair hadn't spoken since she was six, according to the file I'd read last fall. She'd been catatonic since the attack, barely responding to anyone, even Colin. She'd been trapped inside herself for ten years.

Tess's eyes cut from me to the window, and I followed her gaze. Lining the sill were a series of small wooden figurines. Tiny birds in flight—each a different species, painstakingly carved. Some were painted, some stained or varnished. A few were left completely natural.

"You made those for her."

"She used to chase the birds. She'd go outside with bread-crumbs and try to catch them, so they'd teach her how to fly." He glanced over. "Go home, Mo."

Tess's fingers twitched toward the windowsill. Gently, Colin picked up the figure of a hummingbird, set it in her palm, and wrapped her fingers around it. She crooned to it, nonsense words, and something in me stirred at the sound.

"I didn't do it to hurt you," I said.

"Never thought you did. I'm pretty sure you weren't thinking of me at all."

"That's unfair."

"Unfair? You're going to stand in front of my sister and talk about unfair?"

"No. I'm sorry, Colin. For what I did, and for what happened to you and your family. I'm sorry I didn't listen to you, that I betrayed your trust. I was wrong, and I am sorry." I stared at the lamp until the urge to cry passed. "But I won't apologize for making the deal with Billy, and I won't go back on it. Just . . . tell me how to fix this."

"Not everything is fixable," he said, and his voice was weary, eyes shadowed. "You should leave now."

I pressed my hands against my stomach, steadying myself. "Right. Going. It was nice to meet you, Tess."

She didn't respond, her gaze fixed on the hummingbird, her fingers curved loosely around it like a cage.

"It's really beautiful. He's amazing, your brother."

And then I left, because there was nothing else to say.

CHAPTER 20

"You know," Luc said as we walked through the French Quarter, "there is a certain type of man who would use this situation to his advantage."

I laughed to keep myself from crying. "And you are not that type?"

"I am, actually. But I figured I'd point it out to you. Give you fair warning."

"How very noble of you."

"You're sad, and that's a pity. Never like seein' you hurt. But I made my intentions clear, and nothing's changed."

"Except me." Magic inside me like a second heart, heavy with sorrow and sympathy. The future a labyrinth instead of a straight, sure path. And all the rules I'd ever set for myself in shards at my feet. I'd justified my behavior with the same logic as everyone in my family.

"See, that's where we disagree. You're still you. Same girl that went after Darklings in an alley without knowing what they were. Same girl who bit me when I tried to make her hush. It's just that what you're made of used to be stuffed down so deep, you didn't even recognize it."

"You're wrong." And it was a relief, because I'd made so, so many mistakes. I'd changed. The me I used to be would never have been capable of hurting people like this. Parts of me were hardened and cold. Scarred by everything that had happened. But it was a lot easier to believe those parts had been formed by terrible, necessary choices than to think I'd been capable of it all along.

"Did you ever wonder why the magic chose you?" He paused as a horse-drawn carriage full of tourists clopped past, hooves ringing against the pavement. "I do. All the time. The Vessel was dying, but Vee wasn't bound to the source. It could have survived. Been free. The Torrent was never going to destroy the magic, just Arcs. Why did it choose you?"

"It didn't *choose* me. I just happened to be there. Coincidence."

"No such thing," he replied. "The way I figure it, something inside you told the magic you could do this. You were capable. You were the one it was meant for."

"Luc." I tried to draw away, but he caught me by the wrist, held me fast.

"Meant." His voice was as rough as a match struck to flame. "You were meant for this. More than what you thought, or knew, or dreamed about, maybe, but meant all the same. Nothing's changed except that now you know. And you're too honest, deep down, to tell yourself otherwise."

"I lie all the time."

"Not here." He placed his hand over my heart, gentle and weighty, and I was sure he could feel its panicked beats. "And right about now, Mouse, is when I start pressing my case."

"You don't know what's meant and what's not. Not all of it, anyway. Your mom said it was only the destination. Maybe she meant that we were supposed to help the Arcs or save the magic, but not necessarily be together. You could find someone else you wanted to be with. An Arc. Someone who understood . . ." A memory unfolded, a wisp of irritation drifting over my nape as it did. "Someone like Niobe. You two work well together. You obviously have some history. She even told me she has a fondness for you."

Luc seemed to swallow his own tongue. "Niobe. And me. Oh, she'll love that. She'll laugh about that for days."

"Glad you find it so funny. I'm not saying it has to be Niobe. Choose someone you want."

"I want you."

"That's hormones," I said. "Hormones and this stupid prophecy. Not love. I want to be with someone who loves me."

Colin had loved me. And I'd ruined it. But even if we were done, I wasn't going to settle for less.

"You want proof. You want someone to write it all down like a science experiment, an equation, because it's safer that way. Because you know what to expect. And maybe then you won't get hurt."

He tipped my face up to his. "Fit this into your equation, Mouse. I choose you. Fate, entropy, God, science, prophecy, or free will. I don't care about any of it. *I choose you.* I will choose you again tomorrow, and the day after that, and the day after that, all of them, as many days as there are stars."

I broke away, moved out of his reach. "Not today. Don't say those things today, Luc."

"Right. Because if I convince you today, it's an excuse later. You'll tell me it wasn't real, that you were vulnerable, that it was a mistake. So, you need space? Time? You got it."

"Good," I said, unsteady, traitorous heart pounding in my ears.

Frustration darkened his eyes. "I won't kiss you again, Mouse. But when you kiss me, you damn well better mean it. No more excuses. No more running. You kiss me, and it's for keeps."

Annoyance sparked within me. Fear, too, although what I was afraid of seemed too complicated to name. "You're so sure I'll change my mind."

"No. Don't think you need to change your mind at all. You just need to know it better." He took my hand. "Enough fighting. Let's get the Succession under way."

CHAPTER 21

Recognition jolted through me as we appeared outside the Water Arcs' House—a sprawling, white-columned mansion hidden behind topiaries. I'd seen it before in a picture Verity had taken while she was living here. I had a quick moment of vertigo. She'd known this house, spent time training here. Made friends, perhaps. I wondered if there was any trace of her left inside.

It's so strange, the way grief alters you. At first it's deafening, discordant, obscuring everything else. Nothing makes sense, because nothing can get through. And then the noise shifts to an accompaniment, off-key but not overwhelming. And then it blends into the background, altering the tenor of your life but not the central melody. And then something happens, and you're back to the beginning, the cacophony of loss blotting out the world again.

Suddenly, desperately, I missed Verity so much my lungs were crushed by it, and I grabbed the fence for support. I needed her here with me. Not because she'd tell me what to do—although she would, because she always did—but because she'd stick by me. She'd understand, and right now, she might have been the only person on earth who would. Everyone else's perspective was skewed, but Verity would have seen it from my point of view. And she would have stood by me as I figured it out.

Instead, she was gone. I was alone, no matter that Luc's

hand rested on the small of my back, our connection thin but bright. This house was the last place she'd lived. And if it didn't carry Verity's imprint, because her time here had been a single summer, it certainly carried Evangeline's—everything about it had a refined opulence. The lawn lush and perfectly cut, the seashells in the walkways raked smooth. A reflecting pond at one end of the lawn, a fountain at another. Gardenia blossoms, creamy white and rich with scent, covered the shrubs lining the fence.

The pressure of Luc's hand at my back increased, just the faintest touch. "Go ahead," he told me. "Open the gate."

"Isn't it locked?"

"It's spelled. But you're a member of the House, so it'll let you in. Since we're bound, I'm your plus one."

"What about the Quartoren?"

"Special invitation only, because it's the Succession. Hold on a minute."

Swiftly, he opened up a pocket of Between and pulled out the cloth-wrapped dagger, offering it to me handle first.

"I need a weapon?"

"Doubtful. But I won't be able to cast anything once we're inside, and I don't much enjoy the notion of not having a weapon at hand."

"You carry it, then."

"Walk into another House armed? I wouldn't be walking out under my own power. You hold on to it, I'll hold on to you, and everything will go smooth as silk."

In my experience, those words presaged disaster. Every time. Still, I took the blade from him, loosening the cloth enough to inspect the symbols inscribed along the silver handle. It wasn't a large weapon, but it was heavy. I'd seen how sharp it was when I used it on Anton.

Very carefully, I rewrapped the blade and held it away from my body. "What now?"

"Open the gate."

I stretched out my hand, snatched it back, tried again. At the faintest pressure of my fingers against the iron, the magic seemed to thrill, unfurling with a sort of exuberance, and the gate flew open, so hard that it rebounded off the fence and swung back at us.

Luc stopped it with a well-placed foot. "Wouldn't hurt to dial it down a bit."

I scowled at him and stepped through. A few feet away, a burbling stream circled the house and grounds, the water crystalline even in the moonlight. "They have a moat," I said.

He crouched and held a hand over the water. Instantly, it surged up, blue energy swirling at the very edge, and he winced, shaking his fingers as if they stung. "Well, isn't that fine," he said caustically.

"You don't have a moat." I hid a smile.

"Don't need a moat. Too show-offy."

"Totally. You never show off. There's got to be a way around it, though." I crouched down, expecting the same reaction he'd gotten. But my hand slipped easily into the cool water, and I let it rush through my fingers, the magic feeling perfectly at ease. "It feels nice."

He knelt next to me and stuck his hand out—again, the water roiled up. He laced his hand with mine, and it calmed.

"It only lets me touch it if I'm touching you," he said. "Take off your shoes."

"Seriously?"

"It's too wide to jump over, so we can take off our shoes and wade through, or you can ruin a perfectly nice-lookin' pair of boots." He tugged off his own shoes—expensive-looking black leather—and tucked them under one arm, then crooked an elbow at me. "Best not to show up late. Doesn't exactly engender goodwill, you know?"

I pulled off my boots, tucked the dagger inside, and laid a hand on his arm. These days, I needed all the goodwill I could get.

The water was bracingly cold, and the soles of my feet tingled as the magic reacted to the line winding its way through the stream. Three steps later, we were on the other side, putting our shoes back on.

"You want this back now?" I tried to hand him the cloth-wrapped dagger, but he held up his hands in refusal.

"Told you, I can't carry a weapon here. Just . . . put it inside your boot."

Sure. That would work, right up until the moment I sliced my calf wide open.

But I did it, anyway, feeling the blunted outline of the knife against my leg. Slowly, we made our way across the lawn, past elaborate fountains and a koi pond, up the graceful sweep of the front porch. At Luc's nod, I rapped on the door, the crystalline door knocker heavy in my hand.

The door swung open. Inside, the Quartoren stood stiffly, each wearing a ceremonial cloak. Only Dominic looked moderately at ease, but even he seemed ever-so-slightly diminished. Still powerful, but in a crafty way, lean and hungry instead of bold and assured.

Across from them stood three other Arcs, all wearing the pale blue of the Marais, the Water Arcs. They glided forward, and the leader—an Asian woman, her hair a straight midnight fall with one cobalt streak, spoke.

"You are the Vessel and her companion."

"I am," I said. Every time someone addressed me that way, it was a little easier to answer yes. The title rested just a little more comfortably. I wasn't sure what that meant—was I growing into the role, or giving up myself? "I'm Maura Fitzgerald."

"I am Sabine Levaret. This is Iris." She indicated another woman standing nearby. "And Joshua." A portly older man nodded his head. All three wore the same sharp, inquisitive expression I'd grown accustomed to seeing on Pascal. "We are the mages of the Marais, and we welcome you."

Mages were the scholars and scientists of the Arcs. It made sense that they would be the ones presiding over a ceremony to choose the next leader—they had tradition and knowledge on their side, and judging from the hum of energy that came from all three, considerable power, too.

"Thank you," I murmured, feeling conspicuous and childish in my jeans and cardigan. We'd stopped at home so I could ditch my uniform, but now I wished I'd chosen something a little nicer.

"Lucien." Sabine greeted Luc with a bland smile, a subtle reminder that his status here was insignificant. Then she turned back to me. "The rest of our members are gathered outside. Are you ready?"

I glanced at Dominic, who gave the merest hint of a nod. "I think so. I don't have a cloak anymore. Is that a problem?"

"We have one for you."

Iris stepped forward, holding out a mass of pale blue silk. My old one had been white, and I gave Sabine a questioning look.

She smiled gently. "Here, today, you are a Marais."

I shook it out, the material weighty even before I put it on. As I slipped it over my shoulders, Luc stepped forward to help me adjust it.

"The clasp," I said, fumbling with the golden circles.

Luc lifted a hand, a gesture of helplessness. "No magic here," he reminded me.

Sabine stepped forward. "Allow me."

At her touch, the two halves of the circles melted together. With one final tug, I managed to straighten the robe.

"How do I look?" I asked Luc.

"Like you're about to change the world," he said.

"No robe for you?"

"I'm just a bystander. No need to get dressed up."

Sabine cleared her throat and extended an arm toward the hallway. "Shall we begin?"

As we walked, she said, "You must stand with us today, not the Quartoren."

"But we'll enter together," Orla said firmly. "We're trying to send a message, after all."

Luc murmured, "Stay to the side, Mouse. As close to me as you can."

Sabine continued as if she couldn't care less about the Quartoren's message. Probably she didn't. I kind of liked that about her. "We will open the ceremony with the traditional invocation, call forward those who wish to be tested, and pronounce them candidates before their people. Your part is fairly small—the standard responses to the spells—but I would imagine people will be paying attention. I was told you've been practicing the necessary responses?"

I vowed to myself that if I made it through today's ceremony without offending most of the people in the room, I'd be much nicer to Niobe.

"I can manage."

Behind me, Luc made a sound between a snort and a cough.

The mages led us through sitting rooms, a library, and a massive dining room before stopping inside an immense ballroom. The far wall was made entirely of French doors, and through the wavery glass, hundreds of tiny lights glowed, like miniature moons.

In a voice so soft the Quartoren couldn't overhear, Sabine said, "The Marais' future rests in the events that begin tonight. Your future resides here as well, to some degree. We do not profess to fully understand your connection to the source of all magic, but we are aware of the power it grants you. Please make sure to use it wisely tonight, for all our sakes."

I didn't bother to explain that I couldn't use it at all. "I'll do my best."

She looked dubious, but it was all I could promise. The mages took their places at the central three doors. Luc gave my hand a quick, encouraging squeeze and then followed the Quartoren to another door in the far corner of the room. They slipped outside, leaving me alone with the three Water Arcs.

At some unseen signal, the doors opened, and the mages

stepped through in unison. I followed Sabine through the middle door.

The sight outside was almost enough to send me running back through the building. The entire lawn was crammed with Arcs, a sea of blue silk and suspicion. I shrank back, but Sabine turned and caught my eye. Iris and Joshua flanked me, and there was no escape. So I lifted my chin and walked down the veranda steps, to the edge of the crowd, in clear view of Luc.

The mages stopped behind a marble-topped table. In the center rested a glass pen, an inkpot, and a parchment scroll.

I couldn't read what it said, but I didn't need to. Thanks to Niobe's lessons, I already knew it decreed that the names affixed to the sheet were candidates for Matriarch or Patriarch. If selected, they swore to serve the House before all others and be a steward of the magic until their death.

The Houses were hereditary, Niobe had explained—Luc's had been the House of DeFoudre since the beginning of time, one long, unbroken strand of successions. But if prophecy or death resulted in a new family being elevated, the name of the House changed. After this ceremony, the House of Marais would be no longer. The person who was elevated didn't change just their own life, but the life of their descendents.

"Welcome," Sabine called to the crowd. She stretched out her arms, palms up, and began the chant that opened the ceremony. The Arcs responded, and I followed along, the words strange and unwieldy despite all my practice.

I glanced at Luc, who mouthed the words, and I tried to mimic him. But most of the Arcs were concentrating on me, not the ceremony, and the attention made me feel clammy, nearly sick. The only way to cope was to close my eyes, blocking out everyone. I envisioned the words of the invocation written on the blackboards at school, shimmering faintly with power, like stars at twilight. My tongue loosened as I grew more comfortable, and the magic responded by spreading through my body with a soothing warmth.

According to Niobe, these words were a warning about the solemnity of the occasion, the seriousness of the task. It struck me that so little in the Arcs' world was changeable—Bindings, Covenants, and now Successions—everything they did was permanent and unyielding. Was it because they possessed so much power they couldn't act lightly? Or because they believed their actions were dictated by fate and therefore infallible?

As I continued chanting, the magic gathering strength within me, someone in the crowd gasped. Murmurs quickly built and crested, like waves at high tide. I broke off mid-sentence and opened my eyes to see what the problem was—and saw my own skin, luminous in the darkness, the brightest light centered painlessly in my palms.

Luc started forward, but Dominic held him back, a silent argument passing between them.

Sabine broke off, eyebrows raised in a wordless question—was it safe to continue?

The warmth of the magic was already receding, the glow cupped in my hands fading. There didn't seem to be anything wrong—the magic felt contented and easy, leaving me loose limbed. Pascal looked fascinated, not worried. I nodded, and she resumed chanting.

This time I kept my eyes open, trusting in myself and the magic to speak correctly. As I did, the glow resumed, my entire body shining, the light in my cupped hands forming a sphere.

No one spoke. No one even breathed, as if I were a particularly unreliable candle they might extinguish in the slightest wind. I fell silent as the invocation ended, and the shimmer gradually diminished—not entirely, but enough so that I no longer resembled something phosphorescent. I clasped my hands together and tried to look harmless.

It was time for the candidates to come forward and declare themselves, but the crowd was frozen in place. I wondered if they were afraid of me. I looked at Luc for a cue, but he shrugged, brow furrowed in concern.

Traditionally, Niobe told me, the mages would declare first. After a long silence, Sabine stepped forward, signed her name to the parchment, and looked out over the crowd.

"Sabine Levaret," she called, making it sound like a challenge. Her voice carried to the edge of the crowd and rolled back in again. Her gesture seemed to release the tension of the crowd, because the other mages followed in turn, signing their name, stating it to the crowd, and stepping aside.

Slowly, Arcs began to make their way forward and declare. The scroll of parchment continued to unroll, seemingly endless. There was no age limit—some of the Arcs who approached looked my age and some were easily as old as Orla, moving stiffly up the stairs. And judging from the accents I heard, they had come from all over the world.

Finally, the line of candidates slowed to a trickle, then stopped. The mages waited for a long moment, and raised their hands in unison, preparing to suspend the ceremony.

Thunder rolled across the sky. Instinctively, I looked up, expecting another late-afternoon shower.

Instead, Anton strolled forward, cloak slung back over his shoulders, as if he couldn't be bothered to wear it properly. The crowd parted before him like a biblical sea. Hands stuffed in his pockets, nodding genially at people, he seemed unconcerned at the alarm his presence set off.

Luc was at my side instantly, and Anton stopped to study us. "Very sweet," he said. "Useless, of course."

"Touch her and you're a dead man," said Luc.

"How's that?" Anton said. "You're a guest of the House. You have no powers here. You're as helpless as she is."

Inside me, the magic began to panic, and I sought some way to calm it. The cloth-wrapped dagger pressed against my leg, tantalizingly close. "I'm not helpless."

"Nor are we," said Dominic, and he stormed toward us. "You're a criminal. You've broken our laws, and we are within our rights to deal with you as we see fit."

"Not here," said Sabine. Her voice was mild, but her eyes

snapped. "Within the boundaries of this House, our people are sovereign. You may not take arms against him."

Anton smiled. "Always nice to hear the voice of reason."

I bent and slid the dagger from my boot, shaking the cloth away from the blade under the cover of my robe. The magic fear increased as my pulse hammered in my throat.

"This isn't reason," Sabine said, mouth thinning with dislike. "This is tradition."

"A rose by any other name," said Anton. "Since we've established that you can't do anything, I'll be taking that pen now."

I tightened my grip on the dagger. "Why would you want to be on the Quartoren? You want to destroy them."

"And wouldn't it be more fun to see them taken apart from the inside?" he whispered to me. *Anton likes to do his damage up close,* Niobe had said. It wasn't just that he wanted to destroy the Arcs. He wanted to watch them suffer as he did so.

Lightly, he jogged up the steps, then signed his name with a flourish.

"Anton Renard," he called, dropping the pen onto the table with a clatter and strolling back toward me.

I stood fast. "They won't choose you. They know what you are, and they won't choose you."

He leaned in, and it took everything I had not to shrink away. Instead, I drew out the dagger, my hand steady, and pointed it at his throat.

With a smile for the crowd, he stepped in even closer, until the tip was pressing into his skin, about to draw blood.

I wanted to bury the blade deep inside him, but it was too much—too deliberate and too public and too visceral. I couldn't. And Anton had known it all along.

"What I am is the most powerful Arc here. Who else would they choose?" He started to walk away, turning his back on me to underscore how weak and harmless I was.

As the crowd gaped, he traced a door in the air, blue

flames that danced mockingly. Terror turned to fury, and I whirled toward the Quartoren. "Does he really have a shot?"

They exchanged worried looks, not answering me. Luc's hand tightened on mine.

"Anton!"

He glanced back over his shoulder carelessly, as if whatever I had to say wasn't worth his attention. But my mom had taught me, early on, that actions spoke louder than words.

I raced up the steps and snatched the pen from the table, scrawling my name on the paper.

"Maura Fitzgerald," I said, whirling to face the crowd, still holding the dagger.

He scoffed, but there were fissures in the mask of his disdain, rage seeping through. "You're joking."

"I'm a member of this House," I said. "The magic recognized me. And that means I can declare myself for the Quartoren."

Dominic crossed his arms with a satisfied air, but Anton snorted. "You're a child. And you're Flat."

"No," I said, absolute, unshakable conviction ringing in my voice. "I'm the Vessel."

CHAPTER 22

Sometimes, inspiration strikes and the result is genius. Sometimes, the result is failure. And sometimes, the result is a pain in the ass.

In one of the Water Arcs' sitting rooms, Orla was shouting, thumping her cane for emphasis and fluttering her hands in outrage while Dominic tried to soothe her. Meanwhile, Pascal and the mages were deep in discussion, no doubt trying to understand why I'd lit up like a glowworm during the ceremony. Luc sat next to me on the old-fashioned divan, toying with the ends of my hair, deliberately brushing against me every time he reached for the glass of sweet tea on the table in front of us, stretching a casual arm around my shoulders when he settled back. He looked smug. Surprised, but pleasantly so. And at the same time, he looked very, very irritated every time one of the Water Arcs approached—whether they were offering a fresh glass of tea or a greeting, he drummed his fingers and stared, a burning, impatient gaze that had them hurrying away again. As soon as they did, he'd turn back to me, amused.

"Never was one to say I told you so . . ." he began.

"Then don't."

"But I did."

I sat forward, ankles crossed, feeling the strain of the evening in every muscle of my back. "What, exactly, did you tell me? Because I don't remember this ever coming up in conversation."

"You're meant for this. For big things. First time I've seen you take part in your destiny without fighting it. Suits you."

I batted his hand away. My only thought had been to show Anton—and myself—that I wasn't scared. It wasn't until I'd signed my name and felt the lines of water magic rising up to acknowledge me that I realized the enormity of what I'd done. "What you saw was poor impulse control."

"Never had a quarrel with your impulses," he said. "They usually line up pretty nicely with mine. Either way, you gotta be feelin' pretty good now. Putting Anton on notice. Getting hold of the magic."

"That was a fluke. I still can't use it." I stared at my palms. Other than the scar the Darklings had given me, they looked normal. Boring. Any residual magical glow had vanished. And I had no idea how to get through the next stage of the ceremony.

"Practice," he said, with a confidence I didn't share. "We'll work at it. You'll be able to use it soon."

"Not soon enough." But inside me, I shrank from the idea of using magic, even to stop the Seraphim. It would mean I was an Arc, not a Flat. Another irrevocable step into their world, and away from mine.

My world. The one I'd vanished from in a fit of hurt and self-pity. I had no idea if Colin would cover for me, much less stay on as my bodyguard. Chicago had nearly three million people. He could work for Billy and avoid me forever. And it would be forever, because I wouldn't break my promise and endanger him and Tess. Even if he never spoke to me again, I couldn't leave Chicago.

I was about to tell Luc I needed to return home when Pascal and Sabine approached. Dominic spotted the movement and joined us, Orla behind him, wearing her irritation like a second cloak.

"Was it always your intention to declare?" Sabine asked

without preamble. She looked troubled, no doubt at the no-tion that a Flat was in the running to lead her people.

"No! It was an impulse. I don't even know why I did it."

"Perhaps the magic encouraged you," Pascal said, study-ing me keenly.

Luc's fingers tightened on my shoulder. A warning, as if I needed one.

"The magic didn't make me do anything. I was rattled, okay? The whole glow-in-the-dark routine threw me. And Anton showing up didn't exactly calm me down. He wants me dead, and none of you could help."

"Naturally, your solution was to further antagonize him," Orla said. "Do you know what's going to happen as word gets out? Vessel or not, people won't care for the notion of a Flat on the Quartoren."

"They won't pick me." I was almost certain.

"You put on quite a display," said Dominic. "If you can wield that much power, you might be surprised what people will overlook."

"I can't wield anything," I said, uncomfortably aware of the dagger tucked back in my boot again. "Once they realize that, they'll choose someone else."

I just had to make sure the someone wasn't Anton.

"She's okay, right?" Luc asked Pascal. "It's not like be-fore."

Before, when the magic had nearly killed me. I knew it was no longer a danger, but I let Pascal answer, wary of tipping my hand.

"We believe that what happened today was an outward manifestation of your bond with the source. With so many people casting a spell simultaneously, the magic's reaction was visible in you."

"But I didn't do any magic. I just said the words."

"True. The actual castings came from the rest of us. But the magic reacted to your words nevertheless." He seemed to stop himself from saying anything else, but I understood. I'd only channeled everyone else's spell, not cast one of my own.

Dominic slapped his hands together. "What's done is done. Best thing now is to move forward with the ceremony."

"Best for us to go," Luc said quickly, and I knew he was anxious to get me out before anyone guessed the truth.

"Maura," Pascal said, blocking my way. "Are you sure there's nothing else you can tell us about the magic? It could make a difference at the second ceremony. It could be the key to defeating Anton."

That was something I hadn't considered. If I could use the magic, somehow tell it what to do, it would solve every-thing—the Seraphim, the Succession, my place with the Arcs. Maybe communicating with the source was too big a riddle to solve on my own. Maybe I needed help.

Luc sensed my indecision and gripped my hand so hard I felt the bones shift. A game changer, he'd said. A weapon. His warning was more true than ever.

"I really can't," I said.

CHAPTER 23

A s soon as we crossed the gate, leaving the House behind, Luc took me Between to his apartment.

"I need to go home," I said.

"Parents might have something to say about your coat," he said, catching hold of the embroidered edge of my cloak and pulling me in.

I struggled a bit, but he simply wrapped his arms around me. "Hush. I'm not trying anything. You worried me, that's all. Trust me, Mouse. You'll know the difference."

He rested his cheek atop my head, and the stiffness leached from my body. "Pascal knows something's going on," I said.

"Of course he does. Man knows the magic better than anyone except you, I'm guessing."

"I only know that it's alive, Luc. I don't know what to do with it." It was a relief to say the words out loud, one less secret between us, bridging the distance between our worlds.

"We'll work on it together. But in the meantime, you can't tell the Quartoren. If they think you can control the magic, they'll want to use you as a weapon. Don't trust them, okay? Not a one of them."

"What about you?"

He tipped my face up to his—close enough to kiss, but he'd promised not to—and his eyes were somber, moss green. "If you have to ask, it doesn't matter what I say."

Which was either a really clever evasion or his way of letting me set the tone between us. I did trust him. Mostly. About the magic, anyway.

His hands framed my face, traced down my neck, and alarm must have shown in my face, because he smiled, lazy and dangerous. Before I could say anything, he touched the clasp at my throat and it split apart. The cloak tumbled off my shoulders and pooled at my feet.

"What are you doing?"

He tilted his head toward the couch, where my coat and scarf were draped over the corner.

"Right," I said, feeling foolish. Time to go. I slipped my coat on and Luc reached past me for the scarf, draping it around my neck, his fingers deft and sure, slowing as he pulled the fringed ends through the loop. "What's wrong?"

"Thinkin' about how much more enjoyable this process is in reverse." His eyes brightened with mischief, and I smacked his shoulder.

"Not endearing," I said. But in a way, it was. Obvious and clumsy, an attempt to cheer me up—to distract me from the oncoming storm. It didn't work, but I appreciated the thought. "There's going to be hell to pay when I get home."

"You could stay," he offered. This time, there was no teasing note in his voice. Just that melting drawl like bittersweet chocolate, and my heart stuttered. He took my hand in his, rubbed a thumb over my scar. "Maybe it's time to walk away, Mouse."

I pulled my hand away, ignored the minor twang of unhappiness from the magic. "Not yet."

Which was not the same as "no." But he was kind enough not to mention it.

CHAPTER 24

When I arrived home, my father was waiting on the couch, the day's *Trib* spread out in front of him. "It's past curfew," he said. "Your mother was worried."

I checked my watch and winced. "Sorry. I meant to call, but I thought you'd already be in bed."

He snorted. "Have a seat."

"I'm kind of tired," I said. More than kind of, actually. I was exhausted, desperate for the refuge of my bed. "Can we do this tomorrow?"

He pointed to the wing chair.

"Fine." I thumped down, glanced down at the paper on the table. He'd left it open to Nick Petros' column, and my stomach lurched.

"Where were you tonight?" he asked, settling back on the couch and inspecting me carefully.

"Out with a friend."

"Not Donnelly."

"Colin is not feeling very friendly toward me right now."

"You tracked him down, huh? I told you that was a bad idea." He rubbed his forehead. "This friend. Is he connected?"

"I didn't say it was a he."

My dad put his feet up on the coffee table—a sacrilege he could only get away with while my mother slept. "I saw him at the restaurant. Who does he work for?"

So much for keeping Luc secret. But it was proof my uncle hadn't told him about the magic. I wondered briefly about Billy's next move, how he'd try to convince me. My dad made an impatient noise, and I tuned back in. "Nobody. He's not from around here."

"You're sure? People aren't always what they tell you."

"I'm aware of that. He's not connected."

"That's something, anyway." He laced his hands behind his neck. "You know, when I came home, I figured everything would pick up where it had left off. That I could have my old life back."

"Oh, is that what you've been doing? Getting your old life back? I figured it was just garden-variety crime. I didn't realize it was a sentimental thing."

"That's work," he said. "I wanted my family again."

"Have you considered that the two are mutually exclusive?"

"Have you considered that you don't know everything?" he shot back. Then he softened. "Your mother and I . . . it's like I'd never left. Nothing's changed. But you . . . you're different."

"I was five. It was kind of inevitable."

"Anger is one thing, Mo. This is bigger. Your mother sees it, and she worries. Your uncle sees it, and he thinks it's an opportunity. But I see someone who's older than she should be. Harder than she should be. I'm trying to give you something better now."

I lifted a shoulder. The events of the last six months had transformed me, like a strange and wrenching alchemy. Inexplicable and irreversible. And not, in the end, my father's fault. No one's fault but my own.

"I didn't ask you to," I said, but there was no anger in the words this time.

"No. Just like Donnelly didn't ask you to intercede for him with Billy, but you did it anyway. Sometimes you have to do something terrible to prevent something worse. Sometimes you have to let terrible things happen." He slapped his knees and pushed himself off the couch. "Have a little faith in your old man, for once."

"You haven't given me any reason to."

"Twelve years of nuns, and you haven't figured this out yet? That's why it's faith, honey." He headed up the staircase, his footsteps heavy, more tired than he'd let on. "Don't stay up too late."

I'd thought that nothing could be worse than Friday's ride to school—that by Monday morning, Colin would have thawed slightly. He'd had all weekend to think about what I'd done, and he would realize my intentions were good. He'd forgive me—or start to forgive me—and we'd find a way forward, even if the path was rocky.

I was, as usual, wrong.

He didn't look at me. He didn't even seem angry, just . . . impenetrable. I could beat my fists against the wall he'd put up, but there wasn't any point in it. I'd only end up bruised.

I folded my hands in my lap and waited. The longer the silence went on, the harder it was to break. Soon it would be impossible. I wanted to weep, but didn't. If we were going to get through this, it couldn't be a result of Colin feeling sorry for me. We had to be equals. So I matched his silence, setting my teeth against the urge to plead my case.

When we pulled up to school, I reached for the door. "See you later."

"I never lied," he said.

My fingers tightened on the strap of my bag. "What?"

He stared straight ahead. "I never lied to you. Not once."

"I know." I swallowed. "You just refused to tell me the truth."

Without waiting for his response, I slung my bag over my shoulder and headed into school.

The hallways were the same chaotic sea of people as always, and it was old habit to let myself get swept into it, relying on the drama of a thousand other people to hide my own. I kept my head down, threw my stuff in my locker, and made my way to first period. I could anesthetize myself with boredom here. Even if it was only for the day, it would be a relief not to hurt, or to want, or to feel responsible.

Except when I walked in, Niobe was talking to the teacher, managing to look both bored and imperious. They broke off as I approached my desk.

"What did you do this time?" Lena murmured.

"I've kind of lost track," I replied.

With a tilt of her head, Niobe indicated I should come with her. I gathered my books and followed her out.

"First of all," she said, "if you're going to cut school, do me the courtesy of telling me so I can devise an explanation. Every time you disappear, Sister Donna feels compelled to visit me and discuss your progress. It's irritating."

"Sorry to be such an inconvenience," I said, not meaning a word of it. Judging from the arch look she gave me, Niobe didn't fall for it, either. "What else? I'm guessing you heard about the Succession ceremony."

"I did." She gave a small, satisfied smile. "Anton must be incensed."

"Do you think he'll come after me again?"

"You're well guarded. The concealment hides you from the Darklings. His best chance would come during the second half of the ceremony, but he may not have enough support to attack you in such a public fashion."

I was not reassured. "He's done it before."

"Yes. But your display at the ceremony has changed people's perception of you."

"How's that?"

"Before, you were a Flat who had stumbled into someone else's destiny. You'd stopped the Torrent, but your work was done. In most people's eyes, you were disposable. Now you're a force to be reckoned with. They don't know if they should fear you or worship you."

Both choices made me uncomfortable. "Leaving me alone isn't an option?"

Niobe's laugh echoed through the hallway like wind-

chimes. "I don't believe it ever was. But certainly not now."
She ushered me into an empty classroom.

"They won't choose me. I only did it to make Anton
angry." I crossed the room and peered out the window, as if I
could see him coming. The nausea wouldn't go away, the terror I'd felt during the attack at Morgan's returning in icy
waves.

"How comforting to know you've succeeded." She began
to trace symbols on the board, and the magic responded by
calming slightly.

A moment later, Constance appeared in the doorway. "I
got a note?" Her expression was puzzled until she spotted
me, and then it shifted to annoyed. "What now?"

"Training," said Niobe. "This classroom is empty for the
next two hours. You need more time, but—"

"I can't keep skipping class," I said. "Even if you're running interference with the school."

"Perhaps you should have considered that before you disappeared with Luc the other day."

"Luc?" said Constance, closing the door behind her and
locking it with a quick spell. "You cut class to hang out with
Luc? What's your boyfriend say about that?"

Colin wasn't saying anything, and I doubted he was my
boyfriend anymore, but Constance didn't need to know that.
I stood and twisted my hair back into a knot, hands jittery.
"Can we get started, please?"

Niobe finished drawing the symbols on the board, and I
reached out, my fingers hovering over the dusty writing.
They didn't carry the same power as the ones carved into the
table at the Assembly, but I could still feel a faint charge flickering within them, and my hands tingled as if they'd fallen
asleep. Something about the glyphs felt . . . wrong. Off.

"What's today's lesson?"

"The castings you'll use during the second half of the ceremony. These are specific to the candidates."

"A candidate?" Constance echoed, her brows drawing together. "You never said you were going to declare."

"It was a spur-of-the-moment thing."

"You're trying to take Evangeline's place?" There was something sharp and nasty in her voice. "Not really a surprise, I guess. That's kind of your thing, isn't it?"

"My 'thing'? What's that supposed to mean?" I rounded on her, finally fed up with the snotty comments and dirty looks.

Maybe that's all I'd needed to do this whole time, because she stepped back, face smoothing out. "Nothing. But I won't be at the ceremony. Why do I need to practice?"

Niobe answered, "Because unless there's something you've failed to mention, you are not a seer. You may attend a Succession someday, and have cause to know these spells."

Constance flushed. "Not if the Seraphim win. They'll get rid of the Houses."

"Then it's a good thing they won't win," Niobe said, her voice dangerously cheerful. "I'd hate to waste your time."

"We're going to stop them," I said. Niobe was as reassuring as a cobra sometimes, and Constance was still adjusting to the Arcs, still reeling from Verity's death. It made sense that she viewed the world as one giant worst-case scenario. "I promise. Me, and Luc, and the Quartoren, too. We won't let them win."

She bobbed her head and gave me a half smile. "You'll try."

"Better than try, Constance." I touched her shoulder. "I swear it."

Niobe tapped the pointer against the blackboard, and I jerked my gaze back to the front of the room. "You've opened yourself to raw magic before, but during this ceremony you'll be dealing with a single elemental line—water—that has been tempered."

"So it should be easy." That was a nice change of pace. I could use easy, for once. I'd *earned* easy.

"I wouldn't put it that way. It's a test, after all. If you can't wield the magic, you'll fail."

"The only way I fail is if Anton wins." My stomach twisted painfully, and I grabbed at the lectern standing nearby as my legs gave out.

Niobe started toward me and then stopped again, cocking her head like she was listening to music I couldn't hear. Her gaze snapped back to me, and she was at my side in an instant. "Hold on," she said, and there was real fear in her voice as she took my arm.

Instantly, my skin turned slick, jagged panic racing through me. "What's wrong?"

"You and the magic are linked," she said. "Constance, help me get her to a chair."

"I can walk." But I closed my eyes for an instant and memories sprang up—Anton's fingers at my neck, the slash of a Darkling talon through metal, Verity's scream, the fetid smell of death—and the magic thrashed in pain, deep within me. My legs crumpled. "Or not."

Niobe caught me before I hit the ground. "Give me your sweater," she ordered Constance.

I started to tremble—full body shakes, slamming into the floor. "What—"

She slid the sweater beneath my head, kept her hands on my shoulders to hold me still. "If you're hurt, so is the magic. But it works both ways. Try to relax. Breathe through it."

Easy for her to say. I tried to curl up, protecting my stomach, my breath coming too fast and shallow to stay conscious for much longer. "Can they stop it?"

"They're doing everything they can," Niobe said, voice echoing.

Constance dropped to her knees and took my hand. "What's happening to her?"

"They're killing it," I whispered, barely able to force the words out. The magic sent me a relentless parade of images. Darklings, breaking through the walls of the Assembly, shattering the black table, the shifting symbols falling still. Swarming over the beautiful grove of trees and white marble stage of the Allée, cracking open the massive lines surrounding it, sucking out the magic like marrow from a bone. *Marrow from my bones,* just like Anton had said, and I screamed.

Niobe grabbed my hands and began to chant. The pain eased somewhat, and then her words were swallowed up by a great rushing sound, a fresh round of attacks. I begged the magic to please hold on, to fight, to live, my throat raw from shouting. I fought back against the pain, drawing as much of the magic inside me as I could, sheltering it from further assaults.

Gradually, the noise faded. The images were blotted out to a white stillness, like the end of a blizzard, hushed and blindingly bright. I kept my eyes shut, but I could feel the traces of Constance and Niobe's magic drifting across me. I was so cold their spells barely registered.

I don't know how much time passed before the warmth returned, bringing a fresh tingling pain, like recovery from frostbite. The voices strengthened, became clear again, and a third one joined in. I tried to block them out, but one voice was too insistent, shoving past layers of cold and fear and dragging me back to consciousness.

"Mouse. It's okay. Come on back to me. Come on."

The relief I felt at Luc's voice warmed me more than any spell. I bolted upright, sucking down air like I'd been drowning, wracked with gasping sobs. "Darklings!"

"I know. We took care of them. They're gone."

"Darklings? Here?" asked Constance.

"Not here. The Allée. The Assembly. Where the magic's strongest." He chafed his hands over my arms, trying to rub sensation back into them. "We beat them back."

But there was sorrow in his voice, not triumph.

"How many?" Niobe asked, her voice somber.

"Twelve."

"Twelve Darklings?" Constance sounded awed.

Luc shook his head. "Twelve Arcs lost. Quartoren guards."

Constance didn't say anything. None of us did, for a moment. Luc pulled me against his chest. I listened for his heart-beat, and tried to make mine match.

"They were going to kill it," I mumbled. "I felt it dying. I was dying."

He made a shushing noise, the one you use to soothe a fractious child. "It's okay now."

"No." I shoved at him, terror returning in a flash. "I felt it. It was dying, Luc."

He bent, his lips brushing my ear. "It ain't alive, remember?"

I pulled back, and his eyes, bleary and ringed with exhaustion, met mine and held until I'd nodded understanding.

"What did she mean?" Constance asked, gesturing to me. "She's dying?"

"She's not dyin'. She's shook up." I could have answered for myself, but I felt too ragged and shivery. Luc's skin was warm through the linen of his shirt, and I tried to soak it all up, letting their conversation wash over me as if I weren't there.

"She was injured," Niobe said softly. "I tried to heal her, but I couldn't get a strong enough line to draw on."

The second the magic was under attack, it had drawn back into itself, marshaling its energy, trying to hide. I'd done the same, trying to preserve as much of its spark—its life—as I could, balling up on the linoleum floor of the classroom, even as the energy drained out of both of us. An unthinking reflex, the same way the body shunted blood to the essential systems—the heart and lungs—during shock. Now we both needed time to recover.

"Neither could we," Luc said. "It's why there was such a high casualty rate. We had weapons but no magic to channel."

"If the Seraphim had succeeded, they'd have had their Ascendency."

There was grim satisfaction in Luc's voice as he said, "But they didn't. And now people see what they're really about. Might turn the tide in our favor."

I forced my eyelids open, surprised by how heavy they felt. The effort required to speak was more than I could muster. Luc was wrong. Anton didn't need the support of the Arcs. He had Darklings. He had a cult—Evangeline hadn't spoken of him like a politician she was planning to vote for, but rapturously, all blind allegiance and fervent adoration. I'd looked into his eyes, seen the unholy light in them. All he cared about was the Ascendency.

"What happens to Mo now?" Constance asked.

"I'll take her home. Let her rest."

"She can't be left alone," Niobe said. "Not in this state."

"I can stay with her," Constance offered.

"No need," said Luc. "I'll watch her."

"You think I can't be helpful?" She sounded insulted.

"You think I'd trust you to look after her? I wouldn't let you take care of a hamster."

"Luc. Enough." I tugged at his sleeve, but kept my face pressed to his shirtfront. "She's just a kid."

Constance made a huffing noise.

"You've got things here?" he asked Niobe.

"I always do." But the words sounded less acidic than usual, more troubled. I heard their footsteps cross the room, the door opening and closing behind them. "My place or yours?" Luc asked.

"Mine," I croaked. I wanted my bed, and my quilt, and to get out of this uniform, and a chance to confer with the magic. No sleep, though. Sleep was too close to oblivion. Too close to death. "Will you stay with me?"

"Said so not five minutes ago. Don't you remember?"

"Just making sure."

He brushed my hair back from my face. "Be sure of me."

"I am." It was the truth, I realized with a jolt. His expression turned quietly pleased.

He stood, scooping me up without effort. A moment later, we were in my room. "Harder than usual," he mused. "Magic's still recoverin'. So are you." He set me on the bed carefully.

"How long will it take?" I asked.

"To get back to one hundred percent? Not sure. You'll be able to tell before me, more'n likely." He glanced around. "Anyone home this time of day?"

"Everyone's working." I stood up, leg muscles quivering in protest. "Can you get me something to drink? Tea?" Deep inside, where the magic huddled, I was still cold. It was like a layer of permafrost. I needed some way to warm up from the inside out—and a few minutes alone.

"Long as you promise not to keel over."

"Scout's honor." I held up three fingers.

He chuckled. "You as a Girl Scout. Figures. Shame you never showed up on my door selling cookies."

"Tea," I ordered, and shoved him toward the door.

Once I was alone, I changed into pajama pants and an old T-shirt, thick socks and a sweatshirt. Not glamorous, but comfortable and warmer than my uniform. A quick glance in the mirror showed my skin was pale—not creamy, or alabaster, or fine like marble, but the bluish white of skim milk. I thought about trying to brush my hair into submission, but it was clearly a losing battle.

Luc returned as I was crawling back into bed. "Tea," he said, holding out a cup and saucer.

"Thanks." I took them from him. "You used the good china."

"Figured you could stand to be spoiled for once."

"We never use the good china. It's for special occasions."

"You nearly died," he said. "And then you didn't. Special enough for me."

Silly to be so touched by the gesture, but I was. The tea—hot and toothachingly sweet—eased the pain in my throat, sent warmth trickling through my body. The cold receded unevenly, like melting snow. When I'd finished, Luc touched the cup, and with a word it was full again.

"Better?" he asked when I'd drunk it all.

I twisted to set the cup on the nightstand and pulled my

knees to my chest. "How did the Darklings breach the Assembly walls? Orla told me they couldn't."

"Didn't need to. Anton held the damn door open, and they walked right in."

I pictured the table, shattered beyond repair, and the cold crept back. Marguerite had told me once that the Arcs had three sacred places—the Binding Temple, the Allée, and the Assembly—where the magic ran true and strong. All three had been destroyed now. I pressed my face to my knees, feeling weak and helpless all over again.

"We'll stop them," he said. "I promise. Most important thing right now is that you're okay."

"That the magic is okay," I corrected.

"One and the same."

"Not the same. If it was, I could talk to it."

"You can't?"

"It's getting better," I hedged. "Sometimes it's feelings. Sometimes pictures. Memories, even."

"Like what?"

"During the attack, I saw the Allée. I saw the Assembly, too, and the Darklings. Some of it was real time, but some of it was a flashback—like in the Allée, when Anton grabbed me. And the Assembly, when I signed the covenant. And the Darklings . . ."

I broke off, shaking again.

"Enough of that," he said. "Tell me a nice one instead."

I sifted through memories, images the magic had given me during the last few months. "There's a weird one . . ."

"Don't think weird is going to help your mood any," he replied. "Try for nice."

"This is both."

A flash of sunset over endless water, and damp sand cool underfoot. Waves roll in, foamy and white. I dig my toes into the sand, feeling it erode as the waves return to the sea. An instant later, it is night, and a fire crackles, throwing shifting shadows on the rocks encircling it, and the smoke forms

twisting shapes against the indigo sky. The scent of toasting
marshmallows and saltwater fills the air.

"I've never been to a beach like that."

"I have," Luc said slowly. "Long time ago."

I considered the idea, felt it fit into place as neatly as a key
in a lock. "It gave me your memory."

"I'm bound to you. You're bound to the magic. Maybe it
overlaps."

"Maybe." I pulled back to study him. "Was it a happy memory?"

"Yeah." He'd gone far away—back to that beach, I assumed—but his hand ran lightly over my shoulder, the motion as gentle and repetitive as the waves. "Happened when I
was little. Before Theo died. *Maman* had a hankerin' to go to
the beach, so we did. She gets her way, more often than not,"
he said with a fond smile. "So we spent the whole day playing at the water's edge, chasing the tide, skipping rocks. Ate
so many marshmallows I got sick."

"You had me right up to the marshmallows," I said.

"Not my finest hour," he agreed. "But it was a good day.
One of my best."

"Freedom," I said softly. "That's what the magic showed me."

His hand stilled. "Never thought of it that way. Mouse, if
you two can communicate . . . can you tell it what to do?"

"No. I'm getting better at interpreting what it wants.
What it feels. But I'm not in charge. I can't *do* anything."

"You've done plenty. I am startin' to wish your part was
finished. That this could all play out while you and I sat on
the sidelines with some popcorn and watched the show."

"You don't believe that's going to happen."

He smiled ruefully. "Someday, maybe. But right now,
you're both in danger. And sitting back won't do the trick.
The only thing that will is getting rid of Anton."

"Killing him," I said.

I'd killed Evangeline, but it had been an impulse. It hadn't
been a deliberate execution, the sentence for her crimes. It

had been as instantaneous and destructive as a lightning strike, and the repercussions had rolled through my life like the resultant claps of thunder. I didn't regret my decision, but I wasn't proud, either.

Killing Anton would be premeditated. A preemptive strike. A necessary evil, in order to protect the greater good. All true.

All excuses.

It wouldn't matter if it were planned or spur of the moment. I wanted Anton dead, and I no longer felt the need to make excuses about it. I wanted him dead, and by my hand. My thirst for revenge hadn't been slaked with Evangeline's blood. Maybe it wouldn't ever be. But until he lay at my feet and begged to live, the same way I had begged Verity to hang on, I wasn't going to stop.

"I can do that." Now the cold inside me felt good. Right. "Not a problem."

Before he could say more, the front door opened. "Mo?" my mother called. I heard her lock the door, hang her coat in the front closet

"Go!" I hissed, shoving Luc off the bed.

"I'm not leaving," he said, folding his arms.

"Then hide. And take the teacup with you."

"Your counselor called me. She said you had the flu?" Her voice carried up the stairs.

Luc stood, muttering to himself, and shimmered out of sight.

"Closet," I whispered.

"She can't see me." Neither could I, but I could sense him.

"A guy in my bedroom? Trust me, she'll spot you."

The neat rows of school uniforms and church dresses shifted as he stepped inside, then fell still.

"This weather! No wonder you got sick." Mom headed directly for me, laying a hand across my forehead. "You look peaked, but you don't feel warm. Can I get you something?"

"Another pillow, maybe? And another blanket?"

Her brow furrowed. "You're cold?"

"I think it's the fever," I said, trying to look pitiful. It was not a stretch.

"If you say so," she said. "I called your uncle and told him you wouldn't be in tonight. He said you can make it up as soon as you're feeling better."

"Great," I mumbled. A generous Billy was more worrisome than an angry one, in a lot of ways.

"Do you think you could handle some soup?" she asked, fussing with the blankets.

The thought of food made my stomach tighten unpleasantly, but I glanced at the closet and wondered when Luc had eaten last. "I'll try some."

"I'll get started right now." She sounded relieved, which didn't make sense until I realized that the flu was a problem she understood. Something she could treat. Letting her make me soup was as much for her as it was for me so I didn't protest when she bent and kissed my forehead. The scent of pie crust—sugary and familiar—wafted over me, and for an instant I was homesick for a place I hadn't left yet. Because I would leave, and soon. In some ways, I already had.

Luc emerged moments after my mom went downstairs. "You still feelin' lousy?" He reached for my hand, our connection thrumming. "Magic seems stronger."

"The blankets are for you. You're staying, right?"

"You askin' me to sleep over?" He flashed a grin, warming me more than the faded quilt.

"You'd stay even if I said no," I pointed out.

"That I would. But it's nice to be asked." He sat at my desk, flipping through textbooks at random. "You'll miss this place," he said.

I glanced around the room—the gilt and white hand-me-down furniture, the papers and magazines piled on my desk like snowdrifts, the photo collage Verity had made for me junior year. "A little. Maybe. Dorm rooms are kind of notoriously small."

He took a deep breath, held it, let it out. I didn't know if he was gearing up to tell me how I was going to have to leave my old life behind or trying to keep from saying it, like he didn't want to upset me, like I was too fragile to handle what he had to say.

Well, screw that. I'd been hurt, but I would recover. I wasn't fragile. I didn't need protection—from my future or my past—and I was tired of being treated like I did. I flipped back the covers and swung around to face him. "There has to be a plan to take down Anton."

He leaned back, propping his feet on the desk. He looked dangerous and foreign in my childhood bedroom. Totally out of place and completely comfortable at the same time, and I couldn't seem to look anywhere else. "We're working on it. You heard Sabine—the Quartoren can't move against him at the Succession, and that's the only place we know he'll show up."

"Aren't there Water Arcs loyal to the Quartoren? Send them after him."

"We've got some in place. But he's got plenty in his House loyal to the Seraphim. He wouldn't have come to the Succession without people to watch his back. My guess is, he's got enough people there to neutralize ours."

"What about Sabine and the other mages?"

"I'd like to think they're on our side, but they've got to look out for their people. If they believe Anton's the strongest candidate, we can't rely on them. We'll figure something out, Mouse."

"Why not me?"

"No." The words had a stark finality, and my temper flared. "You didn't even think about it."

"Don't need to. You're the one who's not thinkin'. Too risky for you."

"You want me to be safe."

He squinted slightly, his words cautious. " 'Course I do. We need to protect you. And the magic."

"Better to keep me hidden somewhere," I said, letting a dangerous note enter my voice, the thinnest of blades. "I should stay in my room and let you handle it."

"You're twistin' this around. I'm not Cujo."

No, but this conversation was too familiar. "If the shoe fits . . ."

"The shoe most assuredly does not fit. Man clomps around in those work boots, hear him comin' from a mile away. It's not the same thing at all."

"Looks pretty similar from where I'm sitting. Which is on the sidelines. Because neither of you will let me do anything, even though it's my life."

"You know what? I will agree with him on one thing: you have an alarmin' tendency to risk your neck for other people without ever thinkin' of the consequences to yourself."

I shot out of bed. "How's this for consequences? If we don't stop the Seraphim, they're going to keep coming after me and the magic. I'm good at math, Luc. I can calculate odds like you wouldn't believe. And mine are not favorable."

"Then let me protect you."

"I want to protect myself. I want to fight. If I'm going to have a place with the Arcs, I want to define it, not have it dictated to me."

"Nobody's dictating anything. But if you die, so does the magic. And then it's all for nothing." He paused. "I don't want to lose you."

I wasn't his to lose, but I didn't point that out. "You said I'm fated to do big things. To save the magic. Stopping the Seraphim isn't a big thing? Getting rid of Anton?"

"Don't make your whole life about someone else's death, Mouse."

"Like you?" The words slipped out, harsher than I'd meant them to sound, and he looked away. "Everything you do is penance for Theo. Your life is a memorial. There's nothing you do that's just for you."

"The hell there isn't."

"One. Name one thing you do that's for yourself—not the Heir, not the prophecies—something strictly for Luc."

"I'm not kissing you, am I?"

"You don't want to kiss me?" That was a good thing, of

course. Because I certainly didn't want to kiss him, no matter how his eyes were sparking green and how firmly set the line of his mouth was, inviting and infuriating all at once. I didn't want to kiss Luc and it was a relief to hear he felt the same.

He let out a bark of laughter. "I want to kiss you until you see stars. Till you're so lost in us you can't find a way back. And if this was about the prophecy, that's exactly what I'd do. Lock you into this so you can't ever get away. You've got magic flowing through your veins," he said, catching my wrist and pressing his fingers to my pulse. "In your lungs and in your heart, showing you pictures in your brain. I've got you."

His free hand slid through my hair, cupping my face, "Hell, yes, I want to kiss you."

I swallowed, felt his breath feathering across my lips, the gentle touch of his forehead to mine, and my hands found his shoulders—not pulling him in, not pushing him away, just feeling the breadth and the strength of them, the softness of worn linen under my fingers and the heat of his skin beneath.

"I get it now," he said. "You were afraid I didn't want you for you. Only because of the prophecy. Because you're the Vessel, and you wanted me to care about Mo."

I didn't answer, struck dumb at the realization that he knew me so well.

"I'm trying to act separate from the prophecy so you can't question how I feel or what we are. And that means, if the Heir would kiss you, then I can't.

"Besides," he said, easing back. "I promised. And I know you're a fan of keeping promises."

There was a knock on the door. By the time it swung open, Luc was gone, though I could sense him nearby. My parents both entered, my mom bearing a tray of food, my dad laden with spare blankets and a healthy dose of suspicion.

"I think the fever's caught up with you, sweetie. Back into bed." I let her tuck me in again, settled back against the headboard while she placed the tray on my lap. "Soup, saltines, a little Sprite."

"Thanks."

My dad glanced around the room. "Were you on the phone?"

"Um . . ." There was no phone in sight, which made sense, as I'd left it at school. No book bag. But I pointed at a collection of short stories atop my desk. "Spanish," I said. "Translating out loud."

He set the stack of pillows and blankets at the foot of the bed, circled slowly, taking in the room. "Spanish."

"*Sí.*" I took a small sip of soup, bit into a cracker, and gave my mom a thumbs-up.

Her face cleared slightly, the worry lines around her mouth smoothing out. "I'll finish our dinner," she said, touching my dad's shoulder.

"Be there in a minute," he told her, then transferred his attention to me. "Billy wants you to come in tomorrow."

I *knew* he hadn't given up trying to recruit me and Luc. "Did he say why?"

"Delivery, I suppose. Tell him you're sick."

I scoffed. "That's your solution? I can't have the flu for the rest of the year."

"You don't have it now."

I ate more soup and focused on the patchwork of my quilt.

"Mo," my dad said, and the gravity of his tone forced my gaze to his. "Billy's working a new angle. He thinks he's got some way to finish Ekomov permanently, some sort of silver bullet. He's getting cocky, and that's exactly when things will start to go wrong."

"Couldn't happen to a nicer guy," I said. Billy's "silver bullet" was currently hiding in my closet. He wouldn't help my uncle take down Christmas lights, much less the Russian Mob. Which was a relief, until I started to wonder again what lengths Billy would go to in an effort to convince me.

"I agree. But I don't want you caught up in it."

"Too late."

The creases around his eyes seemed deeper, his shoulders more bowed. "I'm asking for your mother. If you want to punish me, can't you find a way that won't hurt her? Or you?"

"I don't want to punish you," I said, surprised to find it was the truth. "I can't stop working for Billy if I want to keep Colin safe. Mom gets it. You should, too. Hell, it's practically a Fitzgerald family tradition."

"Tradition or no, it ends with me."

"Not your call," I said. "I can handle Billy."

"Not from what I've seen." Before I could argue, he held up a hand. "Ekomov wants to know who's on Billy's payroll. That's what the list is."

"I know. He's going to use it like a test, to find out who is loyal and who isn't."

My dad nodded. "A list like that is dangerous. If he asks you to deliver it, stall him. At least until I figure out a plan. Please, Mo."

I bit my lip. Those names were the proof I needed. All the people Billy had paid off? The bribes that let his operation run without interference from the city and the police? If I could get the list to Jenny, Colin and Tess would be free. They could leave. Colin and Tess and me, once upon a time, but that fairy tale was over.

"The only plan I'm interested in is one that helps the Donnellys. I'll hold off if you promise to help them."

"Even if Colin doesn't come back?"

"Even if." But I had to believe he would. I had to believe I could fix this, even though he'd pushed me away.

He squeezed my shoulder gently—and I didn't pull away this time.

After he'd left, Luc reappeared. "Now I know where you get it," he said.

"Get what?" I pushed the tray of food toward him.

"The martyr complex." He took the bowl of soup and sat down at the far end of the bed.

"My mom isn't a martyr."

"Wasn't talking about your mom. Your daddy's tryin' hard to take care of you. Considerin' how ornery you get whenever I try to lend a hand, I have sympathy for the man."

He applied himself to the soup, finishing everything on the tray quickly.

"You're sure you want to stay?" I asked. "It's okay if you go home."

He shook his head. "Not inclined to leave you alone. Besides, who am I to pass up the opportunity to spend the night with a beautiful girl? Wouldn't want word to get out I'd lost my touch."

"No," I said. "We can't have that."

A little while later, I took the tray downstairs, waving away my mom's objections that I was too sick to exert myself. I didn't feel 100 percent, but I was well enough to walk a flight of stairs. And it was infinitely preferable to having another heart-to-heart while Luc listened in.

When I got back, Luc had put together a makeshift bed on the floor. His linen shirt was tossed over the chair, and I wrenched my eyes away from the sight of his bare shoulders, caramel-colored skin over long, lean muscles.

"Please tell me you are wearing pants," I said, skirting the mass of blankets.

"One way to find out for sure."

"I guess it will remain a mystery, then," I said, and slid under the covers.

He stretched out on his back, fingers laced behind his head, and turned to study me. "Tomorrow we go to see the Quartoren," he said.

"Are you going to tell them about the magic?"

"No."

I believed him. There had been no evasion in his answer, no room for shading the truth or hiding behind technicalities. The tension leached from my body, the magic relaxing its stranglehold on my nerves. "Thank you."

He paused. "That's twice."

"Twice what?"

"Twice I've done somethin' just for me. Not sure how it feels quite yet." He rolled his shoulders, like he was trying to dislodge something. " 'Night, Mouse. Sweet dreams."

CHAPTER 25

When I woke the next morning—way earlier than usual, so early the sky was inky blue, the sun a pale smudge on the horizon—Luc was still there.

I flipped back the covers and crept to where he was sleeping, one arm thrown over his head, the other draped across his chest. In all the time I'd known him, I'd never seen him so unguarded. His lashes feathered across his cheeks, softening the harsh lines of his face, the curve of his mouth gentle and unexpectedly sweet. His breathing was slow and regular, even when I edged closer. Our binding felt quiet, different from the crackling energy that typically passed between us.

Even asleep, he radiated heat, and I stretched my hand out, hovering over his skin but not touching, deliberately not letting my gaze drift any farther south. I was definitely not looking at the curve of his hip bone, the way the muscle seemed to cut graceful, dangerous lines into him.

"Didn't your mama teach you it was impolite to stare?"

Before I could react, his hand had snaked over mine, pressing my palm flush against his chest.

Had I thought his skin felt warm? It was practically feverish, and the longer he kept my hand trapped—eyes still closed, breathing unchanged—the more heat spread through me, a flush creeping up my neck and across my face, as if it were contagious.

"I wasn't staring."

"Hmn." He tugged on my hand till I lost my balance and sprawled ungracefully next to him. "I appreciate the initiative, but I'd rather we finish this in your bed."

"Finish?" My voice came out as a squeak, and I scrambled up.

"You weren't starting something?" His tone was teasing. His look was not.

I tugged on the hem of my T-shirt, trying to salvage some dignity. Then I caught sight of my hair in the mirror and gave up. "Absolutely not. I need to get ready for school."

"That excuse won't work today." He stood in one fluid, graceful motion. He *was* wearing pants—jeans, worn soft with age and slung low on the hips—and I felt almost light-headed with relief. It was short-lived, though, because he reached for me, catching a lock of my hair, wrapping the curl around his finger. "You're playing hooky."

"Oh. Right. The Quartoren." And I could breathe again. "I can fake the flu for another day, I guess."

It was easy to convince my mom. She took one look at the color high in my cheeks, my overbright eyes, and sent me back to bed. My dad didn't buy it for a minute, but he and my mom left for the restaurant on time, leaving us alone. Together.

The minute I heard our Taurus rumble down the street, I jumped out of bed, needing more than space between me and Luc. I needed walls. Doors with locks. Because the strange feeling in my stomach wasn't the flu, and he was the only logical explanation.

"I'm taking a shower," I said, and fled down the hallway.

"Want company?" he called after me.

I scrubbed until my skin was pink, letting the water run until it started to cool. When I stepped onto the bath mat, the room was filled with clouds of steam, the mirror too foggy to see my reflection. Intent on escaping Luc, I'd left my robe hanging on the back of my bedroom door. So I wrapped a towel around me, squeezed out my hair, and stepped into the hallway, prepared to boot him out of my room while I dressed.

Colin was halfway up the stairs.

For a split second, I thought I could make it back to the bathroom and hide for the next week or so. But he spotted me before I could act on the impulse, his eyebrows shooting up.

"What are you doing here?" I croaked.

"Your mom said you were sick."

My door was still shut, giving no sign that Luc was within, and I was struck with a very clear idea of how many things could potentially go wrong in the next five minutes. "Not exactly."

"That's what your dad said."

I shifted, water trickling from my hair into the edge of the towel. "But you came to check on me. You were worried?"

"I wanted to make sure you weren't off doing something stupid and reckless."

Annoyance welled up inside me. It was a nice change from despair, so I didn't try to hold it in. "I like to save stupid and reckless for after lunch. Does that work for you?"

"It doesn't," he said, gripping the banister.

"Good thing I'm not asking your permission, then."

"Mo—"

"Took you long enough," said Luc, opening the door. "I was about to come in and—" He broke off as he caught sight of Colin. "Didn't realize we had company."

Colin studied him for a second—bare-footed, bare-chested, hair mussed from sleep—and then looked back at me. I clutched the towel around my chest and said nothing.

"We?" Colin asked. Something I couldn't define crossed his face, chased by cold contempt. "I guess you decided not to wait for lunch."

Before I could respond, Luc sauntered over. He stopped behind me, a shade too close to be innocent, and slicked water off my back with the palm of his hand. His fingers curved over my shoulder, light but unmistakably possessive. "Little busy here, Cujo. Something you needed?"

His needling, cocky tone broke me out of my stupor. Luc was treating this like a game—like he and Colin were competing for me, and he'd just scored.

He had not scored. In any sense of the word. And I wasn't about to let Colin think he had.

"Luc, hands off. Colin, wait downstairs."

For a moment, Luc looked apologetic, like he knew he'd overstepped. Then he released me, and I walked to the bedroom, pretending I was not mortified by the length of my towel.

As soon as the door shut behind me, I yanked clothes out of drawers—jeans, tank, henley, cardigan, all as black as my mood. Layers upon layers, and not just because I'd be jumping between climates today. Not all of Luc's display had been for Colin's benefit. I wanted as much clothing between us as possible.

I pulled my wet hair into a knot and swiped a ChapStick across my lips. That was all the effort I could spare for my appearance right now. Appearances were what had gotten me into trouble in the first place.

Luc knocked on the door. "You decent?"

"I'm dressed." Decent people would not have to deal with this situation. With these feelings. Decent people knew what they wanted. They stuck to the plan.

"Liked the other look better," he said. "Cujo's downstairs. Listen hard enough, you'll hear him frowning."

"He's got a right," I said, not meeting Luc's eyes.

"Does he? I was under the impression you two were done."

"Like you *care*," I snapped. "Like it makes a difference to you."

"Tried to change your mind, sure. But I didn't poach." Luc said. "Now you're fair game."

I shoved at him. "It's not a game! It's my life, and you're treating it like . . ."

I shoved again, unable to find the words. He caught my wrists, held me still, and I couldn't decide if I wanted to punch him in the stomach or weep.

"I'm sorry," he said, so quietly I felt the words vibrating through his chest more than I heard them. "Walked out of

the room, and you looked halfway to broken. Saw your face
go whiter than that towel, like you were bleeding out in front
of me. Figured the best way to make it stop was to make him
hurt, too. Didn't consider it might hurt you more. Instinct.
Not a game."

He was a guy. I wasn't so naive as to think competition
wasn't a factor. But when I drew back, his eyes were clouded
with concern and apology, the typical self-assured gleam
missing, and I felt my temper dissipate.

Dissipate. Not disappear. I took a deep breath and kept my
voice on the stubborn side of firm. "Don't touch me like that
again."

His mouth dropped open in protest, but I shook my head.
"Not to piss Colin off. Not to prove a point. You said if I
kissed you, it had to be for real, and I'm telling you the same
thing. You touch me again, Luc, and it had damn well better
be because you mean it."

His hands tightened on my wrists before letting go entirely.
Movements jerky, he pulled on his shirt. "See, you're acting
like that's a threat. But you know what I hear? You're not entirely averse to the notion."

I swallowed. Thought about the press of his hand against
the damp skin of my back. The thread of magic between us,
simultaneously familiar and unnerving. His insistence that I
could do more—*be* more—than anyone, including me, believed.

"You have to be honest with me. Which means you have
to be honest with yourself."

His fingers flexed as if he wanted to reach for me, but instead he simply looked at me like all the layers I was wearing
didn't exist. "Works both ways, Mouse."

"I know."

I went downstairs, to face Colin and the music.

CHAPTER 26

I'd never gotten used to the sight of Colin standing in my kitchen, leaning against the counter with a coffee cup in hand, scowling into the distance. Every time, it made my breath catch, my pulse jump. Usually, it was a good thing.

Not today.

"You planning on some B&E this afternoon?" he asked, eyeing my all-black outfit.

"Not in my skill set," I said. "I have other things on my plate right now. Stupid and reckless things."

He set the mug down. "Luc told me about the attack. Are you hurt?"

Trust Colin to focus on the least important part of the story. "I'm fine. Nothing happened. With Luc, I mean."

"Not my business if it did."

"No," I said slowly, the urge to plead forgiveness fading. "I guess it's not. But I'm telling you anyway. Why do you think that is?"

"I don't know why you do anything," he said. "If I had to guess, I'd say guilty conscience."

"Pay attention," I snapped. "Nothing. Happened. But you know what? It doesn't matter. You have made your feelings about me abundantly clear. You want nothing to do with me. So, I get to sleep with whomever I want. You don't get to pass judgment. You don't get to make spiteful comments.

You don't even get to make faces about it, because *you're the one that shut me down.*"

"You lied to me."

"To save your life, you ungrateful dumb-ass. And I'm done apologizing." I managed to cross the kitchen, pulled a mug from the cupboard. He was standing in front of the coffeepot. "Move, please."

He folded his arms and stared.

"*Move.*"

"I didn't shut you down."

"The hell you didn't." I elbowed him out of the way and poured myself a cup of coffee. "We haven't spoken in days. Today's the first time you've even looked at me."

"You were kind of an eyeful."

I could feel my cheeks heating again, but I watched him over the rim of the cup. "You've seen more."

"Still a surprise. Luc walked in, and I jumped to conclusions. I didn't mean to hurt you."

"Sure you did." And I wondered why—was it spite, or jealousy? Bad either way, but one held out hope.

He pushed off the counter. "A little."

"A lot."

"I'm sorry." He held my gaze, the apology genuine.

"So am I."

The corner of his mouth twitched, a gesture I knew so well, and one I'd missed so much that my heart constricted. "You said you were done apologizing."

"Haven't we already established I'm a liar?" I asked.

He dragged a hand across his face. "I didn't want you to know about Tess. About what I'd done."

"Why?"

"Because it's ugly. It's like poison, what happened to us. It ruins everything it touches."

"Only because you let it. You made a choice, and it was awful, but it was the best one you had. You saved Tess's life."

Misery flashed across his face. "Some life."

"Would you rather have buried her? And you saved your life, too. Maybe it doesn't matter much to you, but I'm pretty glad."

"You saved mine," he said.

I took another sip of coffee. "I did. I'd do it again."

"I wish you hadn't. But . . . I am grateful. Somehow that got lost in all of this."

"You're welcome," I said. Lots of things had gotten lost. More than I'd realized. Then I asked the question that frightened me most. "Where does this leave us?"

I'd spent seventeen years being the girl with the answers. Straight-A student, my hand always the first in the air, the one who ruined the curve every time. None of it helped me now. In the past week, Colin had transformed from a familiar to foreign territory, and I no longer knew if I was welcome.

He dropped his head, like he was too tired to stay upright anymore. "I know your intentions are good. But it was the one thing I asked you to leave. The *one thing*, Mo. And you couldn't do it. I don't know how to get past that."

I stared at the ceiling, forcing back tears. "I never expected otherwise." I finished my coffee and pushed away from the counter. "Time for me to go."

"Wait." He caught my arm before I could escape. "I'm still pissed. But this plan—drawing out Anton—sounds dangerous."

"It is." And I realized I wanted the danger—not just to survive, or protect the magic, but because it was a distraction. When I was fighting Anton, I couldn't think about Colin, or feel sorry for myself.

"Skip it. We can come up with a new plan. Let Luc handle him while we find a way to protect you and the magic."

If I did that, we were right back where we started. "Not your call."

"It's—"

"Your job? Protecting me from Ekomov is your job. Anything else was because of us. And there is no us. Add this to the list of things in my life that are none of your business."

"Mo. I'm angry. It doesn't change . . ."

"You said you'd never lied to me," I said, low and halting. "Don't start now."

"I love you."

I closed my eyes for a moment, tears collecting beneath my lashes, and bit down on my lip so hard I tasted copper. "I have to go."

I crossed the living room, waiting for him to ask me to stay.

He didn't.

I reached for the door handle, and he finally spoke. "Your uncle wants to see you. Tonight."

"So he can gloat? No, thanks."

"It's not optional. And he doesn't want Luc there, either."

No, he wouldn't want Luc around. It would give me the advantage. Billy gave all sorts of things away—advice, favors, jobs—but never the advantage. Now he'd given me the biggest one of all, and he didn't even realize it. He'd taken away everything I wanted—Colin, a future outside of Chicago, my family's shot at a happy ending. There was nothing left for me to lose, and the awfulness of that truth made me more dangerous than he could possibly guess.

My smile felt as brittle as old veneer and just as ready to crack.

"I'll be by tonight."

CHAPTER 27

If I'd learned anything about Luc from our time together, it was that his silence was the exact opposite of golden. Silence meant red alert. Silence meant something was about to go wrong.

So when we came Between at the Assembly, I was already edgy. He'd said as little as possible since the moment I stepped out of the house—just held out his hand and pulled me through. As I found my feet and let the room settle around me, I understood.

The white anteroom was destroyed, the marble floor shattered, the massive chandelier overhead swinging from only one chain. The scent of beeswax was gone, replaced by something rancid and sour, and I clapped my hand over my nose and mouth to block the smell. The enormous iron doors had long, jagged tears in the metal; one was partly wrenched off the hinges, revealing further destruction within.

Luc put out a hand to support me, but I shook him off and moved into the Assembly itself. The rows of seats had been tossed around the room. The torches ripped out of the walls, that same horrible odor of death, fetid and close, filling the room.

Around me, various Arcs were moving things back into place, the air alive with magic, but I couldn't escape the sorrow that seeped into my bones. I picked my way across the cracked and uneven floor to where the Quartoren stood directing Arcs in the cleanup effort. Orla's pale, wrinkled skin was nearly translucent with fatigue. She leaned heavily on her cane—I'd always assumed she carried it for effect, but today it seemed like the only thing keeping her upright. Next to her, Pascal was covered in dust and blood. His glasses tilted to one side, but he didn't seem to notice. And Dominic directed everything with such clipped, precise movements I knew it was masking a far deeper, more destructive fury. I'd seen Luc do the same, before—when he'd destroyed the Water Tower, when Anton had grabbed me at the Allée. It was the look of someone who was holding on to control by a thread so fine it was nearly invisible. Someone who was about to snap.

On the stage, Marguerite knelt next to the broken remains of the black table. The symbols inscribed in the wood no longer glowed with light—they were motionless, drained of life. The magic mourned, a swell of grief and rage and shock that almost cut off my air.

Dazed, I moved past the Quartoren to join Marguerite, whose cheeks were wet, her artfully coiled hair hanging limply around her face.

"Were you here when it happened?" I asked, sitting beside her.

"Mo!" She reached for my hand. "Should you be up and about?"

"I'm okay. The magic's okay. So sad." I reached out, touching the ebonized wood in a way I'd never been able to before. It was smooth and ordinary now, but I avoided the symbols out of habit.

"I was here at the start. Dominic sent me away once he realized what was happening."

I squeezed her hand. "I'm glad. It must have been terrible."

"I don't know what we'll do. The table's gone. The Allée . . . we'd only just finished rebuilding it. How do we come back from this, Mo? All the old ways, everything we've relied on. It's all gone. What will he take from us next?"

The magic. But I didn't say it. She knew as well as I did—better, even—what Anton's next target would be.

"I didn't foresee this," she murmured, stroking the cracked table like she could fix it. "It's unnatural. It's as much a violation of who we are as Verity's death."

"Maybe that's why you didn't see it," I said. "Because it wasn't supposed to happen. Or maybe it's like you told Luc, and you only see the end result, not the process."

"Perhaps." But she didn't sound convinced. "How is he?"

I glanced over to where he was talking to Dominic, eyebrows lowered, expression fierce. You didn't need to hear their conversation to know it wasn't a happy one. "Worried. Mad."

"You've told him."

"About the magic? He guessed."

"My clever boy." She sighed. "Do you know what you'll do?"

She wasn't just talking about the Seraphim, or the magic, and I answered her in kind. "We're figuring it out."

"So many paths," she said, fingers drifting over the broken wood. "But they're closing. So little time left. And the cost. You won't understand the price until it's too late."

"I've got a pretty good idea of what it's cost me," I said sharply, thinking of Colin's face this morning. "Sorry. That came out wrong."

Marguerite didn't answer. When I looked more closely, her irises were pale and milky. Her words hadn't been idle conversation, but prophecy.

I'd had enough foretelling to last me a lifetime. Now I wanted answers. "What's the cost, Marguerite? Tell me the price. Tell me how to stop it."

"It will not be stopped. Only changed. You cannot save them all."

I froze. "Who? Who do I need to save?"

"You can't," she said, her hands fumbling for mine. "Not all of them. You must listen."

"I *am*. Please," I begged. "Tell me who it is. Tell me how to save them."

"Listen. Then speak." She slumped over as Luc bounded up the stairs toward me and we eased her to the ground. Her bones felt fragile, hollow like a bird's.

"I don't understand," I said, panic mounting at my helplessness. "Marguerite. Please. I don't understand."

Luc took her hands in his, murmuring softly in French, only moving aside to let Dominic through. Marguerite stirred, opening her eyes. "I'm fine, you silly man. Just overset. It's been a hard day."

"I'll take you home," Dominic replied, sparing me a single questioning glance before taking her Between.

"What did she say?" demanded Orla.

I hesitated. If it had been Luc alone, I would have told him everything. But sharing with the Quartoren didn't seem like the best idea. What if Marguerite's words were the final clue, and Pascal realized the truth about the magic? What if one of them was the person she said I couldn't save? She'd told me to speak, but I wasn't ready to tell them.

"Nothing," I said. "We were talking about the attack, and the Seraphim. She got really upset. That's all."

Clearly, they didn't believe me. I gave them my blandest, most insincere smile, nothing else, and they finally drifted away to supervise the rebuilding, looking over their shoulders with obvious suspicion.

Luc sat down at the edge of the stage, his shoulders sagging.

"She'll be okay," I said, joining him. "It *was* a prophecy."

"Figured as much. It's a strange talent. Unpredictable."

"What do you think triggered this one?" Last time, it had been a surge of magic that brought on her trance. But that wasn't the case today.

"You, maybe? The attack? Touching the table?" He made a noise of frustration and studied the ruined Assembly. "Hell, I don't know. Pascal's the scientist, and you're keepin' him in the dark. You going to do the same to me?"

I pulled my knees to my chest and wrapped my arms around them, pulling inward like a turtle in its shell. As if by holding my secrets close, I could forestall disaster. But I knew better, so I let go—my arms falling to my sides, my legs dangling over the edge of the stage. Out of the corner of my eye, I saw the broken table, the jagged ends of the wood, the lifeless symbols, the language of the magic destroyed.

"She said I couldn't save them all."

"Who's them?"

"I don't know. She said a bunch of stuff, Luc. She was talking about paths closing, and how much my choices would cost. She said I can change things but not stop them. That I should listen, that I should speak." I lifted a shoulder, my words thickening with frustration. "It doesn't make sense. It's one or the other, not both."

"Listen to who?"

"Her, I guess." I rested my head on his arm, not sure if I was seeking comfort or giving it.

He let out a laugh—reluctant, but still a laugh, so I counted it as a victory. "*Maman* needs to pick her audience better. You don't listen to a thing anyone says. I'll admit you're turning out a bit on the mouthy side, though."

I smacked him on the leg, and he laughed again, twining his hand with mine before turning serious. "Maybe she was warning you not to go after Anton."

"You're right," I said. "I don't listen."

Dominic reappeared in the anteroom and strode onto the stage, Orla and Pascal trailing him. Luc and I stood, hands still joined.

"She doesn't remember a word," Dominic said. "Said it wasn't a prophecy, just exhaustion."

"Unusual," Pascal mused. "Do you believe her?"

"You suggesting my wife is lying?"

The air in the Assembly had been clearing gradually, the Darkling stench swept away by the fresh gusts of air Orla and her people had created. Now it filled with suspicion and threat, as choking as when I'd first walked in.

"I'm merely pointing out that the situation is wildly different from anything we've dealt with before," Pascal replied after a long pause.

I could feel his gaze on me, probing, trying to find out the truth. I needed to divert his attention. "Why did you want to see me?"

"We need to discuss strategy," Orla said. "You and Anton are in competition for the spot on the Quartoren. We need to figure out a way to ensure you're the next Matriarch."

"Me as Matriarch is a ridiculous idea, and everyone is going to have proof of that as soon as I try to cast a spell. Why would anyone even consider it?"

"The alternative is Anton."

Not if I could help it. "There were nearly fifty names on that list. They could choose someone completely different."

"Mouse," said Luc. "Think about it. In your government, you elect the person you think will make you strong, right? Whatever the office, you want the person powerful enough to make things happen for you."

"I live in Chicago," I pointed out. "This is not really the place you want to hold up as a model of politics at its finest."

"Arcs are no different," Dominic said. "The Water Arcs want someone who will come on the Quartoren and keep them strong—they've been at a disadvantage since Evangeline died, and it's clear things are changing. They want to make sure their next leader can make things happen. You're the Vessel. You stopped the Torrent. Bound yourself to the magic. They know you've got power, whether it's magic or not. As for Anton . . . they've seen what he can do. Like it or not, you two are the front-runners."

"What if Anton wasn't in the race at all?"

Orla sighed deeply, as if the answer was painful. "Then they'd choose you."

"Maybe. Maybe not. We need to get rid of Anton."

"We?" asked Dominic, condescendingly. "You have a plan? By all means, let's hear it."

I planted my feet on the crumbling stage and crossed my arms. "I take out Anton."

Beside me, Luc shook his head. Pascal looked doubtful, Orla repulsed—but Dominic looked intrigued, and he was the one I needed to convince. The others would fall in line.

"You know I'm right. He'll come after me at the Succession, because it's where you can't guard me. And he thinks I'm weak, so he won't be expecting any resistance."

"It's a sacrilege," Orla said. "To defile a Succession . . ."

"He's done it plenty of times before," I said. "I'm the best shot you have at stopping him."

Pascal cleared his throat. "What if you fail? And he kills you?"

"He can't kill me if he wants the Ascendency. He can put me in a coma, or Riven me until I have the IQ of a garden slug. But I'm not going to sit around and wait for it. At least this way, I've got a chance."

"It's fine for you to say you're willing," Dominic countered. "But in the moment, can you bring yourself to do it? You had an opportunity to slit the man's throat and you couldn't do it. Why would this time be different?"

"*I'm* different," I said evenly. "It won't be a problem this time."

He inclined his head. A look passed between the three of them, an unspoken communication. Finally Dominic said, "Do it."

"You can't—" Luc began.

Dominic loomed over him. "I can do whatever I damn well please. You ain't the Patriarch yet—I am, and that means my word is law. If this is what we need to do to stop the Seraphim, so be it." And then, in a voice so low that only

Luc and I heard it, he said, "Don't be stupid. You need to be thinkin' of what's best for your people now. Remember where your loyalties lie."

I'd known Dominic would have an angle—and that he'd try to use Luc. But it couldn't change my plans for Anton. Dealing with the Quartoren would have to wait.

Around us, people worked to restore the room—mending what they could, sending the rest into the vast emptiness of Between—but no one had touched the table. It lay in pieces on the other side of the stage, and while Dominic stared Luc down, Orla and Pascal straining to hear what was said, I walked over to it and knelt, just as Marguerite had done.

This was the worst part, I knew instinctively. The language of the magic rendered mute, and inside me the magic felt as splintered as the wood. It yearned to reach out, and so I did, placing my hand on the table leg closest to me, pressing the scar on my palm to the grain of the wood. The Darkling's wound had been the point of entry for the magic, back when Verity had transferred her power to me. Maybe I could send it out the same way.

The magic swelled a bit within me, like the opening note of a symphony.

Startled, I yanked my hand away. The magic fell silent again. Across the stage, Pascal shifted, and I tried to look innocent.

When he turned back to Luc and Dominic, I stretched my hand out again, opening myself to the images coursing through me—a stirring of a breeze, clouds gathering over parched earth, the tide creeping higher along a beach, the strike of a match against a box. As if pulled by a magnet, the tips of my fingers brushed against the tracks carved into the surface. The faintest glow shone through the wood, like the embers of a fire thought long dead.

If I could restore this table, it would make everything okay. I was certain of it. I could fix the Quartoren, the Seraphim, Luc's own knotty destiny—the idea that I could solve all of it with a little furniture repair was ludicrous but unshakeable, the belief so strong it knocked down my resistance. "More. Come on. Please."

But the tremulous light didn't increase. I chewed my lip in frustration.

Pascal broke away from the group. "What have you done?"

"Nothing! I touched it, that's all. It lit up."

"The Darklings drained every ounce of magic from the table," he said. "Once they'd finished, it was nothing but ancient wood. It couldn't hold against the onslaught."

"Maybe they didn't drain all the magic."

"Perhaps." He tapped it lightly, but there was no answering glow. "Or perhaps you can do more than you realize. Try again."

The rest of the group joined us. Luc touched my shoulder, our connection strong and reassuring. I slid my hand over the path of a glyph, closing my eyes, listening as hard as I could, but all I heard was Orla's indrawn breath. Luc's grip tightened in surprise, and I opened my eyes to see the wood glowing brighter than before. The magic surged, and I dug down inside myself, trying to push more power into the table.

Instead, the light dimmed and flickered.

"Don't rush it," Luc murmured, but I wanted so badly to make everything go back to the way it had been. I tried to envision myself ordering the magic, the way an owner might scold a recalcitrant dog, but the glow disappeared entirely. The magic folded itself up and retreated inside me, leaving a cold, desolate space in its wake.

"What happened?" asked Orla. "The symbols were returning. What did you do wrong?"

"I don't know." Of course Orla would blame me. I turned to Luc, feeling unmoored by the magic's retreat. "I tried. Even when the magic wouldn't respond, I tried forcing it. It wouldn't . . ."

Wouldn't listen.

"Try again," urged Dominic.

I clutched Luc's hand and stood up. "I need to rest," I told the Quartoren. "Maybe when I'm stronger. When the magic's at full strength again."

"Sure," said Luc. "Sensible. I'll take her home."

He guided me down the stairs and back to the anteroom, an urgency to his movements I couldn't quite decipher. I turned to look at the table one more time, felt a longing so strong it nearly strangled me, and then Luc pulled me Between.

CHAPTER 28

I didn't know when I'd lost the ability to lie to Luc. It should have been a relief—I'd kept so many truths clutched to my chest that it should have felt like freedom. Instead, I felt exposed. Raw. Like I'd given him an advantage I could never reclaim.

If Luc knew all my secrets, how could I keep a safe distance between us?

Definitely something to worry about, but at the moment, there was only one secret he was pursuing. And it had nothing to do with my feelings.

"Thought you needed to rest, Mouse. You sure you're up for visiting your uncle?"

We'd come Between a few blocks from Morgan's, on a quiet residential street with plenty of trees to hide our arrival. I braced a hand against the rough bark of an oak and waited for the world to settle. "He's expecting me. C'mon."

I started down the sidewalk, and he caught my arm. "What spooked you at the Assembly?"

"I was tired, that's all." I couldn't look at him when I spoke.

"You almost had it," he said. "The table was responding to you. I felt how hard you were working, how much you wanted it. Why stop?"

"Because the more I pushed, the more the magic resisted. Your mom wanted me to listen to it, right? So I did."

He crossed his arms and leaned against a nearby tree, watching me closely. "The magic said you needed to get the hell out of Dodge?"

"Pascal's nearly figured the truth. If I'd stayed at the Assembly much longer, he would have put it together. They can't know the magic and I are communicating. Not yet."

"I get it," he said slowly. "But they won't. And we're running out of options."

"Your mom said I should listen *and* speak. Does she mean I should speak to it? Tell it what to do?"

"Makes sense. You're the one it chose, so you're the one who should control it." His fingers dug into the tree bark, like he was as unsteady as me. "Do you know how much power you'll have? Controlling raw magic? What people would do to get hold of you?"

A tremor ran through me at the implication. "I couldn't control it today," I pointed out.

"Could be you need practice. Or you have to give it a bigger push."

No. We were on the wrong track. I knew it with the same certainty that had prompted me to repair the table. "It was working, right? The symbols were coming back. And when you joined in, it got stronger."

Luc nodded. "Kind of the point of bein' the Four-In-One."

Right. *The Four-In-One, the Vessel bound.* As the Vessel, I could work with Air, Earth, and Water. No Arc had ever had three talents. And once Luc and I were bound, I could use fire lines as well. It was why I had been able to renew the lines when they were crumbling, why I'd been able to bond with the magic without destroying the balance between the Houses.

It was also the reason Luc believed we were meant to be together. But this was not the time to consider the ramifications for our relationship. "At the end, when I was really trying, something felt . . . off. Like it was slipping away from me." Like water cupped in my hand, trickling through my fingers. "I held it as tightly as I could, and pushed, but it just . . . left."

"Is it still gone?"

"It's keeping a distance. Like it's skittish. The magic *wanted* me to touch the table, Luc. It was so sad, and when the symbols started to come back, it was happy again. Relieved. Why stop? I did what it wanted. That's why I pushed so hard."

"Listen," he murmured. "Listen and speak."

He mouthed the words, repeating them over and over, pacing back and forth as he tried to work it out. Then he stopped, a grin spreading across his face, eyes lighting with comprehension.

"You know what happened?" I didn't see anything remotely funny about the situation.

"I've got a guess. Maybe the magic chose you 'cause you've got so much in common."

"I don't—"

I broke off as he stepped closer, nudging me back toward the tree. He bent his head to mine, his breath stirring my hair, his voice soft. "You want me."

"This isn't really the time," I said, and placed my hand on his chest, about to shove him away.

He drew back enough to meet my eyes. "You're scared it's not right. You're worried about getting hurt. You're worried about Cujo. It's complicated. So you let me get close, like this. Because you want me, and you like the fact I want you. You like the hum in your blood and the shiver down your back and the butterflies in your stomach. But only on your terms. If I came at you full force, you'd run until your lungs gave out. If I push, you shut down. You tell me no. I push hard enough, and you tell me not ever."

"Can we please do this later?" My traitorous blood was humming, just as he'd said, at the truth in his words.

He shoved his hair out of his eyes, the gesture impatient, the moment gone. "Don't you see? Magic's doing the same thing. The harder you push, the more it pulls back. Even if you're doing what it wants."

Without realizing it, I'd curled my fingers around the edge of his leather coat. I let go, very deliberately, and pulled my own jacket closer around me. "Then what's the point?"

"She said you should speak."

"I begged. I pleaded. I explained. What else could I do?"

"Those symbols were the purest forms of the magic," he said. "It's like a game of telephone. Every time someone casts a spell, they change it a little bit. Their own inflections and accents and voice. It's never an exact duplicate of the original. But you've got a direct line. At the Succession, you spoke the words, and they were the truest I'd ever heard."

"I can't say them now," I reminded him. "It wasn't really me speaking, it was . . ."

I broke off as understanding hit me in the face like a bucket of ice water.

"I spoke for the magic."

He shook his head ruefully. "You know, I have never once won an argument with my mother. She's always right."

"Must be irritating," I said. He was standing so close that I could see the pulse beating in his throat. "You being so confident and all."

"Would be, if she wasn't so sure about us." He stepped back, and I could breathe again. "Your move, Mouse."

I started down the sidewalk toward Morgan's, and he fell into step beside me. "You think I have to speak for the magic? Translate?"

"Makes sense, doesn't it? If the magic's as smart as you say, you're the perfect fit—you were able to bond with it, but you can't use it. You don't even want to. Who better to act as its voice than someone who won't twist it around and use it for their own purposes?"

Deep within me, his words resonated. I didn't know what to feel about it. "And on the topic of purposes," I said, "what was Dominic talking about? That you should do what's best for your people?"

"Doesn't signify. This is bigger. We need to figure out what the magic wants."

"I'm actually more interested in what Dominic wants right now. Because anytime he starts making pronouncements about what's best, he's never referring to what's best for me."

"Forget about Dominic."

"I would like nothing better. But he's after something, and he wants you to get it for him. What is it?"

He dragged a hand through his hair and met my eyes. "You."

Come to think of it, I liked it better when Luc was able to lie to me.

CHAPTER 29

"Dominic's after me." Because Anton, the Seraphim, and two organized crime families weren't enough. I needed Luc's dad gunning for me, too. I walked faster. "Perfect."

"Not like that. He wants you to be on the Quartoren."

"I know that," I said. "Better me than Anton, right?"

"Taking down Anton is a short-term gain. A big one, sure enough. He's thinking long term. With you on the Quartoren, and us bound . . . it makes the House of DeFoudre stronger."

"I'm not going to cut him slack because you and I are together." I paused, hearing what I'd said. "We're not even together. He knows that, right?"

"He figures it's only a matter of time. Like I said, *Maman* ain't often wrong."

"It would be years before you were on the Quartoren, right?"

"Probably. But even so, that kind of connection between Houses would put the Fire Arcs in control for decades. We'd have half the Quartoren sewn up."

"Wouldn't the Water Arcs benefit, too?"

"Sure. But DeFoudres have always held a seat on the Quartoren. When the table was formed and the Quartoren established, we were there. Politics and power struggles are in our blood. Your uncle's not a bad teacher, but his business is small potatoes compared to this."

"I see." And I did—or most of it, anyway. I couldn't out-maneuver Dominic—I was too new to this world. He'd find ways to manipulate me, even if I kept my guard up. "What do you think?"

He lifted a shoulder, almost surly. "I don't know."

"Really? It seems pretty clear-cut. Either you want me on the Quartoren or you don't."

"I want Anton stopped. I want the Seraphim scattered on the wind like the ashes of a campfire. I want *you*, Mouse."

"There's your answer," I said. Relief broke over me like a wave. "Wasn't so hard."

He continued, eyes fixed straight ahead. "But I also want what's best for my people. I'm obligated to do right by my House. If I don't, I'm not much of an Heir—and Theo died for nothing. It has to matter. I took up this life for him, and I need it to mean something."

I understood the sentiment too well. After all, I'd felt the same after Verity had died. But I also knew how easy it was to lose yourself along the way. Marguerite's concern over Luc made perfect sense now. "That's the Heir talking."

"That's a man who's seen good people sacrificed on ac-count of fate and doesn't want it to be in vain. If you think that's only my title, and not who I am deep down, you don't know me at all."

"I know both sides of you. What I don't know is who will be standing next to me at that ceremony. Because if it's Luc, I can trust you with my life. And if it's the Heir, I can't trust you at all."

His face hardened. "I don't take kindly to ultimatums."

"And I don't like being played." I hitched my bag over my shoulder. Morgan's was a block away, and I felt the wards part to let us through. "Speaking of which, I have to go see my uncle."

"Let me come along."

"He said to come alone." Somehow, it seemed even more

important to keep my two lives separate now that Billy knew about the Arcs. Like too much contact would endanger both of them. "It might be better if you waited out here."

"I'll cloak myself. He won't even notice me."

I pressed my lips together. It would be safer, definitely. He'd drop the concerned uncle act he kept putting on for Luc's benefit, and I could get more information about the list of names that everyone was so interested in.

"You can't react," I said finally. "He's horrible, okay? He'll say things you won't like, he'll threaten me—but you have to stay hidden, no matter what."

A grin ghosted his face. "Sounds familiar."

It was, actually. Months ago, we'd gone to the Dauphine and he'd left me at the bar with nearly identical instructions. Of course, while he'd been in a booth chatting with Niobe, the Seraphim had come after me. "Let's hope it ends a little better this time around."

"Let's," he said dryly.

By the time we reached the front door, Luc had vanished. I could feel him a few steps behind me as I entered.

"Go ahead back, Mo. He's waiting for you," said Charlie. Normally, his moon-eyed face was wreathed in smiles. Now it was a mask of good cheer that didn't quite cover the worry underneath.

"Thanks." I wound around clusters of people, ducked under the uplifted tray of one of the usual waitresses, and made my way back. The temptation to look for Luc was overwhelming, but I kept my eyes on my uncle, seated in his booth. Showing fear would be the worst thing I could do.

"Feeling better?" Billy asked as I slid into the seat. "Your mother was worried about you."

"Fabulous." I sat down, steeling myself to look composed despite the tangle of nerves inside me.

"Glad to hear it. Your mother says you and Donnelly are on the outs."

"He knows about our deal." The words tasted like ash.

"Ah. Never say I didn't warn you, Mo."

"Did you hear me say that?"

"Ah, well. You've plenty of other options at hand." He pretended to think for a moment. "Like that young man from the alley. Luc. I'm sure he has many fine qualities."

"Wow." I made a show of checking my watch. "That took even less time than I expected. Luc's not going to help you. Can I leave now?"

"You haven't heard me out!" he said as I slid out of the booth. "The lad's obviously taken with you. He'd lend us a hand, if you were the one asking."

"Shame I won't be asking, then." It was humiliating to listen to Billy's machinations, knowing Luc was on the other side of the booth's wall, hearing everything.

"Not even for Donnelly's sake?" There was a crafty note to the words, and I paused in the middle of buttoning my coat.

"We had a deal." So foolish to think Billy would honor it. But he'd always done business on the strength of his word. It was the one thing he wouldn't break. He'd lie outright, but he never went back on a promise. Magic had changed the rules. Again.

"Sit down," he said.

After a moment, I obeyed. "You gave me your word."

"And I've kept it. Think of this as a renegotiation of terms. I brought you in because I needed someone who could help me deal with Ekomov. You've done well enough, but he's still a complication. If we could be rid of him entirely, there'd be no need for you to continue working for me."

Like I really believed he'd let me go. "Get to the part about Colin."

He lifted a shoulder, negligently. "I want Ekomov removed. You want to start over someplace fresh, with Donnelly at your side. If you can wrangle your new friend into helping me with my situation, that's exactly what the two of you can do. I'll even provide for Tess, wherever you end up."

The high wooden sides of the booth seemed to close in, blocking out the rest of the world. All I could see was Billy, dangling my dream in front of me. Freedom. A future with Colin. We could go to New York; we could go to Des Moines, we could go . . . anywhere. We could have the life I'd constructed in my head before everything fell apart, filled with lazy Sunday afternoons and Friday nights at the movies. He'd teach me to drive the truck and keep me company while I did my coursework. We'd be happy. My entire body seemed lighter at the prospect, suffused with a mixture of hope and relief, like I could slip right out of my skin and be free. I could have my life back, even better than before.

All I had to do was ask Luc to kill for me.

I could feel the bubbling happiness evaporate at the idea. I tried to justify it—I'd killed Evangeline. I was planning on killing Anton. Why should Yuri Ekomov be any different? He'd been nice enough to me, but he wasn't a good man. He was a criminal. He'd ordered countless deaths. He was threatening my neighborhood. Eliminating Ekomov would make the world a better place—and my family, in particular, would benefit. Would it really be so wrong?

I didn't feel light anymore. I felt weighed down by something dark and sticky, the hunger for vengeance heavy within me.

But this wasn't vengeance, it was greed. Manipulation. Billy using me, me using Luc. It was wrong.

The things I'd done had been my choices, and mine alone. How could I ask Luc to kill someone in cold blood, so I could be with another guy? I couldn't imagine anything more selfish. I couldn't imagine what it would do to us.

Luc stood a few feet away, hidden from everyone but me, waiting for my response. Our connection was as taut as my nerves, but utterly silent. This was my call, he seemed to be saying. But I couldn't make a decision like this for him. I'd tried that with Colin and it had ruined us. I wouldn't take that chance again.

"No."

Billy blinked at me. "No?"

"No. I will not ask Luc to take out Ekomov for you. I will not use the magic to help you. I will not use the Donnellys' futures as a bargaining chip with you. I have *learned* from my mistakes, unlike everyone else in this family." I stood up, slinging my bag over my shoulder.

Rage twisted his features. "You'll make all new mistakes, then. And this *is* a mistake for you, Mo. You'll regret this moment."

"Not as much as you," I said. "Are we finished?"

He caught sight of someone over my shoulder and his expression changed from intimidating to irritated.

"We certainly are. Tomorrow," he said. "Delivery. Don't be late."

"I'm never late," I said, and left. The bar was starting to fill up, but I searched the room, looking for an indication of what had rattled Billy. Charlie was scowling, and it didn't take long for me to see why—the two cops who'd harassed my father the day after his return were standing at the bar, scanning the room. One of them caught my eye, nudged his partner, and nodded at me.

They knew who I was. And I was willing to bet they knew I was working with Jenny. Before their attention gave me away, I ducked my head and left, Luc hidden at my side.

CHAPTER 30

"We need to talk about that?" Luc asked, when we were far enough away that he could shed the concealment spell.

"Not even a little," I said. I needed time to absorb what I'd done and why. The impulse that had seized me was too fragile for words, and too important to risk. So we walked in silence back to my house, Luc's hand gentle on my arm, his concern palpable.

"Thank you," he said finally. "Cost you some, that meeting."

You won't understand the price until it's too late. I shivered and tucked my nose deeper in my scarf. "Everything costs," I said, the thick wool making my voice muzzy and indistinct.

"You could have taken the deal. Left with Cujo. Gone to New York, the way you and Vee had planned. He was givin' you a shot at your dream, and you turned it down."

"Maybe it's time to wake up," I said. So much for not discussing it. "I'm not going to ask you to kill a man in cold blood. Not for my sake. This isn't your fight. It's not even your world."

"You turned him down for my sake?"

It wasn't a lie to tell him no. I had turned down Billy's offer for lots of reasons. I didn't want to follow in my uncle's footsteps. I didn't want to use the people I cared about as leverage, or dictate the terms of Colin's life simply because I could. And maybe I'd turned it down for Luc and me, too, as a way of ensuring any possible future we had was untainted by my family or his duties. But telling him that would set off more discussions. And decisions. I settled instead for a slanted truth. "Partly."

"Why you gotta do that?" he asked. "You can't keep sacrificing yourself for other people, Mouse. Not even me."

"You should be thrilled," I said. "Isn't this what you wanted? For me to choose a life with the Arcs?"

"This is you giving up your life to save everyone else. You have got to stop, Mouse. Your life matters, and if you keep acting like it doesn't, everyone's going to suffer. Look at the bigger picture."

"I'm sorry," I said, lacing my voice with a sweetness I didn't feel. "I was under the impression you wanted me to sacrifice my Flat life so that I could speak for the magic, stop the Seraphim, and take a seat on the Quartoren. Now you're saying I should just do what I want? God, Luc. You think the entire reason I exist is to give a voice to the magic, like my own doesn't even matter. Even the name is an insult—the Vessel. Like I'm empty without the magic. Like I'm *nothing*."

My muscles were clenched and shaking with anger—not at Luc, but at my own helplessness—and I quickened my steps. Turning down Billy's offer was the right thing to do, but part of me mourned the future I'd just given up. All I wanted now was to go home.

Luc caught up to me just across the street from my house. He grabbed me by the shoulders and spun me to face him. "You're not nothing. You are strong and smart and stubborn as hell. I have watched you do amazing things without the magic, and it's only made me love you more." His voice turned sharper, as if he was angry, too. "But you have got to stop running from this. You're so afraid that magic is going to take over your life, you're letting fear do it instead—and that's even worse. Don't. Find something else to define you."

"Like what?" I had spent my entire life defined by other

people. By my past. Luc defined himself by his fate. None of those options appealed to me.

"Your choices," he said, and touched my lips with a single finger. "And you've got to make 'em for yourself, and soon, or people are going to take those choices away."

"Do you have choices?"

"Some. Now I'm trying to do right by them."

Across the street, my mother peered out the picture window. "I should go."

"Mouse," he said as I started home. "Thank you."

"For what?"

"Thinking of me."

I didn't tell him how impossible it was to do otherwise, lately.

CHAPTER 31

"Who was that boy?" my mother demanded as I hung up my coat. Apparently we weren't going to wait to start the interrogation.

I'd kept Luc apart from my life for as long as I could, but if I had even the slightest hope of keeping my Flat life, it was time to introduce him. Gradually. "A guy I know."

"You were walking with him."

"Yes, Mom. We were walking. People do it all the time."

"And what does Colin have to say about this?"

I tried to keep my voice steady. "Colin has very little to say to me right now. Or hadn't you noticed?"

The thin, hard line of her mouth softened a bit. "I'd hoped you two would be able to sort through all of that."

Not for the first time, I wondered how much my mom truly saw. More than I gave her credit for, obviously, if she knew how bad things were between us. "You said to give him some space. Dad said to give him some space. Behold, space."

"Taking up with some strange boy is not what we meant. Making Colin jealous is not the way to go about winning him back."

"I'm not trying to make him jealous." If I'd wanted to make him jealous, I would have let him think more had happened between me and Luc than truly had. "And Luc's not a strange boy."

"Luc? That's his name? How do you know him?"

I touched the scar on my palm. "He was a friend of Verity's."

"Good heavens, Mo. I thought we'd put that behind us." She pressed a fist against her heart, concern deepening the lines around her mouth. I knew what she was thinking—after Verity's death, I'd disappeared somewhere she couldn't follow and come back full of secrets. Now I was slipping away again, without Colin to pull me back.

"It's never going to be behind me, Mom." No matter what my motives were now, it had all started in that alley. My path changed in that instant. I had changed. Forever.

"I'm not saying you should forget about her. But it's not healthy to dwell on the past. Not when you should be thinking about your future."

"I am thinking about it," I said through gritted teeth. "I don't think about anything else."

"Let it go, Annie," said my father, emerging from the basement. "What did Billy want to see you about?"

"My work schedule," I said carefully. "He needs me tomorrow."

My father's scowl made it clear he understood which job I was referring to—and that he didn't approve. "And you agreed?"

"I didn't have much of a choice."

My mother huffed and busied herself with dinner. "As long as it doesn't interfere with your schoolwork. I don't want you thinking you can let your grades slip just because you're graduating. Or because of boys, Mo. You're too sensible for that."

Before I could respond, there was a knock at the door. My parents exchanged glances.

"It seems a little late for company," my mom said. "Is it Colin?"

"I doubt it," I muttered, and opened the door. "Hey!"

Lena stood shivering on the porch. "Bad time?"

"Excellent time." Any excuse to avoid talking to my parents. "Come on in. What's up?"

"I brought your homework," she said. "And your cell. And a well-developed sense of curiosity."

"Lena, come in!" said my mom. "Would you like to stay for dinner? I made plenty."

"I wish I could," she said. "Maybe another time?"

"Of course," my mom replied, and stood in the doorway, clearly not interested in leaving us alone to chat.

"Come on upstairs," I said. "You can fill me in."

"I have had a very weird day" she said as I closed the door behind us. "First, Constance Grey keeps asking me if I've heard from you. If I know what's wrong or when you're coming back. I am assuming the girl has your phone number and knows how to dial, so why is she asking me? She doesn't even like you. Then your guidance counselor pulls me out of class to ask if I'll bring your stuff home, since you went home sick. Except everyone knows you weren't sick, because if you were, Colin would have come and picked you up. But he showed up at school, right on schedule, and I had to tell him you were gone. Which means she's covering for you. Again, weird."

I said nothing.

"And then there's your phone. Which has been ringing constantly. I finally answered it, and whoever was on the other end hung up. And then called back. Weirdness abounds."

I pulled my phone out of the bag and checked it. Jenny Kowalski. Which meant something was going on, and she either needed my help or wanted to warn me. Either way, bad news. I wondered if the cops at Morgan's this afternoon were there for me or my dad.

"Thanks for bringing this back."

She threw herself down on the chair. "So. Is this one of those times where you tell me it's complicated and you can't explain, and you're really sorry?"

I didn't even bother to answer.

"Okay," she said. "But tell me this much: whenever you pull this routine, Luc's involved. Is he back?"

"Yes."

"And are you two . . ."

"I don't know."

"You and Colin are really done, then?"

I pressed a hand against my stomach, as if it might stop the nausea that swamped me every time I asked myself that question. "He's really angry, Lena. Like, he might never stop being angry. I can't fix it."

"So Luc's your rebound?"

"Luc is . . ." More than a rebound. More than an alternative, even. Luc was all the things I could be, and all the things that scared me, and all the things I'd ever dreamed about in the most secret, most hidden places of my heart. Which made him more dangerous than anything else in my life, Mob or magic. "Complicated."

Lena toyed with a pencil on my desk. "How much trouble are you in?"

I nudged the phone and met her eyes. "A lot."

"You should let me help you out."

"It's not that simple." I couldn't expose Lena to the Arcs— and I wouldn't expose her to the Outfit. "It's too dangerous."

"Mo. Listen to me. Let me help you *out*."

The intensity of her expression—pinched with worry, color high on her olive skin—made me realize what she was saying. She didn't mean she'd pass along messages or cover for me when I skipped class. She could give me another way out—a new identity, a fresh start. But there was no hiding from the magic, even if I wanted to.

And I didn't want to. There was too much at stake in both of my worlds. If I left, I wanted it to be because I was heading toward something, not running away.

"I appreciate it. But I have to see this through."

She bit her lip. "You're sure? We can make you disappear."

"I don't want to disappear anymore."

"Okay," she said after a long minute. "Then you'd better get cracking on Calc. Test tomorrow."

I groaned.

"See? Now you wish you'd said yes, don't you?" We headed back downstairs and she gave me a quick hug. "Tell me if you change your mind, okay?"

"I won't. But thanks."

After dinner, I went upstairs and listened to all ten of Jenny's messages. They were nearly identical—the only difference was that each sounded more panicked than the last.

"It's me. Listen, I just got a call from Nick. He says to forget about the records for The Slice. Or Morgan's. Everything." She was holding back tears, without much success, her frustration palpable even in voice mail. "They thank us for our help, but the investigation will proceed without our involvement, and oh, hey, they're sorry about my dead dad."

I heard her blow her nose, take a deep breath, and continue. "They're cutting us out of the loop, Mo. I think they're going to move soon, and they don't want us involved. You need to be ready. And so does your boyfriend."

I flopped back on the bed, ignoring the tightness in my chest at the reminder that Colin wasn't my boyfriend anymore, trying to formulate a plan. The police wouldn't go after Colin, I was almost sure. Billy had long ago cut him out of anything important, anything illegal. The minute he'd realized we were together, Billy had decided Colin wasn't loyal enough to be trusted. My mom, of course, would be protected. She might have an idea of what was going on, but she hadn't participated. She'd been kept in the dark, used again and again.

Which left my dad. And he'd thrown himself back into life with the Outfit with such enthusiasm, no one would question his loyalty to my uncle. He might not have been back for very long, but he'd certainly managed to ingratiate himself with the Forellis again, and I didn't doubt there was a mountain of evidence against him already.

I'd begged him not to, and he'd ignored me, even after the police had made it clear they were watching. He'd been so convinced he was doing right by us, making up for lost time. And now we'd lose him all over again.

Unless I warned him.

The danger was that he'd tell Billy. He'd realize I was working with the police, and he'd choose the Outfit over me. Again.

But he might not. He might decide to run. Maybe he'd even convince my mom to go with him. But if he didn't—if he stayed loyal to Billy and the Forellis, he'd be heading back to Terre Haute, and my mom would be devastated.

I didn't know what to do. Tell my dad and risk my shot at Billy, or stay quiet and send him back to prison?

I reached for my phone by instinct, dialed the numbers before I realized what I was doing.

"What's wrong?" Colin asked, answering on the first ring.

I closed my eyes and lost myself in the safe, familiar sound. It was so tempting to pour out all of my worries, let him tell me what to do, let him take care of it.

But I'd told him I could take care of myself. Calling him in the middle of the night to fix my life was admitting I couldn't. And I wasn't ready to admit that, or go back to being the sheltered schoolgirl he'd met a lifetime ago.

"Nothing," I lied. Everything. Including us. "I'm going to school tomorrow. I figured you'd want to know."

"You called me at . . ." I heard the rustling of sheets as he sat up, no doubt reaching for the alarm clock. "Midnight? To tell me that? What happened when you met with Billy?"

Of course he knew about the meeting. He'd probably been watching Morgan's the whole time. "He wanted to renegotiate our deal. I said no."

"Why?"

"I figured you would not appreciate me making decisions about your future without talking to you. Or at all."

"You figured right," he said. "What did he want from you?"

"He wants the magic. To take down Ekomov, he says, but he'd keep hammering until he was running the entire Outfit."

"And you said no." Grim satisfaction carried through the connection. "He's not going to give in."

"Neither am I."

There was a long silence. I listened to the sound of his breathing, deep and regular, let myself relax into the rhythm of it. For a second, things were good again.

"You and Luc saw the Quartoren today."

My eyes snapped open, hearing a wealth of questions in his blunt statement, only a few of which I knew how to answer. "We have a plan. You won't like it."

"I never do. Will it make a difference what I say?"

"Not this time."

"Did it ever?"

I exhaled slowly. "Every day. From the minute we met."

"That's something, anyway." The line fell quiet again. "It's late, Mo. Go to sleep."

The weary dismissal felt like a slap. "Sure. Sorry to have woken you." But I didn't hang up the phone.

"Was there something else?" he asked.

My resolve weakened. There was an awful, echoing sensation in my chest, and I pressed a fist against my mouth to keep from begging for another chance.

"Mo." He paused. "What is it?"

"Nothing. Sorry."

"You sure?"

"I'll see you in the morning," I said softly. This time, I did hang up.

CHAPTER 32

I'd never been the kind of girl who got so caught up in drama that I ignored school. But the drama in my life these days went beyond the usual worries—what had happened at someone's party, the latest round of dating musical chairs, who'd been gossiping about whom—so maybe it was understandable that I'd let homework and journalism and all my other responsibilities slip without realizing it.

Realization hit me full force the next day at school, when I had no lab report written up for Chemistry, no Spanish translation ready, and I left at least a third of my calc test blank. I could explain it away as senior slump, maybe. Or the lingering effects of being out sick. But the fact was, nothing at school held the kind of weight it used to. It didn't even have the appeal. I still found the puzzle of differential equations and molar reactions engaging—I liked working my way through the problems, seeing the elegance of the solution forming in front of me. Constant. Orderly. Reassuring. But they were no longer enough to distract me from the other problems in my life.

Which didn't stop me from freezing, deer-in-the-headlights style, when I logged into my e-mail during Journalism and found a reply from NYU's admissions department.

Lena slid into the seat next to me as the final bell rang. "Bad news?"

"Don't know." I held the mouse in a death grip but couldn't seem to click on the message.

She peered at the monitor. "You have to open it," she said.

"Do I?"

"Mo. It's NYU. You've been waiting years for this."

"It doesn't matter," I said, throat tight. "I'm stuck here either way."

"But don't you want to know? Even if you have to decline, don't you want to know—"

"What I could have had?" The words sounded bitter, even to my ears. "I'm not sure that's such a great idea."

"Then focus on what you *can* have. Either way, open the damn e-mail. The not-knowing will make you crazy. It'll hold you back."

I didn't move.

"You want me to open it for you?"

"No." Slowly, deliberately, I pushed the pointer across the screen and clicked the link.

"Dear Ms. Fitzgerald," I read, voice shaking, "We are pleased to offer you a spot in New York University's class of. . . ."

Lena squealed and threw her arms around me. "You did it! Please, please, *please* let me be there when you tell Jill. I'm begging you. She's going to lose her mind."

I didn't say anything.

She let go, million-watt grin fading. "You're not happy. You should be happy, Mo."

I was. I wanted to call Verity, jump up and down, shriek with laughter and start shopping for my dorm room. Make a spreadsheet of my classes for the next four years. But I couldn't do any of those things. Verity was gone. The path we'd laid out was closed to me now. Thinking about it would eat me alive. I could feel it already, the same slithering hunger that reared up every time I thought about going after Anton. Dwelling on what I'd lost would only give it strength, until it took me over completely.

"I told you, it doesn't matter. I can't go."

"But you got in. You can celebrate a little, right? This is what you and Verity always wanted. And maybe you'll find a way."

"Maybe," I said, with an unsteady laugh. "God, it would have pissed Jill off, wouldn't it? Being stuck with me for another four years."

Lena watched me silently. I closed my eyes, shook my head once, and opened them again. "Anyway. Better get to work, right?"

I logged out and turned to face the room. Around us, people were writing stories, popping out to do interviews, arguing cheerfully about the layout. Lena took a breath and looked at the list of articles still to be turned in. "You finished that editorial?"

I didn't need to rummage through my bag to know the answer. "No. I meant to, but . . ."

"Things got crazy."

"I'm sorry. I'll crank it out right now."

She waved a hand. "I'll make one of the juniors do it. Good practice for them."

I watched her approach one of the girls standing near the printer, who nodded eagerly at the chance for a front-page story.

Nick Petros was used to writing front-page stories, I thought—the juicier the better. And now he was telling Jenny we couldn't help with the case against Billy. Something didn't make sense.

"Can I make a call in your office?" I asked Ms. Corelli, the newspaper advisor. "It's a little loud out here for an interview."

"Don't touch my chocolate stash," she warned, but waved me into the tiny room. Nick's card was still pinned to the bulletin board, a souvenir from his visit to our class last fall. I dialed, hands shaking, and was surprised when he picked up on the second ring.

"Petros." There was the sound of hunt-and-peck typing in the background.

"It's Mo Fitzgerald," I said, and waited.

"Mo." The typing stopped. "What's wrong?"

"You told Jenny we weren't part of the investigation anymore."

"You're minors," he said. "You're too young to be involved."

"It didn't bother you before," I pointed out. "What changed?"

He sucked in air with a whistling sound. "We're at a sensitive juncture. There's a lot happening, and it's better if you two stay out of it. You did good work, but you need to leave it alone now."

"I can still help! There's a list, Nick. People my uncle's bought off. People who work for him. You said you needed proof, and I can get it for you. I just need a little time."

"No. Look, Mo. I didn't get into this with Jenny, but I'll tell you, because I think you're smart enough to see the bigger picture. The people in charge of the investigation are very clear. You are not to be involved. Period."

"But the list . . ."

"We know about the list, and we'll get it. But you're out, Mo. I'm sorry."

I thought about Jenny's choked, tearful voice in the message. The frustration she must have felt. "Yeah. That's what you told Jenny, right? Do you really think that helps her? She lost her dad, Nick. She needs to see this through."

His voice was kind, in a gruff sort of way, but absolutely firm. "Jenny needs to let this go, and so do you. I'm sorry, Mo. It's done."

He hung up the phone, and I sat for a moment, stunned. The bigger picture? Taking down Billy and the Forellis was the bigger picture, and that list was the key. I was their best chance at getting it.

And I wasn't giving up.

Colin was waiting for me after school, the red truck sitting amid midwinter slush like a Christmas ornament that had yet to be packed away. I squared my shoulders and climbed in.

"Where to?" he asked.

A few degrees warmer than icy politeness, but a long way from normal. Colin kept his hands at ten and two, his eyes on the road, and his guard up.

"Morgan's."

"Another delivery." It wasn't a question, so I didn't bother to answer. "I wish you wouldn't do this."

"My life," I said, staring out the window. I wondered what the weather was like in New York. Wondered if, some- day, I'd see it. "My decision."

"I guess it is. Doesn't mean I don't worry. Or want to help."

"You don't want to help me," I said softly. "You want to do it for me."

"You make it sound like I want to hurt you."

"I know you wouldn't. But keeping me safe . . . it's not enough. It's not how I want to spend my life, sheltered and on the sidelines. Not anymore. I don't want other people de- ciding how I should live, or what I can do."

"You signed all of those choices over to Billy," he pointed out.

"I'm going to bring Billy down," I said. "And then I'll leave. You won't have to worry anymore. You'll be free of all of it."

"I will always worry about you," he said, jabbing at the buttons on the dash.

"I know." And I knew what was coming—the speech where he let me down gently. Where we promised to stay friends. I hated it. I wanted to cover my ears. To stop time. To jump out of the truck while it was still moving. Anything to stave off the inevitable. "It's okay. You don't need to . . ."

He cut me off. "I'm so angry with you I can't see straight."

"You have a right." I bowed my head. It hurt to speak, but I forced the words out. "I'm sorry."

He pulled over. "I don't . . . I can't get past the mad."

I nodded.

"But I will. I love you, Mo."

I felt the tears welling up, escaping down my cheeks. "I know. That's not the problem."

"Don't say that." He brushed away my tears but more followed. "We can fix it."

"You can't fix me. I'm not broken, just . . . changed. I have this magic, and I can do something with it. Something amazing. I *want* to, Colin, even if it's dangerous. But you hate it. All of it. The magic, and the Arcs, and everything I've been working to save."

He didn't deny it.

"It's never going to stop, you know. I'm tied to the magic for the rest of my life. It's part of me, and you hate it. And if we were together . . ."

"I wouldn't hate you."

"No. But you'd be miserable because of me. And I'd start to regret what I'd done, and who I'd become, even though it's this incredible thing, because it made you unhappy. I can't do that. I can't afford to regret my whole life. And I don't want to resent you for making me feel that way."

"I wouldn't." He kissed me, and I tried to memorize the feeling of his mouth, the taste of him, the circle of his arms keeping the rest of the world at bay for just a moment longer. "It's a job. At the end of the day, you put it aside, and we're together. We can make it work."

"The magic is part of me. I can't put it aside." Wouldn't, even if I could.

"So it's the magic that's to blame."

"No. It's me."

"And Luc."

I shook my head, covered his hands with mine. "That would be easier, wouldn't it? But it's not Luc."

"What, then?"

"We'd end up damaging each other. You can't build a life with someone who's constantly running off into danger, because it'll make you insane. And I can't build a life with someone who wants me to give up a huge part of myself, and thinks it's for my own good. It will ruin us. I don't want us to be ruined, Colin. I'd rather be done now, while you don't hate me, than wait for the day that you do. That's not a life, it's waiting for the ax to fall."

"Mo . . ."

"Tell me I'm wrong." I was crying openly, breath coming in raggedy hitches. "You can't, can you?"

He drew back, slumping against his door. "So I'm supposed to shut off how I feel about you?"

"I don't know. I don't know what comes next."

"And you think I do?"

I flinched at the harshness in his voice, swiped at my tears, and said nothing.

He started the truck again, and we finished the trip to Morgan's in miserable silence.

After he parked, he said, "Do you want another bodyguard? It would probably make Billy's day."

"I don't need a bodyguard." My head throbbed from all the crying, and I rubbed my temples.

"You've got two crime families interested in you. I might not be able to protect you from the magic, but I can still keep an eye out for Forelli and Ekomov."

"You'd stay?" I didn't believe it. Didn't deserve it. Didn't know if I could handle it.

"You think I could leave? I told you before. The most important thing is making sure you're safe."

"And once Billy's done? Then what?"

"Then . . . I don't know. It's not for you to worry about." The reproach was clear in his voice, and I could feel the lines of our relationship being redrawn, the rules rewritten to take in this new reality.

I ducked my head. "Are you coming with me for the delivery?"

"Didn't I just answer that?"

I nodded and went inside.

"What the hell's wrong with you?" my uncle said the minute I stepped into the back room. "You look terrible."

"Do you have something for me or not?"

"Here." He handed me a thumb drive, small enough to tuck into my pocket.

I turned it over in my hands. It was navy blue with white lettering, a tiny St. Brigid's crest embossed on the side. The same kind you could buy at the school store. "I take it this is supposed to be mine?"

"Verisimilitude," he said, looking way too pleased with himself. "You copied files off the computer here while I was out dealing with the police."

"The police were here?" There'd been no sign of them when I came in. Then again, I wasn't really looking.

"All the time these days. They like to harass your father and me, for all the good it will do them. Waste of my tax dollars."

"Yeah. It's an outrage. So, what's on here?"

"Payroll, of a sort." The list, then. The one Jenny needed, that my dad had warned me about. Billy made a shooing motion. "Go on with you. I've a timetable to keep."

"It's not like he's going anywhere," I said. But I pocketed the drive and headed out again.

My father caught me at the door. "He gave you the list?"

"So much for stalling," I said.

"Give it to me," my dad said. "You're upset. You shouldn't be dealing with Ekomov like this."

There was a dull ache in my chest, but I ignored it. No matter what Nick said, and no matter what happened to me and Colin, I had to honor my deal with Billy. "I'm fine. But this is a huge gamble. Why risk letting Ekomov have these names?"

"He thinks the payoff's worth it. Like I said, it's his silver bullet," he said.

"No. This is his backup plan." The Arcs had been Billy's silver bullet, not a computer file. And my uncle was canny and cagey, but he wasn't a gambler. He wouldn't risk something like this if he wasn't assured it would eliminate Ekomov. I'd expected him to come up with a new way of threatening me, and instead he'd gone in a different direction entirely. It didn't make sense, but I was so wrung out from the conversation with Colin, I couldn't figure it out.

"You don't need to do this," my dad said. "Let me handle it."

The door to the back room swung open. "She'll be fine, Jack," called my uncle. "But they're expecting her."

I grabbed the delivery cart and shrugged. "I can handle Ekomov."

"Never doubted it for a minute," Billy said, coming to stand next to my dad. "Mo's a girl of many talents."

As soon as I stepped outside, Colin climbed out of the truck. "Took a long time."

"Got waylaid by my dad. Who has suddenly sprung a conscience."

"I'm not sure how sudden it is," he said. His eyes were shuttered, dark and impossible to read. He turned up his collar and we started off. The sun was setting, the heavy blanket of clouds turning everything dim and dingy, the cars throwing slush against the curb with a hissing sound, the shops and restaurants and offices casting feeble yellow glows that barely reached the sidewalk. "He's been worried about you ever since he got back. I think it started before then, even."

"So he went to work for Billy?"

"Easier to look out for you if he's on the inside."

Memories stirred uneasily. "He said you'd look out for me if something happened to him."

"Yeah. That was before . . ." He jerked his head back in the direction of the truck. Before I'd betrayed his trust, destroyed our relationship, stomped all over his heart. Not hard to imagine that Colin might feel unenthusiastic at the prospect now.

"You don't need to," I said quickly. "That's not why I asked. It's just a weird thing to say, isn't it? Like he thinks something might happen to him."

"First, I *would* look after you. That doesn't end because we're not together. But you made it pretty clear you don't need it. Second, your dad picked a dangerous line of work, and he knows it. He made a plan, and hopes like hell he won't need it."

"Is that what you did? For Tess?"

Colin scrubbed a hand through his hair. "If something happened to me, Tess wouldn't notice. But, yeah, I made sure she'd be taken care of."

"You're a good brother to her." A good person. The best I'd ever known. God, I missed him already.

He didn't respond. When we reached the door of Shady Acres, he put a hand out for the cart. "I'll come inside with you."

"It has to be like usual. He can't know you know."

Colin frowned.

"I've done it a hundred times," I said, and his scowl deepened. "Okay, not a hundred. Ten, maybe. Fifteen, tops."

Edie buzzed us in. He held the door while I wrestled the cart through.

"Five minutes," I said, and headed down the hallway, past the library and the game room. They were all quiet, the residents likely having dinner. I could smell the faint aroma of pot roast and overcooked green beans overlying the pine-scented cleaner. My nerves prickled. Even the magic was on edge. *Do the job and get out,* I told myself. Billy was up to something, but right now all I could think about was the hollowness inside me where Colin had once been.

I wanted to scream so badly my throat ached with the effort of keeping it in. I wasn't feeling regret, because I knew with an awful, thudding certainty I had done the right thing. But it wasn't supposed to be like this. If you loved someone, that was supposed to take away all the obstacles. Give you the strength to overcome whatever difficulties you had. Make you better and stronger and truer. Colin had pushed me to find my voice and take charge of my life and make my own path—and then that path had taken me away from him. Maybe my English teacher would call it irony. I called it unfair.

I pushed open the swinging door of the kitchen. Normally,

Ekomov waited until I'd started unloading the cart before entering, but today he stood at the counter, age-spotted hands curling over the top of his cane, the wrinkles on his face sagging heavily. He'd always been old—older than Billy, older than Orla. But I'd never mistaken him for frail or helpless. Only dangerous. The courtly mannerisms, the offers of help—they were an indulgence. He could afford to be generous with me because he knew I was trapped.

But today, he was only old, and the look on his face was decidedly ungenerous.

"You're late," he said.

"Busy afternoon," I said, and started setting the pies on the counter, lining up the boxes neatly to calm myself.

"I have always thought it . . . odd . . . that you would choose to betray your uncle. That you would put so little value on family."

I thought about what Colin had said, that my dad had rejoined Billy because he wanted to protect me from the inside. About how my mom had given up her dreams and her husband to give me a solid future. Putting Billy in jail was the best thing I could do for my family and the Donnellys. But Ekomov was watching me carefully, so I kept my expression neutral.

"My uncle doesn't value me," I said, trying for nonchalant despite the tightening of my nerves. *Go,* the magic seemed to urge, sending me the image of a mouse scampering across an open field, an eagle poised to strike. *Go now.*

"He sends you here. That suggests he values you greatly."

"Because I deliver pies?" I injected a note of exasperation into my voice. I finished stacking the white cardboard boxes, pocketed the payment envelope just like usual. "He doesn't even know you're here."

"Oh, my dear Mo. I wish that were true." He sounded genuinely sad. "For both our sakes."

I edged away, toward the door leading back to the lobby. I needed to escape. To buy myself some time. "Here," I said, tossing the flash drive on the counter. "I brought this. Files from the office computer. I copied them while the police were harassing my dad."

My dad, who had not wanted me to come here. I was beginning to think he was right.

"You were supposed to arrive earlier," Ekomov said again.

"I'm sorry. It was a bad day." I twisted my fingers together, glancing at the door. "I hope I didn't waste your time."

He lifted his shoulders, let them fall again heavily. "We waited. I learned many things I would not have otherwise known."

"Great," I hissed as the corner of the cabinet banged my hip. "Like I said, the drive's got—wait. *We?*"

"We," he said. "I did not wait alone."

The far door, the one that led to the dining room, swung open.

"Hello, Mo." Anton smiled, sunny as a spring morning.

CHAPTER 33

My mouth dropped open, but I couldn't get a full breath. "You?"

"Surprise," Anton said, with barely restrained glee.

"Mr. Ekomov," I said, "this man . . . I don't know what he promised you, but he is dangerous. You can't trust him. Believe me when I tell you that you do not want to work with him."

"I'm not," Ekomov said. "We had a good amount of time to talk, waiting for you. I am not the one working with your Mr. Anton."

"He's not mine." I paused. "What did you talk about?"

"All sorts of things," Anton said. "You, specifically. Yuri was *so* disheartened to realize you were working for your uncle. He'd thought you were estranged."

"We are."

"And yet you've been working for him all along."

I closed my eyes for a brief second, opened them to see the resignation on Ekomov's face. Resignation, not anger. The realization unnerved me. "I had to protect Colin. I couldn't say no."

"Now, that's not quite true," said Anton, wagging a finger at me as if I were a child caught in a lie. I chopped down the cherry tree. I ate the last cookie. I work for my mobster uncle, not you. "You told him no just the other day. Ungrateful, when you consider all he's done for you. Anyone would take offense."

And then I understood. "Son of a bitch. He figured he'd team up with you instead."

You'll regret this moment, Billy had said.

"What's that saying you're so fond of?" Anton said to Ekomov, who was leaning heavily on the cane, his face like clay. "The enemy of my enemy . . ."

"Is my friend," Ekomov replied. "I am not so fond of it lately."

"If it's any consolation, he turned me down the first time I offered a partnership. Thought he could get through to you. Happily, you did the honorable thing and said no. But that's all water under the bridge, isn't it?" said Anton, dusting his hands. "Shall we move on?"

"You don't have to do this," I said, feeling sick. "He's an innocent bystander."

"Hardly innocent," said Anton. Ekomov shrank back.

"Please," I said softly.

"You wouldn't honestly sacrifice yourself for this man, would you? That Flat I've seen you with, certainly. Your family. Your friends. Luc DeFoudre." He paused, tapping his chin thoughtfully. "That would be interesting. Do you think he'd let you do it? I doubt it. But this man? You'd hand yourself over to save his life?"

"He doesn't deserve to die." Ekomov was shuffling toward the back door. If I could distract Anton long enough, maybe he could escape. I could feel Anton drawing on a nearby line, gathering the magic he needed. "You don't need to do this."

He studied me. "You're right, I suppose. On both counts."

My legs trembled with the urge to flee, but I locked them. Showing fear would only encourage him. Ekomov had nearly reached the open door.

"But I don't really care." He flung out an arm, and a deep-blue bolt sliced through the air, striking Ekomov in the chest. He barely had time to look surprised. He grunted, then crumpled, his body spinning from the force of the blast. His cane clattered on the linoleum, and then he was just a sad, limp mass, his face the same color as the dingy snow outside.

The magic jerked and twisted, rising up within me. The earlier whisper—*go now run go run now*—built to a shriek inside my head, so loud I couldn't tell if I was screaming, too, backing away from Anton, shaking and sick to my stomach.

"Easy enough," he said, and I could barely hear him over the tumult in my head. "He didn't suffer, you know. It didn't hurt. Much."

"You didn't have to kill him!"

"What sort of person would I be if I didn't keep my word? I promised your uncle I'd help him cement his position in exchange for a chance to see you alone."

I reached out for Luc, and Anton tsk'd. "Don't bother," he said. "I'll just pull you Between before he gets here. And I wouldn't recommend rushing a Rivening. It makes mistakes almost inevitable."

"Inevitable." This couldn't possibly be my fate. There had to be a way out. But Anton was strolling toward me in his slightly rumpled suit, a manic light in his eyes. I backed away, trying to find the knife block, but it was halfway across the room. Too far to reach.

He grabbed me, fingers biting into my upper arms, and shoved me against the countertop until the edge dug into my back. I thrashed from side to side, kicking and snarling, and he grabbed my hair, twisting it painfully, slamming my head into the cabinet until black dots swam before my eyes. Fueled by my own terror and the magic's, I fought to stay conscious. He threw me across the room and I landed inches away from Ekomov's body, his brown eyes sightless and dull.

"Stupid. Stupid Flat." He straightened the cuffs of his navy suit jacket, watching me with a clinical coldness. I felt him drawing on the lines, knew he was readying another blast. He couldn't kill me, but he could knock me out or immobilize me. I'd be at his mercy.

He didn't have any mercy.

I scuttled backward on hands and knees, whimpering as I brushed against Ekomov's icy hand.

And then there was a new noise, a crack that hung in the air, almost as deafening as the magic. And then another. And another.

Anton's hands fell to his sides, the blue light cupped in his fingers dissipating into mist, and red seeped across the crisp white of his shirt. He grunted and toppled over.

Colin stood in the doorway, gun in hand.

"Are you okay?"

I gasped, and he crossed the room in three strides, pulling me up, urging me out the door. My feet tangled together as I stumbled toward him.

"We need to go," Colin said. "He's dead."

Anton lay faceup on the linoleum, blood pooling around him, but he wasn't dead. I felt him tugging on the lines, saw a pale blue glow spreading over his chest. "Not dead. Healing."

Colin's grip tightened. "Then we really need to go."

"Wait!" I skirted around the two bodies and snatched up the thumb drive as Anton rolled to his side. His pull on the lines was sluggish and his spells were mumbled, but he was healing too quickly for us to escape. We needed time. I snatched up Ekomov's cane from the floor and swung at his head like I was batting cleanup.

He fell still again, but the lines twitched intermittently, all the proof I needed that he wasn't dead. I needed to do a lot more damage, but Colin was hauling on my arm. "*Now,* Mo."

We ran down the corridor, past the front desk. Edie looked up in alarm.

"Is everything okay? I thought I heard—"

"I knocked over some stuff," I said. "Pots and pans. I cleaned it up."

Colin wasn't wasting time on niceties with Edie. Hand on my back, he hustled me out the door. We burst onto the darkened street, the sudden noise of everyday life disorienting. I halted, trying to get my bearings, feeling for any tension in the lines that would indicate the Seraphim were nearby. Aside from the faint, erratic pull from Anton as he healed himself, there was nothing. Even the Quartoren's protective wards were gone, and I cursed myself for not having noticed it before.

"Can I borrow that gun?" I asked, setting off for the bar.

"Not in this lifetime," he said. "You can't go back to Morgan's."

"Billy sold me out. He handed me over to Anton in exchange for his getting rid of Ekomov. I am *definitely* going back in there. And I will finish this."

"Ekomov is dead. The cops will be here soon, and once they figure out who Ekomov really is, they will be all over Billy. You were the last person to see him alive. The damn delivery cart is still in the kitchen. Your prints are everywhere—including on his cane. You cannot be here right now."

I jammed my hands in my pockets and kept walking.

"We need to get out of here," he insisted. "We'll deal with Billy later, I swear."

"No. We deal with him now. This minute." I gripped the thumb drive so hard that the crest of St. Brigid's was probably permanently embossed into my skin. "But not here."

Moments later, we were speeding down I-57, away from Morgan's and the wreckage of my family, toward the only way I could think of to stop him. Jenny Kowalski, who could give the drive to the police. With the list of Billy's contacts and bribes, they'd have all the proof they needed.

"You should call your mom," Colin said.

"And tell her what? 'Your brother put a hit out on me, and I have to go destroy the criminal organization he works for, so don't hold dinner'?"

"She's going to worry. Your house isn't safe right now. Billy's going to be looking for you."

"Looking for you, too." A pang of regret struck me. "You can't go home, either, can you?"

"It's the first place he'll look for us."

I thought about the beautiful furniture he'd made, the pride he'd taken in transforming a broken-down warehouse into a rough-hewn sanctuary. Who knew how long before he could go back. Or if he could at all.

"I'm sorry."

"Don't be. It was always a possibility." So like Colin, to consider the situation from every angle, cover every outcome. Thorough and careful. "I never thought he'd actually hurt you, Mo. That was the one thing I banked on."

"He's desperate. That makes him dangerous." The words reminded me of something Luc had said. I needed to warn Luc. He'd know what the next move against Anton should be. Tentatively, I felt along our connection, but my concentration flitted away before I could do much more than envision the chain between us. I'd missed something important in Colin's words. There was an angle he hadn't seen. A soft spot that Billy could dig into.

I grabbed his arm. "Tess."

He glanced over, his face blank.

"*Tess,*" I said. "He'll go after her next."

"He wouldn't—"

"I'm family, Colin, and that wasn't enough to protect me. You're all the protection she has."

He wrenched the wheel so hard I slid into the door.

The rush-hour traffic was thinning, and we sped across town. All of Colin's attention was focused on the road, and I tried to will the cars out of our way, change the lights to green. I tried magic, and prayer, and sheer concentration, with no clue whether any of them helped.

We'd hit three greens in a row, sailing down Kedzie, picking up speed, and I touched his leg gently. "We've got a head start," I reminded him. "He might not even know yet."

"Might?" was all he said, and pressed down on the gas.

Suddenly there was a flash, as if lightning had struck a few feet beyond the car, and when our eyes cleared, someone was standing in the middle of the road, just out of the street lamp's yellow circle.

Colin swore and stomped on the brake. Tires squealed as the truck fishtailed. Momentum slammed me into the dash, seat belt jerking tight across my chest.

"Jesus," he said. "You okay?"

I fumbled for the seat belt, trying to force air into my lungs again. "Yeah. Did you hit them?"

The street was deserted, and I could feel the thrum of the lines, like an echo. Someone had done magic—big magic—at the moment of impact.

The knock at the window practically levitated me out of my seat.

"Sorry about that," Luc said when I opened the door. "You know how hard it is to come Between in a moving vehicle?"

CHAPTER 34

I launched myself out of the truck and grabbed Luc's sleeve. "I couldn't kill him. I wanted to, but everything happened so fast and we had to get out and Ekomov's dead, and he's going after Tess and we have to *go*, Luc, or it'll be too late."

He drew back and looked at me for a moment, then at Colin. "Which he are you talkin' about?"

"All of them. I don't have time to explain."

"I need to get to my sister," Colin said. "Get in and you can catch him up on the way."

Luc pursed his lips. "Faster for all three of us to go Between."

"We can't leave the truck," Colin said. "We'll need to get around later."

"You and Luc go," I said. "I'll take the truck and meet you there."

Colin shook his head. "You can barely drive. And I'm not leaving you on your own."

"I'll be fine. Worry about Tess right now."

"Cujo's got a point. I don't know exactly what you did to Anton, but he is gunning for you. I can't leave you alone, Mouse."

"Go with him," Colin said roughly. "Tess met you once. She's heard me talk about you. It might be enough to keep her calm until I get there."

"But Billy's guys . . ."

"Are probably on their way." Colin met Luc's eyes. "She's my baby sister. She is literally all I have in the world."

There was a moment I couldn't understand and clearly was not a part of, and then Luc nodded, lacing his fingers with mine. "I'll take care of her."

We came through in the lounge—the same one Luc had waited in before, and I tried not to think about how badly my earlier visit had gone. He kept my hand firmly in his, and the concealment shimmered over us before I'd reoriented myself from the jump Between.

"Down there," I said. "Do you want to come in with me?"

"Told you, I'm not leaving you alone again."

Tess's door stood open slightly, and I paused. "Someone's in there."

Luc pushed me behind him, the tips of his fingers sending out tiny sparks.

"Figures," I heard someone say. "She's a freaking vegetable. How are we gonna get her out if she won't walk? I'm not carrying her scrawny ass to the car."

"There's got to be a wheelchair around here somewhere."

The other man's grumbling grew louder as he approached the door, and as he came through, Luc spoke a few words, casting a spell to conceal the entire area. The fight didn't take long—Luc was efficient and brutal. A punch to the kidneys, a knee to the groin, and an elbow to the face, and the guy slumped to the floor.

"Is he dead?"

"No." Bending down, Luc hooked his hands under the guy's armpits and dragged him to a nearby supply closet, shoving him in unceremoniously and locking the door with a quick wave. I thought we'd sneak into Tess's room and take the second thug by surprise, but Luc was done with sneaking. He strode through the corridor and shoved the door open.

Before the man inside could find his feet, Luc flung a crimson bolt across the room and knocked him from his chair, as smoothly as if he'd planned it.

"Watch her," Luc said. "I'll get rid of the trash."

Tess was sitting in the same wheelchair as before—but she was plainly terrified. Hectic color dotted her pale cheeks, and her fingers clenched the armrest, her knuckles white.

"Tess," I said, crouching down. "Tess, it's Mo. Colin's friend? Do you remember me?"

She didn't answer, but her chest heaved as she struggled for air.

"They're gone," I said. "Luc made those men leave. They won't come back. You're safe now."

She made small, frightened animal sounds, and my heart broke at the sight of her, trapped, alone in her fear. "Colin's coming. He sent us to help, but he's coming, I promise."

Her eyes stopped their panicked rolling and fixed on mine.

"Colin," I repeated. "He's coming. He'll be here soon, okay? Just hold on."

Luc came back. "All finished. How's she doin'?"

"Better," I said, trying to keep my voice upbeat. "Luc, this is Tess Donnelly. Tess, this is Luc."

He placed his hand over hers. "Pleasure to meet you, Tess. Big brother'll be here any minute."

Her gaze switched to the menagerie on the windowsill.

"Here," I said, seized with inspiration. I balanced the hummingbird figurine in the palm of my hand. "Colin made you this, didn't he?"

Her fingers twitched. I took her hand, placed the bird on her palm, like Colin had. As she started to croon again, Luc's brow furrowed, watching her with undisguised curiosity.

"She's been like this for how long?"

The spots of color on Tess's cheeks faded to a more natural blush, and she stroked her fingertip along the hummingbird's back. "More than ten years. We have to get her out of here, Luc."

"Better be someplace far away," he said. "Soon as your uncle figures out his boys got no follow-through, he'll send more. What happened today?"

"Billy sold me out. I went to make a delivery and Anton ambushed me, killed the guy Billy's been in competition with."

"And Cujo shot him?"

"Yes. He's healed by now."

"Outstandin'. Next time finish the job, will you?"

"Gladly."

Colin burst through the door. "Tess? You're okay?" I shifted out of the way, and he knelt in front of her.

"You're fine, aren't you, Tess? But we should go," I said.

"Go? She can't go anywhere." Colin glanced over, incredulous.

I tugged at the sleeve of his jacket until he followed me to a corner, out of earshot. "There were two guys here when we arrived. Luc sealed them in a broom closet, but there's going to be more. We need to leave."

"I'm not leaving until I've handled Billy."

It was pointless to argue, like having a debate with a boulder. "Great. Let's do that. But in the meantime, we cannot stay here, and you know it."

"Hell, Mo. If you have ideas about who can hide Tess while we go after Billy, I am all ears."

Across the room, Luc was putting on a show for Tess, sending the hummingbird floating through the air, creating a tiny firework display in his palm. The frantic, terrified look was gone, and she almost seemed to respond to him.

I massaged my temples. We needed someone who'd help but not ask questions. And a place Billy wouldn't find them.

New Orleans was out—Colin wouldn't leave until Billy was dealt with, and he wouldn't let Tess go so far away. But I had one friend who was almost as good at hiding as me. I pulled out my phone and dialed.

Lena answered, sounding slightly out of breath. "Hello?"

"Hey. Were you running?"

"Conditioning for soccer," she said, and paused to gulp water noisily. "What's up?"

"You said if I ever needed to disappear, you could help."

There was another pause. When she spoke, her voice was tight. "Be really sure, Mo. If you back out, you'll put a lot of people at risk."

"Not me. Colin. And his sister."

"But not you."

I swallowed. "No."

Colin touched Tess on the shoulder, speaking to her in a low, soothing voice, and more of the tension eased from her thin frame. Her eyes flickered between him and Luc, who cupped a flame in his hand, making it take on different shapes—a dragonfly, a pirouetting dancer, each creation delicate and full of movement.

"His sister needs supervision. She's not sick, exactly, but she can't stay by herself."

"Would I be correct in assuming I should not ask a lot of questions?"

"Yes. But Lena . . . it's dangerous. People are looking for them."

"If people weren't looking, they wouldn't need to hide. Give me an hour."

I sat down on the hospital bed, ran my fingers over the soft pink blanket, and reminded myself that Colin and Tess's freedom was exactly what I'd been working toward. The best thing for everyone. Me included.

Across the room, Luc caught my eye, raising his eyebrows meaningfully. Before I could decipher the look, Colin approached me. Luc turned away, focusing on Tess again.

"Well?" Colin asked.

"I called Lena," I said. "She'll find us a place to hide Tess, and when you guys are ready, she'll help you start over somewhere else."

I tried to sound enthusiastic, like it was a brilliant plan, but I couldn't quite make it work.

He tapped my phone. "Call your mom."

"Billy will be looking for me."

"All the more reason to call. Your mom knows what he is."

"What if she tells him where I am?"

"She won't. Call her. Ease her mind a little."

She answered on the first ring. "Mo? Thank heavens! Are you all right? Where are you?"

"Is Billy there?"

"Your father called a few minutes ago. They're on their way over. He said you took something of your uncle's? Mo, what is going on? Are you with Colin? Are you safe?"

"Mom . . . I'm okay. But it's not a good idea for me to come home right now. I have some stuff I have to do first."

"You're in trouble, aren't you?"

I didn't answer.

Her voice broke as she said, "I've tried to keep you safe, all these years. I thought if I could watch over you, it would be enough. Your father wanted us to leave, but I couldn't bear the thought of starting over without him. But he was right, wasn't he? You're not safe at all."

"Not yet," I said. "But I will be. I have to go now. Don't tell Billy I called."

"Sweetheart—"

"I love you," I said, and hung up the phone.

Across the room, Luc was hiding Tess's figurines in pockets of Between, then bringing them out again, and her mouth curved up slightly. Colin watched, surprised. "He's good with her."

"He has a certain charm," I conceded. "We should pack her stuff. Be ready to go when Lena calls."

"She doesn't have much," he said, and gestured to an empty duffle bag near the door. "Whatever fits, we take."

"I'll do it. You visit with her. She likes that more than Luc's tricks, you know."

He moved as if he was going to touch me. At the last minute, he seemed to think better of it, and he went to sit with Tess instead.

Mechanically, I moved stacks of T-shirts and yoga pants to the duffle bag, throwing in handfuls of socks and underwear, wondering how Colin and Tess would survive. I'd upended their lives without meaning to, without even considering the effect my actions would have on them. Now they had to rebuild everything from scratch. All because of me.

Luc's hand slid over mine. "Why don't you rest?"

"I need to make sure they're all set."

"They're set. You're makin' everyone jumpy."

"I ruined their lives," I said.

"This wasn't you," he said. "This was Anton. And your uncle. And before that, it was the man who hurt that girl. This was a long line of people who did selfish things, but none of them were you. Worst thing you did was fall for Cujo, and while I question your taste, it's not a hangin' offense."

Silently, I folded and refolded one of Tess's innumerable pink T-shirts.

"Mouse, listen. There's a way I can help, if you think Cujo'll be amenable."

"He wants to go after Billy himself."

"I was thinkin' more along the lines of his sister. You told me part of what's keepin' her locked up in her head is psychological."

"Her stepfather abused her when she was little. This is how she copes. It's a defense mechanism."

"But part of it's not psychological, right? There was trauma to her brain."

I nodded. "He beat her, too. It was pretty bad, and she was so young . . . the damage was permanent."

Tess sat with her hands cupped loosely around the bird figurine. The sharp angle of her shoulder blade through the T-shirt emphasized her thinness. She looked fragile and defenseless, and Colin hovered over her, watching out the window for any sign of trouble as he wrapped her tiny menagerie in paper towels, ready to pack away.

Luc touched my chin, drawing my attention back to him. "Maybe I can fix it. Heal her."

I shook my head. "She's had those injuries for years. We don't even know how much of the damage is actually physical."

"I tried to get a feel for it, but I won't know for sure until I actually try. But considerin' what they're up against, it's worth a shot, isn't it?"

"You have to clear it with Colin," I warned.

When Luc explained, Colin's expression was stony, his guard up. "She can't be cured," he said. "You think they haven't tried? Therapy and tests and medication. Nothing helped. You're telling me a goddamn spell will erase what he did to her?"

I thought Luc would take offense, but his eyes were solemn. "Magic has limits, just like anything else. But I could help. The parts that are banged up . . . I can heal them. Won't fix the damage to her soul, but it's a start."

"Why?" He looked at me for an instant, then back at Tess.

"Because I can," Luc said.

"You want leverage with Mo. You want to use my sister to prove you're a good guy."

"Never said I was a good guy." I watched Luc tamp down on the anger that was smoldering beneath the surface. "This has nothing to do with Mouse. Not for me, anyway. I understand you've got reservations about me, on account of how you two shook out, but let's be real clear: I didn't steal your girl. She doesn't belong to anyone but herself."

Colin stared at him, eyes nearly black with emotion.

Luc shrugged and met his gaze. "Only thing that matters right now is that I can help your sister. You want to hold a grudge, fine. But I don't think you hate me enough to make her suffer for it."

A muscle in Colin's jaw jumped, and his fingers flexed slightly, like he was about to reach out and throttle Luc. Quickly, I stepped between them.

"You know he won't hurt her." I laid my palm against his jaw, the stubble rasping against my skin. "Please, Colin. Let him try."

His eyes met mine. "I never thought I owned you. Did I make you think that?"

"Never. Not once."

"Good," he said, and his voice shook a little.

"We're running out of time," I said. "Let him help Tess."

He turned to Luc. "Yeah. Of course. Anything you can do."

Luc blew out a breath. "Let's get started, then."

Colin nodded in understanding. Luc sat opposite Tess, their knees nearly touching, and placed his hands gently over her head. She started at his touch. "Won't hurt a bit," he murmured.

Colin's muscles were clenched, and I reached for his hand, squeezed as hard as I could. After a moment, he squeezed back.

Luc began to speak, and the casting appeared to twine around Tess's head like plumes of smoke. The magic responded cautiously at first, growing brighter and more confident as Luc worked. Luc's gaze went inward as the spell shimmered around them, and Tess's eyes drifted shut. Her lips moved as if she were echoing Luc's words, individual strands of hair lifting like she was charged with static electricity. She swayed backward, and Colin started to move in, but I tugged him back.

Luc worked for a long time. Longer than he ever had with me, even during my worst injuries. Sweat beaded at his hairline, trickled down his face. The skin was drawn tightly over his face, the veins in his temple standing out. I fought the urge to go to him.

The physical damage he healed would be converted to a magical hurt, and Luc would take it on himself. Since he and

Tess weren't bound, much of the energy would be lost in the transfer between them, and Luc would recover quickly. I'd always liked knowing exactly how things worked, but now as I watched him take that pain into himself, I reconsidered. My free hand gripped the bed rail, trying to steady myself against the fear.

And then it was done. He dropped his hands and slumped back in the chair, exhaling heavily. Tess swayed for a moment more and fell still, hands in her lap, then turned shining eyes toward us.

"Tess? Are you . . ." Colin crossed the room, took her hands in his. "How do you feel?"

She blinked at him, pale eyes watchful under sandy lashes.

"It's me, honey."

"Colin." She lifted one hand and touched his face. "You're here."

He ducked his head, wrapped his arms around her. "Yeah," he said, voice rasping. "I'm here. Missed you, baby girl."

"You told me to hang on." Her voice was barely a whisper, but we were all spellbound.

"And you did." He stood, took her hands again. "Can you stand up? We're going on a trip."

Her body went rigid. "I don't want to go home."

"We're never going back there. I promise." He turned to Luc, still sitting in the chair. "I can't—"

Luc waved a hand. "Glad to help. She's a special girl, your sister. You take care of her."

"I will."

Tess stood and walked to Luc, visibly concentrating on each step. "You're Luc."

He nodded, watching her warily.

"I felt you in here," she said, a hand drifting over her brow. "Colin said to hang on, and I did. You came to get me."

"Somethin' like that," he mumbled. She bent and pressed her lips to his cheek, the soft, heavy kiss of a child, and retreated to the protective circle of Colin's arm.

The two men exchanged looks. "She still needs help," Luc said. "Tell Mouse, once you land. I know some people."

Before I could ask what kind of help he thought Tess might need—and who, exactly, he thought could help her, the phone rang. I checked the number. Lena.

"Hey," I said, stepping away from the group. "All set?"

"For now. Colin should ditch the truck first," she said. "It's pretty distinctive."

I winced. "Got it. No truck. And you have someone to help with his sister?"

"Yeah. Me," Lena said, and gave me the address. "See you there."

She hung up the phone, and I turned to face the rest of the group. "Time to go. But we can't take the truck."

Colin straightened. "I'll know if we're being followed."

"Lena says no. What if someone spots it?"

"How the hell are we supposed to get there? How am I supposed to get around the city?"

"The same way I got around before I met you," I said. "CTA."

"Tess hasn't been outside of this place for eleven years. A city bus is not how she should reacclimate."

"You two," Luc said, shaking his head. "No creativity at all. What's your favorite color, Miss Tess?"

"Pink," she said promptly.

A wicked grin crossed Luc's face. "Pink it is."

"Absolutely not," I said, catching on. "The idea is to be inconspicuous. Black."

He shook his head glumly. "You never let me have any fun."

I folded my arms and stared him down.

"Fine. Black. Now, let's get a move on."

We trailed out to the parking lot as the sun was setting, and Colin helped Tess into the truck. "It'll be a squeeze to fit us all in," he said.

"Better we part ways now," said Luc. "Succession's tonight. Plenty to do."

"What about Billy?" Colin said. "It's not over, Mo."

I felt for the thumb drive, still safe in my pocket. "Not yet. But it will be. Luc's right about the Succession—you two meet up with Lena at the safe house. I'll check in when we're done." I elbowed Luc. "The truck?"

He placed his hand on the hood, muttered a few words, and the paint rippled under his touch, darkening to black. Tess gasped in delight.

The guys shook hands. "Have a good life, Cujo. Don't anticipate we'll be crossin' paths again."

"I guess not. Thank you," Colin said, and tilted his head toward me. "Keep her safe. Even if she says she doesn't need it."

Luc nodded and strolled over to Tess, giving us some privacy. Colin turned back to me, hooking his thumbs in his pockets. "It's pointless to argue with you, isn't it? To tell you not to go down there with him?"

"Pretty much. I'm sorry," I said softly. "Bringing all of this down on the two of you. Ruining your lives."

"You gave me back Tess," he said firmly. "Just make sure you come back, okay? Luc gets a pass, but the rest of them . . . they aren't worth dying for."

No, but the magic was worth living for. And that's what I intended to do. "I'll call you as soon as it's done," I said, giving him a hug, relishing the strength of his arms as they locked around me.

"Be careful," he whispered into my hair. "You come back, and we take down Billy. Got it?"

"Got it," I said, inhaling the scent of soap and canvas and Colin.

He climbed into the truck and pulled out of the parking lot. I clenched my teeth, trying to keep it together, and watched until the taillights faded away.

"You did good," Luc said. "Finding them a safe place."

"So did you."

He shrugged, as if healing Tess was no big deal. I knew differently. "It's time to go, Mouse."

"One last stop," I said. "I need to swing by a friend's place."

CHAPTER 35

Jenny Kowalski lived in Noble Square, on the northwest side of the city. Her street looked similar to mine—a mixture of bungalows and two-flats on narrow lots, half-melted snowmen stubbornly clinging to the front lawns. The biggest difference was the ever-hopeful Cubs flags hanging listlessly in the night breeze—in my neighborhood, an offense punishable by egging. Jenny's ancient blue Civic was parked on the street. I swallowed painfully at the memory of Kowalski, and hoped like crazy that he knew, somehow, what I was about to do.

I jabbed at the doorbell and waited for a response, glancing over my shoulder to where Luc waited on the sidewalk. I'd insisted on coming alone. I didn't want to spook Jenny, but the shock on her face turned to alarm the instant she recognized me.

"Can I come in?" I didn't wait for an answer, just barreled right inside and waved to Jenny's mom and sister, sitting at the kitchen table. On one wall was a family portrait, four daughters clustered around their parents, Kowalski in the center with his arm looped around the waist of his wife. He looked resigned, in a good-natured way, completely unaware how little time he had left.

"I know," she said, following my gaze. "So awkward."

"It's perfect," I said.

She shrugged, clearly unwilling to reminisce with me. "You

look like shit. And you didn't call. How did you even know where I lived?"

"I didn't want anyone to know I was coming."

"Paranoid much?"

"After the day I've had? Survival instinct."

She started to roll her eyes at me, and I held out the flash drive. "Give this to Nick and his people. And do it fast. Tonight would be good."

She examined it. "I'm going to assume this isn't your Lit homework. Nick said we were off the investigation, remember?"

"After this, I will be. You can't contact me again," I said. "Don't come by school, or my house—anywhere. It's not safe."

The expression on her face made it obvious she wasn't concerned with safety. I knew too well how grief could push aside what had once seemed important. How it could make you reckless and selfish for the noblest of reasons. I ached for Jenny, because she wouldn't stop grieving until she had answers. Ones I could never give her.

I looked again at the family portrait. "Your dad loved you so much. More than he hated Billy."

"The job was his life," she said, chin wobbling the slightest bit.

"No. This was his job." I gestured to the drive clutched in her hand. "*You* were his life. He'd be proud of you for finishing his work. But he wouldn't want you to keep doing it, Jenny. He would want your life to be about something more than revenge and hatred. It's a lousy way to live."

"That's a little rich, coming from you. Aren't you doing this for Verity?"

Once, yes. But it had become more. "Do you remember what I told you the first day you came into The Slice?"

"You said your uncle didn't kill my dad."

"It's true. The files on that drive are enough to put Billy away for the rest of his life. Marco Forelli, too. But there's nothing on there to tie either of them to Verity or your dad."

"You erased them. You're still protecting him." But an uncertain note had entered her voice.

"Believe me, Billy is the last person in the world I would protect. Second-to-last," I amended, thinking of Anton. "The files aren't there because they don't exist. He wasn't involved."

Luc whistled, as if he was hailing a cab. Time to go. "Don't come around me again, Jenny. I am pretty damn close to radioactive right now."

"You can't stop me," she said.

"No. But I can't help you, either. Give the drive to Nick, and let it go."

I turned to leave, and she said, "Mo—"

I paused.

"My dad . . . he liked you. He thought you were a good kid, and you got caught up in stuff you couldn't handle. He said you had a lot more in you than your uncle realized."

I looked at the picture of Kowalski on the wall. "He was right."

I headed outside, back to Luc. We started walking, moving out of Jenny's sight before we went Between.

"What did you give her?" he asked.

"Insurance. If I don't come back, they'll still be able to dismantle Billy's operation. Put him in jail."

"It'll send your daddy back to Terre Haute."

The moon was so full and bright overhead, the bare trees cast shadows like vines at our feet. "I can't save everyone. You told me that."

"So I did," he mused. "But the only person you need to save tonight is yourself, okay? Anyone else is gravy. We all clear?"

"Crystal."

CHAPTER 36

The trip into the Water Arcs' House was the same as before—gate, stream, fumbling with my stupid ceremonial robe. Dagger from Luc, tucked into my boot.

Through the windows, we could see the Quartoren, milling about, trying to look as if they were in charge. Dominic, of course, pulled it off better than the others, but he paced the room, peering about as if he expected Anton to pop up any moment.

"Don't see why we couldn't go back to my place first," Luc said. "Hell of a day for you. Might be nice to stop and catch your breath."

I was running on adrenaline at this point—that, and the urging of the magic, a visceral tugging, impossible to ignore. I couldn't let myself think about today's events. Thinking would lead to feeling, and that was a luxury I could not afford right now. Billy's betrayal, Colin's new life. Handing over information that would send my father back to prison. I would mourn later.

"If I stop, I'll fall over." I marched across the glinting-black lawn, the moonlight turning the water to pools of silver. "I need to focus on the ceremony. And Anton. The rest will wait."

"Poor Mouse," he said. "You've been tryin' so hard to put all the different parts of your life in neat little boxes. Friends in one and family in another and magic in a third. You've probably got a box just for me, don't you?"

"So what if I do?" I brushed a stray curl out of my face. "You're the one who said I had to choose between them."

"I did," he agreed. "But hard as you're workin' to keep everything separate, they just keep overlapping. I'm not saying you don't have a destiny. You do, and it's with us. I'm as sure of that as I am my own name. But when this is over, maybe your life can be a mix of Arc and Flat. Like you."

"I don't have much of a life to go back to after today," I said.

"Then we make a new one," he said. "A little overlap wouldn't kill me, either."

The door to the House opened, and Sabine stepped onto the front porch, peering into the darkness until she spotted the pale blue of my cloak. She raised a hand, beckoning us forward.

"Showtime," I said, and we climbed the steps hand in hand.

"The House is assembled," Sabine said, her delicate features pinched with worry. "We may begin."

"Should we go over the plan one last time?" Dominic asked.

"I know what I need to do," I replied, careful to keep my expression impassive, despite the fury churning underneath. Dominic wanted to play me—to use me as a way to ensure his own hold on power for generations to come. I was nothing more than a pawn to him.

I was nobody's pawn.

What I needed to do didn't match up with Dominic's plans as completely as he thought. I wasn't loyal to this House or any other. I wasn't loyal to the Quartoren or the Arcs. I was loyal to the magic, and tonight, I would do everything in my power to ensure its safety.

Luc picked up on my mood, because he broke away from the formal lines we'd fallen into and made a show of adjusting my cloak, tracing the gold designs embroidered on the edge.

"Remember what I said," he told me. "I don't care what happens to the rest of them. You keep yourself safe."

"I will."

He leaned forward until his mouth was an inch from my ear. "I'd kiss you, but I promised not to."

"You're very honorable," I said.

"Not really."

"What if I kissed you?" My words were impulsive, prompted by nerves and the recklessness he always brought out in me, but my tone was not.

He drew back, the gold flecks in his eyes mesmerizing. "In front of all these people? Didn't know you were such an exhibitionist."

"I . . ." I could feel the blush warming my skin.

He smiled grimly. "Ask me again after we get out of this."

"Maura," said Sabine. "It's time."

We trailed out onto the massive veranda, gleaming crystals like lanterns dotting the lawn. Under the flickering lights, the Arcs' silk robes gave the impression of gently moving water.

The eyes that tracked my movements were anything but gentle. They ranged from curious to alarmed to openly hostile. My steps were leaden as I took my place at the edge of the crowd.

On the marble-topped table stood a glass basin filled with water and the parchment scroll I'd signed before. On the other side of the basin, a piece of sea glass, one edge chipped to form a crude knife, rested atop a neat stack of white linen squares.

I searched the crowd again. No sign of him.

Yet.

At some unseen signal, Sabine lifted her hands and began the chant to resume the ceremony. The rest of us joined in, and I felt the same surge of magic, saw my skin begin to shine, heard the crowd's murmurs. This time, Sabine didn't pause.

As soon as the invocation was finished, the magic settled back under my skin. My fingertips still glowing as the power traced through my veins.

Sabine's name was the first on the list. Iris picked up the glass knife, murmured a blessing, and handed it to Sabine. I hoped the magic would choose her. Choose anyone. Make my job here easier.

Calmly, Sabine drew the edge of the rock across her palm. The blood welled up in a thick line and she squeezed, letting the drops fall into the basin below. It billowed through the water like crimson smoke, diffusing slowly. My stomach clenched at the sight. When it was completely dissolved, she stretched her cut hand over the surface of the water and began the spell, opening herself to the massive ley lines bordering the House.

I'd taken raw magic into myself more than once. Tempered magic was easier, but it was a little bit like saying that sticking your finger in an electrical socket was easier than getting struck by lightning.

Sabine jerked once, her eyes rolling back, and then she recovered, continuing the spell. The air quivered with the force of it, the water in the bowl roiling as she spoke, struggling to channel the power effectively.

This was the test, Niobe had explained, a public demonstration of how well the candidate worked with the magic. It showed his strength and skill, because everyone here could read the lines. Sometimes the candidate was too weak to direct the magic once it was mixed with his blood, and it consumed him. Sabine seemed to be managing it well enough, casting a finely wrought blue lattice in the air, delicate but steady. It looked like the wards of protection Luc had placed around me, but Luc's wards always glittered, a constant, shifting array of light, as if they were truly made of fire. Sabine's were quieter—a faint, will-o'-the-wisp glimmer. I didn't know if that was because she lacked strength or because she wasn't a showoff. Either way, it seemed obvious that Sabine was competent. Not outstanding, but capable enough.

Gradually, the lattice faded away. Joshua handed her a linen cloth to bind her hand, because you weren't supposed to heal a wound from a Succession ceremony. Sabine stepped back, and Iris moved forward to take her place. Sabine's test was over, and the Succession was under way.

I watched Iris and Joshua's tests, and then the rest of the candidates proceeded toward the stage, one at a time. Each of them took the magic inside themselves and built a lattice— some were sloppy, the lines jagged as a child's drawing, and some were gracefully curved. Some were orderly to the point of being rigid, and some were so weak you could barely see them. But none of the spells had the vitality of Luc's magic.

Whenever Luc cast a spell, the magic moved—flickering and dancing, full of light. I'd always thought it was the nature of fire-based ley lines, but now I understood it was because the magic responded to him. He might not have known it was sentient, but that shimmer was a sign they were working together—not just Luc imposing his will on the lines, but a partnership.

That's why he was the Heir. Whether the Arcs here understood the meaning behind it, they, too, knew it was essential.

Magic was as unique as a fingerprint, I realized. Every single lattice looked different—the structure, the brightness, the degree of movement within the lines. They revealed everything about the person working the spell. By adding their blood to the casting, each person's essence was captured perfectly, displaying their truest nature. This ceremony was the Arc equivalent of a polygraph.

The testing continued, but none of the candidates blew me away. A few could barely withstand the magic and were knocked unconscious and carried offstage. There was never an instance where the magic reared up, grabbed my attention, and said, *That one.* I began to worry, as we worked our way through the list of names, that Anton would, in fact, be the one. That he would put on such a display of power that the Water Arcs wouldn't be able to resist naming him as their leader. I could speak for the magic, but I couldn't speak for the entire House. The crowd grew restless. Finally, Sabine called Anton's name. Luc scanned the crowd, ready to spring. The Quartoren stood in silence, Orla gripping her cane, Pascal studying the scene through half-closed eyes, more intent on the activity in the lines than on the ground. Dominic watched me.

Inside me, the magic twanged a warning, and I sent a wave of reassurance back toward it, just as Sabine called Anton's name again.

This time, the crowd parted to let him through.

He strode past me, hood thrown back, every hair immaculate, betraying no sign that he'd been shot three times in the chest. But his eyes were pools of malice, and I stepped back as he passed.

He took the knife from Sabine, tilted it back and forth to catch the light, and tested the edge against his thumb. He turned and aimed the point at me, smirking.

"Any day now," I muttered, hands balled into fists.

He drew the blade across his hand without hesitation, without betraying any pain, and let the blood fall freely into the basin

I don't know what I expected—for it to sizzle like holy water on a vampire, maybe. Something clichéd, some outward manifestation of his evil. But the crimson drops merely spread through the water, tinting it a repulsive pink. His mouth stretched into a horrible grin as he took the magic inside himself, barely flinching.

His eyes dilated as the full force of the power hit him, but he took it in stride, even pausing to survey the crowd. It was a calculated gesture, a deliberate show of strength, and then he began chanting. At first the words were soft, impossible to make out, but as the wards took shape, it became clear that the other candidates' workings had been child's play. The blue flame was darker than the others, but the light and magic running over the surface gave it an unearthly sheen.

The lines formed a nearly impenetrable lattice, the spaces between the lines so narrow I doubted I could get a hand through. He let the construct hang in the air for a moment, and then it exploded, blinding everyone momentarily.

When my vision cleared, Luc was standing between me and Anton, who chuckled. "You're forgetting your place, boy."

Luc's fingers flexed, but I nudged him. "Not yet."

"Soon," he said, not taking his eyes off of Anton.

Silently, Iris handed Anton the scrap of linen to bind his hand. He surveyed the crowd as he tied it, as smug as if he'd already won.

"Next," he called, and moved to the foot of the stairs, forcing me to pass within reach. As I climbed the steps, he positioned himself in front of the crowd like a general leading an army. I wondered how many Seraphim stood with him. How many targets I had painted on me. And I wondered what would happen when my blood hit the water and I set the magic loose.

CHAPTER 37

I could have chosen to make a fresh wound—to use the glass knife on my other hand and leave the scar from Verity's attack. But it was that scar—the Darkling scar—that had started me on this journey, transferred her destiny to me. It seemed fitting to open it again now, at the end.

Because I was pretty sure this was going to be the end. I just didn't know what kind of ending it was yet.

I set my jaw as the blade bit in, refusing to give Anton the satisfaction of seeing me whimper. Scarlet drops rippled through the water, and I waited for Sabine's signal before I began. But instead of chanting the spell everyone else had, I felt for the lines, opened myself up to them, and invited the magic inside me once again.

The rush of energy was staggering, but I managed to stay upright. The magic churned through me like a waterfall, turning my skin light and my eyes sightless. I spoke in the language of the Arcs, musical and silvery, distinctly Water based this time, the words rushing and tumbling from my mouth.

I didn't know how I could suddenly be fluent in this language—but every word was pure and correct, an exact translation of the magic's thoughts, a declaration of freedom and triumph and life. It was like a dam had broken and pure energy poured forth. It wasn't a spell—I didn't shape the magic or direct it. There was no glowing lattice, no magical fingerprint. I simply lit up like the scoreboard after a grand slam, the magic brilliant and unmistakably alive within me.

The truth revealed, my secret displayed for everyone to see. Especially Anton, who'd put it together before anyone else.

When the magic finally quieted, leaving me spent and shaking on the stage, Anton wore a horrible, catlike grin on his face.

I didn't bother waiting for Joshua to hand me the bandage. I wrapped up my hand in the crackling silence, unable to look up, or at Luc, or anywhere except the blood soaking through the snowy fabric.

"I came here for you," Anton said conversationally, breaking the silence. "The Succession's a quaint little honor. But you're the real prize. Even more so now that I know what you've been hiding."

"You don't care about these people," I said, staring down at him. "You want to destroy them."

"I want to usher in a new age. Houses are meaningless. Our bloodlines are polluted. The Quartoren work to serve their own interests first. Even this ceremony . . . it's a mockery of what it once was. In olden times, those who wished to be tested risked their lives for the privilege of serving our people. The spilling of blood was literal, not figurative, and the one who survived was the one chosen to lead. We've become weak. Debased."

"People vote," I said. "They have a say in their future. How is that a bad thing, to let the members of a House determine its path?"

"Because they don't deserve it," he said. "You want to be a scientist. This is evolution. I'm merely helping it along, making sure the strong are the ones who carry us forward. Those capable of handling the burden of greatness. Everyone else should be sloughed off. They're useless."

"What about me, then? I'm not even an Arc. I'm not useful to you."

"You're the most useful thing of all," he said. "It's through you that we'll release the magic and wipe the slate clean. You've shown us what we can be, how strong, and pure, and powerful. All we have to do is release the magic."

"I won't let you," I said, reaching for the dagger in my boot.

"No? Not even if it saves the ones you love?" He reached behind him, pulling a cloaked, visibly trembling figure from the crowd. "Poor thing. She thinks you'll save her. Again. But I think you're callous enough to let me spill her blood right here. You've already let an innocent die for you once today. What's one more?"

He pulled back the cloak, and Constance stood in his grasp, pale and tearful, blue eyes so like Verity's, begging me for help.

I set the dagger on the table. "Mouse," said Luc, his voice low, a warning. "Stick to the plan."

The only person you need to save tonight is yourself. But Luc hadn't counted on this. Verity's sister. You had to hand it to Anton. He played his cards well.

"Ekomov wasn't innocent. And he didn't die for me. Kind of a different situation here," I said, and moved down the steps, careful and deliberate.

"Think," said Luc. "Don't do this."

I met Constance's gaze, noting the quivering of her chin, the tears trembling on her lashes. "I know what I'm doing."

Dominic stepped forward. "Don't take another step, Maura."

"You cannot act here, Dominic," Sabine said.

"Neither can you," Anton said to her, cheerily. "Or I'll kill the girl."

He would. He'd kill everyone here to get a shot at me. To take me over, just like he'd done with Jill, and force me to release the magic.

Constance made a strangled noise and I moved closer, hands held up in a gesture of surrender. As soon as I was within reach, he shoved Constance to the ground and clamped a hand around my wrist, dragging me toward him.

I didn't bother to resist.

"For someone with such potential, Maura Fitzgerald, you are dreadfully predictable." His breath was hot against my cheek, but it made me feel cold, his fingers clammy against my skin. "You should work on that."

"I told you," said Constance, climbing to her feet and moving to stand just behind Anton's shoulder. "Mo the Martyr. Works every time."

CHAPTER 38

If Anton hadn't been holding on to me so tightly, I would have slapped the smirk off Constance's face right then and there.

"Damn it, Constance. You're supposed to be smart."

She tossed her hair back and unfastened the blue cloak she'd been wearing, kicking it away.

"Smart enough to fool you," she said. "Did you really think you and I were good, Mo? You let Verity die—you ran and left her to fight the Darklings all alone. She died because she was trying to save your worthless ass."

"Darklings that Anton sent," I said. "Why am I the bad guy when he's the one who had her killed?"

Constance was still trembling, but with rage. Not fear. She practically spat at me. "Verity wouldn't listen to them. If she'd listened, and joined the Seraphim when they asked her, it would have been okay. But she was too worried about getting back to you and your stupid plans for New York. And then she was dead, and you stole her life. You slipped right into it like she'd never existed. You took her boyfriend. And then you killed my aunt so you could take her place here."

"Evangeline was working with them. She betrayed Verity. What the hell is wrong with you, Constance?"

"You don't understand this world," she replied. "You don't like it. You don't even respect it. He's trying to make it better. Stronger. And all you do is interfere."

"You are such a moron," I said. "You know what else? You have a terrible memory. Last time we fought, I kicked your ass. And I'm going to do it again, as soon as I'm finished here."

Anton wrenched my arm around so that I was facing him again. "Then let's begin."

"Be careful what you wish for," I said as he clapped his hands along my temples. It felt as if he were actually digging through my brain, icy fingers plucking out random memories, and the sensation made me gag. But I was prepared this time. I gave him the worst memories I had—holding Verity's body as she died, the Darklings reaching for me in the park, the sight of Kowalski burning up in the magic, Ekomov slumped on the floor of the nursing home. The very worst of what I'd seen, I gave to him in vivid color. When he reached for more, I didn't fight. Instead I let the full strength of the magic—its intelligence, its power, the untempered force I'd once taken inside myself—coalesce into one furious stream of energy, and I poured it directly into his mind.

He was so greedy he didn't even realize what was happening at first. He soaked up the magic, his glee and avarice unbridled, until it overwhelmed him. When he finally tried to draw back, the magic wouldn't let him, forcing its way through the Rivening, turning against him. I spoke the words the magic gave to me—warning and outrage and punishment—visceral, powerful words that sliced through his defenses and hollowed him out, filled him with raw magic.

I felt the power of it, and for the barest moment, I thought about stopping. But then I thought about Verity, and the future he'd taken from her, all the memories she'd never make. The life she should have had.

The life I should have had.

I did not stop.

Luc had told me that raw magic killed Arcs from the inside out. The bigger their talent, he'd said, the longer it took. Anton was strong—he'd staked his claim as leader of the Seraphim on his power. But now, it prolonged his suffering.

When the Darklings breached the walls of the House, it was Anton—raw magic streaming from his eyes and mouth and fingertips and chest—that they went for. Even when his screaming turned to their language, and he begged for them to stop, directed them toward me, they ignored him, snatched him up in their talons, and his screams turned incoherent.

The Darklings ripped him apart. I didn't look away, though many of the Arcs did. The magic recognized the moment Anton's heart stopped. Lightning fast, it retreated to the lines, sealing itself away from the Darklings. Anton was dead, and I fell to the ground, spent.

And then the Darklings were among us, and the battle began.

Quartoren Guards threw off their robes and began to fight. The rest of the Water Arcs summoned their own weapons from Between. But I was too tired to fight now, and my dagger was onstage, too far away to be of any use.

Luc reached me before the first Darkling struck, hauling me to my feet and pulling me inside. I stared out the ballroom doors at the violence raging outside.

"It's done," he said, standing beside me.

I felt the cold hunger rise up and squeeze my heart, releasing another icy flood of grief, reminding me of all I'd lost. For a moment, I was lost, too, wanting to find a new target. And then I felt Luc's hand, warm in mine, and I realized I didn't want the coldness within me any longer.

"Yeah," I said, "it is."

We found a sitting room and curled up on the couch. The sounds of the fighting were muted, but Luc kept staring at the arched doorway like he longed to dash through it. "I don't like missing this," he said. "I should be out there."

"But you can't fight on the grounds of another House, right? Even though we're bound?"

He made a noise of frustration deep in his throat. "No."

"Good." I didn't want to risk losing him after everything we'd survived. I glanced up and grimaced as the Quartoren swept into the room. "You can protect me from your dad."

"That I can do," Luc said, and moved to intercept Dominic, who was shouting about my recklessness and how I'd endangered the magic.

Orla sat down in a silk-covered chair and eyed me critically. "You knew Constance Grey was a traitor."

We won't let them win, I'd told her.

And she'd smiled and said, *You'll try.*

"I didn't, actually. I just had a feeling, when he brought her out. So I gambled." And won. Or lost, depending on how you looked at it.

"Surely there was some sign," Orla pressed.

"Anton kept finding me. At school. At Morgan's. Even at Ekomov's. I wasn't using magic, or tapping into the lines, so he shouldn't have been able to find me so easily. Even Luc said so. I figured someone who knew my schedule was tipping him off."

"And you didn't suspect Niobe?"

"No. I kept thinking about the first attack at St. Brigid's. Constance was casting a spell at the exact same moment Anton was Rivening Jill. I thought it was a coincidence, but it was actually a diversion. She was helping him get close to me." I leaned back, shaking my head. "All the times we spoke . . . she never blamed the Seraphim for Verity's death— only me. And she was never afraid they would come after her. Constance *always* worries about herself first, but even after the attacks, she wasn't scared."

You're the one they want, she'd said.

"I should have monitored her more closely." Orla's lips thinned. "We can't keep her from the House, but there will be consequences. I promise you that."

"Do what you want," I said. "She's not my responsibility anymore."

"She's still on the grounds," Pascal said. "She can't cross the boundaries without a Water Arc taking her through. Assuming she survives the Darklings."

"She'll survive," I said wearily. She'd get someone to take her to safety. This Constance, the one I didn't know, was a survivor. My heart ached for the girl she'd been. The one I'd considered my own little sister, who'd tagged along after us and played Barbies, who'd helped us make cookies in the Greys' light-filled kitchen and burned her mouth because she was too impatient to let them cool.

"How long have you known the magic is alive?" Pascal asked. "You must have been communicating for some time to have refined your abilities so much."

"Since we were bound. I don't know how it happened."

"I have a theory," he said. "If you'd like to hear it."

I nodded. Luc rejoined me on the couch while Dominic silently fumed across the room.

Pascal said, "When the magic used Verity's blood as a conduit—transferred her role as the Vessel to you—it recognized that you were not an Arc. In that moment, I believe the magic saw an opportunity. Someone who could withstand its force but not use it. Who could speak for the magic without imposing her will upon it. More important, it also felt how very alone you were. It felt a kinship—it has spent eternity in isolation. The magic chose you to be its voice precisely because you were the only person it believed could understand it."

"It wanted me all along? Not Verity?" Six months ago, I wouldn't have believed him. But now, considering everything we'd been through and everything we'd done, it seemed right. Fitting.

"Verity was meant for one purpose only: to be the Vessel. To stop the Torrent. I can't guess what would have come after that, had she lived. But in the end, she was not the Vessel. You made that destiny your own, and the path since then has been yours alone." He looked at Luc for an instant, then smiled at me.

"The Darklings are retreating," said Dominic. "We'll proceed with the ceremony as soon as they're gone."

"Should have expected Anton would bring them through the boundaries," Luc muttered.

"It's poetic justice that they finished him off after he'd done so much damage with them," Orla said. I had to agree.

"If I were a gambling man," Dominic said, "I'd say it's a pretty safe bet you'll be elevated to the Quartoren. The Water Arcs have seen what you can do—they'd be fools not to. Guess we're the fools now."

"What's wrong?" I asked sweetly. "I thought you wanted me on the Quartoren. Wasn't that the whole point of this? You figured if I was a Matriarch, you could keep me in line. You should have listened to Luc."

Luc smiled at his father and draped an arm over my shoulders. "I've been trying to keep her in line since the day we met," he said. "She ain't an Arc, but she's still a force of nature. I'm not the one you need to listen to. She is."

Sabine entered the room, her robe ripped and blood-stained, her expression grim. "The Darklings have been vanquished. It would be good to conclude the ceremony now. My people are eager to put these events behind us."

"People should listen to me," I said to Luc. A certainty had crept over me in the last few minutes, and the magic thrummed approval.

"That would be my suggestion."

We stepped out onto the veranda again. The basin sat empty before us. The Arcs, disheveled and battle-scarred, stood in ragged lines before us. The bodies of the fallen lay in a neat row at the foot of the steps, their cloaks like shrouds, the last casualties in the war against the Seraphim. I bowed my head at the sight and said the Hail Mary under my breath, lifelong instinct taking over.

Then I looked up at the array of battle-hardened faces in front of me, and took a deep breath, and spoke. For *myself*.

"In a moment, you will walk up these steps and decide who you want to lead this House forward into a new age. You need someone strong and wise and loyal. Someone who will fight for this House and its people in all things.

"I am not that person.

"Do not choose me. I won't fight for you. I can't. My loyalty is not with you, or any House. My loyalty is to the magic. You have to choose a new path today, and it should not be set by me." Then I stepped back; looked at Sabine's startled, lovely face; and held my hand over the water.

"Sabine Levaret," I said, loud enough for my voice to carry to the back of the crowd. Deliberately, I crossed the stage and took Luc's hand, and let the voting begin.

Each member of the House approached, filing up the steps in a silent, undulating line that stretched to the back of the grounds. One by one, they stretched a hand over the basin and whispered a name, and a single droplet of water fell from their fingertips into the basin. Gradually, it filled, the water inside turning the blue of a tropical sea.

"Sabine?" he asked me. "Her spell wasn't much to write home about."

"The magic responded to her. She's smart. She's strong. She might not be showy, but she stood up to your father."

"Good point. Want to get out of here?" Luc murmured. "Your part's done. Quartoren will do the induction privately later on."

"Do you think anyone would notice?"

"Do you care?"

I shook my head, and he led me through the empty rooms to the front lawn. It was like sneaking out, and I couldn't help laughing, giddy with relief. We slipped off our shoes and waded through the stream, pushed through the gate, and stood on the deserted street.

"They're the House of Levaret now," he said. "New name."

"New world." Not just for them. The magic unfurled itself, slipping free of the tight bonds of fear that had constrained it since the attack, growing stronger with every breath. I had the faint, nagging feeling I'd left something undone, but for now, it was enough that we'd restored the balance.

Luc's expression was pensive. "Take you home?" he asked.

I thought about the disaster that awaited me back in Chicago. Ekomov was dead, Billy was on the warpath. My mom was probably frantic, and the police had to be closing in. If I went back, I'd be heading straight into chaos. It was too much for one day. "Not yet. Can we go back to your place?"

He lifted an eyebrow as he cut a door Between. "You stopped Anton, stood up to my father, and decreed a new Matriarch, Mouse. We can do anything you want."

As he spoke, he took my hands, preparing to bring us through. At the last minute, just before we fell into nothingness, I stepped closer and fit my mouth over his.

CHAPTER 39

Going Between always left me dizzy, but this time, the room was spinning for an entirely different reason. The instant we landed, Luc's hands were tangling in my hair, sliding down my back, pressing me into the heat of his body while I opened my mouth and drew him closer. It was fierce and hot and glorious, a power that had nothing to do with the magic surging through me, and I broke the kiss long enough to drag in a breath and say, "More."

He stepped away, and my eyes flew open. His face had turned sharp and wary. Not exactly the reaction I was hoping for.

"What the hell was that?" he asked, dragging the back of his hand across his mouth.

"If you have to ask, I'm doing something wrong." I shoved my hair back, trying to hold on to the heat leaching away.

"You kissed me."

"Yes. Glad we're on the same page."

"We ain't," he said, and stalked past me. "You need to go home. Get some rest."

"I kissed you, and your response is to tell me it's naptime? Is this a joke?" A horrible thought struck me. "Is this because of the Quartoren? Because I told them not to choose me?"

"I'm *glad* you're not the new Matriarch. Last thing I want is you feeling roped into staying here."

"What, then?"

"You didn't mean it," he said. "I know you, Mouse. Better than you know yourself, I'm starting to think. And that kiss was adrenaline. That was emotions running high and you needing to do something with them. That was you trying to grab hold of something solid after a bad, bad day. But that was most assuredly not about you and me. Don't you remember what I told you?"

I remembered. Perfectly. "You said the next time I kissed you, I needed to mean it."

"I won't do this," he said, and he refused to meet my eyes. "I will not do this and then in a few days, when the world's settled back into place and you've found your feet, the first thing you do is run away."

"Luc . . ."

"I *can't*," he said, and stepped back. The hallway was narrow enough that I could have easily caught him, but the wild, fearful look on his face stopped me. "You do this every damn time."

The accusation stung. It was completely true. Walking away from Luc—or telling him to leave—had become a specialty of mine. And I didn't know how to convince him this time was different.

"I do," I agreed. "I did, anyway. But the world's not going to settle back in place. Not the way it was before. And I'm okay with that. Better than okay."

I caught the tips of his fingers in mine. He glanced up at me quickly and looked down again, but not before I caught the hope that flashed across his features.

"It's not done. The magic isn't finished with me. I still have to deal with my uncle. I have months of school left. I haven't even picked a college, Luc. I got into NYU," I added, feeling bashful at the admission.

"I'm glad," he said, not looking glad at all. "I know how much you wanted it."

"I used to. Now . . . I don't know. Nothing's settled at all. Except this. Us. No more running." I brushed a kiss along the sharp line of his cheekbone, even as he twisted away. "No more excuses." Another kiss, whisper soft, along his jaw. His hair felt cool and slippery as I slid my hand along the back of his head.

"For keeps." I touched my lips to his, lightly, and then paused as a sliver of fear worked its way under my skin. "If that's what you want, too. Me, I mean. If you want me. Because if it's not . . . if you've changed your mind . . ." My nerves kicked in and so did the babbling, even as his eyes turned green and gold and heated. "I'd understand that. I wouldn't like it, but I'd understand it. I'd probably even deserve it, and you could go off with Niobe, or someone—"

His hands closed over my hips, backing me up until my spine hit the wall behind us. "Tell me you mean it," he said when our mouths were almost touching. "Tell me."

"I mean it," I said, and closed my eyes, waiting for the pressure of his lips on mine.

It didn't happen, and I opened my eyes again. "Seriously, Luc?"

"Kiss me," he said, his voice strangled. "I made a promise, remember? Trying to be a man of my word here, but you're making it a challenge."

My mouth curved, and I licked my lips just to watch his pupils dilate. "Technically, it's your turn. I kissed you when we went Between. I kissed you thirty seconds ago. That's twice in a row. I'm not sure I should be the one doing all the work here."

"Hell on fire, woman. You want to talk about work? I've been chasing after you since the day we met. Now kiss me and mean it, Maura Fitzgerald."

So I did.

Soft like the last time, but now his lips moved against mine—with mine—and the warmth spread through me like a drug, like a fever, my skin heating as I tasted him, burnt sugar and the sea and something blazing brightly between us. "I mean it," I said, nipping along his jaw, my fingers trailing over his face, like I might memorize it. His hands were in my hair, on my throat, tugging at the cloak I was still wearing, and he cursed softly when the clasp wouldn't give way.

He swallowed the laugher that burbled up before I could stop it, his mouth hungrier and hotter than before, shoving back the heavy silk, his hips pressing me harder into the wall. He murmured something, his forehead against my shoulder, and the clasp at my throat split in two, the material pooling at our feet, and I felt so light without it I nearly floated away.

His lips touched my pulse, and I slid my hands under his shirt, feeling hard lines of muscle, feeling him tremble at my touch, and I reveled in the sensation, the way the heat flashed and built between us. When his hands found the hem of my shirt, crept higher, it was like reaching a boiling point.

"Wait." I pushed him away and he staggered, his mouth moist and swollen where I'd nipped him, face flushed, hair tumbling into his eyes. He was so familiar and so new, all at once, I lost my breath. "Could we—"

"It's too fast," he said, shoving a hand through his hair. "You're right. We can wait. Take some time. As much as you need."

I clapped a hand over his mouth. "I was going to ask if we could move this to your bedroom."

He froze, eyebrows arching in surprise.

"Your bedroom," I said. "Where there is a bed. You might not have noticed, but I've been on my feet all night, and I would like to not be on my feet. In your bed."

He yanked me toward him, his face serious but his eyes smiling, and kissed me so thoroughly I almost forgot what I'd asked. But then he started walking me backward toward the bedroom, the hard planes of his body never breaking contact with mine, one hand splayed wide against my back, and it became impossible to forget what I'd just asked him.

We fell onto the bed, still kissing, his mouth everywhere, his hands everywhere, my clothing landing somewhere behind us with a soft whooshing sound, and I tugged at the buttons of his shirt, laughing when I heard them pop. When I

trailed my fingers across his stomach, reaching for the waistband of his jeans, he stopped me.

"I believe you," he said.

"That's good." I reached for him again, and he took my
hand, held it over his heart.

"No, Mouse." He kissed me once, waited for me to look
at him. "What I'm sayin' is, you don't have to prove anything
to me."

"Glad to hear it," I said. "Let go of my hand."

"Maura."

That stopped me. "You never call me Maura. Only when
things are really bad. Please don't tell me things are bad.
Please don't—" *Don't tell me no.* God, he could tell me anything but that. Not when I wanted him this much, not when
I'd finally let myself fall.

His smile was crooked, his gaze on my bare skin practically leaving scorch marks. "Beautiful girl in my bed, trying
to divest me of my clothing and my virtue? How is that possibly bad?"

"Your virtue?"

"My clothing, anyway." He sobered. "I want it to be perfect. Maybe perfect means waiting a little bit. Being sure."

"I'm sure of you," I said softly, laying my head on his
chest, walking my fingers up his arm. "It's perfect because it's
you. It's us. It could be awful, and it would still be perfect. I
don't want to wait, Luc. I just want you."

He exhaled, his fingers tightening on my hip, and his
mouth sealed against mine. "Been waitin' on you for so
damn long," he mumbled, shucking off his jeans, pushing me
back onto the bed, acres of snowy linen smooth and cool
against my bare back, while his mouth was searingly hot, his
hands roaming over me like he was memorizing my skin.
"Thought it was a dream. You sure this ain't a dream?"

I bit his shoulder and he jerked his head up, mock-scowling.
"Not a dream," I said, and pulled him back down, feeling the
heat and the strength of him against me, and his hands—the
fingers so clever, finding the places that made me giggle and

the places that made me gasp and the places that made the whole world go blurry, that made me arch my back, and if he hadn't had his mouth on mine, I would have begged.

He drew back, skin glowing like amber, and his eyes drank me in, like he'd been in the desert for weeks and weeks, and I felt the same way watching the light play over his body. He reached for the drawer of the nightstand and rolled back toward me. "I can stop now," he said, voice tight, body tense despite the gentle, exquisite movements of his hand against me. "But not if we keep goin' down this path."

"Don't you dare," I said. "Don't you dare stop."

I pulled him down again, and he brushed kisses against my forehead, my cheeks, my eyelids, and when I finally caught his mouth with mine, I poured all of the wanting and the hunger and the joy into him I possibly could, spun those same feelings out to him through our binding. And then he was moving on top of me and inside me and the heat went from a flash to an inferno, burning away everything except the two of us, something fine and sharp and sweet and painful building up within me. He said my name and my eyes flew open to find him watching me, and I broke beneath him, the world going brilliant and dark all at once.

It was quiet except for the sound of his breathing, ragged in my ear. My hands slicked down his back and he shifted to the side, drew me into his arms.

"See?" I whispered, tipping my head back to kiss him. "Like I said. Perfect."

He smoothed the damp tendrils of hair from my face, drew a thumb across my lips. "Did I hurt you?"

I lifted a shoulder. "A little. Worth it, though."

He skimmed a hand along my rib cage, over my hip bone, and then circled his fingers around my wrist, the bond bright and stronger than it had ever been before. It had saved my life, our bond. More than once, it had brought me back from the heart of the magic, given me strength and consolation and power. And now, it brought me Luc's words the instant before he spoke them.

"I love you," he said.

I propped myself on an elbow, feeling more naked than I had a few minutes ago, and hid behind a joke. "You've got the order wrong. You're supposed to say that *before*, to convince me."

"I'll remember that next time," he said, his tone matching mine. He touched his forehead to mine. "I love you, Mouse, and it's got nothing to do with what we did. It's just you. It's always been you."

Lacing our fingers together, he said, "I know you've got plenty left to deal with back home. I'll wait as long as you need."

"I need you," I said. "For keeps, remember? I'll deal with everything else, and then I'll come back."

"We will," he corrected. "Together. I like the sound of that."

"Good." I yawned, clapped a hand over my mouth, and he grinned.

"The rest of the world will keep," he said. "Sleep now."

I curled myself into him and didn't try to protest. "Together."

When I woke, the room was dim, and Luc's expression was wolfish and charming.

"Sleep well?" he asked, his hand sliding over me.

"What time is it?" I bolted upright and clutching the sheet to my chest. "Oh, God. Have I slept a whole day?"

"Middle of the morning. I was going to wake you in a bit. Your phone's been beeping like crazy. Like one of those little robot pets."

I climbed out of bed, managed to wrap the sheet around me like a giant towel. Luc's grin widened. "Why so shy?"

"I'm naked under here." I padded out to the living room, looking for where I'd dumped my bag when we came in.

"It's a good look for you. You weren't like this before."

"You distracted me. With kissing. And stuff." I rummaged

through pens and scraps of paper, hairclips and a granola bar.

"And stuff." He chuckled. "That an invitation?"

I grabbed for my phone and scrolled through. Missed calls, plenty of texts. Colin, Lena, my mom. Nick Petros. A single text from Jenny.

"I don't want to deal with this." I sat down on the couch.

"Then don't," he said. "Stay here. With me."

"I have to stop Billy. My mom's in danger, you know. If he'll go after me, he'll go after her."

"Let me take care of him."

I shook my head. If I asked Luc to do that, it would be because I was too scared to handle it myself. I wanted to be the person he thought I could be, strong and capable. I didn't need Billy to die. I just needed him to be out of my family's life. "My uncle. My fight."

He nodded unhappily. "When do we leave?"

CHAPTER 40

"Come inside," I said to Luc, standing at the door to the screen porch. We'd come Between at the side of the house, checking for cars. Even my mom's Taurus was gone, but I could see her through the windows, head bent over the sink, scrubbing furiously.

"You sure this is the right time for introductions?" Luc asked. "Might be a lot for her to take in, considerin'."

There was never going to be a good time to tell my mom about Luc. Instead, I opened the door and he followed behind, looking almost nervous. Luc, who never looked nervous. Who owned every room he walked into within seconds. And the prospect of meeting my mom turned his skin pale under the golden hue. It was oddly touching.

"Mo!" My mom whirled as we entered, squeezing the sponge so tightly that rivulets of soap ran down her arm. "Where have you been? We've been frantic!"

"I'm sorry." I knew how it looked—out all night, my hair wet from a hasty shower, wearing one of Luc's cashmere sweaters while he hovered at my shoulder. And for once, the situation was exactly as it seemed. I didn't even try to tell her she shouldn't worry, because I realized I'd been out of the loop for an entire day. She had all sorts of things to worry about, and Luc was the least of it.

"Where's Billy? And Dad?"

"Where have you been?" she asked again, voice shrill, and her eyes were filled with tears.

"Where are they, Mom?"

"Your uncle's probably at the bar. Your father's driving around looking for you. Where's Colin? He's supposed to be taking care of you."

"He had to leave." I kept my voice steady. For the best, I reminded myself.

Her gaze slid to Luc, openly hostile. "I can see why."

"Colin has a sister. Did you know that?"

"A sister? He never said . . . he should have brought her to visit."

"She was sick. Too sick to visit. She's better now, but they need a fresh start. They're gone, Mom."

Her lips pressed together, hands still wringing a dishcloth till it nearly split. "And who's this, then?"

"Luc DeFoudre," he said, stepping forward and offering his hand. "Pleasure to meet you, ma'am."

It had to be the accent, I decided. The accent, or the way his smile managed to be solemn yet beguiling, or the way he bowed slightly, like a courtier. Whatever trick he used, my mom thawed a few degrees—from arctic to merely wintry—and considering how very bad things were at the moment, that was an incredible victory.

"You're a friend of Mo's?"

"Yes'm."

"Well, Luc," she said. "We are having a slight family . . . situation right now. Perhaps you could come for dinner in a few weeks, and we could get to know you a little better. But for now, I'm going to have to ask you to excuse us."

Closing ranks. Putting on the veneer of propriety that she'd adopted most of my life. Impossible to pretend everything was okay, so she'd shifted to damage control, with a practiced smoothness.

Luc nodded politely. "I appreciate that, ma'am. But I'm afraid I can't leave."

"Oh?"

"Not if Mo's in trouble. Not if she might need help."

"What Mo needs," my mother said, "is someone who can take care of her. Protect her."

"She's not much inclined to let anyone do that," Luc said. "Wish she would, but I've learned it's better not to argue with her when she's got her mind made up."

"I can take care of myself," I said.

"Never said you couldn't," he replied. "But I might come in handy."

My mom set the dishcloth down and gripped the edge of the sink with both hands, seemingly arguing with herself. Finally, she turned back to us.

"Are you hungry? I can put together some sandwiches, if you'd like."

She'd been too upset to cook. She must have been out of her mind with worry, and I was about to make it worse.

"I can't stay," I began, but the phone rang, making us both jump.

"Maybe it's your father," she said, and lunged for the phone, cutting it off midring. From the way her face fell, I knew it wasn't Dad, and she held the handset out to me. "Billy," she said, her voice devoid of emotion.

"You have something that doesn't belong to you," he said when I'd taken the phone.

My mom watched me like she used to when I'd come home from a party—not that I'd gone to many, but she'd always stayed up, looking for any evidence of drinking or boys— vodka on my breath, shirt buttoned incorrectly. There'd never been anything for her to find. But I slipped into the other room, and before she could follow, Luc intercepted her.

"I could do with one of those sandwiches," he said. "And a cup of coffee, if it's not too much trouble. We both could, come to think of it. Not sure when I last saw her eat."

Clever Luc. I walked to the other side of the living room, peered out the windows. The street was empty—if Billy had people watching the house, they were well hidden. I turned my attention back to the phone.

"I don't have it. I did exactly what you told me to when I walked in there—I gave it to Ekomov."

"Don't play games with me. They didn't find it on his body. Or in the room."

"Things got a little crazy there at the end. Hard to keep track of a little thing like a flash drive when someone's trying to kill you."

"He said he wouldn't kill you. He wanted information."

"And then he wanted me dead. You saw what Anton sent after me in the alley. Darklings aren't big on talking."

His voice was icy. "It was business."

"I am *family.*"

"If you were family, you'd have helped. Every step of the way, you put someone else before us. The police identification. Donnelly. The Arcs—they're not even your people, and you chose them over your own kin. You made your feelings crystal clear, and so I did what I had to do to protect what's mine."

"Call someone who cares," I said.

But before I could hang up the phone, he said, "You care. I believe they call that an Achilles' heel, don't they? You care about all sorts of people—Donnelly and his sister, for example. And your mother."

"Colin and Tess are gone," I said, fear gathering at the nape of my neck.

"They can't have gotten too far in one day. Not with Tess in her condition. Not without help, and I can well imagine who you turned to this time. Lena, isn't it? Her family's got a talent for making people disappear without an ounce of magic."

"Leave her alone."

"Can you imagine what would happen if people started prying into their business? Years of jail time, I'd imagine. For all the people involved. When did your friend turn eighteen, I wonder?"

"It's a stupid disk drive," I said. "It's some files."

"Files that many people in this city—important people,

powerful people—have an interest in. You've pushed too much this time, Mo. You've angered too many people. If you return the drive, tonight, I can stave off the worst of the damage. If you don't, I can't protect you, or anyone else you care about. Lena, Donnelly . . . even your mother. It will be out of my hands, Maura Kathleen, and on your head."

"I don't—" have the drive, I almost said, and stopped. If he thought I had the drive, I had leverage. And one last chance to stop him. I climbed the stairs to my room. "I don't know how you live with yourself."

He chuckled. "Quite comfortably, as it happens. Bring the drive now. I'd like this finished."

The buzz of the dial tone filled my ear.

"Not as much as I would," I muttered, and rummaged in my desk until I found another St. Brigid's thumb drive, identical to the one he'd given me. Then I returned to the kitchen, where my mom and Luc were each pretending to eat a roast beef sandwich, the squat jar of horseradish between them. I set the phone back on the base.

"I have to go out for a little while."

My mother dropped her sandwich. "You just got back! Your father's still out looking for you, Mo. We'll call him. Let him take care of this."

"He can't. I won't be long. Stay here until I come back."

"I am your mother! I don't know what gives you the idea that you can order me around, but you have it absolutely backward, young lady. I want to know what's going on. This minute."

"Billy thinks I have something of his."

"You stole from him?" she said, clearly horrified.

"No—he gave it to me. Now he wants it back." I rubbed at my forehead. "It's complicated, okay? But I need to go see him. I'll be back as soon as I can."

"Mo, sweetheart." She pressed a fist against her mouth, like she was holding back words. "Be careful."

Luc followed me outside. "You gave Jenny the drive. Why not let the police handle it now?"

"He's going after the people I love. My friends. My family. I'm not waiting for the police." I slung my bag over my shoulder and started down the sidewalk.

"Your uncle's a bad man, and he needs to be dealt with, but Mouse, I am begging you. Let someone else do it."

I whirled. "You knew this is why I was coming back. Why are you trying to talk me out of it now?"

"Because we're good now, you and I. We're finally good, and the magic is safe, and you are scaring the hell out of me." He took my face in his hands, and I understood the source of his fear

"I love you, too." Just saying the words out loud gave me strength. "And when this is done, you are taking us somewhere wonderful. The ocean. I have never seen the ocean in my life, and I think it's about time."

"The ocean," he said, swallowing hard. "You gonna wear a bikini?"

"You could probably talk me into it."

"Rather talk you out of it," he grumbled.

"That too." I kissed him, slow and careful until my blood started to heat and his hands edged under my shirt, and the kiss turned fast and hard and desperate.

Then I broke away and headed for Morgan's, promising myself it would be the last time.

CHAPTER 41

We could have gone Between, I guess, but I needed the time to make a plan. The air smelled like earth and melting snow despite the chill wind. "It smells like spring," I said, surprised. When had winter ended?

Luc drew in a deep breath, humoring me. "Never lived somewhere with seasons. Wouldn't mind giving it a try. If you wanted."

"Leave New Orleans?" I'd never considered the notion that Luc might move somewhere else. He'd always seemed tied to the city. Then again, we hadn't had time to consider our future at all, really.

"I'm not on the Quartoren yet," he said. "Easy enough to pop in when they need us."

It would be so easy to walk with Luc and plan our future, now that we had one. But the plans I needed to make now were a little more immediate and a lot less fun.

"Don't much trust your uncle," Luc said. "Figure he's not inviting you down to Morgan's for a drink."

"No," I said. "But he won't hurt me. Not if you're there." I touched his arm. "I hate to ask this of you."

"You changed your mind? You want me to take him out?"

"No. But if you could look threatening. Do the thing where the sparks come out of your hand. The sword wouldn't be a bad touch."

"My usual charming self, then."

"Exactly. The drive I gave Jenny—it should be enough to lock him up, and based on what she's said, they'll move in pretty quickly. I just need to keep things under control for a little longer."

"Easy as pie," he said, stopping midstride. "You know, you haven't mentioned your daddy in all of this."

I understood my father, finally. I had learned easily you could trap yourself—make one bad decision with the best of intentions, and watch your life slide out of control as a result. "He didn't know about Anton. I'm sure of it. Billy wanted to keep the magic for himself. As for the rest . . . he's my dad. He's not happy about working for Billy again, but he went ahead and did it. I think he knows it's going to end badly, but he's stuck."

"You still angry?"

We walked another block before I answered. "Hurt, I guess. I wish my mom and I had been enough for him. Or maybe he thought he wasn't enough for us. Either way . . . I can't help him now."

He squeezed my hand in silent understanding.

"So, we go in," Luc said. "You'll give him the drive? Even though it's fake?"

"I want Billy to think he's won," I said. "I want to see him think he's beaten me, and give me that smug look, and then I want to see his face when I take it all away. When I tell him the cops have the real drive, and he's finished. He's taken so much from me, Luc. From my mom. I want to see him realize that I've taken every last thing from him."

Luc blinked, shook his head. "You're vergin' on blood-thirsty, Mouse. Unexpected."

"Does that bother you?"

"Not at all. Thinking maybe you missed your calling for the Quartoren, though. You'd make Dominic either very nervous or very proud."

"I prefer nervous."

"Figured you might."

CHAPTER 42

Morgan's was empty.

Morgan's was never empty.

Except for now. No customers at the tables, no Charlie wiping down the bar. No ESPN on the plasma. Empty and quiet and dark.

Until two men stepped out of the shadows on either side of the door.

"Take him out front," Billy called, sliding out of the booth and strolling across the room. "I didn't invite *him,* Mo."

"Luc stays, or we both go. Your pick."

"My bar. My rules," he said, his voice wavering with rage. He brought it back under control with an effort. "Your friend isn't welcome here."

"Like to see you make me leave," Luc said easily, his hand still twined with mine.

"Did you enjoy the sandwich? Roast beef, wasn't it?" he said. "My sister does a lovely job with them. She always includes just the right amount of horseradish."

"Horseradish?" I stared for a moment, and then it hit me. "You've been watching the house. You called the landline, not my cell. You knew the moment we came home."

The grin stretched clear across his face but never reached his eyes.

"And *that,*" he said to Luc, "is how I make you leave."

"Mouse?" Luc asked. My call, he was telling me. He'd do whatever I asked.

Billy pulled his phone from his pocket and waggled it at me. "You're too young to remember this," he said conversationally. "But the phone companies used to have a slogan. 'Reach out and touch someone.' Shall I reach out, Mo?"

The magic went on alert, and my pulse galloped. I couldn't look at Luc, or I'd break. "It'll be fine," I said to him.

"Of course it will," Billy said. "So long as everyone behaves properly."

"I'll be okay." I brushed my lips over Luc's cheek and whispered, "Help my mom."

He flexed his fingers, like he was about to cast a working, and walked out, the two guys trailing behind.

"Now," said Billy. "Let's get down to business, shall we? Or would you like one last drink before the war?"

"War's over," I said, forcing myself not to look out the window toward Luc. "You lost. The police are coming for you, Uncle Billy. They have enough to nail you even without the drive. You can drag this out longer, I guess, but in the end, you'll be going to prison."

He sat on the barstool, expansive and unconcerned. "Your mother always said you were better at science than history. Don't you know how this plays out?"

"If you think my dad's going to take the fall for you again, you're crazy."

"I think your father will do anything to protect his family. You get that from him, you know. This belief that you can save everyone. The Donnellys, your friend Lena. I would imagine your hunger to find Verity's killers was penance for not saving her."

A flare of anger obscured my vision for an instant. "I really don't think you should talk to me about Verity."

"You couldn't save Joseph Kowalski, either, could you? That, by the way, truly wasn't my doing."

"I know."

"So it would appear that history repeats itself. We'll carry on, just as we always have." He sat back with a smug, satisfied look. Not taking his eyes off me, he called, "How does that sound to you, Jack?"

There was a noise from the back room. Heavy, tired footsteps, and my father appeared. "Sounds like you've got everything planned out, Billy."

"Dad?" I stared, baffled. He'd heard everything? And he was taking Billy's side?

"Mo." He sighed, shaking his head. "I wish I could say I was happy to see you."

"Mom said you were out looking for me."

"Wasn't hard to figure out where you'd end up," he said. "I told you to not to take that drive. Did you think I was joking?"

"You don't understand. You don't know what he's done." I had to make him understand. Make him see how bad this was. Convince him to help me.

Before I could tell him about Mom, Billy cut me off. "It doesn't matter. Hand it over, Mo."

I didn't move, and he slapped the bar open-palmed, so hard the glasses jumped. "Now. Unless you want me to tell Marco Forelli you've decided to go from stubborn to suicidal."

"Dad?"

"Do it," he said tonelessly. "And then leave."

"Why are you doing this?" I willed myself not to cry, but the hurt was deeper and more painful than I'd anticipated.

"To protect you and your mother. The way I should have all along."

I blinked, shook my head, and threw the drive onto the bar. "So much for being a changed man."

Billy snorted. "People don't change, Maura Kathleen. Look at you. For all your bravado, you still do exactly what's expected."

I gritted my teeth. "Don't be so sure."

"You came right over here, didn't you? Brought the drive, just like I told you to. And now you'll come back to work for us, as expected." He scooped it up and smiled.

My temper, thin and brittle, snapped into a hundred pieces. "I brought you *a* drive. Not *the* drive."

"What do you mean?" Billy said. My father's head jerked up.

"Enjoy the files," I said. "My physics teacher really liked the presentation on dark matter. I'd ask you what you think of it, but you'll both be in jail."

Billy gaped at me, and I tried to feel the satisfaction I'd anticipated. The triumph. Instead, it left a sharp, vinegary taste in my mouth, especially when I looked at my dad.

"The police have the drive and your files," I said. "You're holding my junior year portfolio."

"You gave it to the police?" asked my father. He didn't seem shocked, just confused.

"Close enough."

"You stupid, stupid girl! Forelli will kill you—he'll kill all of us. Don't you see what you've done?" Billy stood so abruptly the stool toppled over, and went behind the bar. Face splotched with red, hands shaking, he pulled a bottle of Bushmills off the top shelf and poured a glass. He downed it in one go and pointed a trembling finger at me. "You're a ghost," he said. "You died the minute you handed over the drive. So did your family."

He exchanged a glance with my father. "She's killed us all, Jack. What now?"

"I'll deal with her at home. She's my responsibility." He folded his arms, glaring at me.

Billy poured another glass. "You've been too soft with her from the moment you got back. She's a danger to us; she has been from the start. You've no idea what she's been up to. I'm the one who kept her in line."

"I'll take care of her," my dad said again, moving toward me, but I backed away, banging into a table.

"Sure, and I'll tell Marco what? She's grounded? You've taken away her television privileges? We need to control the damage. Prove she was working alone. He needs to know we're loyal." He rounded on me. "You were such a darling girl, once upon a time."

I saw Billy grimace, his idea of an apology. I saw him bend slightly, reaching beneath the counter.

When he straightened, all I saw was the gun.

CHAPTER 43

The sound of the safety clicking off was louder than I'd expected. Like someone snapping their fingers right next to your eardrum, a high harsh sound.

"You don't want to shoot me." Reasons, eminently logical, flooded my brain. Luc would kill him. Colin would kill him. Forelli would still blame him for the drive. Murder charges carried a stiffer penalty than racketeering. He'd lose the bar. He'd lose everything.

But my mouth wouldn't work. And the wild, vacant look in his eyes said logic wasn't going to be much use. Billy's rage had carried him light-years past reason.

"We all have choices," my dad said, stepping in front of me. "And hurting my daughter would be the worst one you ever made."

I sagged against the table. My father gave me a faint, weary smile over his shoulder. "It's going to be okay, sweetheart."

Never had I wanted to believe him more.

He kept his hands up, easy, nonthreatening, but there was steel in his voice when he said, "Put the gun down."

"We need to minimize the damage," my uncle said.

"Mo," my father said, as if Billy hadn't spoken. "Leave."

I glanced toward the front door, too scared to breathe.

"Don't take a step," Billy said. "Jack, we have a situation. It needs to be dealt with."

"It will be," my father promised. Something was transforming him—the stoop of his shoulders disappearing, the lines around his eyes determined instead of defeated. "You're going to let Mo leave. You're going to call off the men at the house. And then I will deal with you."

Billy's hand trembled. "You know I'd never hurt Annie, not truly."

"You've got two guys covering my home, and they're both carrying. I can have my people take them out now, but I'd rather not put my wife in harm's way. *My wife,* you bastard. My wife and my daughter. I trusted you to look after them."

"Your people?" Billy asked, and the gun steadied. "And who are your people, that you come into my bar and tell me what to do?"

"Me, to start with." The door to the storeroom, the one that connected Morgan's to The Slice, slammed wide open. Colin strode in, and I could breathe again.

Billy looked between the three of us, confusion plain on his face. "You left town."

"Not quite yet," Colin said. He held out his hand for me. "Come on, Mo."

I couldn't stop watching the waves of hatred rolling off my dad. So much anger, so carefully restrained, as if he was waiting for something.

"You used my wife. My child. That was never part of our deal," my dad said, taking a slow, menacing step forward.

"I've protected them."

"You *used* them. I've seen the records. I know what you've done with the restaurant's books, even after you signed the business over to Annie. I told her not to let you help with the taxes, to keep all her files separate, but she has a blind spot for you. Always has."

"It was nothing," Billy said. "Barely worth the effort, really. I just kept running cash through until it was squeaky clean, same as I'd always done, and she never noticed the difference."

"And burning down The Slice?"

"The money came in handy, of course. But we needed Mo on our side. And it showed people how badly things would go, if they cast their lot with the wrong team."

"So you burned down my wife's restaurant to intimidate people—including Mo—and to get a little insurance money?"

"These are difficult times. I do what's necessary to protect what's mine."

"So do I." My dad turned to me, deliberately putting his back to Billy and the gun. "You did good, sweetheart. But you should have listened to Nick."

"Nick? You know . . ." Suddenly, it made sense. The early release. The secret phone calls. His insistence that I didn't understand what he was doing. "You were working for the police?"

"The FBI. Part of the deal was that you and the Kowalski girl weren't supposed to participate anymore."

"Nick said they didn't need us. Because they had you." *The bigger picture,* Nick had told me. And I'd never seen it. I'd treated my dad like a criminal. My voice shook. "You should have told me."

"I didn't even tell your mother. I had to make you doubt me. It was the best way to convince Billy and Marco that I was truly back. I'm sorry."

"It's okay," I said. "It's good. Not good. But manageable, right?" The words tumbled out as relief swept over me. He'd chosen us. That's what mattered. He'd chosen us over the Outfit. We could fix this, and be a family again. A fresh start, like he'd said. I grabbed his hand. "It's okay. We'll call the police and they'll arrest Billy and everything will be fine. We can go—" *Home,* I was going to say, but Billy's outrage, loud enough to rattle the bottles on the shelves, drowned me out.

"You bastard!"

"Gun!" Colin shouted. My dad shoved me to the ground with a grunt, the sound of the gunshot impossibly loud and close. He staggered, dropped, and I scrambled across the floor to him, screaming, seeing the dark stain spreading across his denim shirt, not caring about Billy anymore.

Gunshot. Pressure on the wound. Stop the bleeding. I'd paid attention in health class. I knew first aid. I could fix this.

Colin dove toward me, but Billy fired again, the noise splitting the air like someone had gone Between, but it wasn't Luc—it was me. The bullet slammed into my shoulder and the magic flared crazily, shrieking in protest. Colin took aim at Billy just as people in helmets and bulky vests burst in. The room spun as the magic shuddered, and Colin dropped the gun, shouting something to the cops, easing me back, and stripping off his jacket to press against my shoulder.

"Gunshot," I mumbled to Colin as time slowed to a crawl. "Pressure on the wound."

I looked past him. Billy was still holding the gun, aiming at me again, snarling and holding everyone at bay. He'd lost it completely. He'd kill me before the cops could stop him.

He jerked back at the same time I heard more gunshots—four sharp explosions like the Fourth of July—and disappeared behind the bar.

I twisted my head to the side and saw my father, half-sitting, Colin's gun slipping from his hand, blood pooling around him. He collapsed.

"No!" Somehow, I shook Colin off and crawled to my father, panting, the magic wailing and frantic, keening loss, and I wanted to keen, too, but all I could say was his name, and beg him to stay.

People didn't stay.

I'd done this before. I knew. People didn't stay. Not like this. Not with so much blood, and I'd sent Luc away. I screamed for him now, felt my father's hand touch mine.

"Wish I'd done that twelve years ago," he said, the words grinding out of him, costing him so much. "Never should've left."

"You're here now," I said. "Just stay, okay? Don't go. Hang on a little longer. We can fix this."

I needed Luc. I needed the magic. I needed time. God, why wasn't there ever enough time?

He tried to smile but only one corner of his mouth lifted, and his eyes met mine again, hazel and infinitely sad. "Liar."

"Daddy, don't." My tears were lost in the stain spreading across his chest.

"You go now. Far away. And be . . . extraordinary, okay?" His breath rattled, his voice faded. "Love you, sweetheart."

"I love you, too. Daddy, please. I'm sorry. Please. Don't—"

The EMTs elbowed us out of the way, urging me onto a stretcher, and I was fighting them off but my shoulder hurt so, so much, and everything started to go black. I felt Colin pick me up and carry me outside, and Luc was there, shoving his way through the crowd of people, blazing with fear and love.

"Mouse!" His hand was on my shoulder, but I pushed him toward the door. "My dad. Luc. Inside." And he was gone again, and the dark came back.

CHAPTER 44

There were so many lights and so many horrible noises—wailing and shrieking—and the sensation of hurtling through space, and I hurt so much I didn't want to breathe. I didn't open my eyes, but saw the ocean, the line of damp sand, the endless waves cresting against the horizon. Ancient hills shrouded in mist, weathered and lovely. A field of wildflowers, blossoms nodding and stirring in the breeze, azure sky dotted with clouds stretching overhead. Peaceful sights. Calming sights. A sending from the magic, the only kind of healing it could provide.

When I finally opened my eyes, it was to the last thing I wanted to see.

Hospital. Emergency room. I'd done this before and was not looking forward to a repeat.

"Hey." Luc said, standing in the curtained doorway. "You're awake."

His face was haggard, haunted. "No," I said, turning my head to keep from seeing what was written there.

"I tried," he said softly. "It was too late."

I closed my eyes, felt the tears spilling over.

"I'm sorry," he said, and his voice broke. "I'm so sorry. I tried—"

"I know." *Can't fix dead,* he'd told me ages ago.

He didn't say anything else for a long time, but I felt the gentle stroke of his hand over my hair, wordless consolation.

"My mom?"

"*Maman*'s there. Took care of your uncle's guys, called her to keep your mom company while I came back to you." He paused. "They had so many people watching the bar I couldn't get through—not even with a concealment. I should have gone Between. Should have chanced it."

"Billy would have freaked. Started shooting anyway. It's not your fault."

If it was anyone's fault, it was mine—I was the one who'd egged Billy on, flaunted the fact I'd switched out the drives. If I hadn't pushed him. If my dad hadn't admitted he was working for FBI. If Colin hadn't surprised us. If Luc had stayed. So many ifs, and none of them made a difference. None of them changed the truth. My father was dead, and only now did I realize who he truly was.

You won't understand until it's too late. I'd thought Marguerite was talking about the magic, or taking my place with the Quartoren. But it had been this moment all along. Not even my Flat life could escape her predictions. I couldn't separate the two anymore.

"Does my mom know?"

"Cujo told her. Police were mighty interested in him, but he managed to sneak off." He tried to smile but failed. "Might have had a little help. He figured it might come easier if she heard it from him instead of the police."

"She needs me." I struggled to sit up, and he slipped an arm around my waist.

"Let me heal your arm," he said. "Please."

"It's fine."

"They patched you up, but it's going to hurt like hell for the next couple weeks. I couldn't . . ." He stopped, searching for the words. "You'll hurt plenty no matter what, but this I can fix. I need to."

I nodded and he pulled the hospital gown to the side, baring my shoulder and the thick gauze pad taped over it. Gently, he peeled the bandage away and his fingers hovered over the wound.

I kept my eyes shut. I'd seen enough blood today.

When he spoke, it was as if the magic had been waiting for him, drawing the words in eagerly, rising up to meet him. The warmth spread along my back and down my arm, and I could feel our connection respond, his love and concern a tangible presence.

He touched his lips to the top of my shoulder and drew the thin blue gown back up.

"My clothes?"

"Not in any condition to be worn again," he said. "Niobe brought you some things."

St. Brigid's sweats and a T-shirt, and he glanced away, giving me privacy as I dressed.

"Home," I said softly, and he nodded, helping me to my feet.

I slipped my arms around his neck, still unsteady, and breathed in the scent of him, spice and smoke and saltwater. *Safe now,* I told myself, and that's when I cried.

He didn't say anything, just held on while I sobbed and sobbed, because my dad was never coming back and neither was Verity, and I hated fate more than I ever had before, because I didn't know how to go on and I didn't believe it could tell me a path.

Inside me, the magic hummed a steady reassurance, a comfort, a promise that whatever was ahead of me, I wouldn't be alone. Luc's heartbeat told me the same thing.

After a long time, there were no more tears. I drew back, wiping at my cheeks, and he cradled my face in his hands, brushing away the dampness, pressing kisses against my swollen lids, and my breathing slowed.

"Ready?"

I shook my head. No. Never.

"Then I'll stay close," he promised.

CHAPTER 45

There was no way to gauge the mood inside my house, to prepare for what I was walking into. The shades were drawn, a thin yellow line edging the windows, and the house was quiet. I trudged up the front steps, Luc at my side, the doorknob turning easily under my hand.

Inside, my mom sat on the edge of the couch, brittle as old glass. Marguerite sat next to her, her delicate hands encasing my mom's work-reddened ones. Colin sat in the chair opposite, elbows on knees, miserable.

"Mo!"

"Mom," I said. "I . . ."

She stood, and Colin jumped to his feet, ready to catch her if she seemed unsteady. I shot him a look of gratitude.

"Your father? He's really gone?" she said, her voice tremulous with disbelief.

I pressed my lips together and nodded, throat too clogged to speak.

"Billy?"

I didn't know if she was asking whether Billy was dead, or if he'd been the one responsible. The answer was the same. I didn't need to say the words. She looked at my face, and she knew the truth.

She gave a cry—a soft, warbling sound that cut right through me—and sank back to the couch. I lurched forward. Strange, how I thought my tears would have run dry by now. I should have known better.

"Mo, sit with your mother," said Marguerite. "Boys, help me make tea."

I sat, and took my mother's hand, and tried to be as strong for her as my dad had been for me.

"What are we going to do?" she asked as we huddled together, clutching me like I was the only thing she had left in the world. Maybe I was. "What do we do now?"

"I don't know." That wasn't true. I did know. But saying it out loud seemed cruel.

You lived. That's what you did. When you loved someone and they died and the world stopped spinning on its axis and gravity failed and everything tasted like ashes and rage, you lived. Not always well, or happily. Sometimes it was just forcing yourself to take one more breath, or one more step. Sometimes you wished you didn't. But in the end, you lived. Because they couldn't. And you owed it to them.

You lived.

CHAPTER 46

"I have to leave," said Colin. We stood on the porch. He'd hugged my mom, said good-bye to Marguerite, nodded at Luc. The light from the kitchen barely illuminated his face, and I switched on the lamp. I wanted to see him clearly. I wanted him to see me.

"Your dad called me, right after you and Luc had left. He explained everything then. I swear, Mo, I didn't know about the FBI before then, or I would have told you. I'd figured he was trying to find a way to get you out of the deal, that's all. Trading himself for you."

"He did," I said softly.

He touched my cheek, tentative. "He was right. You did good."

I rubbed at my eyes, gritty from too many tears. "You're the one who came back. You didn't need to."

"How many times have I told you—I want you to be safe. And happy." He glanced over my shoulder, into the house. "You could come with us, if you wanted. We can start over somewhere else. Be happy."

I tried to smile, but it wouldn't come. "You told me once that you always wanted a quiet life. Do you remember?"

He nodded.

"You deserve that," I said. "I want that for you. So much."

"But not for you, right?" He closed his eyes briefly, pain

evident on his face, and something twisted inside me, the tears starting fresh. "I thought you might say that."

"I want you to have a really good life, okay?"

He kissed me gently, his lips solid and real against mine. "I will try. Just . . . promise me something, Mo."

"Name it."

"You have a really amazing one. Do all the things you never believed you could. Do even more." He laughed a little. "And give Luc all the hell you can. Which is a lot. I should know."

"Done," I said.

He nodded and let himself out. I stood at the top of the steps, hugging myself against the cold, and watched him leave. He looked back once, and I lifted a hand in farewell, knowing it would be the last time I saw him.

Then he was gone.

I turned off the light and sat on the ancient couch in the dark, and listened to the sound of the snow melting off the eaves, and prayed—to God, or the magic, or fate, or anyone else that was listening—that he'd be safe, and happy, and not hate me.

After a little while, Luc came out and sat down on the other end of the couch.

"He ask you to go with him?"

"Yes."

He picked at the arm of the couch, breaking off a cracked piece of wicker and setting it aflame like a tiny candle. "You want to go?"

"I'm here," I said, watching the flame throw shadows over his face. "What do you think?"

He jerked a shoulder. "I think your mama needs you right now. But down the road . . ."

I concentrated, pushed enough magic into our connection to make it visible, and lifted my hand, the silver filament glowing between us. "I choose you," I said. "You. And me. For keeps."

* * *

Later, after the police had come with solemn faces and practiced sympathy, after Father Armando had come to pray and bear witness, after my mom had made her way upstairs alone, refusing help, I lay on the couch, my head on Luc's lap, his fingers twined with mine.

"You should rest," Marguerite said. "You've been so strong, but your mother will need you even more tomorrow. When all of this sinks in."

"I think she knew," I said. "All along, she knew it wouldn't last."

"She was making all those plans," Luc said. "Expandin' the restaurant. Talkin' about the future. Why would she do that if she thought it wouldn't happen?"

"Maybe because she was afraid it wouldn't? Like she thought, if she could just make it perfect, it would stick. I don't know what she'll do about the restaurant now." I didn't know if she would cling more tightly to it, the anchor that had held her steady for the last twelve years, or if it would be too much, a reminder of everything that had gone wrong, dragging her under the surface of her grief.

"Time enough to decide," said Marguerite, her hands folded in front of her. "For now, you need sleep."

"Close your eyes, Mouse, I'll stay as long as you need."

My eyes drifted shut, and Luc tugged the afghan over my shoulders. Too painful to think of my father, to watch the images that played in my mind, so I tuned into the magic instead, let it direct my thoughts, let my mind wander out along the lines, looking for something that might soothe the raw edges of my grief.

Instead, I saw the Assembly, the Quartoren seated in their ornamental chairs, a new table before them like a blank slate. They were complete, ready to start a new era for the Arcs. Stable magic, the Torrent Prophecy averted, the Seraphim defeated . . . they were frozen as if in a tableau, Dominic still the leader, Sabine poised and watchful next to him. Orla, fussy and demanding to be heard, and Pascal, distracted as usual.

At the edge of the stage was the shattered table, the pieces piled haphazardly, exactly as we'd left them after Marguerite's prophecy. Sadness swept over me again, yet another sign of all we'd lost. But the magic didn't respond in kind. Instead, it quickened my blood, overlaid the sorrow with yearning.

I shifted, uncomfortable with the sensation, trying to will it away, but the magic only grew more insistent. I opened my eyes, hoping to dispel the images.

"Shhh . . ." Luc stroked my hair, but I struggled to sit up. "What's wrong?"

"The magic. It wants something." Affirmation bloomed like a flower inside me.

"Wants you to nap, more'n likely."

"No. Can we go to the Assembly?"

"You feel the need to stare down the Quartoren one more time?"

"The magic's not done talking. It's the table, Luc. I have to fix the table."

"It's been broken for days. Another one won't hurt."

"Please," I said. "Take me to the Assembly. I need to see it for myself."

"Maman?"

"I'll stay with Mo's mother," she said. "Good luck, Mo."

The Assembly was almost completely restored, the ruined table the only reminder of the Darklings' attack.

"Son," said Dominic as we approached. "Maura. Something we can help you with?" The cautious sympathy in his voice made it clear he knew about my dad.

"No," I said, letting go of Luc's hand to kneel next to the pile of ebony wood.

"We're about to induct Sabine," he said. "You're more than welcome to watch, but we'd like to get down to it."

I didn't reply. Instead, I studied the symbols, trying to understand the interplay between them and the magic. One by one, the Quartoren left their seats and crossed the stage, Pascal first, peering at me through his glasses.

"Mouse?" Luc asked. "What are you doing?"

I could feel the Quartoren exchanging glances, deciding whether or not to humor me. "I can fix it," I said. "The magic wants me to. It's what your mom said: Listen and speak."

His arms came around me. "You don't have to fix everything. Sometimes we can't, okay? Sometimes we just have to let it go. There are things even magic can't do. You know that."

I rested my forehead on his chest. Gone was gone. He was right. There was no way to repair this table.

But I could make a new one.

A new table. A new Quartoren. A new age, as Marguerite had predicted.

"Do you trust me?" I kept my voice low, my head still tucked under his chin.

"Of course."

"I know what the magic wants me to do, but I need your help."

His eyes met mine, oddly calm, absolutely sure. "I'm all yours."

I stood and walked to the table where the Quartoren had been sitting. It was a single, solid expanse of ebonized wood, smooth and even. I felt a tingling along my spine, exactly where Luc had placed his hand.

"That's for the Quartoren," blustered Dominic. "I'll be the first to admit you have more leeway than most, but some things aren't meant for you."

"This is," I said. "Be quiet, Dominic. *I'm talking.*"

I closed my eyes, and the graceful, twisting lines of a glyph sprang up, as clear and pristine in my mind as if it were real. Without looking, I drew a copy on the tabletop with clean, purposeful strokes, waiting for the magic to recognize it.

Luc started, and I opened my eyes to see light breaking through where I'd traced, tiny pinpricks where my finger had touched, fine as dust motes. I leaned down and blew gently, and flecks of wood scattered. More scratch than carving, but the mark was indelible.

"Again," Luc whispered, as if he was afraid he'd break my concentration. He didn't need to worry. I retraced the markings, opening myself fully to the lines crisscrossing the room, my hand shaking with the influx of power. Luc's talent bolstered my own, and the words began to take shape.

At first, the magic felt diffuse, blurred at the edges, like a silhouette held too far from the light. But I stretched myself, listening to what it said with my entire body, the power growing sharper, coming into focus, and the wood was transformed at my touch. With each pass, more flaked away, the carving more pronounced, the light shining more brightly.

Still, the design was static. Beautiful, luminescent with power, but it wouldn't move. It didn't have the same vitality as the old table. The magic urged me to draw more shapes, and I began to work around the table, creating whatever glyphs the magic gave me. Symbols from every House, every element. Some resembled spells I'd learned for the Succession, and some were completely new.

I could sense the Quartoren edging closer, heard the confusion in their voices, but tuned them out. All I wanted to hear was the magic. Anything else was a distraction, would alter the symbols I was carving into the table. My arms trembled with the effort, my breathing coming in fits and starts. Luc buoyed me, enabling me to continue the painstaking work.

Time passed, and I moved around the table, my confidence increasing with each completed glyph, all the way down the massive table legs, light streaming out, illuminating the farthest corners of the Assembly. When I'd carved the last symbol, my mind went quiet and blank, and I sagged back against Luc, exhausted. But the magic wasn't done. The symbols were inert, unmoving. They needed something else.

They needed my voice.

I chose the ones that were most familiar—symbols I'd learned from Niobe—and began to recite them. Despite my halting, cumbersome speech, they grew brighter. The more I spoke, the more easily the words came, ones I'd never heard before flowing as easily as rosary prayers, and I realized—the magic was giving the language of the Arcs to me. I understood them perfectly now, the same absolute comprehension I'd felt during the Torrent, and when I'd bound myself to the magic.

But this time, there was no chance of getting lost, because the magic was inside me, centered deep within, simultaneously infinite and contained. I didn't need to lose myself in the magic to succeed; I simply needed to join it. It was my voice the magic had needed to coax the symbols to life, clear and perfect and vibrant. My words—the exact translation of the magic's needs—took root and began to grow. As I spoke, I pulled power from the lines and poured it into the symbols. Gradually, they came alive, magic pulsing like a heartbeat in each, giving them a specific hue. Ruby for fire, sapphire for water, emerald for earth, gold for air.

And something else.

Something new.

Something the magic and I had created together.

Some of the symbols—the most complicated shapes of all, the ones the Quartoren stared at in fascination—glittered diamond-bright and began to shift and slide over the tabletop, picking up speed, the effect rippling out to the other glyphs until we were all bathed in a whirl of colors, the signs streaming over the tabletop too quickly to distinguish.

Alive. That's what they were now—some portion of the magic's life force captured within the table, and some portion of mine as well. There was a place for me at the table now, I understood. The magic and its language were imprinted on my soul as deeply as they were in that table. This moment, this task—this had been what I was meant to do all along.

Eventually, the compulsion to chant slowed, the words tapering off, the symbols' movement less frenetic. Orla sighed, a mixture of awe and delight, while Pascal and Sabine examined the symbols. My legs started to give way, and Luc guided me to one of the Quartoren chairs.

"Thanks," I rasped, rubbing at my throat.

"You changed the magic," Dominic said accusingly. "Again."

I shook my head. The lines were as strong and flexible as ever, the source steady and powerful. But I'd done enough talking. Dominic could wait.

Pascal, though, had already figured it out. "You reformed the table."

I nodded.

"The Quartoren's restored, then," said Dominic. "About damn time."

"Not restored," Pascal said, catching my eye. *"Reformed."*

Orla's brow furrowed delicately. "Like the table."

Sabine was still inspecting the symbols. "Some of these don't correspond to a specific House," she said. "They're directly from the source."

"The source is alive," I said. "For as long as the Arcs have existed, you've treated the magic as a power plant, not as a living being. That's wrong. It wants to help you, but it needs a voice. The magic needed someone to protect it, because you're pledged to protect your House."

My own voice petered out, and I looked to Pascal to continue.

"It chose Maura. In reforming the table, the Quartoren has been reformed as well. The four Houses no longer compose the Quartoren Entire. Maura has taken up a seat as well."

"She stepped aside," Dominic protested. "She refused to serve as Matriarch. And now she creates her own position?"

"Didn't you pay attention?" Luc asked. "She couldn't represent a single House when she has ties to all of them. It would have tipped the balance. But now . . ."

"Now her seat is not tied to a House, but to the magic itself," said Sabine.

I looked at each of them in turn. "From here on out, the magic has a say in what you do. How things are run."

"The magic—" Dominic began, but I shoved out of the chair and stood directly in front of him, arms folded across my chest.

"The magic speaks through me. You can either adjust or hand the reins off to Luc."

Next to me, Luc flinched. "Prefer to wait, if it's all the same to you."

Dominic scowled. "What if something happens to you? What if the Seraphim re-form? You're not immortal."

I touched the spot on my shoulder where the bullet had struck me, saw blood still caked under my fingernails. "Definitely not immortal."

"A succession," put in Sabine. "Just as with any other seat. A ceremony, or a prophecy. A child."

"We don't need to worry about that," I said quickly. "Not for a long time. And as for the Seraphim . . . they needed Anton. He was the force behind them, and watching him self-destruct was the most effective way of ending them.

"It comes down to this. I don't care what you call it—the Quartoren or Congress or the High Council of Mystical Woo-Woo—but the magic has a place now. And I'm its representative. From now on, whatever decisions you make take the will of the magic into account. That's how we go forward, or we don't go forward at all."

One by one, the Quartoren nodded. Dominic and Orla with obvious reluctance, Pascal and Sabine out of sheer fascination. The new era had started.

CHAPTER 47

Nothing fascinates people like death. The stream of visitors through our living room was constant, exhausting. I spent the next few days accepting condolences and casseroles, shielding my mom from too many questions, planning the funeral and my future. I spent the nights curled next to Luc on my narrow bed. When the nightmares came—and they did, because not even the magic could take away the things I'd seen—he was there, replacing them with soft words and gentle warmth and promises that daylight would come again.

The funeral was packed, but my mom and I stood apart from everyone else. She clutched my arm as the casket was lowered, as Father Armando spoke the words of the service, as a raw spring wind whipped around us. Luc and Marguerite stood nearby. Behind them, the Quartoren watched, faces solemn and respectful, and I nodded my thanks.

After the crowd dispersed, the last of them straggling down the drive, Jenny Kowalski stepped out from behind a nearby tree. I should have been surprised, but I'd watched her father's funeral from a distance. It seemed fitting she should do the same.

"It sucks beyond belief, doesn't it?" Her eyes were red-rimmed, and I knew her tears were for both of us. "I'm sorry."

"Thanks," I said, meaning it. She understood in a way no one else had.

"Nick—" She jerked her head to where Nick Petros stood,

a short distance down the road. "He says they've taken Marco Forelli into custody. That he won't be able to get out this time. Your dad's wiretaps, plus the records . . . it's everything they needed."

"I'm glad." I was trying to be, anyway. Trying to care. My dad had died because he was trying to protect me—not just from Billy's gun, but from the life he'd left me exposed to, twelve years ago. Remembering that made the grief a little more manageable. Made it easier to put aside guilt and focus on helping my mom.

"What now?" she asked.

"Still figuring that out." The heels of my shoes sank a little in the half-thawed ground, and I shifted. "How about you?"

"The usual. School. Track. I have another year before I graduate. I've got time." She ran a hand over her ponytail. "Good luck, Mo."

"You too."

After she'd left, Luc returned. "Your mom went on ahead with the priest. I told her I'd see you home."

"Do you think we should tell her?"

"About the Arcs?" He considered as we wandered through the cemetery. I didn't take the path back to the gates. Instead, I turned toward the section where Verity was buried, Luc at my side. "Eventually. When she's steadier. When you've decided what to do."

I nodded, my footsteps slowing as we approached the gravestone with Verity's name engraved on it. The white marble felt cold and still under my hands, such a misguided tribute for someone so vibrant and vital.

"Do you think she knew?" I asked him. "In the alley, do you think she knew she was passing along the magic to me?"

He studied the grave, the bright shoots of new daffodils and tulips beginning to push through the earth.

"I think she knew it was the right thing to do. She didn't need to know why. She loved you, and that was all the reason she needed."

CHAPTER 48

Over my mother's protests, I went back to school the following Monday.

"Everyone will talk," she said. "And Father Armando said you could wait as long as you needed."

"Everyone's already talking." In truth, what I needed was normalcy. The Quartoren hadn't made many demands on my time. They'd need me for big issues, not the day-to-day routines of managing inter-House relations and rounding up the remaining Seraphim. I had sat at home for days, watching my mother fill out forms and write thank-you notes and do everything in her power to keep busy enough that she didn't notice my father's absence.

If there'd been a service for Billy, no one mentioned it to us. Morgan's was shut down, work had halted on The Slice. It was as if we were waiting for someone to flip the switch and restore our regular life, but no one had yet.

The waiting was making me crazy. Normal, I decided, would be nice.

I realized my mistake as soon as I climbed onto the CTA bus that would take me to school. Colin had driven me all year. I missed the truck. Missed the smell of fresh coffee and sawdust and soap that had greeted me every morning for months, the familiar rumble of the engine. The bus had squeaky brakes and a pneumatic *whoosh* every time someone boarded, and the air smelled of sweaty vinyl and Lysol. I gripped the strap of my bag and swayed as we lumbered toward St. Brigid's.

My feet dragged on the pavement after I got off, and I forced myself not to look for a flash of rust-spotted red. Instead I focused on the clusters of girls in the courtyard. Despite the chill that lingered, winter not quite ready to relinquish its grip, they all had bare legs under their uniforms, anticipating warm weather. Like if they dressed the part, the weather would follow. I understood the impulse. Act as if things were okay, and they might be.

A hush fell as I passed by. Lena must have been waiting, because she popped through the front doors and linked her arm with mine, staring down everyone in the courtyard as she did so.

"You should have told me you were coming back," she said. "I would have picked you up."

"Last-minute decision," I said. "Have I missed much?"

"Nothing new here." Lena had come to the funeral, and we'd talked a few times, but I hadn't felt up to a long conversation. "How are you holding up?"

"I'm getting there. Three months to go, right? I can do three months."

"Of course you can." We trudged to my locker, and Jill McAllister stopped by.

"Sorry about your dad," she said, tipping her head to the side, all faux sincerity. I fought the urge to smash her nose in with my textbook. "And NYU. I guess it wasn't meant to be, huh?"

As if I cared about this stupid feud with Jill, after everything else. "What are you talking about?"

"They sent out the final acceptance letters," she said.

"I know. I got in."

She gaped. "You didn't say anything."

"Why would I tell you?" I fished a notebook out of my locker and slammed it, the noise making her jump. "I don't need your permission. I don't need your good opinion. The only thing I have ever needed from you was to get the hell out of my way. So do it."

I stared at her until she caved, sidling across the hall, trying to act like it was her idea in the first place.

"Nice," said Lena, hurrying after me. "You're not going to New York, are you?"

"NYU was always what I'd planned on doing with Verity. I thought I owed that to her."

"And now?"

"Now I'm going to do what I want. I owe her that, too." Happiness. I owed her my happiness, and I wasn't going to find it chasing after ghosts.

"Good," she said. "Will you stay here?"

"I need a change of scenery."

Lena paused, eyes troubled. "Speaking of new vistas . . . I heard from Colin."

"Tell me," I said, heart contracting.

"He wanted me to tell you they're good. They're safe. It's very quiet."

I grabbed her arm. "He said that? Those exact words?"

"Yeah. He made me repeat it back to him, just to be sure."

I let out a breath, steadied myself against the wall.

"He can't contact me again, Mo. He shouldn't have done it this time. It's really risky for everyone involved."

"Sure. Absolutely. Thanks for passing it along." I could have asked more. Could have demanded to know where he was, or how to track him down. Lena would have told me, if I'd needed it. But we'd said good-bye. His message was a gift, meant to ease my conscience, and I took it gratefully.

CHAPTER 49

Constance must have been lying in wait. I'd known she was hovering nearby all day, but it wasn't until Lena and I had split up—her to Latin, me to Spanish—that she finally approached me.

"Mo . . ." she said, eyes filling with tears, lower lip trembling. "I can explain."

"You could," I agreed. "But I don't care."

"I missed Verity so much. Anton told me that she could have run away, in the alley that night. She stayed to protect you."

"She did," I said bluntly. "She gave up her life to protect me. And when I made the Covenant, I risked mine to protect you."

"I'm sorry," she wailed. "I got . . . confused. I couldn't think straight and I didn't know who to trust. And you wouldn't tell me stuff. You kept secrets. About Evangeline, and Luc . . . and I couldn't trust you."

"The feeling's mutual," I said. "You're not sorry, Constance. You're sorry you got caught. That you bet on the wrong team."

Her eyes were ice blue, more like Evangeline's than Verity's. I marveled that I hadn't seen it before. Her mouth twisted. "And you're going to lord it over me, aren't you? Make me beg for forgiveness, now that you're on the Quartoren. Make me pay."

"Nope," I said, shifting the bag on my shoulder. "My duty to you was finished when the Covenant ended. You're proficient with the magic. Niobe stayed on to help you as a favor, but you've had enough training. You're on your own."

"You can't kick me out. Just because you're on the Quartoren doesn't mean you can banish me."

"I don't intend to. Fend for yourself, Constance. Orla can't revoke your right to the House, although I imagine she'll make your time there pretty unpleasant. But I don't care. About your explanations or your excuses or your problems. We all make choices," I said. "The trick is learning to live with them. Now it's your turn."

It hurt me to say it, to know that I was leaving Verity's sister unprotected. But I'd carried her—and my guilt—as far as I could. Constance was on her own.

She stared at me, disbelief turning her face blank, then furious. And then she flounced off.

"Tough love?" Niobe asked from behind me.

"Do you think she'll be okay?" I thought about the Arcs at the homeless shelter, wondered if Constance would end up like them.

"I think it is not your responsibility. You saved her from the magic, but you can't save her from herself." She sighed. "Sometimes people's lives are finely balanced—she has a great deal of power, and she could wield it for good or ill. Or she could choose to leave us entirely. It's up to her."

"Not fate? Constance gets free will?" I didn't bother to hide my skepticism.

"As free as any of us."

"But you believe in fate."

"And you do not. Yet here we both are, in lives completely different from what we'd expected, exactly as we should be. Leave Constance to figure out her destiny, and instead, enjoy your own."

CHAPTER 50

"We need to think about our future," my mom said over dinner a few nights later.

"Okay." I set my fork down. I'd been doing nothing but thinking about my future—namely, how much I wished it was already here. And how to explain to my mother that it didn't lie in Chicago.

"I don't want to reopen The Slice," she said. "It's too hard, Mo, going back there."

"I understand." I hadn't been back to either the restaurant or Morgan's. On the bus ride to school each morning, I made sure to sit on the opposite side and stared out the window until we'd gone three more stops. "What do you want to do?"

She folded the napkin into a perfect square, touched it to the corner of her eye. "I don't know, exactly. I can cook. Manage a restaurant. Manage any sort of shop, I suppose."

"That's a good start. There's got to be a place around here that could use you."

"But I don't want to be here."

I choked a little on my water. "Excuse me?"

"Your father always wanted a fresh start," she said. "To go somewhere new. It's time for that."

"But all of your friends are here. You've lived in Chicago all your life. All your memories . . ." I trailed off, understanding.

"We could go somewhere together," she said. "You and I. The Fitzgerald Girls. You've got your pick of schools. Your father had a life insurance policy. It wasn't very large, but if we sell the house, and I work, we'll get by."

For the first time since my father's death, she looked hopeful. Telling her no would be the cruelest possible thing I could say—but the truth was, I needed a different kind of fresh start, not just the same life in a new location.

She must have seen it on my face, because she waved a hand, as if erasing her words. "Or not," she said quickly. "I don't want to be a burden, Mo. I'm not trying to keep tabs on you. I'm just afraid that the minute you move out, I'll lose you. I'll never see you again."

"Of course you'll see me," I said. "I'll come back all the time. Breaks and holidays. Weekends, even."

"Not if you're all the way across the country. I want to be somewhere I can see you easily. What if you're in New York and I'm in California? It's not as if you can fly across the country at the drop of a hat."

But I could. Luc could, anyway. She just didn't know it. I'd have to tell her about the magic eventually, but not while she was still reeling from so many revelations. She needed to be somewhere she wouldn't feel alone but she wouldn't feel judged. Where I could visit without raising suspicions.

My smile felt genuine for the first time in a week. "How do you feel about New Orleans?"

CHAPTER 51

"You promised me the ocean," I said when Luc appeared in my bedroom a few nights later. "I distinctly remember you said we could go to the ocean."

"It's past midnight," he pointed out. "But it ain't too late, considerin' the time difference. You got a swimsuit?"

"No."

"I was hoping you'd say that." He held out his hand, an invitation, but I tugged him into the bed instead.

"Mouse," he protested, landing next to me. The ancient bedsprings groaned in protest. "Your mother's in the next room. That's a little too much risk, even for me."

He stretched out and I tucked my head against his shoulder. "She's asking me about the future. Everyone is. They all have ideas."

"And what about your ideas?" He slid a hand along my leg.

"It's funny. The whole time I've known you, I wanted to make my own choices. But now, I can go anywhere I want. Do anything. It's overwhelming. There are so many possibilities, I don't know how to choose."

"Don't, then."

"I have to," I said. "Otherwise I'm stuck."

"You don't have to decide everything all at once," he pointed out. "Choose one thing, Mouse. One thing you want."

"You," I said immediately.

"That's a given," he said, but he looked pleased. "Something else."

"The ocean," I said, thinking of endless waves and endless sky and the sun glinting like diamonds. All that freedom and light, room to move in any direction. I could spill out all of the sadness I'd been carrying for so long, and the water would wash it away. Power and peace, all in one. "Start there."

"Works for me. And when we get there, we figure out the next thing."

"What about college?"

"It's a big ocean, Mouse. I'm bettin' there's at least one nearby."

"We just . . . choose," I said, trying to wrap my head around the concept. "We don't plan?"

"You've made plans," he said. "You used them like a shield, a way to make sure your life stayed safe and small. Did they work?"

I shook my head, blinking back tears.

"Let's try it this way. You've spent so long doing what's right for everyone else. This time, pick what's right for you."

I twined my fingers with his. "What about fate?"

He kissed me, full of laughter and promise and love. "You don't believe in it."

"You do."

"You're my fate. Remember what she said—the destination is fixed? That's us. We're the destination. And I don't care where the journey takes us, as long as I'm with you. Ocean, city, middle of the damn desert. Let's have an adventure, Mouse. Let's make our own fate."

He kissed me again, a different kind of kiss, and when I opened my eyes, it was under a blanket of stars, infinite and bright, and the magic within me just as vast. I kissed him back, and the world began anew.

Later, when he'd fallen asleep on the beach, the driftwood from the fire burning low, I watched him. The waves washed over the sand in a quiet rhythm, the stars traced a path across the sky. I thought about Verity, how desperately I'd wanted to avenge her, and how that one choice had set off a chain re-action that had transformed two worlds. If I'd listened to Luc that first night, my life would have continued on—safe and quiet and utterly ordinary. I would never have met Colin, or killed Evangeline, or bonded with the magic, or lost my fa-ther. Verity's death had changed my life, but only because I let it. Because I'd sacrificed, and fought, and made myself into someone new. Someone strong. Someone whose future was as limitless as the water stretching out before me.

I felt for the binding on my wrist, the one that tied me to Luc. It had brought me back from magic and grief, brought him back from a duty that had overtaken his life. The con-nection between us was constant as the sunrise, edging up over the horizon, the choice that made all the others possible. He was my home now, no matter where our path led.

"Luc," I whispered, as the sun rose. "Wake up."

He mumbled something and wrapped his arm around my waist.

"Wake up." I poked him with a bare toe. "New day. New adventures."

"Yeah?" he asked, propping himself up on one elbow, voice thick with sleep. "What are we gonna do?"

I watched the sky change, the water tipped with gold, and felt the magic stretch and rise within me, a greeting and a testing, all potential and bright power.

"Everything."

FOOD FOR THOUGHT

1. At the beginning of *Bound,* Mo says, "In the end, people have to make their own choice. Even if it's a terrible one." What makes a choice terrible—the intention or the outcome? And when is a terrible choice necessary or right? How do you make difficult decisions in your own life?

2. Mo's anger over her father's return affects their relationship throughout the book. Is she unfairly holding a grudge, considering that he went to prison to protect her family, or is she right not to trust him? If someone betrays your trust or hurts you deeply, how do you forgive them—or is true forgiveness even possible?

3. Luc wonders why Mo's mother made plans to expand the restaurant if she knew that the family's "fresh start" wouldn't last, and Mo replies, "Maybe because she was afraid it wouldn't." When Mo's father suggests they start over in another city, however, Mrs. Fitzgerald resists. Is her behavior optimistic or unrealistic? Given the choice between something familiar but less than ideal and something completely unknown, how do you decide?

4. Constance justifies her betrayal of Mo as revenge for Verity's sacrifice and Evangeline's death. And while Mo could have chosen to punish Constance in kind, she cuts ties instead. Did Mo act out of sentimentality or some other reason? When is vengeance justifiable, and when is it simply an excuse? Do you think Constance can redeem herself?

5. When Colin finds out Mo secretly traded her future for his family's safety, he ends their relationship, despite having done something similar when he started working for Billy. Is he holding her to an unfair double standard, or

does he have a right to be angry? Would it have been better for Mo to tell him from the outset? Is he more upset about her duplicity or the effect her actions will have on her life?

6. Mo chooses not to get back together with Colin because she thinks they'll end up resenting each other. Do you think Colin's insistence that Mo's safety is more important than anything else would ultimately come between them? By the end of the book, how are their worldviews different? Is it possible to have a long-term future with someone who wants a fundamentally different lifestyle from yours?

7. Mo accuses Luc and the Arcs of thinking she is nothing without the magic. Is it only her connection to the magic that makes Mo special, or is there something intrinsically heroic about her? What makes a person heroic: their abilities or their decisions?

8. Despite the parallels in their situations, Luc is reluctant to tell Mo the story of how he became the Heir. Why? Considering his own history, do you think he was more or less likely to empathize with Mo? Why? If you overcome a difficult situation, does it make you more sympathetic toward others in the same position, or do you assume they should be able to overcome their troubles as you did?

9. Mo tells Jenny Kowalski she should stop investigating her father's death because he would have wanted her to move on with her life. Do you think Jenny will listen to that advice? How do you move on from a loss if you can't have the closure you wanted?

10. Because of her own family history, Lena is very accepting of Mo's need for secrecy. Were they able to forge a true friendship despite Mo's refusal to reveal the Arcs? Was it the right thing for Mo to do? Do you need to know

everything about someone's life in order to trust them and consider them a real friend, or can people hold things back and still be honest?

11. In the end, Mo decides against attending NYU and the University of Chicago, opting for another school entirely. What were her reasons? Do you agree with them? How do you know when a goal you've set for yourself is no longer a good one?

12. At the beginning of *Torn*, Mo says that fate is an excuse for people who don't want to take responsibility for their own actions. Do you think her views changed by the end of *Bound*? Did Luc's? Were Mo's decisions dictated by fate, or could she have chosen differently? Do you believe fate plays a role in your life?